D1709747

1

The Parent's Assistant; Or, Stories for Children

by Maria Edgeworth

Copyright © 3/15/2016
Jefferson Publication

ISBN-13: 978-1530577118

Printed in the United States of America

Table of Contents

PREFACE

ADDRESSED TO PARENTS

Our great lexicographer, in his celebrated eulogium on Dr. Watts, thus speaks in commendation of those productions which he so successfully penned for the pleasure and instruction of the juvenile portion of the community.

'For children,' says Dr. Johnson, 'he condescended to lay aside the philosopher, the scholar, and the wit, to write little poems of devotion, and systems of instruction adapted to their wants and capacities, from the dawn of reason to its gradation of advance in the morning of life. Every man acquainted with the common principles of human action will look with veneration on the writer who is at one time combating Locke and at another time making a catechism for *children in their fourth year*. A voluntary descent from the dignity of science is perhaps the hardest lesson which humility can teach.'

It seems, however, no very easy task to write for children. Those only who have been interested in the education of a family, who have patiently followed children through the first processes of reasoning, who have daily watched over their thoughts and feelings—those only who know with what ease and rapidity the early associations of ideas are formed, on which the future taste, character, and happiness depend, can feel the dangers and difficulties of such an undertaking.

Indeed, in all sciences the grand difficulty has been to ascertain facts—a difficulty which, in the science of education, peculiar circumstances conspire to increase. Here the objects of every experiment are so interesting that we cannot hold our minds indifferent to the result. Nor is it to be expected that many registers of experiments, successful and unsuccessful, should be kept, much less should be published, when we consider that the combined powers of affection and vanity, of partiality to his child and to his theory, will act upon the mind of a parent, in opposition to the abstract love of justice, and the general desire to increase the wisdom and happiness of mankind. Notwithstanding these difficulties, an attempt to keep such a register has actually been made. The design has from time to time been pursued. Though much has not been collected, every circumstance and conversation that have been preserved are faithfully and accurately related, and these notes have been of great advantage to the writer of the following stories.

The question, whether society could exist without the distinction of ranks, is a question involving a variety of complicated discussions, which we leave to the politician and the legislator. At present it is necessary that the education of different ranks should, in some respects, be different. They have few ideas, few habits, in common; their peculiar vices and virtues do not arise from the same causes, and their ambition is to be directed to different objects. But justice, truth, and humanity are confined to no particular rank, and should be enforced with equal care and energy upon the minds of young people of every station; and it is hoped that these principles have never been forgotten in the following pages.

As the ideas of children multiply, the language of their books should become less simple; else their taste will quickly be disgusted, or will remain stationary. Children that live with people who converse with elegance will not be contented with a style inferior to what they hear from everybody near them.

All poetical allusions, however, have been avoided in this book; such situations only are described as children can easily imagine, and which may consequently interest their feelings. Such examples of virtue are painted as are not above their conception of excellence, or their powers of sympathy and emulation.

It is not easy to give *rewards* to children which shall not indirectly do them harm by fostering some hurtful taste or passion. In the story of 'Lazy Lawrence,' where the object was to excite a spirit of industry, care has been taken to proportion the reward to the exertion, and to demonstrate that people feel cheerful and happy whilst they are employed. The reward of our industrious boy, though it be money, is only money considered as the means of gratifying a benevolent wish. In a commercial nation it is especially necessary to separate, as much as possible, the spirit of industry and avarice; and to beware lest we introduce Vice under the form of Virtue.

In the story of 'Tarlton and Loveit' are represented the danger and the folly of that weakness of mind, and that easiness to be led, which too often pass for good nature; and in the tale of the 'False Key' are pointed out some of the evils to which a well-educated boy, on first going to service, is exposed from the profligacy of his fellow-servants.

In the 'Birthday Present,' and in the character of Mrs. Theresa Tattle, the *Parent's Assistant* has pointed out the dangers which may arise in education from a bad servant or a common acquaintance.

In the 'Barring Out' the errors to which a high spirit and the love of party are apt to lead have been made the subject of correction, and it is hoped that the common fault of making the most mischievous characters appear the most *active* and the most ingenious has been as much as possible avoided. *Unsuccessful* cunning will not be admired, and cannot induce imitation.

It has been attempted, in these stories, to provide antidotes against ill-humour, the epidemic rage for dissipation, and the fatal propensity to admire and imitate whatever the fashion of the moment may distinguish. Were young people, either in public schools or in private families, absolutely free from bad examples, it would not be advisable to introduce despicable and vicious characters in books intended for their improvement. But in real life they *must* see vice, and it is best that they should be early shocked with the representation of what they are to avoid. There is a great deal of difference between innocence and ignorance.

To prevent the precepts of morality from tiring the ear and the mind, it was necessary to make the stories in which they are introduced in some measure dramatic; to keep alive hope and fear and curiosity, by some degree of intricacy. At the same time, care has been taken to avoid inflaming the imagination, or exciting a restless spirit of adventure, by exhibiting false views of life, and creating hopes which, in the ordinary course of things, cannot be realised.

THE ORPHANS

Near the ruins of the castle of Rossmore, in Ireland, is a small cabin, in which there once lived a widow and her four children. As long as she was able to work, she was very industrious, and was accounted the best spinner in the parish; but she overworked herself at last, and fell ill, so that she could not sit to her wheel as she used to do, and was obliged to give it up to her eldest daughter, Mary.

Mary was at this time about twelve years old. One evening she was sitting at the foot of her mother's bed spinning, and her little brothers and sisters were gathered round the fire eating their potatoes and milk for supper. 'Bless them, the poor young creatures!' said the widow, who, as she lay on her bed, which she knew must be her deathbed, was thinking of what would become of her children after she was gone. Mary stopped her wheel, for she was afraid that the noise of it had wakened her mother, and would hinder her from going to sleep again.

'No need to stop the wheel, Mary, dear, for me,' said her mother, 'I was not asleep; nor is it *that* which keeps me from sleep. But don't overwork yourself, Mary.' 'Oh, no fear of that,' replied Mary; 'I'm strong and hearty.' 'So was I once,' said her mother. 'And so you will be again, I hope,' said Mary, 'when the fine weather comes again.'

'The fine weather will never come again to me,' said her mother. ''Tis a folly, Mary, to hope for that; but what I hope is, that you'll find some friend—some help—orphans as you'll soon all of you be. And one thing comforts my heart, even as I *am* lying here, that not a soul in the wide world I am leaving has to complain of me. Though poor I have lived honest, and I have brought you up to be the same, Mary; and I am sure the little ones will take after you; for you'll be good to them—as good to them as you can.'

Here the children, who had finished eating their suppers, came round the bed, to listen to what their mother was saying. She was tired of speaking, for she was very weak; but she took their little hands as they laid them on the bed, and joining them all together, she said, 'Bless you, dears—bless you; love and help one another all you can. Good night!—good-bye!'

Mary took the children away to their bed, for she saw that their mother was too ill to say more; but Mary did not herself know how ill she was. Her mother never spoke rightly afterwards, but talked in a confused way about some debts, and one in particular, which she owed to a schoolmistress for Mary's schooling; and then she charged Mary to go and pay it, because she was not able to *go in* with it. At the end of the week she was dead and buried, and the orphans were left alone in their cabin.

The two youngest girls, Peggy and Nancy, were six and seven years old. Edmund was not yet nine, but he was a stout-grown, healthy boy, and well disposed to work. He had been used to bring home turf from the bog on his back, to lead carthorses, and often to go on errands for gentlemen's families, who paid him a sixpence or a shilling, according to the distance which he went, so that Edmund, by some or other of these little employments, was, as he said, likely enough to earn his bread; and he told Mary to have a good heart, for that he should every year grow able to do more and more, and that he should never forget his mother's words when she last gave him her blessing and joined their hands all together.

As for Peggy and Nancy, it was little that they could do; but they were good children, and Mary, when she considered that so much depended upon her, was resolved to exert herself to the utmost. Her first care was to pay those debts which her mother had mentioned to her, for which she left money done up carefully in separate papers. When all these were paid away, there was not enough left to pay both the rent of the cabin and a year's schooling for herself and sisters which was due to the schoolmistress in a neighbouring village.

Mary was in hopes that the rent would not be called for immediately, but in this she was disappointed. Mr. Harvey, the gentleman on whose estate she lived, was in England, and in his absence all was managed by a Mr. Hopkins, an agent, who was a *hard man*.1 The driver came to Mary about a week after her mother's death and told her that the rent must be brought in the next day, and that she must leave the cabin, for a new tenant was coming into it; that she was too young to have a house to herself, and that the only thing she had to do was to get some neighbour to take her and her brother and her sisters in for charity's sake.

The driver finished by hinting that she would not be so hardly used if she had not brought upon herself the ill-will of Miss Alice, the agent's daughter. Mary, it is true, had refused to give Miss Alice a goat upon which she had set her fancy; but this was the only offence of which she had been guilty, and at the time she refused it her mother wanted the goat's milk, which was the only thing she then liked to drink.

Mary went immediately to Mr. Hopkins, the agent, to pay her rent; and she begged of him to let her stay another year in her cabin; but this he refused. It was now September 25th, and he said that the new tenant must come in on the 29th, so that she must quit it directly. Mary could not bear the thoughts of begging any of the neighbours to take her and her brother and sisters in *for charity's sake*; for the neighbours were all poor enough themselves. So she bethought herself that she might find shelter in the ruins of the old castle of Rossmore, where she and her brother, in better times, had often played at hide and seek. The kitchen and two other rooms near it were yet covered in tolerably well; and a little thatch, she thought, would make them comfortable through the winter. The agent consented to let her and her brother and sisters go in there, upon her paying him half a guinea in hand, and promising to pay the same yearly.

Into these lodgings the orphans now removed, taking with them two bedsteads, a stool, chair, and a table, a sort of press, which contained what little clothes they had, and a chest in which they had two hundred of meal. The chest was carried for them by some of the charitable neighbours, who likewise added to their scanty stock of potatoes and turf what would make it last through the winter.

These children were well thought of and pitied, because their mother was known to have been all her life honest and industrious. 'Sure,' says one of the neighbours, 'we can do no less than give a helping hand to the poor orphans, that are so ready to help themselves.' So one helped to thatch the room in which they were to sleep, and another took their cow to graze upon his bit of land on condition of having half the milk; and one and all said they should be welcome to take share of their potatoes and buttermilk if they should find their own ever fall short.

The half-guinea which Mr. Hopkins, the agent, required for letting Mary into the castle was part of what she had to pay to the schoolmistress, to whom above a guinea was due. Mary went to her, and took her goat along with her, and offered it in part of payment of the debt, but the schoolmistress would not receive the goat. She said that she could afford to wait for her money till Mary was able to pay it; that she knew her to be an honest, industrious little girl, and she would trust her with more than a guinea. Mary thanked her; and she was glad to take the goat home again, as she was very fond of it.

Being now settled in their house, they went every day regularly to work; Mary spun nine cuts a day, besides doing all that was to be done in the house; Edmund got fourpence a day by his work; and Peggie and Annie earned twopence apiece at the paper-mills near Navan, where they were employed to sort rags and to cut them into small pieces.

When they had done work one day, Annie went to the master of the paper-mill and asked him if she might have two sheets of large white paper which were lying on the press. She offered a penny for the paper; but the master would not take anything from her, but gave her the paper when he found that she wanted it to make a garland for her mother's grave. Annie and Peggy cut out the garland, and Mary, when it was finished, went along with them and Edmund to put it up. It was just a month after their mother's death.

It happened, at the time the orphans were putting up this garland, that two young ladies, who were returning home after their evening walk, stopped at the gate of the churchyard to look at the red light which the setting sun cast upon the window of the church. As the ladies were standing at the gate, they heard a voice near them crying, 'O mother! mother! are you gone for ever?' They could not see any one; so they walked softly round to the other side of the church, and there they saw Mary kneeling beside a grave, on which her brother and sisters were hanging their white garlands.

5

The children all stood still when they saw the two ladies passing near them; but Mary did not know anybody was passing, for her face was hid in her hands.

Isabella and Caroline (so these ladies were called) would not disturb the poor children; but they stopped in the village to inquire about them. It was at the house of the schoolmistress that they stopped, and she gave them a good account of these orphans. She particularly commended Mary's honesty, in having immediately paid all her mother's debts to the utmost farthing, as far as her money would go. She told the ladies how Mary had been turned out of her house, and how she had offered her goat, of which she was very fond, to discharge a debt due for her schooling; and, in short, the schoolmistress, who had known Mary for several years, spoke so well of her that these ladies resolved that they would go to the old castle of Rossmore to see her the next day.

When they went there, they found the room in which the children lived as clean and neat as such a ruined place could be made. Edmund was out working with a farmer, Mary was spinning, and her little sisters were measuring out some bogberries, of which they had gathered a basketful, for sale. Isabella, after telling Mary what an excellent character she had heard of her, inquired what it was she most wanted; and Mary said that she had just worked up all her flax, and she was most in want of more flax for her wheel.

Isabella promised that she would send her a fresh supply of flax, and Caroline bought the bogberries from the little girls, and gave them money enough to buy a pound of coarse cotton for knitting, as Mary said that she could teach them how to knit.

Inquired what it was she most wanted.

Inquired what it was she most wanted.

The supply of flax, which Isabella sent the next day, was of great service to Mary, as it kept her in employment for above a month; and when she sold the yarn which she had spun with it, she had money enough to buy some warm flannel for winter wear. Besides spinning well, she had learned at school to do plain work tolerably neatly, and Isabella and Caroline employed her to work for them; by which she earned a great deal more than she could by spinning. At her leisure hours she taught her sisters to read and write; and Edmund, with part of the money which he earned by his work out of doors, paid a schoolmaster for teaching him a little arithmetic. When the winter nights came on, he used to light his rush candles for Mary to work by. He had gathered and stripped a good provision of rushes in the month of August, and a neighbour gave him grease to dip them in.

One evening, just as he had lighted his candle, a footman came in, who was sent by Isabella with some plain work to Mary. This servant was an Englishman, and he was but newly come over to Ireland. The rush candles caught his attention; for he had never seen any of them before, as he came from a part of England where they were not used. Edmund, who was ready to oblige, and proud that his candles were noticed, showed the Englishman how they were made, and gave him a bundle of rushes.[2]

The servant was pleased with his good nature in this trifling instance, and remembered it long after it was forgotten by Edmund. Whenever his master wanted to send a messenger anywhere, Gilbert (for that was the servant's name) always employed his little friend Edmund, whom, upon further acquaintance, he liked better and better. He found that Edmund was both quick and exact in executing commissions.

One day, after he had waited a great while at a gentleman's house for an answer to a letter, he was so impatient to get home that he ran off without it. When he was questioned by Gilbert why he did not bring an answer, he did not attempt to make any excuse; he did not say, 'There was no answer, please your honour' or, 'They bid me not wait' etc.; but he told exactly the truth; and though Gilbert scolded him for being so impatient as not to wait, yet his telling the truth was more to the boy's advantage than any excuse he could have made. After this he was always believed when he said, 'There was no answer' or, 'They bid me not wait'; for Gilbert knew that he would not tell a lie to save himself from being scolded.

The orphans continued to assist one another in their work according to their strength and abilities; and they went on in this manner for three years. With what Mary got by her spinning and plain work, and Edmund by leading of carthorses, going on errands, etc., and with little Peggy and Anne's earnings, the family contrived to live comfortably. Isabella and Caroline often visited them, and sometimes gave them clothes, and sometimes flax or cotton for their spinning and knitting; and these children did not *expect* that, because the ladies did something for them, they should do everything. They did not grow idle or wasteful.

When Edmund was about twelve years old, his friend Gilbert sent for him one day, and told him that his master had given him leave to have a boy in the house to assist him, and that his master told him he might choose one in the neighbourhood. Several were anxious to get into such a good place; but Gilbert said that he preferred Edmund before them all, because he knew him to be an industrious, honest, good-natured lad, who always told the truth. So Edmund went into service at *the vicarage*; and his master was the father of Isabella and Caroline. He found his new way of life very pleasant; for he was well fed, well clothed, and well treated; and he every day learned more of his business, in which at first he was rather awkward. He was mindful to do all that Mr. Gilbert required of him; and he was so obliging to all his fellow-servants that they could not help liking him. But there was one thing which was at first rather disagreeable to him: he was obliged to wear shoes and stockings, and they hurt his feet. Besides this, when he waited at dinner he made such a noise in walking that his fellow-servants laughed at him. He told his sister Mary of his distress, and she made for him, after many trials, a pair of cloth shoes, with soles of platted hemp.[3] In these he could walk without making the least noise; and as these shoes could not be worn out of doors, he was always sure to change them before he went out; and consequently he had always clean shoes to wear in the house.

It was soon remarked by the men-servants that he had left off clumping so heavily, and it was observed by the maids that he never dirtied the stairs or passages with his shoes. When he was praised for these things, he said it was his sister Mary who should be thanked, and not he; and he showed the shoes which she had made for him.

Isabella's maid bespoke a pair immediately, and sent Mary a piece of pretty calico for the outside. The last-maker made a last for her, and over this Mary sewed the calico vamps tight. Her brother advised her to try platted packthread instead of hemp for the soles; and she found that this looked more neat than the hemp soles, and was likely to last longer. She platted the packthread together in strands of about half an inch thick, and these were sewed firmly together at the bottom of the shoe. When they were finished they fitted well, and the maid showed them to her mistress.

Isabella and Caroline were so well pleased with Mary's ingenuity and kindness to her brother, that they bespoke from her two dozen of these shoes, and gave her three yards of coloured fustian to make them of, and galloon for the binding. When the shoes were completed, Isabella and Caroline disposed of them for her amongst their acquaintance, and got three shillings a pair for them. The young ladies, as soon as they had collected the money, walked to the old castle, where they found everything neat and clean as usual. They had great pleasure in giving to this industrious girl the reward of her ingenuity, which she received with some surprise and more gratitude. They advised her to continue the shoemaking trade, as they found the shoes were liked, and they knew that they could have a sale for them at the *Repository* in Dublin.

Mary, encouraged by these kind friends, went on with her little manufacture with increased activity. Peggy and Anne platted the packthread, and basted the vamps and linings together ready for her. Edmund was allowed to come home for an hour every morning, provided he was back again before eight o'clock. It was summer time, and he got up early, because he liked to go home to see his sisters, and he took his share in the manufactory. It was his business to hammer the soles flat; and as soon as he came home every morning he performed his task with so much cheerfulness, and sang so merrily at his work, that the hour of his arrival was always an hour of joy to the family.

Mary had presently employment enough upon her hands. Orders came to her for shoes from many families in the neighbourhood, and she could not get them finished fast enough. She, however, in the midst of her hurry, found time to make a very pretty pair, with neat roses, as a present for her schoolmistress, who, now that she saw her pupil in a good way of business, consented to receive the amount of her old debt. Several of the children who went to her school were delighted with the sight of Mary's present, and went to the little manufactory at Rossmore Castle, to find out how these shoes were made. Some went from curiosity, others from idleness; but when they saw how happy the little shoemakers seemed whilst busy at work, they longed to take some share in what was going forward. One begged Mary to let her plat some packthread for the soles; another helped Peggy and Anne to baste in the linings; and all who could get employment were pleased, for the idle ones were shoved out of the way. It became a custom with the children of the village to resort to the old castle at their play hours; and it was surprising to see how much was done by ten or twelve of them, each doing but a little at a time.

One morning Edmund and the little manufacturers were assembled very early, and they were busy at their work, all sitting round the meal chest, which served them for a table.

'My hands must be washed,' said George, a little boy who came running in; 'I ran so fast that I might be in time, to go to work along with you all, that I tumbled down, and look how I have dirtied my hands. Most haste worst speed. My hands must be washed before I can do anything.'

Whilst George was washing his hands, two other little children, who had just finished their morning's work, came to him to beg that he would blow some soap bubbles for them, and they were all three eagerly blowing bubbles, and watching them mount into the air, when suddenly they were startled by a noise as loud as thunder. They were in a sort of outer court of the castle, next to the room in which all their companions were at work, and they ran precipitately into the room, exclaiming, 'Did you hear that noise?'

'I thought I heard a clap of thunder,' said Mary, 'but why do you look so frightened?'

As she finished speaking, another and a louder noise, and the walls round about them shook. The children turned pale and stood motionless; but Edmund threw down his hammer and ran out to see what was the matter. Mary followed him, and they saw that a great chimney of the old ruins at the farthest side of the castle had fallen down, and this was the cause of the prodigious noise.

The part of the castle in which they lived seemed, as Edmund said, to be perfectly safe; but the children of the village were terrified, and thinking that the whole would come tumbling down directly, they ran to their homes as fast as they could. Edmund, who was a courageous lad, and proud of showing his courage, laughed at their cowardice; but Mary, who was very prudent, persuaded her brother to ask an experienced mason, who was building at his master's, to come and give his opinion whether their part of the castle was safe to live in or not. The mason came, and gave it as his opinion that the rooms they inhabited might last through the winter, but that no part of the ruins could stand another year. Mary was sorry to leave a place of which she had grown fond, poor as it was, having lived in it in peace and contentment ever since her mother's death, which was now nearly four years; but she determined to look out for some other place to live in; and she had now money enough to pay the rent of a comfortable cabin. Without losing any time, she went to the village that was at the end of the avenue leading to *the vicarage*, for she wished to get a lodging in this village because it was so near to her brother, and to the ladies who had been so kind to her. She found that there was one newly built house in this village unoccupied; it belonged to Mr. Harvey, her landlord, who was still in England; it was slated, and neatly fitted up inside; but the rent of it was six guineas a year, and this was far above what Mary could afford to pay. Three guineas a year she thought was the highest rent for which she could venture to engage. Besides, she heard that several proposals had been made to Mr. Harvey for this house, and she knew that Mr. Hopkins, the agent, was not her friend; therefore she despaired of getting it. There was no other to be had in this village. Her brother was still more vexed than she was, that she could not find a place near him. He offered to give a guinea yearly towards the rent out of his wages; and Mr. Gilbert spoke about it for him to the steward, and inquired whether, amongst any of those who had given in proposals, there might not be one who would be content with a part of the house, and who would join with Mary in paying the rent. None could be found but a woman who was a great scold, and a man who was famous for going to law about every trifle with his neighbours. Mary did not choose to have anything to do with these people. She did not like to speak either to Miss Isabella or Caroline about it, because she was not of an encroaching temper; and when they had done so much for her, she would have been ashamed to beg for more. She returned home to the old castle, mortified that she had no good news to tell Anne and Peggy, who she knew expected to hear that she had found a nice house for them in the village near their brother.

'Bad news for you, Peggy,' cried she, as soon as she got home. 'And bad news for you, Mary,' replied her sisters, who looked very sorrowful. 'What's the matter?' 'Your poor goat is dead,' replied Peggy. 'There she is, yonder, lying under the great corner stone; you can just see her leg. We cannot lift the stone from off her, it is so heavy. Betsy (*one of the neighbour's girls*) says she remembers, when she came to us to work early this morning, she saw the goat rubbing itself and butting with its horns against that old tottering chimney.'

'Many's the time,' said Mary, 'that I have driven the poor thing away from that place; I was always afraid she would shake that great ugly stone down upon her at last.'

The goat, who had long been the favourite of Mary and her sisters, was lamented by them all. When Edmund came, he helped them to move the great stone from off the poor animal, who was crushed so as to be a terrible sight. As they were moving away this stone in order to bury the goat, Anne found an odd-looking piece of money, which seemed neither like a halfpenny, nor a shilling, nor a guinea.

'Here are more, a great many more of them,' cried Peggy; and upon searching amongst the rubbish, they discovered a small iron pot, which seemed as if it had been filled with these coins, as a vast number of them were found about the spot where it fell. On examining these coins, Edmund thought that several of them looked like gold, and the girls exclaimed with great joy—'O Mary! Mary! this is come to us just in right time—now you can pay for the slated house. Never was anything so lucky!'

But Mary, though nothing could have pleased her better than to have been able to pay for the house, observed that they could not honestly touch any of this treasure, as it belonged to the owner of the castle. Edmund agreed with her that they ought to carry it all immediately to Mr. Hopkins, the agent. Peggy and Anne were convinced by what Mary said, and they begged to go along with her and her brother, to take the coins to Mr. Hopkins. On their way they stopped at the vicarage, to show the treasure to Mr. Gilbert, who took it to the young ladies, Isabella and Caroline, and told them how it had been found.

It is not only by their superior riches, but it is yet more by their superior knowledge, that persons in the higher rank of life may assist those in a lower condition.

Isabella, who had some knowledge of chemistry, discovered, by touching the coins with nitric acid, that several of them were of gold, and consequently of great value. Caroline also found out that many of the coins were very valuable as curiosities. She recollected her father's having shown to her the prints of the coins at the end of each king's reign in Rapin's *History of England*; and upon comparing these impressions with the coins found by the orphans, she perceived that many of them were of the reign of Henry the Seventh, which, from their scarcity, were highly appreciated by numismatic collectors.

Isabella and Caroline, knowing something of the character of Mr. Hopkins, the agent, had the precaution to count the coins, and to mark each of them with a cross, so small that it was scarcely visible to the naked eye, though it was easily to be seen through a magnifying glass. They also begged that their father, who was well acquainted with Mr. Harvey, the gentleman to whom Rossmore Castle belonged, would write to him, and tell him how well these orphans had behaved about the treasure which they had found. The value of the coins was estimated at about thirty or forty guineas.

A few days after the fall of the chimney at Rossmore Castle, as Mary and her sisters were sitting at their work, there came hobbling in an old woman, leaning on a crab stick that seemed to have been newly cut. She had a broken tobacco-pipe in her mouth; her head was wrapped up in two large red and blue handkerchiefs, with their crooked corners hanging far down over the back of her neck, no shoes on her broad feet, nor stockings on her many-coloured legs. Her petticoat was jagged at the bottom, and the skirt of her gown turned up over her shoulders to serve instead of a cloak, which she had sold for whisky. This old woman was well known amongst the country people by the name of *Goody Grope*;4 because she had for many years been in the habit of groping in old castles and in moats,5 and at the bottom of a round tower6 in the neighbourhood, in search of treasure. In her youth she had heard some one talking in a whisper of an old prophecy, found in a bog, which said that before many

St. Patrick's days should come about,
There would be found
A treasure under ground,
By one within twenty miles around.

This prophecy made a deep impression upon her. She also dreamed of it three times: and as the dream, she thought, was a sure token that the prophecy was to come true, she, from that time forwards, gave up her spinning-wheel and her knitting, and could think of nothing but hunting for the treasure that was to be found by one '*within twenty miles round*.'

Year after year St. Patrick's day came about without her ever finding a farthing by all her groping; and, as she was always idle, she grew poorer and poorer; besides, to comfort herself for her disappointments, and to give her spirits for fresh searches, she took to drinking. She sold all she had by degrees; but still she fancied that the lucky day would come, sooner or later, *that would pay for all*.

Goody Grope, however, reached her sixtieth year without ever seeing this lucky day; and now, in her old age, she was a beggar, without a house to shelter her, a bed to lie on, or food to put into her mouth, but what she begged from the charity of those who had trusted more than she had to industry and less to *luck*.

'Ah, Mary, honey! give me a potato and a sup of something, for the love o' mercy; for not a bit have I had all day, except half a glass of whisky and a halfpenny-worth of tobacco!'

Mary immediately set before her some milk, and picked a good potato out of the bowl for her. She was sorry to see such an old woman in such a wretched condition. Goody Grope said she would rather have spirits of some kind or other than milk; but Mary had no spirits to give her; so she sat herself down close to the fire, and after she had sighed and groaned and smoked for some time, she said to Mary, 'Well, and what have you done with the treasure you had the luck to find?' Mary told her that she had carried it to Mr. Hopkins, the agent.

'That's not what I would have done in your place,' replied the old woman. 'When good luck came to you, what a shame to turn your back upon it! But it is idle talking of what's done—that's past; but I'll try my luck in this here castle before next St. Patrick's day comes about. I was told it was more than twenty miles from our bog, or I would have been here long ago; but better late than never.'

9

'Well, and what have you done with the treasure you had the luck to find?'

'Well, and what have you done with the treasure you had the luck to find?'

Mary was much alarmed, and not without reason, at this speech; for she knew that if Goody Grope once set to work at the foundation of the old castle of Rossmore, she would soon bring it all down. It was in vain to talk to Goody Grope of the danger of burying herself under the ruins, or of the improbability of her meeting with another pot of gold coins. She set her elbow upon her knees, and stopping her ears with her hands, bid Mary and her sisters not to waste their breath advising their elders; for that, let them say what they would, she would fall to work the next morning, '*barring* you'll make it worth my while to let it alone.'

'And what will make it worth your while to let it alone?' said Mary; for she saw that she must either get into a quarrel or give up her habitation, or comply with the conditions of this provoking old woman.

Half a crown, Goody Grope said, was the least she could be content to take. Mary paid the half-crown, and was in hopes that she had got rid for ever of her tormentor, but she was mistaken, for scarcely was the week at an end before the old woman appeared before her again, and repeated her threats of falling to work the next morning, unless she had something given to her to buy tobacco.

The next day and the next, and the next, Goody Grope came on the same errand, and poor Mary, who could ill afford to supply her constantly with halfpence, at last exclaimed, 'I am sure the finding of this treasure has not been any good luck to us, but quite the contrary; and I wish we never had found it.'

Mary did not yet know how much she was to suffer on account of this unfortunate pot of gold coins. Mr. Hopkins, the agent, imagined that no one knew of the discovery of this treasure but himself and these poor children; so, not being as honest as they were, he resolved to keep it for his own use. He was surprised some weeks afterwards to receive a letter from his employer, Mr. Harvey, demanding from him the coins which had been discovered at Rossmore Castle. Hopkins had sold the gold coins, and some of the others; and he flattered himself that the children, and the young ladies, to whom he now found they had been shown, could not tell whether what they had seen were gold or not, and he was not in the least apprehensive that those of Henry the Seventh's reign should be reclaimed from him as he thought they had escaped attention. So he sent over the silver coins and others of little value, and apologised for his not having mentioned them before, by saying that he considered them as mere rubbish.

Mr. Harvey, in reply, observed that he could not consider as rubbish the gold coins which were amongst them when they were discovered; and he inquired why these gold coins, and those of the reign of Henry the Seventh, were not now sent to him.

Mr. Hopkins denied that he had ever received any such; but he was thunderstruck when Mr. Harvey, in reply to this falsehood, sent him a list of the coins which the orphans had deposited with him, and exact drawings of those that were missing. He informed him that this list and these drawings came from two ladies who had seen the coins in question.

Mr. Hopkins thought that he had no means of escape but by boldly persisting in falsehood. He replied, that it was very likely such coins had been found at Rossmore Castle, and that the ladies alluded to had probably seen them; but he positively declared that they never came to his hands; that he had restored all that were deposited with him; and that, as to the others, he supposed they must have been taken out of the pot by the children, or by Edmund or Mary on their way from the ladies' house to his.

The orphans were shocked and astonished when they heard, from Isabella and Caroline, the charge that was made against them. They looked at one another in silence for some moments. Then Peggy exclaimed—'*Sure!* Mr. Hopkins has forgotten himself strangely. Does not he remember Edmund's counting the things to him upon the great table in his hall, and we all standing by? I remember it as well as if it was this instant.'

'And so do I,' cried Anne. 'And don't you recollect, Mary, your picking out the gold ones, and telling Mr. Hopkins that they were gold; and he said you knew nothing of the matter; and I was going to tell him that Miss Isabella had tried them, and knew that they were gold? but just then there came in some tenants to pay their rent, and he pushed us out, and twitched from my hand the piece of gold which I had taken up to show him the bright spot which Miss Isabella had cleaned by the stuff that she had poured on it? I believe he was afraid I should steal it; he twitched it from my hand in such a hurry. Do, Edmund; do, Mary—let us go to him, and put him in mind of all this.' 'I'll go to him no more,' said Edmund sturdily. 'He is a bad man—I'll never go to him again. Mary, don't be cast down—we have no need to be cast down—we are honest.' 'True,' said Mary; 'but is not it a hard case that we, who have lived, as my mother did all her life before us, in peace and honesty with all the world, should now have our good name taken from us, when——' Mary's voice faltered and stopped. 'It can't be taken from us,' cried Edmund, 'poor orphans though we are, and he a rich gentleman, as he calls himself. Let him say and do what he will, he can't hurt our good name.'

Edmund was mistaken, alas! and Mary had but too much reason for her fears. The affair was a great deal talked of; and the agent spared no pains to have the story told his own way. The orphans, conscious of their own innocence, took no pains about the matter; and the consequence was, that all who knew them well had no doubt of their honesty; but many, who knew nothing of them, concluded that the agent must be in the right and the children in the wrong. The buzz of scandal went on for some time without reaching their ears, because they lived very retiredly. But one day, when Mary went to sell some stockings of Peggy's knitting at the neighbouring fair, the man to whom she sold them bid her write her name on the back of a note, and exclaimed, on seeing it—'Ho! ho! mistress; I'd not have had any dealings with you, had I known your name sooner. Where's the gold that you found at Rossmore Castle?'

It was in vain that Mary related the fact. She saw that she gained no belief, as her character was not known to this man, or to any of those who were present. She left the fair as soon as she could; and though she struggled against it, she felt very melancholy. Still she exerted herself every day at her little manufacture; and she endeavoured to console herself by reflecting that she had two friends left who would not give up her character, and who continued steadily to protect her and her sisters.

Isabella and Caroline everywhere asserted their belief in the integrity of the orphans, but to prove it was in this instance out of their power. Mr. Hopkins, the agent, and his friends, constantly repeated that the gold coins were taken away in coming from their house to his; and these ladies were blamed by many people for continuing to countenance those that were, with great reason, suspected to be thieves. The orphans were in a worse condition than ever when the winter came on, and their benefactresses left the country to spend some months in Dublin. The old castle, it was true, was likely to last through the winter, as the mason said; but though the want of a comfortable house to live in was, a little while ago, the uppermost thing in Mary's thoughts, now it was not so.

One night, as Mary was going to bed, she heard some one knocking hard at the door. 'Mary, are you up? let us in,' cried a voice, which she knew to be the voice of Betsy Green, the postmaster's daughter, who lived in the village near them.

She let Betsy in, and asked what she could want at such a time of night.

'Give me sixpence, and I'll tell you,' said Betsy; 'but waken Anne and Peggy. Here's a letter just come by post for you, and I stepped over to you with it; because I guessed you'd be glad to have it, seeing it is your brother's handwriting.'

Peggy and Anne were soon roused, when they heard that there was a letter from Edmund. It was by one of his rush candles that Mary read it; and the letter was as follows:—

'Dear Mary, Nancy, and little Peg—Joy! joy!—I always said the truth would come out at last; and that he could not take our good name from us. But I will not tell you how it all came about till we meet, which will be next week, as we are (I mean, master and mistress, and the young ladies—bless them!—and Mr. Gilbert and I) coming down to the vicarage to keep Christmas; and a happy Christmas 'tis likely to be for honest folks. As for they that are not honest, it is not for them to expect to be happy, at Christmas, or any other time. You shall know all when we meet. So, till then, fare ye well, dear Mary, Nancy, and little Peg.—Your joyful and affectionate brother, Edmund.'

To comprehend why Edmund is joyful, our readers must be informed of certain things which happened after Isabella and Caroline went to Dublin. One morning they went with their father and mother to see the magnificent library of a nobleman, who took generous and polite pleasure in thus sharing the advantages of his wealth and station with all who had any pretensions to science or literature. Knowing that the gentleman who was now come to see his library was skilled in antiquities, the nobleman opened a drawer of medals, to ask his opinion concerning the age of some coins, which he had lately purchased at a high price. They were the very same which the orphans had found at Rossmore Castle. Isabella and Caroline knew them again instantly; and as the cross which Isabella had made on each of them was still visible through a magnifying glass, there could be no possibility of doubt.

The nobleman, who was much interested both by the story of these orphans, and the manner in which it was told to him, sent immediately for the person from whom he had purchased the coins. He was a Jew broker. At first he refused to tell them from whom he got them, because he had bought them, he said, under a promise of secrecy. Being further pressed, he acknowledged that it was made a condition in his bargain that he should not sell them to any one in Ireland, but that he had been tempted by the high price the present noble possessor had offered.

At last, when the Jew was informed that the coins were stolen, and that he would be proceeded against as a receiver of stolen goods if he did not confess the whole truth, he declared that he had purchased them from a gentleman, whom he had never seen before or since; but he added that he could swear to his person, if he saw him again.

Now, Mr. Hopkins, the agent, was at this time in Dublin, and Caroline's father posted the Jew, the next day, in the back-parlour of a banker's house, with whom Mr. Hopkins had, on this day, appointed to settle some accounts. Mr. Hopkins came—the Jew knew him—swore that he was the man who had sold the coins to him; and thus the guilt of the agent and the innocence of the orphans were completely proved.

A full account of all that happened was sent to England to Mr. Harvey, their landlord, and a few posts afterwards there came a letter from him, containing a dismissal of the dishonest agent, and a reward for the honest and industrious orphans. Mr. Harvey desired that Mary and her sisters might have the slated house, rent-free, from this time forward, under the care of ladies Isabella and Caroline, as long as Mary or her sisters should carry on in it any useful business. This was the joyful news which Edmund had to tell his sisters.

All the neighbours shared in their joy, and the day of their removal from the ruins of Rossmore Castle to their new house was the happiest of the Christmas holidays. They were not envied for their prosperity; because everybody saw that it was the reward of their good conduct; everybody except Goody Grope. She exclaimed, as she wrung her hands with violent expressions of sorrow—'Bad luck to me! bad luck to me! —Why didn't I go sooner to that there Castle? It is all luck, all luck in this world; but I never had no luck. Think of the luck of these *childer*, that have found a pot of gold, and such great, grand friends, and a slated house, and all: and here am I, with scarce a rag to cover me, and not a potato to put into my mouth!—I, that have been looking under ground all my days for treasure, not to have a halfpenny at the last, to buy me tobacco!'

'That is the very reason that you have not a halfpenny,' said Betsy. 'Here Mary has been working hard, and so have her two little sisters and her brother, for these five years past; and they have made money for themselves by their own industry—and friends too—not by luck, but by——'

'Phoo! phoo!' interrupted Goody Grope; 'don't be prating; don't I know as well as you do that they found a pot of gold, *by good luck*? and is not that the cause why they are going to live in a slated house now?'

'No,' replied the postmaster's daughter; 'this house is given to them *as a reward*—that was the word in the letter; for I saw it. Edmund showed it to me, and will show it to any one that wants to see. This house was given to them "*as a reward for their honesty.*"'

LAZY LAWRENCE

In the pleasant valley of Ashton there lived an elderly woman of the name of Preston. She had a small neat cottage, and there was not a weed to be seen in her garden. It was upon her garden that she chiefly depended for support; it consisted of strawberry beds, and one small border for flowers. The pinks and roses she tied up in nice nosegays, and sent either to Clifton or Bristol to be sold. As to her strawberries, she did not send them to market, because it was the custom for numbers of people to come from Clifton, in the summer time, to eat strawberries and cream at the gardens in Ashton.

Now, the widow Preston was so obliging, active, and good-humoured, that every one who came to see her was pleased. She lived happily in this manner for several years; but, alas! one autumn she fell sick, and, during her illness, everything went wrong; her garden was neglected, her cow died, and all the money which she had saved was spent in paying for medicines. The winter passed away, while she was so weak that she could earn but little by her work; and when the summer came, her rent was called for, and the rent was not ready in her little purse as usual. She begged a few months' delay, and they were granted to her; but at the end of that time there was no resource but to sell her horse Lightfoot. Now Lightfoot, though perhaps he had seen his best days, was a very great favourite. In his youth he had always carried the dame to the market behind her husband; and it was now her little son Jem's turn to ride him. It was Jem's business to feed Lightfoot, and to take care of him—a charge which he never neglected, for, besides being a very good-natured, he was a very industrious boy.

'It will go near to break my Jem's heart,' said Dame Preston to herself, as she sat one evening beside the fire stirring the embers, and considering how she had best open the matter to her son, who stood opposite to her, eating a dry crust of bread very heartily for supper.

'Jem,' said the old woman, 'what, art hungry?' 'That I am, brave and hungry!'

'Ay! no wonder, you've been brave hard at work—Eh?' 'Brave hard! I wish it was not so dark, mother, that you might step out and see the great bed I've dug; I know you'd say it was no bad day's work—and oh, mother! I've good news: Farmer Truck will give us the giant strawberries, and I'm to go for 'em to-morrow morning, and I'll be back afore breakfast.'

'God bless the boy! how he talks!—Four mile there, and four mile back again, afore breakfast.' 'Ay, upon Lightfoot, you know, mother, very easily; mayn't I?' 'Ay, child!' 'Why do you sigh, mother?' 'Finish thy supper, child.' 'I've done!' cried Jem, swallowing the last mouthful hastily, as if he thought he had been too long at supper—'and now for the great needle; I must see and mend Lightfoot's bridle afore I go to bed.'

To work he set, by the light of the fire, and the dame having once more stirred it, began again with 'Jem, dear, does he go lame at all now?' 'What, Lightfoot! Oh la, no, not he!—never was so well of his lameness in all his life. He's grown quite young again, I think, and then he's so fat he can hardly wag.' 'God bless him—that's right. We must see, Jem, and keep him fat.' 'For what, mother!' 'For Monday fortnight at the fair. He's to be—sold!' 'Lightfoot!' cried Jem, and let the bridle fall from his hand; 'and *will* mother sell Lightfoot?' '*Will*? no: but I *must*, Jem.' 'Must! who says you *must*? why *must* you, mother?' 'I must, I say, child. Why, must not I pay my debts honestly; and must not I pay my rent, and was not it called for long and long ago; and have not I had time; and did not I promise to pay it for certain Monday fortnight, and am not I two guineas short; and where am I to get two guineas? So what signifies talking, child?' said the widow, leaning her head upon her arm. 'Lightfoot *must* go.'

Jem was silent for a few minutes—'Two guineas, that's a great, great deal. If I worked, and worked, and worked ever so hard, I could no ways earn two guineas *afore* Monday fortnight—could I, mother?' 'Lord help thee, no; not an' work thyself to death.' 'But I could earn something, though, I say,' cried Jem proudly; 'and I *will* earn *something*—if it be ever so little, it will be *something*—and I shall do my very best; so I will.' 'That I'm sure of, my child,' said his mother, drawing him towards her and kissing him; 'you were always a good, industrious lad, *that* I will say afore your face or behind your back;—but it won't do now—Lightfoot *must* go.'

Jem turned away struggling to hide his tears, and went to bed without saying a word more. But he knew that crying would do no good; so he presently wiped his eyes, and lay awake, considering what he could possibly do to save the horse. 'If I get ever so little,' he still said to himself, 'it will be *something*, and who knows but landlord might then wait a bit longer? and we might make it all up in time; for a penny a day might come to two guineas in time.'

But how to get the first penny was the question. Then he recollected that one day, when he had been sent to Clifton to sell some flowers, he had seen an old woman with a board beside her covered with various sparkling stones, which people stopped to look at as they passed, and he remembered that some people bought the stones; one paid twopence, another threepence, and another sixpence for them; and Jem heard her say that she got them amongst the neighbouring rocks: so he thought that if he tried he might find some too, and sell them as she had done.

Early in the morning he wakened full of this scheme, jumped up, dressed himself, and, having given one look at poor Lightfoot in his stable, set off to Clifton in search of the old woman, to inquire where she found her sparkling stones. But it was too early in the morning, the old woman was not at her seat; so he turned back again, disappointed. He did not waste his time waiting for her, but saddled and bridled Lightfoot, and went to Farmer Truck's for the giant strawberries.

A great part of the morning was spent in putting them into the ground; and, as soon as that was finished, he set out again in quest of the old woman, whom, to his great joy, he spied sitting at her corner of the street with her board before her. But this old woman was deaf and cross; and when at last Jem made her hear his questions, he could get no answer from her, but that she found the fossils where he would never find any more. 'But can't I look where you looked?' 'Look away, nobody hinders you,' replied the old woman; and these were the only words she would say.

Jem was not, however, a boy to be easily discouraged; he went to the rocks, and walked slowly along, looking at all the stones as he passed. Presently he came to a place where a number of men were at work loosening some large rocks, and one amongst the workmen was stooping down looking for something very eagerly; Jem ran up and asked if he could help him. 'Yes,' said the man, 'you can; I've just dropped, amongst this heap of rubbish, a fine piece of crystal that I got to-day.' 'What kind of a looking thing is it?' said Jem. 'White, and like glass,' said the man, and went on working whilst Jem looked very carefully over the heap of rubbish for a great while.

'Come,' said the man, 'it's gone for ever; don't trouble yourself any more, my boy.' 'It's no trouble; I'll look a little longer; we'll not give it up so soon,' said Jem; and after he had looked a little longer, he found the piece of crystal. 'Thank'e,' said the man, 'you are a fine little industrious fellow.' Jem, encouraged by the tone of voice in which the man spoke this, ventured to ask him the same questions which he had asked the old woman.

'One good turn deserves another,' said the man; 'we are going to dinner just now, and shall leave off work—wait for me here, and I'll make it worth your while.'

Jem waited; and, as he was very attentively observing how the workmen went on with their work, he heard somebody near him give a great yawn, and, turning round, he saw stretched upon the grass, beside the river, a boy about his own age, who, in the village of Ashton, as he knew, went by the name of Lazy Lawrence—a name which he most justly deserved, for he never did anything from morning to night. He neither worked nor played, but sauntered or lounged about restless and yawning. His father was an ale-house keeper, and being generally drunk, could take no care of his son; so that Lazy Lawrence grew every day worse and worse. However, some of the neighbours said that he was a good-natured poor fellow enough, and would never do any one harm but himself; whilst others, who were wiser, often shook their heads, and told him that idleness was the root of all evil.

'What, Lawrence!' cried Jem to him, when he saw him lying upon the grass; 'what, are you asleep?' 'Not quite.' 'Are you awake?' 'Not quite.' 'What are you doing there?' 'Nothing.' 'What are you thinking of?' 'Nothing.' 'What makes you lie there?' 'I don't know—because I can't find anybody to play with me to-day. Will you come and play?' 'No, I can't; I'm busy.' 'Busy,' cried Lawrence, stretching himself, 'you are always busy. I would not be you for the world to have so much to do always.' 'And I,' said Jem, laughing, 'would not be you for the world, to have nothing to do.'

They then parted, for the workman just then called Jem to follow him. He took him home to his own house, and showed him a parcel of fossils, which he had gathered, he said, on purpose to sell, but had never had time enough to sell them. Now, however, he set about the task; and having picked out those which he judged to be the best, he put them in a small basket, and gave them to Jem to sell, upon condition that he should bring him half of what he got. Jem, pleased to be employed, was ready to agree to what the man proposed,

13

provided his mother had no objection. When he went home to dinner, he told his mother his scheme, and she smiled, and said he might do as he pleased; for she was not afraid of his being from home. 'You are not an idle boy,' said she; 'so there is little danger of your getting into any mischief.'

Accordingly Jem that evening took his stand, with his little basket, upon the bank of the river, just at the place where people land from a ferry-boat, and the walk turns to the wells, and numbers of people perpetually pass to drink the waters. He chose his place well, and waited nearly all the evening, offering his fossils with great assiduity to every passenger; but not one person bought any.

'Hallo!' cried some sailors, who had just rowed a boat to land, 'bear a hand here, will you, my little fellow, and carry these parcels for us into yonder house?'

Jem ran down immediately for the parcels, and did what he was asked to do so quickly, and with so much good-will, that the master of the boat took notice of him, and, when he was going away, stopped to ask him what he had got in his little basket; and when he saw that they were fossils, he immediately told Jem to follow him, for that he was going to carry some shells he had brought from abroad to a lady in the neighbourhood who was making a grotto. 'She will very likely buy your stones into the bargain. Come along, my lad; we can but try.'

The lady lived but a very little way off, so that they were soon at her house. She was alone in her parlour, and was sorting a bundle of feathers of different colours; they lay on a sheet of pasteboard upon a window seat, and it happened that as the sailor was bustling round the table to show off his shells, he knocked down the sheet of pasteboard, and scattered all the feathers. The lady looked very sorry, which Jem observing, he took the opportunity, whilst she was busy looking over the sailor's bag of shells, to gather together all the feathers, and sort them according to their different colours, as he had seen them sorted when he first came into the room.

'Where is the little boy you brought with you? I thought I saw him here just now.' 'And here I am, ma'am,' cried Jem, creeping from under the table with some few remaining feathers which he had picked from the carpet; 'I thought,' added he, pointing to the others, 'I had better be doing something than standing idle, ma'am.' She smiled, and, pleased with his activity and simplicity, began to ask him several questions; such as who he was, where he lived, what employment he had, and how much a day he earned by gathering fossils.

'This is the first day I ever tried,' said Jem; 'I never sold any yet, and if you don't buy 'em now, ma'am, I'm afraid nobody else will; for I've asked everybody else.'

'Come, then,' said the lady, laughing, 'if that is the case, I think I had better buy them all.' So, emptying all the fossils out of his basket, she put half a crown into it.

Jem's eyes sparkled with joy. 'Oh, thank you, ma'am,' said he, 'I will be sure and bring you as many more, to-morrow.' 'Yes, but I don't promise you,' said she, 'to give you half a crown, to-morrow.' 'But, perhaps, though you don't promise it, you will.' 'No,' said the lady, 'do not deceive yourself; I assure you that I will not. *That*, instead of encouraging you to be industrious, would teach you to be idle.'

Jem did not quite understand what she meant by this, but answered, 'I'm sure I don't wish to be idle; what I want is to earn something every day, if I knew how; I'm sure I don't wish to be idle. If you knew all, you'd know I did not.' 'How do you mean, *if I knew all*?' 'Why, I mean, if you knew about Lightfoot.' 'Who's Lightfoot?' 'Why, mammy's horse,' added Jem, looking out of the window; 'I must make haste home, and feed him afore it gets dark; he'll wonder what's gone with me.' 'Let him wonder a few minutes longer,' said the lady, 'and tell me the rest of your story.' 'I've no story, ma'am, to tell, but as how mammy says he must go to the fair Monday fortnight, to be sold, if she can't get the two guineas for her rent; and I should be main sorry to part with him, for I love him, and he loves me; so I'll work for him, I will, all I can. To be sure, as mammy says, I have no chance, such a little fellow as I am, of earning two guineas afore Monday fortnight.' 'But are you willing earnestly to work?' said the lady; 'you know there is a great deal of difference between picking up a few stones and working steadily every day, and all day long.' 'But,' said Jem, 'I would work every day, and all day long.' 'Then,' said the lady, 'I will give you work. Come here to-morrow morning, and my gardener will set you to weed the shrubberies, and I will pay you sixpence a day. Remember, you must be at the gates by six o'clock.' Jem bowed, thanked her, and went away.

It was late in the evening, and Jem was impatient to get home to feed Lightfoot; yet he recollected that he had promised the man who had trusted him to sell the fossils, that he would bring him half of what he got for them; so he thought that he had better go to him directly; and away he went, running along by the water-side about a quarter of a mile, till he came to the man's house. He was just come home from work, and was surprised when Jem showed him the half-crown, saying, 'Look what I got for the stones; you are to have half, you know.' 'No,' said the man, when he had heard his story, I shall not take half of that; it was given to you. I expected but a shilling at the most, and the half of that is but sixpence, and that I'll take. 'Wife, give the lad two shillings, and take this half-crown.' So the wife opened an old glove, and took out two shillings; and the man, as she opened the glove, put in his fingers and took out a little silver penny. 'There, he shall have that into the bargain for his honesty—honesty is the best policy—there's a lucky penny for you, that I've kept ever since I can remember.' 'Don't you ever go to part with it, do ye hear!' cried the woman. 'Let him do what he will with it, wife,' said the man. 'But,' argued the wife, 'another penny would do just as well to buy gingerbread; and that's what it will go for.' 'No, that it shall not, I promise you,' said Jem; and so he ran away home, fed Lightfoot, stroked him, went to bed, jumped up at five o'clock in the morning, and went singing to work as gay as a lark.

Four days he worked 'every day and all day long'; and every evening the lady, when she came out to walk in her gardens, looked at his work. At last she said to her gardener, 'This little boy works very hard.' 'Never had so good a little boy about the grounds,' said the gardener; 'he's always at his work, let me come by when I will, and he has got twice as much done as another would do; yes, twice as much, ma'am; for look here—he began at this 'ere rose-bush, and now he's got to where you stand, ma'am; and here is the day's work that t'other boy, and he's three years older too, did to-day—I say, measure Jem's fairly, and it's twice as much, I'm sure.' 'Well,' said the lady to her gardener, 'show me how much is a fair good day's work for a boy of his age.' 'Come at six o'clock and go at six? why, about this much, ma'am,' said the gardener, marking off a piece of the border with his spade.

'Then, little boy,' said the lady, 'so much shall be your task every day. The gardener will mark it off for you; and when you've done, the rest of the day you may do what you please.'

Jem was extremely glad of this; and the next day he had finished his task by four o'clock; so that he had all the rest of the evening to himself. He was as fond of play as any little boy could be; and when he was at it he played with all the eagerness and gaiety imaginable; so as soon as he had finished his task, fed Lightfoot, and put by the sixpence he had earned that day, he ran to the playground in the village, where he found a party of boys playing, and amongst them Lazy Lawrence, who indeed was not playing, but lounging upon a gate, with his thumb in his mouth. The rest were playing at cricket. Jem joined them, and was the merriest and most active amongst them; till, at last, when quite out of breath with running, he was obliged to give up to rest himself, and sat down upon the stile, close to the gate on which Lazy Lawrence was swinging.

'And why don't you play, Lawrence?' said he. 'I'm tired,' said Lawrence. 'Tired of what?' 'I don't know well what tires me; grandmother says I'm ill, and I must take something—I don't know what ails me.' 'Oh, pugh! take a good race—one, two, three, and away—and you'll find yourself as well as ever. Come, run—one, two, three, and away.' 'Ah, no, I can't run, indeed,' said he hanging back heavily; 'you know I can play all day long if I like it, so I don't mind play as you do, who have only one hour for it.' 'So much the worse for you. Come now, I'm quite fresh again, will you have one game at ball? do.' 'No, I tell you I can't; I'm as tired as if I had been working all day long as hard as a horse.' 'Ten times more,' said Jem, 'for I have been working all day long as hard as a horse, and yet you see I'm not a bit tired, only a little out of breath just now.' 'That's very odd,' said Lawrence, and yawned, for want of some better answer; then taking out a handful of halfpence,—'See what I got from father to-day, because I asked him just at the right time, when he had drunk a glass or two; then I can get anything I want out of him—see! a penny, twopence, threepence, fourpence—there's eightpence in all; would not you be happy if you had *eightpence*?' 'Why, I don't know,' said Jem, laughing, 'for you don't seem happy, and you *have eightpence*.' 'That does not signify, though. I'm sure you only say that because you envy me. You don't know what it is to have eightpence. You never had more than twopence or threepence at a time in all your life.'

Jem smiled. 'Oh, as to that,' said he, 'you are mistaken, for I have at this very time more than twopence, threepence, or eightpence either. I have—let me—see—stones, two shillings; then five days' work that's five sixpences, that's two shillings and sixpence; in all, makes four shillings and sixpence; and my silver penny, is four and sevenpence—four and sevenpence!' 'You have not!' said Lawrence, roused so as absolutely to stand upright, 'four and sevenpence, have you? Show it me and then I'll believe you.' 'Follow me, then,' cried Jem, 'and I'll soon make you believe me; come.' 'Is it far?' said Lawrence, following half-running, half-hobbling, till he came to the stable, where Jem showed him his treasure. 'And how did you come by it—honestly?' 'Honestly! to be sure I did; I earned it all.' 'Lord bless me, earned it! well, I've a great mind to work; but then it's such hot weather, besides, grandmother says I'm not strong enough yet for hard work; and besides, I know how to coax daddy out of money when I want it, so I need not work. But four and sevenpence; let's see, what will you do with it all?' 'That's a secret,' said Jem, looking great. 'I can guess; I know what I'd do with it if it was mine. First, I'd buy pocketfuls of gingerbread; then I'd buy ever so many apples and nuts. Don't you love nuts? I'd buy nuts enough to last me from this time to Christmas, and I'd make little Newton crack 'em for me, for that's the worst of nuts, there's the trouble of cracking 'em.' 'Well, you never deserve to have a nut.' 'But you'll give me some of yours,' said Lawrence, in a fawning tone; for he thought it easier to coax than to work—'you'll give me some of your good things, won't you?' 'I shall not have any of those good things,' said Jem. 'Then, what will you do with all your money?' 'Oh, I know very well what to do with it; but, as I told you, that's a secret, and I shan't tell it anybody. Come now, let's go back and play—their game's up, I daresay.'

Lawrence went back with him, full of curiosity, and out of humour with himself and his eightpence. 'If I had four and sevenpence,' said he to himself, 'I certainly should be happy!'

The next day, as usual, Jem jumped up before six o'clock and went to his work, whilst Lazy Lawrence sauntered about without knowing what to do with himself. In the course of two days he laid out sixpence of his money in apples and gingerbread; and as long as these lasted, he found himself well received by his companions; but at length the third day he spent his last halfpenny, and when it was gone, unfortunately some nuts tempted him very much, but he had no money to pay for them; so he ran home to coax his father, as he called it.

When he got home he heard his father talking very loud, and at first he thought he was drunk; but when he opened the kitchen door, he saw that he was not drunk, but angry.

'You lazy dog!' cried he, turning suddenly upon Lawrence, and gave him such a violent box on the ear as made the light flash from his eyes; 'you lazy dog! See what you've done for me—look!—look, look, I say!'

Lawrence looked as soon as he came to the use of his senses, and with fear, amazement, and remorse beheld at least a dozen bottles burst, and the fine Worcestershire cider streaming over the floor.

'Now, did not I order you three days ago to carry these bottles to the cellar, and did not I charge you to wire the corks? answer me, you lazy rascal; did not I?' 'Yes,' said Lawrence, scratching his head. 'And why was not it done, I ask you?' cried his father, with renewed anger, as another bottle burst at the moment. 'What do you stand there for, you lazy brat? why don't you move, I say? No, no,' catching hold of him, 'I believe you can't move; but I'll make you.' And he shook him till Lawrence was so giddy he could not stand. 'What had you to think of? What had you to do all day long, that you could not carry my cider, my Worcestershire cider, to the cellar when I bid you? But go, you'll never be good for anything; you are such a lazy rascal—get out of my sight!' So saying, he pushed him, out of the house door, and Lawrence sneaked off, seeing that this was no time to make his petition for halfpence.

The next day he saw the nuts again, and wishing for them more than ever, he went home, in hopes that his father, as he said to himself, would be in a better humour. But the cider was still fresh in his recollection; and the moment Lawrence began to whisper the word 'halfpenny' in his ear, his father swore with a loud oath, 'I will not give you a halfpenny, no, not a farthing, for a month to come. If you want money, go work for it; I've had enough of your laziness—go work!'

At these terrible words Lawrence burst into tears, and, going to the side of a ditch, sat down and cried for an hour; and when he had cried till he could cry no more, he exerted himself so far as to empty his pockets, to see whether there might not happen to be one halfpenny left; and, to his great joy, in the farthest corner of his pocket one halfpenny was found. With this he proceeded to the fruit-woman's stall. She was busy weighing out some plums, so he was obliged to wait; and whilst he was waiting he heard some people near him talking and laughing very loud.

'See what you've done for me—look!—look, look, I say!'

'See what you've done for me—look!—look, look, I say!'

The fruit-woman's stall was at the gate of an inn yard; and peeping through the gate in this yard, Lawrence saw a postilion and a stable-boy, about his own size, playing at pitch farthing. He stood by watching them for a few minutes. 'I began but with one halfpenny,' cried the stable-boy, with an oath, 'and now I've got twopence!' added he, jingling the halfpence in his waistcoat pocket. Lawrence was moved at the sound, and said to himself, 'If *I* begin with one halfpenny I may end, like him, with having twopence; and it is easier to play at pitch farthing than to work.'

So he stepped forward, presenting his halfpenny, offering to toss up with the stable-boy, who, after looking him full in the face, accepted the proposal, and threw his halfpenny into the air. 'Head or tail?' cried he. 'Head,' replied Lawrence, and it came up head. He seized the penny, surprised at his own success, and would have gone instantly to have laid it out in nuts; but the stable-boy stopped him, and tempted him to throw it again. This time Lawrence lost; he threw again and won; and so he went on, sometimes losing, but most frequently winning, till half the morning was lost. At last, however, finding himself the master of three halfpence, he said he would play no more.

The stable-boy, grumbling, swore he would have his revenge another time, and Lawrence went and bought his nuts. 'It is a good thing,' said he to himself, 'to play at pitch farthing; the next time I want a halfpenny I'll not ask my father for it, nor go to work neither.' Satisfied with this resolution, he sat down to crack his nuts at his leisure, upon the horse-block in the inn yard. Here, whilst he ate, he overheard the conversation of the stable-boys and postilions. At first their shocking oaths and loud wrangling frightened and shocked him; for Lawrence, though *lazy*, had not yet learned to be a *wicked* boy. But, by degrees, he was accustomed to the swearing and quarrelling, and took a delight and interest in their disputes and battles. As this was an amusement which he could enjoy without any sort of exertion, he soon grew so fond of it, that every day he returned to the stable yard, and the horse-block became his constant seat. Here he found some relief from the insupportable fatigue of doing nothing, and here, hour after hour, with his elbows on his knees and his head on his hands, he sat, the

16

spectator of wickedness. Gaming, cheating, and lying soon became familiar to him; and, to complete his ruin, he formed a sudden and close intimacy with the stable-boy (a very bad boy) with whom he had first begun to game.

The consequences of this intimacy we shall presently see. But it is now time to inquire what little Jem had been doing all this while.

One day, after Jem had finished his task, the gardener asked him to stay a little while, to help him to carry some geranium pots into the hall. Jem, always active and obliging, readily stayed from play, and was carrying in a heavy flower pot, when his mistress crossed the hall. 'What a terrible litter!' said she, 'you are making here—why don't you wipe your shoes upon the mat?' Jem turned to look for the mat, but he saw none. 'Oh,' said the lady, recollecting herself, 'I can't blame you, for there is no mat.' 'No, ma'am,' said the gardener, 'nor I don't know when, if ever, the man will bring home those mats you bespoke, ma'am.' 'I am very sorry to hear that,' said the lady; 'I wish we could find somebody who would do them, if he can't. I should not care what sort of mats they were, so that one could wipe one's feet on them.'

Jem, as he was sweeping away the litter, when he heard these last words, said to himself, 'Perhaps I could make a mat.' And all the way home, as he trudged along whistling, he was thinking over a scheme for making mats, which, however bold it may appear, he did not despair of executing, with patience and industry. Many were the difficulties which his '*prophetic eye*' foresaw; but he felt within himself that spirit which spurs men on to great enterprises, and makes them 'trample on impossibilities.' In the first place, he recollected that he had seen Lazy Lawrence, whilst he lounged upon the gate, twist a bit of heath into different shapes; and he thought that, if he could find some way of plaiting heath firmly together, it would make a very pretty green, soft mat, which would do very well for one to wipe one's shoes on. About a mile from his mother's house, on the common which Jem rode over when he went to Farmer Truck's for the giant strawberries, he remembered to have seen a great quantity of this heath; and, as it was now only six o'clock in the evening, he knew that he should have time to feed Lightfoot, stroke him, go to the common, return, and make one trial of his skill before he went to bed.

Lightfoot carried him swiftly to the common, and there Jem gathered as much of the heath as he thought he should want. But what toil! what time! what pains did it cost him, before he could make anything like a mat! Twenty times he was ready to throw aside the heath, and give up his project, from impatience of repeated disappointments. But still he persevered. Nothing *truly great* can be accomplished without toil and time. Two hours he worked before he went to bed. All his play hours the next day he spent at his mat; which, in all, made five hours of fruitless attempts. The sixth, however, repaid him for the labours of the other five. He conquered his grand difficulty of fastening the heath substantially together, and at length completely finished a mat, which far surpassed his most sanguine expectations. He was extremely happy—sang, danced round it—whistled—looked at it again and again, and could hardly leave off looking at it when it was time to go to bed. He laid it by his bedside, that he might see it the moment he awoke in the morning.

And now came the grand pleasure of carrying it to his mistress. She looked fully as much surprised as he expected, when she saw it, and when she heard who made it. After having duly admired it, she asked how much he expected for his mat. 'Expect!—Nothing, ma'am,' said Jem; 'I meant to give it you, if you'd have it; I did not mean to sell it. I made it in my play hours, I was very happy in making it; and I'm very glad, too, that you like it; and if you please to keep it, ma'am, that's all.' 'But that's not all,' said the lady. 'Spend your time no more in weeding in my garden, you can employ yourself much better; you shall have the reward of your ingenuity as well as of your industry. Make as many more such mats as you can, and I will take care and dispose of them for you.'

'Thank'e, ma'am,' said Jem, making his best bow, for he thought by the lady's looks that she meant to do him a favour, though he repeated to himself, 'Dispose of them, what does that mean?'

The next day he went to work to make more mats, and he soon learned to make them so well and quickly, that he was surprised at his own success. In every one he made he found less difficulty, so that, instead of making two, he could soon make four, in a day. In a fortnight he made eighteen.

It was Saturday night when he finished, and he carried, at three journeys, his eighteen mats to his mistress's house; piled them all up in the hall, and stood with his hat off, with a look of proud humility, beside the pile, waiting for his mistress's appearance. Presently a folding-door, at one end of the hall, opened, and he saw his mistress, with a great many gentlemen and ladies, rising from several tables.

'Oh! there is my little boy and his mats,' cried the lady; and, followed by all the rest of the company, she came into the hall. Jem modestly retired whilst they looked at his mats; but in a minute or two his mistress beckoned to him, and when he came into the middle of the circle, he saw that his pile of mats had disappeared.

'Well,' said the lady, smiling, 'what do you see that makes you look so surprised?' 'That all my mats are gone,' said Jem; 'but you are very welcome.' 'Are we?' said the lady, 'well, take up your hat and go home then, for you see that it is getting late, and you know Lightfoot will wonder what's become of you.' Jem turned round to take up his hat, which he had left on the floor.

But how his countenance changed! the hat was heavy with shillings. Every one who had taken a mat had put in two shillings; so that for the eighteen mats he had got thirty-six shillings. 'Thirty-six shillings,' said the lady; 'five and sevenpence I think you told me you had earned already—how much does that make? I must add, I believe, one other sixpence to make out your two guineas.'

'Two guineas!' exclaimed Jem, now quite conquering his bashfulness, for at the moment he forgot where he was, and saw nobody that was by. 'Two guineas!' cried he, clapping his hands together,—'O Lightfoot! O mother!' Then, recollecting himself, he saw his mistress, whom he now looked up to quite as a friend. 'Will *you* thank them all?' said he, scarcely daring to glance his eyes round upon the company; 'will *you* thank 'em, for you knew I don't know how to thank 'em *rightly*.' Everybody thought, however, that they had been thanked *rightly*. 'Now we won't keep you any longer, only,' said his mistress, 'I have one thing to ask you, that I may be by when you show your treasure to your mother.'

'Come, then,' said Jem, 'come with me now.' 'Not now,' said the lady, laughing; 'but I will come to Ashton to-morrow evening; perhaps your mother can find me a few strawberries.'

'That she will,' said Jem; 'I'll search the garden myself.'

He now went home, but felt it a great restraint to wait till to-morrow evening before he told his mother. To console himself he flew to the stable:—'Lightfoot, you're not to be sold on Monday, poor fellow!' said he, patting him, and then could not refrain from counting out his money. Whilst he was intent upon this, Jem was startled by a noise at the door: somebody was trying to pull up the latch. It opened, and there came in Lazy Lawrence, with a boy in a red jacket, who had a cock under his arm. They started when they got into the middle of the stable, and when they saw Jem, who had been at first hidden by the horse.

'We—we—we came,' stammered Lazy Lawrence—'I mean, I came to—to—to——' 'To ask you,' continued the stable-boy, in a bold tone, 'whether you will go with us to the cock-fight on Monday? See, I've a fine cock here, and Lawrence told me you were a great friend of his; so I came.'

Lawrence now attempted to say something in praise of the pleasures of cock-fighting and in recommendation of his new companion. But Jem looked at the stable-boy with dislike, and a sort of dread. Then turning his eyes upon the cock with a look of compassion, said, in a low voice, to Lawrence, 'Shall you like to stand by and see its eyes pecked out?' 'I don't know,' said Lawrence, 'as to that; but they say a cockfight's a fine sight, and it's no more cruel in me to go than another; and a great many go, and I've nothing else to do, so I shall go.' 'But I have something else to do,' said Jem, laughing, 'so I shall not go.' 'But,' continued Lawrence, 'you know Monday is a great Bristol fair, and one must be merry then, of all the days in the year.' 'One day in the year, sure, there's no harm in being merry,' said the stable-boy. 'I hope not,' said Jem; 'for I know, for my part, I am merry every day in the year.' 'That's very odd,' said Lawrence; 'but I know, for my part, I would not for all the world miss going to the fair, for at least it will be something to talk of for half a year after. Come, you'll go, won't you?' 'No,' said Jem, still looking as if he did not like to talk before the ill-looking stranger. 'Then what will you do with all your money?' 'I'll tell you about that another time,' whispered Jem; 'and don't you go to see that cock's eyes pecked out; it won't make you merry, I'm sure.' 'If I had anything else to divert me,' said Lawrence, hesitating and yawning. 'Come,' cried the stable-boy, seizing his stretching arm, 'come along,' cried he; and, pulling him away from Jem, upon whom he cast a look of extreme contempt; 'leave him alone, he's not the sort.'

'What a fool you are,' said he to Lawrence, the moment he got him out of the stable; 'you might have known he would not go, else we should soon have trimmed him out of his four and sevenpence. But how came you to talk of four and sevenpence? I saw in the manger a hat full of silver.' 'Indeed!' exclaimed Lawrence. 'Yes, indeed; but why did you stammer so when we first got in? You had like to have blown us all up.' 'I was so ashamed,' said Lawrence, hanging down his head. 'Ashamed! but you must not talk of shame now you are in for it, and I shan't let you off; you owe us half a crown, recollect, and I must be paid to-night, so see and get the money somehow or other.' After a considerable pause he added, 'I answer for it he'd never miss half a crown out of all that silver.' 'But to steal,' said Lawrence, drawing back with horror; 'I never thought I should come to that—and from poor Jem, too—the money that he has worked so hard for, too.' 'But it is not stealing; we don't mean to steal; only to borrow it; and if we win, which we certainly shall, at the cock-fight, pay it back again, and he'll never know anything about the matter, and what harm will it do him? Besides, what signifies talking? you can't go to the cock-fight, or the fair either, if you don't; and I tell ye we don't mean to steal it; we'll pay it by Monday night.'

Lawrence made no reply, and they parted without his coming to any determination.

Here let us pause in our story. We are almost afraid to go on. The rest is very shocking. Our little readers will shudder as they read. But it is better that they should know the truth and see what the idle boy came to at last.

In the dead of the night, Lawrence heard somebody tap at his window. He knew well who it was, for this was the signal agreed upon between him and his wicked companion. He trembled at the thoughts of what he was about to do, and lay quite still, with his head under the bedclothes, till he heard the second tap. Then he got up, dressed himself, and opened his window. It was almost even with the ground. His companion said to him, in a hollow voice, 'Are you ready?' He made no answer, but got out of the window and followed.

When he got to the stable a black cloud was just passing over the moon, and it was quite dark. 'Where are you?' whispered Lawrence, groping about, 'where are you? Speak to me.' 'I am here; give me your hand.' Lawrence stretched out his hand. 'Is that your hand?' said the wicked boy, as Lawrence laid hold of him; 'how cold it feels.' 'Let us go back,' said Lawrence; 'it is time yet.' 'It is no time to go back,' replied the other, opening the door: 'you've gone too far now to go back,' and he pushed Lawrence into the stable. 'Have you found it? Take care of the horse. Have you done? What are you about? Make haste, I hear a noise,' said the stable-boy, who watched at the door. 'I am feeling for the half-crown, but I can't find it.' 'Bring all together.' He brought Jem's broken flower-pot, with all the money in it, to the door.

The black cloud had now passed over the moon, and the light shone full upon them. 'What do we stand here for?' said the stable-boy, snatching the flower-pot out of Lawrence's trembling hands, and pulled him away from the door.

'Good God!' cried Lawrence, 'you won't take all. You said you'd only take half a crown, and pay it back on Monday. You said you'd only take half a crown!' 'Hold your tongue,' replied the other, walking on, deaf to all remonstrances—'if ever I am to be hanged, it shan't be for half a crown.'

Lawrence's blood ran cold in his veins, and he felt as if all his hair stood on end. Not another word passed. His accomplice carried off the money, and Lawrence crept, with all the horrors of guilt upon him, to his restless bed. All night he was starting from frightful dreams; or else, broad awake, he lay listening to every small noise, unable to stir, and scarcely daring to breathe—tormented by that most dreadful of all kinds of fear, that fear which is the constant companion of an evil conscience.

He thought the morning would never come; but when it was day, when he heard the birds sing, and saw everything look cheerful as usual, he felt still more miserable. It was Sunday morning, and the bell rang for church. All the children of the village, dressed in their Sunday clothes, innocent and gay, and little Jem, the best and gayest amongst them, went flocking by his door to church.

'Well, Lawrence,' said Jem, pulling his coat as he passed, and saw Lawrence leaning against his father's door, 'what makes you look so black?' 'I?' said Lawrence, starting; 'why do you say that I look black?' 'Nay, then,' said Jem, 'you look white enough now, if that will please you, for you're turned as pale as death.' 'Pale!' replied Lawrence, not knowing what he said, and turned abruptly away, for he dared not stand another look of Jem's; conscious that guilt was written in his face, he shunned every eye. He would now have given the world to have thrown off the load of guilt which lay upon his mind. He longed to follow Jem, to fall upon his knees and confess all.

Dreading the moment when Jem should discover his loss, Lawrence dared not stay at home, and not knowing what to do, or where to go, he mechanically went to his old haunt at the stable yard, and lurked thereabouts all day, with his accomplice, who tried in vain to quiet his fears and raise his spirits by talking of the next day's cock-fight. It was agreed that, as soon as the dusk of the evening came on, they should go together into a certain lonely field, and there divide their booty.

In the meantime, Jem, when he returned from church, was very full of business, preparing for the reception of his mistress, of whose intended visit he had informed his mother; and whilst she was arranging the kitchen and their little parlour, he ran to search the strawberry beds.

'Why, my Jem, how merry you are to-day!' said his mother, when he came in with the strawberries, and was jumping about the room playfully. 'Now, keep those spirits of yours, Jem, till you want 'em, and don't let it come upon you all at once. Have it in mind that to-morrow's fair day, and Lightfoot must go. I bid Farmer Truck call for him to-night. He said he'd take him along with his own, and he'll be here just now—and then I know how it will be with you, Jem!' 'So do I!' cried Jem, swallowing his secret with great difficulty, and then tumbling head over heels four times running.

A carriage passed the window, and stopped at the door. Jem ran out; it was his mistress. She came in smiling, and soon made the old woman smile, too, by praising the neatness of everything in the house.

We shall pass over, however important as they were deemed at the time, the praises of the strawberries, and of 'my grandmother's china plate.'

Another knock was heard at the door. 'Run, Jem,' said his mother. 'I hope it's our milk-woman with cream for the lady.' No; it was Farmer Truck come for Lightfoot. The old woman's countenance fell. 'Fetch him out, dear,' said she, turning to her son; but Jem was gone; he flew out to the stable the moment he saw the flap of Farmer Truck's greatcoat.

'Sit ye down, farmer,' said the old woman, after they had waited about five minutes in expectation of Jem's return. 'You'd best sit down, if the lady will give you leave; for he'll not hurry himself back again. My boy's a fool, madam, about that there horse.' Trying to laugh, she added, 'I knew how Lightfoot and he would be loth enough to part. He won't bring him out to the last minute; so do sit ye down, neighbour.'

The farmer had scarcely sat down when Jem, with a pale, wild countenance, came back. 'What's the matter?' said his mistress. 'God bless the boy!' said his mother, looking at him quite frightened, whilst he tried to speak but could not.

She went up to him, and then leaning his head against her, he cried, 'It's gone!—it's all gone!' and, bursting into tears, he sobbed as if his little heart would break. 'What's gone, love?' said his mother. 'My two guineas—Lightfoot's two guineas. I went to fetch 'em to give you, mammy; but the broken flower-pot that I put them in and all's gone!—quite gone!' repeated he, checking his sobs. 'I saw them safe last night, and was showing 'em to Lightfoot; and I was so glad to think I had earned them all myself; and I thought how surprised you'd look, and how glad you'd be, and how you'd kiss me, and all!'

His mother listened to him with the greatest surprise, whilst his mistress stood in silence, looking first at the old woman and then at Jem with a penetrating eye, as if she suspected the truth of his story, and was afraid of becoming the dupe of her own compassion.

'What's the matter?' said his mistress. 'God bless the boy!' said his mother.

'This is a very strange thing!' said she gravely. 'How came you to leave all your money in a broken flower-pot in the stable? How came you not to give it to your mother to take care of?' 'Why, don't you remember?' said Jem, looking up in the midst of his tears—'why, don't you remember you, your own self, bid me not tell her about it till you were by?' 'And did you not tell her?' 'Nay, ask mammy,' said Jem, a little offended; and when afterwards the lady went on questioning him in a severe manner, as if she did not believe him, he at last made no answer. 'O Jem! Jem! why don't you speak to the lady?' said his mother. 'I have spoke, and spoke the truth,' said Jem proudly; 'and she did not believe me.'

Still the lady, who had lived too long in the world to be without suspicion, maintained a cold manner, and determined to wait the event without interfering, saying only that she hoped the money would be found, and advised Jem to have done crying.

'I have done,' said Jem; 'I shall cry no more.' And as he had the greatest command over himself, he actually did not shed another tear, not even when the farmer got up to go, saying he could wait no longer.

Jem silently went to bring out Lightfoot. The lady now took her seat, where she could see all that passed at the open parlour-window. The old woman stood at the door, and several idle people of the village, who had gathered round the lady's carriage examining it, turned about to listen. In a minute or two Jem appeared, with a steady countenance, leading Lightfoot, and, when he came up, without saying a word, put the bridle into Farmer Truck's hand. 'He *has been* a good horse,' said the farmer. 'He *is* a good horse!' cried Jem, and threw his arm over Lightfoot's neck, hiding his own face as he leaned upon him.

At this instant a party of milk-women went by; and one of them, having set down her pail, came behind Jem and gave him a pretty smart blow upon the back. He looked up. 'And don't you know me?' said she. 'I forget,' said Jem; 'I think I have seen your face before, but I forget.' 'Do you so? and you'll tell me just now,' said she, half opening her hand, 'that you forget who gave you this, and who charged you not to part with it, too.' Here she quite opened her large hand, and on the palm of it appeared Jem's silver penny.

'Where?' exclaimed Jem, seizing it, 'oh, where did you find it? and have you—oh, tell me, have you got the rest of my money?' 'I know nothing of your money—I don't know what you would be at,' said the milk-woman. 'But where—pray tell me where—did you find this?' 'With them that you gave it to, I suppose,' said the milk-woman, turning away suddenly to take up her milk-pail. But now Jem's mistress called to her through the window, begging her to stop, and joining in his entreaties to know how she came by the silver penny.

'Why, madam,' said she, taking up the corner of her apron, 'I came by it in an odd way, too. You must know my Betty is sick, so I came with the milk myself, though it's not what I'm used to; for my Betty—you know my Betty?' said she, turning round to the old woman, 'my Betty serves you, and she's a tight and stirring lassy, ma'am, I can assure——' 'Yes, I don't doubt it,' said the lady impatiently; 'but about the silver penny?' 'Why, that's true; as I was coming along all alone, for the rest came round, and I came a short cut across yon field—no, you can't see it, madam, where you stand—but if you were here——' 'I see it—I know it,' said Jem, out of breath with anxiety. 'Well—well—I rested my pail upon the stile, and sets me down awhile, and there comes out of the hedge—I don't know well how, for they startled me so I'd like to have thrown down my milk—two boys, one about the size of he,' said she, pointing to Jem, 'and one a matter taller, but ill-looking like; so I did not think to stir to make way for them, and they were like in a desperate hurry: so, without waiting for the stile, one of 'em pulled at the gate, and when it would not open (for it was tied with a pretty stout cord) one of 'em whips out with his knife and cuts it——Now, have you a knife about you, sir?' continued the milk-woman to the farmer. He gave her his knife. 'Here, now, ma'am, just sticking, as it were here, between the blade and the haft, was the silver penny. The lad took no notice; but when he opened it, out it falls. Still he takes no heed, but cuts the cord, as I said before, and through the gate they went, and out of sight in half a minute. I picks up the penny, for my heart misgave me that it was the very one my husband had had a long time, and had given against my voice to he,' pointing to Jem; 'and I charged him not to part with it; and, ma'am, when I looked I knew it by the mark, so I thought I would show it to *he*,' again pointing to Jem, 'and let him give it back to those it belongs to.' 'It belongs to me,' said Jem, 'I never gave it to anybody—but——' 'But,' cried the farmer, 'those boys have robbed him; it is they who have all his money.' 'Oh, which way did they go?' cried Jem, 'I'll run after them.'

'No, no,' said the lady, calling to her servant; and she desired him to take his horse and ride after them. 'Ay,' added Farmer Truck, 'do you take the road, and I'll take the field way, and I'll be bound we'll have 'em presently.'

Whilst they were gone in pursuit of the thieves, the lady, who was now thoroughly convinced of Jem's truth, desired her coachman would produce what she had ordered him to bring with him that evening. Out of the boot of the carriage the coachman immediately produced a new saddle and bridle.

How Jem's eyes sparkled when the saddle was thrown upon Lightfoot's back! 'Put it on your horse yourself, Jem,' said the lady; 'it is yours.'

Confused reports of Lightfoot's splendid accoutrements, of the pursuit of thieves, and of the fine and generous lady who was standing at dame Preston's window, quickly spread through the village, and drew everybody from their houses. They crowded round Jem to hear the story. The children especially, who were fond of him, expressed the strongest indignation against the thieves. Every eye was on the stretch; and now some, who had run down the lane, came back shouting, 'Here they are! they've got the thieves!'

The footman on horseback carried one boy before him; and the farmer, striding along, dragged another. The latter had on a red jacket, which little Jem immediately recollected, and scarcely dared lift his eyes to look at the boy on horseback. 'Good God!' said he to himself, 'it must be—yet surely it can't be Lawrence!' The footman rode on as fast as the people would let him. The boy's hat was slouched, and his head hung down, so that nobody could see his face.

At this instant there was a disturbance in the crowd. A man who was half-drunk pushed his way forwards, swearing that nobody should stop him; that he had a right to see—and he *would* see. And so he did; for, forcing through all resistance, he staggered up to the footman just as he was lifting down the boy he had carried before him. 'I *will*—I tell you I *will* see the thief!' cried the drunken man, pushing up the boy's hat. It was his own son. 'Lawrence!' exclaimed the wretched father. The shock sobered him at once, and he hid his face in his hands.

There was an awful silence. Lawrence fell on his knees, and in a voice that could scarcely be heard made a full confession of all the circumstances of his guilt.

'Such a young creature so wicked!' the bystanders exclaimed; 'what could put such wickedness in your head?' 'Bad company,' said Lawrence. 'And how came you—what brought you into bad company?' 'I don't know, except it was idleness.'

While this was saying, the farmer was emptying Lazy Lawrence's pockets; and when the money appeared, all his former companions in the village looked at each other with astonishment and terror. Their parents grasped their little hands closer, and cried, 'Thank God! he is not my son. How often when he was little we used, as he lounged about, to tell him that idleness was the root of all evil.'

As for the hardened wretch, his accomplice, every one was impatient to have him sent to gaol. He put on a bold, insolent countenance, till he heard Lawrence's confession; till the money was found upon him; and he heard the milk-woman declare that she would swear to the silver penny which he had dropped. Then he turned pale, and betrayed the strongest signs of fear.

'We must take him before the justice,' said the farmer, 'and he'll be lodged in Bristol gaol.'

'Oh!' said Jem, springing forwards when Lawrence's hands were going to be tied, 'let him go—won't you?—can't you let him go?' 'Yes, madam, for mercy's sake,' said Jem's mother to the lady; 'think what a disgrace to his family to be sent to gaol.'

His father stood by wringing his hands in an agony of despair. 'It's all my fault,' cried he; 'brought him up in *idleness*.' 'But he'll never be idle any more,' said Jem; 'won't you speak for him, ma'am?' 'Don't ask the lady to speak for him,' said the farmer; 'it's better he should go to Bridewell now, than to the gallows by and by.'

Nothing more was said; for everybody felt the truth of the farmer's speech.

Lawrence was eventually sent to Bridewell for a month, and the stable-boy was sent for trial, convicted, and transported to Botany Bay.

During Lawrence's confinement, Jem often visited him, and carried him such little presents as he could afford to give; and Jem could afford to be *generous*, because he was *industrious*. Lawrence's heart was touched by his kindness, and his example struck him so forcibly that, when his confinement was ended, he resolved to set immediately to work; and, to the astonishment of all who knew him, soon became remarkable for industry. He was found early and late at his work, established a new character, and for ever lost the name of *'Lazy Lawrence*.'

THE FALSE KEY

Mr. Spencer, a very benevolent and sensible man, undertook the education of several poor children. Among the best was a boy of the name of Franklin, whom he had bred up from the time he was five years old. Franklin had the misfortune to be the son of a man of infamous character; and for many years this was a disgrace and reproach to his child. When any of the neighbours' children quarrelled with him, they used to tell him that he would turn out like his father. But Mr. Spencer always assured him that he might make himself whatever he pleased; that by behaving well he would certainly, sooner or later, secure the esteem and love of all who knew him, even of those who had the strongest prejudice against him on his father's account.

This hope was very delightful to Franklin, and he showed the strongest desire to learn and to do everything that was right; so that Mr. Spencer soon grew fond of him, and took great pains to instruct him, and to give him all the good habits and principles which might make him a useful, respectable, and happy man.

When he was about thirteen years of age, Mr. Spencer one day sent for him into his closet; and as he was folding up a letter which he had been writing, said to him, with a very kind look, but in a graver tone than usual, 'Franklin, you are going to leave me.' 'Sir!' said Franklin. 'You are now going to leave me, and to begin the world for yourself. You will carry this letter to my sister, Mrs. Churchill, in Queen's Square. You know Queen's Square?' Franklin bowed. 'You must expect,' continued Mr. Spencer, 'to meet with several disagreeable things, and a great deal of rough work, at your first setting out; but be faithful and obedient to your mistress, and obliging to your fellow-servants, and all will go well. Mrs. Churchill will make you a very good mistress, if you behave properly; and I have no doubt but you will.' 'Thank you, sir.' 'And you will always—I mean, as long as you deserve it—find a friend in me.' 'Thank you, sir—I am sure you are——' There Franklin stopped short, for the recollection of all Mr. Spencer's goodness rushed upon him at once, and he could not say another word. 'Bring me a candle to seal this letter,' said his master; and he was very glad to get out of the room. He came back with the candle, and, with a stout heart, stood by whilst the letter was sealing; and, when his master put it into his hand, said, in a cheerful voice, 'I hope you will let me see you again, sir, sometimes.' 'Certainly; whenever your mistress can spare you, I shall be very glad to see you; and remember, if ever you get into any difficulty, don't be afraid to come to me. I have sometimes spoken harshly to you; but you will not meet with a more indulgent friend.' Franklin at this turned away with a full heart; and, after making two or three attempts to express his gratitude, left the room without being able to speak.

He got to Queen's Square about three o'clock. The door was opened by a large, red-faced man, in a blue coat and scarlet waistcoat, to whom he felt afraid to give his message, lest he should not be a servant. 'Well, what's your business, sir?' said the butler. 'I have a letter for Mrs. Churchill, *sir*,' said Franklin, endeavouring to pronounce his *sir* in a tone as respectful as the butler's was insolent.

The man, having examined the direction, seal, and edges of the letter, carried it upstairs, and in a few minutes returned, and ordered Franklin to rub his shoes well and follow him. He was then shown into a handsome room, where he found his mistress—an elderly lady. She asked him a few questions, examining him attentively as she spoke; and her severe eye at first and her gracious smile afterwards, made him feel that she was a person to be both loved and feared. 'I shall give you in charge,' said she, ringing a bell, 'to my housekeeper, and I hope she will have no reason to be displeased with you.'

The housekeeper, when she first came in, appeared with a smiling countenance; but the moment she cast her eyes on Franklin, it changed to a look of surprise and suspicion. Her mistress recommended him to her protection, saying, 'Pomfret, I hope you will keep this boy under your own eye.' And she received him with a cold 'Very well, ma'am,' which plainly showed that she was not disposed to like him. In fact, Mrs. Pomfret was a woman so fond of power, and so jealous of favour, that she would have quarrelled with an angel who had got so near her mistress without her introduction. She smothered her displeasure, however, till night; when, as she attended her mistress's toilette, she could not refrain from expressing her sentiments. She began cautiously: 'Ma'am, is not this the boy Mr. Spencer was talking of one day— that has been brought up by the *Villaintropic Society*, I think they call it?'—'Philanthropic Society; yes,' said her mistress; 'and my brother gives him a high character: I hope he will do very well.' 'I'm sure I hope so too,' observed Mrs. Pomfret; 'but I can't say; for my part, I've no great notion of those low people. They say all those children are taken from the very lowest *drugs* and *refuges* of the town, and surely they are like enough, ma'am, to take after their own fathers and mothers.' 'But they are not suffered to be with their parents,' rejoined the lady; 'and therefore cannot be hurt by their example. This little boy, to be sure, was unfortunate in his father, but he has had an excellent education.' 'Oh, *education*! to be sure, ma'am, I know. I don't say but what *education* is a great thing. But then, ma'am, *education* can't change the *natur* that's in one, they say; and one that's born naturally bad and low, they say, all the *education* in the world won't do no good; and, for my part, ma'am, I know I knows best; but I should be afraid to let any of those *Villaintropic* folks get into my house; for nobody can tell the *natur* of them aforehand. I declare it frights me.' 'Pomfret, I thought you had better sense: how would this poor boy earn his bread? he would be forced to starve or steal, if everybody had such prejudices.'

Pomfret, who really was a good woman, was softened at this idea, and said, 'God forbid he should starve or steal, and God forbid I should say anything *prejudiciary* of the boy; for there may be no harm in him.'

'Well,' said Mrs. Churchill, changing her tone, 'but, Pomfret, if we don't like the boy at the end of the month, we have done with him; for I have only promised Mr. Spencer to keep him a month upon trial: there is no harm done.' 'Dear, no, ma'am, to be sure; and cook must put up with her disappointment, that's all.' 'What disappointment?' 'About her nephew, ma'am; the boy she and I was speaking to you for.' 'When?' 'The day you called her up about the almond pudding, ma'am. If you remember, you said you should have no objections to try the boy; and upon that cook bought him new shirts; but they are to the good, as I tell her.' 'But I did not promise to take her nephew.' 'Oh no, ma'am, not at all; she does not think to *say that*, else I should be very angry; but the poor woman never let fall a word, any more than frets that the boy should miss such a good place.' 'Well, but since I did say that I should have no objection to try him, I shall keep my word; let him come to-morrow. Let them both have a fair trial, and at the end of the month I can decide which I like best, and which we had better keep.'

Dismissed with these orders, Mrs. Pomfret hastened to report all that had passed to the cook, like a favourite minister, proud to display the extent of her secret influence. In the morning Felix, the cook's nephew, arrived; and, the moment he came into the kitchen, every eye, even the scullion's, was fixed upon him with approbation, and afterwards glanced upon Franklin with contempt—contempt which Franklin could not endure without some confusion, though quite unconscious of having deserved it; nor, upon the most impartial and cool self-examination, could he comprehend the justice of his judges. He perceived indeed—for the comparisons were minutely made in audible and scornful whispers—that Felix was a much handsomer, or as the kitchen maid expressed it, a much more genteeler gentlemanly looking like sort of person than he was; and he was made to understand that he wanted a frill to his shirt, a cravat, a pair of thin shoes, and, above all, shoe-strings, besides other nameless advantages, which justly made his rival the admiration of the kitchen. However, upon calling to mind all that his friend Mr. Spencer had ever said to him, he could not recollect his having warned him that shoe-strings were indispensable requisites to the character of a good servant; so that he could only comfort himself with resolving, if possible, to make amends for these deficiencies, and to dissipate the prejudices which he saw were formed against him, by the strictest adherence to all that his tutor had taught him to be his duty. He hoped to secure the approbation of his mistress by scrupulous obedience to all her commands, and faithful care of all that belonged to her. At the same time he flattered himself he should win the goodwill of his fellow-servants by showing a constant desire to oblige them. He pursued this plan of conduct steadily for nearly three weeks, and found that he succeeded beyond his expectations in pleasing his mistress; but unfortunately he found it more difficult to please his fellow-servants, and he sometimes offended when he least expected it. He had made great progress in the affections of Corkscrew, the butler, by working indeed very hard for him, and doing every day at least half his business. But one unfortunate night the butler was gone out; the bell rang: he went upstairs; and his mistress asking where Corkscrew was, he answered that he was gone out. 'Where to?' said his mistress. 'I don't know,' answered Franklin. And, as he had told exactly the truth, and meant to do no harm, he was surprised, at the butler's return, when he repeated to him what had passed, at receiving a sudden box on the ear, and the appellation of a mischievous, impertinent, mean-spirited brat.

'Mischievous, impertinent, mean!' repeated Franklin to himself; but, looking in the butler's face, which was a deeper scarlet than usual, he judged that he was far from sober, and did not doubt but that the next morning, when he came to the use of his reason, he would be sensible of his injustice, and apologise for his box of the ear. But no apology coming all day, Franklin at last ventured to request an explanation, or rather, to ask what he had best do on the next occasion. 'Why,' said Corkscrew, 'when mistress asked for me, how came you to say I was gone out?' 'Because, you know, I saw you go out.' 'And when she asked you where I was gone, how came you to say that you did not know?' 'Because, indeed, I did not.' 'You are a stupid blockhead! could you not say I was gone to the washerwoman's?' 'But *were* you?' said Franklin. 'Was I?' cried Corkscrew, and looked as if he would have struck him again: 'how dare you give me the lie, Mr. Hypocrite? You would be ready enough, I'll be bound, to make excuses for yourself. Why are not mistress's clogs cleaned? Go along and blacken 'em, this minute, and send Felix to me.'

From this time forward Felix alone was privileged to enter the butler's pantry. Felix became the favourite of Corkscrew; and, though Franklin by no means sought to pry into the mysteries of their private conferences, nor ever entered without knocking at the door, yet it was his fate once to be sent of a message at an unlucky time; and, as the door was half-open, he could not avoid seeing Felix drinking a bumper of red liquor, which he could not help suspecting to be wine; and, as the decanter, which usually went upstairs after dinner, was at this time in the butler's grasp, without any stopper in it, he was involuntarily forced to suspect they were drinking his mistress's wine.

Nor were the bumpers of port the only unlawful rewards which Felix received: his aunt, the cook, had occasion for his assistance, and she had many delicious *douceurs* in her gift. Many a handful of currants, many a half-custard, many a triangular remnant of pie, besides the choice of his own meal at breakfast, dinner, and supper, fell to the share of the favourite Felix; whilst Franklin was neglected, though he took the utmost pains to please the cook in all honourable service, and, when she was hot, angry, or hurried, he was always at hand to help her; and in the hour of adversity, when the clock struck five, and no dinner was dished, and no kitchen-maid with twenty pair of hands was to be had, Franklin would answer to her call, with flowers to garnish her dishes, and presence of mind to know, in the midst of the commotion, where everything that was wanting was to be found; so that, quick as lightning, all difficulties vanished before him. Yet when the danger was over, and the hour of adversity had passed, the ungrateful cook would forget her benefactor, and, when it came to his supper time, would throw him, with a carelessness that touched him sensibly, anything which the other servants were too nice to eat. All this Franklin bore with fortitude; nor did he envy Felix the dainties which he ate, sometimes close beside him: 'For,' said he to himself, 'I have a clear conscience, and that is more than Felix can have. I know how he wins cook's favour too well, and I fancy I know how I have offended her; for since the day I saw the basket, she has done nothing but huff me.'

The history of the basket was this. Mrs. Pomfret, the housekeeper, had several times, directly and indirectly, given the world below to understand that she and her mistress thought there was a prodigious quantity of meat eaten of late. Now, when she spoke, it was usually at dinner time; she always looked, or Franklin imagined that she looked, suspiciously at him. Other people looked more maliciously; but, as he felt himself perfectly innocent, he went on eating his dinner in silence.

But at length it was time to explain. One Sunday there appeared a handsome sirloin of beef, which before noon on Monday had shrunk almost to the bare bone, and presented such a deplorable spectacle to the opening eyes of Mrs. Pomfret that her long-smothered indignation burst forth, and she boldly declared she was now certain there had been foul play, and she would have the beef found, or she would know why. She spoke, but no beef appeared, till Franklin, with a look of sudden recollection, cried, 'Did not I see something like a piece of beef in a basket in the dairy?—I think——'

The cook, as if somebody had smote her a deadly blow, grew pale; but, suddenly recovering the use of her speech, turned upon Franklin, and, with a voice of thunder, gave him the lie direct; and forthwith, taking Mrs. Pomfret by the ruffle, led the way to the dairy, declaring she could defy the world—'that so she could, and would.' 'There, ma'am,' said she kicking an empty basket which lay on the floor—'there's malice for you. Ask him why he don't show you the beef in the basket.' 'I thought I saw——' poor Franklin began. 'You thought you saw!' cried the cook, coming close up to him with kimboed arms, and looking like a dragon; 'and pray, sir, what business has such a one as you to think you see? And pray, ma'am, will you be pleased to speak—perhaps, ma'am, he'll condescend to obey you—ma'am, will you be pleased to forbid him my dairy? for here he comes prying and spying about; and how, ma'am, am I to answer for my butter and cream, or anything at all? I'm sure it's what I can't pretend to, unless you do me the justice to forbid him my places.'

Mrs. Pomfret, whose eyes were blinded by her prejudices against the folks of the *Villaintropic Society*, and also by her secret jealousy of a boy whom she deemed to be a growing favourite of her mistress's, took part with the cook, and ended, as she began, with a firm persuasion that Franklin was the guilty person. 'Let him alone, let him alone!' said she, 'he has as many turns and windings as a hare; but we shall catch him yet, I'll be bound, in some of his doublings. I knew the nature of him well enough, from the first time I ever set my eyes upon him; but mistress shall have her own way, and see the end of it.'

These words, and the bitter sense of injustice, drew tears at length fast down the proud cheek of Franklin, which might possibly have touched Mrs. Pomfret, if Felix, with a sneer, had not called them *crocodile tears*. 'Felix, too!' thought he; 'this is too much.' In fact, Felix had till now professed himself his firm ally, and had on his part received from Franklin unequivocal proofs of friendship; for it must be told that every other morning, when it was Felix's turn to get breakfast, Felix never was up in decent time, and must inevitably have come to public disgrace if Franklin had not got all the breakfast things ready for him, the bread and butter spread, and the toast toasted; and had not, moreover, regularly, when the clock struck eight, and Mrs. Pomfret's foot was heard overhead, run to call the sleeping Felix, and helped him constantly through the hurry of getting dressed one instant before the housekeeper came downstairs. All this could not but be present to his memory; but, scorning to reproach him, Franklin wiped away his crocodile tears, and preserved a magnanimous silence.

The hour of retribution was; however, not so far off as Felix imagined. Cunning people may go on cleverly in their devices for some time; but although they may escape once, twice, perhaps ninety-nine times, what does that signify?—for the hundredth time they come to shame, and lose all their character. Grown bold by frequent success, Felix became more careless in his operations; and it happened that one day he met his mistress full in the passage, as he was going on one of the cook's secret errands. 'Where are you going, Felix?' said his mistress. 'To the washerwoman's, ma'am,' answered he, with his usual effrontery. 'Very well,' said she. 'Call at the bookseller's in—stay, I must write down the direction. Pomfret,' said she, opening the housekeeper's room door. 'have you a bit of paper?' Pomfret came with the writing-paper, and looked very angry to see that Felix was going out without her knowledge; so, while Mrs. Churchill was writing the direction, she stood talking to him about it; whilst he, in the greatest terror imaginable, looked up in her face as she spoke; but was all the time intent on parrying on the other side the attacks of a little French dog of his mistress's, which, unluckily for him, had followed her into the passage. Manchon was extremely fond of Felix, who, by way of pleasing his mistress, had paid most assiduous court to her dog; yet now his caresses were rather troublesome. Manchon leaped up, and was not to be rebuffed. 'Poor fellow—poor fellow—down! down! poor fellow!' cried Felix, and put him away. But Manchon leaped up again, and began smelling near the fatal pocket in a most alarming manner. 'You will see by this direction where you are to go,' said his mistress. 'Manchon, come here—and you will be so good as to bring me—down! down! Manchon, be quiet!' But Manchon knew better—he had now got his head into Felix's pocket, and would not be quiet till he had drawn from thence, rustling out of its brown paper, half a cold turkey, which had been missing since morning. 'My cold turkey, as I'm alive!' exclaimed the housekeeper, darting upon it with horror and amazement. 'What is all this?' said Mrs. Churchill, in a composed voice. 'I don't know, ma'am,' answered Felix, so confused that he knew not what to say; 'but——' 'But what?' cried Mrs. Pomfret, indignation flashing from her eyes. 'But what?' repeated his mistress, waiting for his reply with a calm air of attention, which still more disconcerted Felix; for, though with an angry person he might have some chance of escape, he knew that he could not invent any excuse in such circumstances, which could stand the examination of a person in her sober senses. He was struck dumb. 'Speak,' said Mrs. Churchill, in a still lower tone; 'I am ready to hear all you have to say. In my house everybody shall have justice; speak—but what?' 'But,' stammered Felix; and, after in vain attempting to equivocate, confessed that he was going to take the turkey to his cousin's; but he threw all the blame upon his aunt, the cook, who, he said, had ordered him upon this expedition.

The cook was now summoned; but she totally denied all knowledge of the affair, with the same violence with which she had lately confounded Franklin about the beef in the basket; not entirely, however, with the same success; for Felix, perceiving by his mistress's eye that she was on the point of desiring him to leave the house immediately; and not being very willing to leave a place in which he had lived so well with the butler, did not hesitate to confront his aunt with assurance equal to her own. He knew how to bring his charge home to her. He produced a note in her own handwriting, the purport of which was to request her cousin's acceptance of 'some *delicate cold turkey*,' and to beg she would send her, by the return of the bearer, a little of her cherry-brandy.

Mrs. Churchill coolly wrote upon the back of the note her cook's discharge, and informed Felix she had no further occasion for his services, but, upon his pleading with many tears, which Franklin did not call *crocodile tears*, that he was so young, that he was under the dominion of his aunt, he touched Mrs. Pomfret's compassion, and she obtained for him permission to stay till the end of the month, to give him yet a chance of redeeming his character.

Mrs. Pomfret, now seeing how far she had been imposed upon, resolved, for the future, to be more upon her guard with Felix, and felt that she had treated Franklin with great injustice, when she accused him of malpractices about the sirloin of beef.

Good people, when they are made sensible that they have treated any one with injustice, are impatient to have an opportunity to rectify their mistake; and Mrs. Pomfret was now prepared to see everything which Franklin did in the most favourable point of view; especially as the next day she discovered that it was he who every morning boiled the water for her tea, and buttered her toast—services for which she had always thought she was indebted to Felix. Besides, she had rated Felix's abilities very highly, because he made up her weekly accounts for her; but unluckily once, when Franklin was out of the way, and she brought a bill in a hurry to her favourite to cast up, she discovered that he did not know how to cast up pounds, shillings, and pence, and he was obliged to confess that she must wait till Franklin came home.

But, passing over a number of small incidents which gradually unfolded the character of the two boys, we must proceed to a more serious affair.

Corkscrew frequently, after he had finished taking away supper, and after the housekeeper was gone to bed, sallied forth to a neighbouring alehouse to drink with his friends. The alehouse was kept by that cousin of Felix's who was so fond of 'delicate cold turkey,' and who had such choice cherry-brandy. Corkscrew kept the key of the house door, so that he could return home whenever he thought proper; and, if he should by accident be called for by his mistress after supper, Felix knew where to find him, and did not scruple to make any of those excuses which poor Franklin had too much integrity to use.

All these precautions taken, the butler was at liberty to indulge his favourite passion, which so increased with indulgence that his wages were by no means sufficient to support him in this way of life. Every day he felt less resolution to break through his bad habits; for every day drinking became more necessary to him. His health was ruined. With a red, pimpled, bloated face, emaciated legs, and a swelled, diseased body, he appeared the victim of intoxication. In the morning, when he got up, his hands trembled, his spirits flagged, he could do nothing until he had taken a dram—an operation which he was obliged to repeat several times in the course of the day, as all those wretched people *must* who once acquire this habit.

He had run up a long bill at the alehouse which he frequented; and the landlord, who grew urgent for his money, refused to give further credit.

One night, when Corkscrew had drunk enough only to make him fretful, he leaned with his elbow surlily upon the table, began to quarrel with the landlord, and swore that he had not of late treated him like a gentleman. To which the landlord coolly replied, 'That as long as he had paid like a gentleman, he had been treated like one, and *that* was as much as any one could expect, or, at any rate, as much as any one would meet with in this world.' For the truth of this assertion he appealed, laughing, to a party of men who were drinking in the room. The men, however, took part with Corkscrew, and, drawing him over to their table, made him sit down with them. They were in high good-humour, and the butler soon grew so intimate with them that, in the openness of his heart, he soon communicated to them not only all his own affairs, but all that he knew, and more than all that he knew, of his mistress's.

His new friends were by no means uninterested by his conversation, and encouraged him as much as possible to talk; for they had secret views, which the butler was by no means sufficiently sober to discover.

Mrs. Churchill had some fine old family plate; and these men belonged to a gang of housebreakers. Before they parted with Corkscrew, they engaged him to meet them again the next night; their intimacy was still more closely cemented. One of the men actually offered to lend Corkscrew three guineas towards the payment of his debt, and hinted that, if he thought proper, he could easily get the whole cleared off. Upon this hint, Corkscrew became all attention, till, after some hesitation on their part, and repeated promises of secrecy on his, they at length disclosed their plans to him. They gave him to understand that, if he would assist in letting them into his mistress's house, they would let him have an ample share in the booty. The butler, who had the reputation of being an honest man, and indeed whose integrity had hitherto been proof against everything but his mistress's port, turned pale and trembled at this proposal, drank two or three bumpers to drown thought, and promised to give an answer the next day.

He went home more than half-intoxicated. His mind was so full of what had passed, that he could not help bragging to Felix, whom he found awake at his return, that he could have his bill paid off at the alehouse whenever he pleased; dropping, besides, some hints which were not lost upon Felix.

In the morning Felix reminded him of the things which he had said; and Corkscrew, alarmed, endeavoured to evade his questions by saying that he was not in his senses when he talked in that manner. Nothing, however, that he could urge made any impression upon Felix, whose recollection on the subject was perfectly distinct, and who had too much cunning himself, and too little confidence in his companion, to be the dupe of his dissimulation. The butler knew not what to do when he saw that Felix was absolutely determined either to betray their scheme or to become a sharer in the booty.

The next night came, and he was now to make a final decision; either to determine on breaking off entirely with his new acquaintances, or taking Felix with him to join in the plot.

His debt, his love of drinking, the impossibility of indulging it without a fresh supply of money, all came into his mind at once and conquered his remaining scruples. It is said by those whose fatal experience gives them a right to be believed, that a drunkard will sacrifice anything, everything, sooner than the pleasure of habitual intoxication.

How much easier is it never to begin a bad custom than to break through it when once formed!

The hour of rendezvous came, and Corkscrew went to the alehouse, where he found the housebreakers waiting for him, and a glass of brandy ready poured out. He sighed—drank—hesitated—drank again—heard the landlord talk of his bill, saw the money produced which would pay it in a moment—drank again—cursed himself, and, giving his hand to the villain who was whispering in his ear, swore that he could not help it, and must do as they would have him. They required of him to give up the key of the house door, that they might get another made by it. He had left it with Felix, and was now obliged to explain the new difficulty which had arisen. Felix knew enough to ruin them, and must therefore be won over. This was no very difficult task; he had a strong desire to have some worked cravats, and the butler knew enough of him to believe that this would be a sufficient bribe. The cravats were bought and shown to Felix. He thought them the only things wanting to make him a complete fine gentleman; and to go without them, especially when he had once seen himself in the glass with one tied on in a splendid bow, appeared impossible. Even this paltry temptation, working upon his vanity, at length prevailed with a boy whose integrity had long been corrupted by the habits of petty pilfering and daily falsehood. It was agreed that, the first time his mistress sent him out on a message, he should carry the key of the house door to his cousin's, and deliver it into the hands of one of the gang, who were there in waiting for it. Such was the scheme.

Felix, the night after all this had been planned, went to bed and fell fast asleep; but the butler, who had not yet stifled the voice of conscience, felt, in the silence of the night, so insupportably miserable that, instead of going to rest, he stole softly into the pantry for a bottle of his mistress's wine, and there drinking glass after glass, he stayed till he became so far intoxicated that, though he contrived to find his way back to bed, he could by no means undress himself. Without any power of recollection, he flung himself upon the bed, leaving his candle half hanging out of the candlestick beside him. Franklin slept in the next room to him, and presently awaking, thought he perceived a strong smell of something burning. He jumped up, and seeing a light under the butler's door, gently opened it, and, to his astonishment, beheld one of the bed curtains in flames. He immediately ran to the butler, and pulled him with all his force to rouse him from his lethargy. He came to his senses at length, but was so terrified and so helpless that, if it had not been for Franklin, the whole house would soon inevitably have been on fire. Felix, trembling and cowardly, knew not what to do; and it was curious to see him obeying Franklin, whose turn it now was to command. Franklin ran upstairs to awaken Mrs. Pomfret, whose terror of fire was so great that she came from her room almost out of her senses, whilst he, with the greatest presence of mind, recollected where he had seen two large tubs of water, which the maids had prepared the night before for their washing, and seizing the wet linen which had been left to soak, he threw them upon the flames. He exerted himself with so much good sense, that the fire was presently extinguished.

Everything was now once more safe and quiet. Mrs. Pomfret, recovering from her fright, postponed all inquiries till the morning, and rejoiced that her mistress had not been awakened, whilst Corkscrew flattered himself that he should be able to conceal the true cause of the accident.

'Don't you tell Mrs. Pomfret where you found the candle when you came into the room,' said he to Franklin. 'If she asks me, you know I must tell the truth,' replied he. 'Must!' repeated Felix, sneeringly; 'what, you *must* be a tell-tale!' 'No, I never told any tales of anybody, and I should be very sorry to get any one into a scrape; but for all that I shall not tell a lie, either for myself or anybody else, let you call me what names you will.' 'But if I were to give you something that you would like,' said Corkscrew—'something that I know you would like?' repeated Felix. 'Nothing you can give me will do,' answered Franklin, steadily; 'so it is useless to say any more about it—I hope I shall not be questioned.' In this hope he was mistaken; for the first thing Mrs. Pomfret did in the morning was to come into the room to examine and deplore the burnt curtains, whilst Corkscrew stood by, endeavouring to exculpate himself by all the excuses he could invent.

Mrs. Pomfret, however, though sometimes blinded by her prejudices, was no fool; and it was absolutely impossible to make her believe that a candle which had been left on the hearth, where Corkscrew protested he had left it, could have set curtains on fire which were at least six feet distant. Turning short round to Franklin, she desired that he would show her where he found the candle when he came into the room. He took up the candlestick; but the moment the housekeeper cast her eye upon it, she snatched it from his hands. 'How did this candlestick come here? This was not the candlestick you found here last night,' cried she. 'Yes, indeed it was,' answered Franklin. 'That is impossible,' retorted she, vehemently, 'for I left this candlestick with my own hands, last night, in the hall, the last thing I did, after you,' said she, turning to the butler, 'was gone to bed—I'm sure of it. Nay, don't you recollect my taking this *japanned candlestick* out of your hand, and making you to go up to bed with the brass one, and I bolted the door at the stair-head after you?'

This was all very true; but Corkscrew had afterwards gone down from his room by a back staircase, unbolted that door, and, upon his return from the alehouse, had taken the japanned candlestick by mistake upstairs, and had left the brass one in its stead upon the hall table.

'Oh, ma'am,' said Felix, 'indeed you forget; for Mr. Corkscrew came into my room to desire me to call him betimes in the morning, and I happened to take particular notice, and he had the japanned candlestick in his hand, and that was just as I heard you bolting the door. Indeed, ma'am, you forget.' 'Indeed, sir,' retorted Mrs. Pomfret, rising in anger, 'I do not forget; I'm not come to be *superannuated* yet, I hope. How do you dare to tell me I forget?' 'Oh, ma'am,' cried Felix, 'I beg your pardon, I did not—I did not mean to say you forgot, but only I thought, perhaps, you might not particularly remember; for if you please to recollect——' 'I won't please to recollect just whatever you please, sir! Hold your tongue; why should you poke yourself into this scrape; what have you to do with it, I should be glad to know?' 'Nothing in the world, oh nothing in the world; I'm sure I beg your pardon, ma'am,' answered Felix, in a soft tone; and, sneaking off, left his friend Corkscrew to fight his own battle, secretly resolving to desert in good time, if he saw any danger of the alehouse transactions coming to light.

Corkscrew could make but very blundering excuses for himself; and, conscious of guilt, he turned pale, and appeared so much more terrified than butlers usually appear when detected in a lie, that Mrs. Pomfret resolved, as she said, to sift the matter to the bottom. Impatiently did she wait till the clock struck nine, and her mistress's bell rang, the signal for her attendance at her levee. 'How do you find yourself this morning, ma'am?' said she, undrawing the curtains. 'Very sleepy, indeed,' answered her mistress in a drowsy voice; 'I think I must sleep half an hour longer—shut the curtains.' 'As you please, ma'am; but I suppose I had better open a little of the window shutter, for it's past nine.' 'But just struck.' 'Oh dear, ma'am, it struck before I came upstairs, and you know we are twenty minutes slow—Lord bless us!' exclaimed Mrs. Pomfret, as she let fall the bar of the window, which roused her mistress. 'I'm sure I beg your pardon a thousand times—it's only the bar—because I had this great key in my hand.' 'Put down the key, then, or you'll knock something else down; and you may open the shutters now, for I'm quite awake.' 'Dear me! I'm so sorry to think of disturbing you,' cried Mrs. Pomfret, at the same time throwing the shutters wide open; 'but, to be sure, ma'am, I have something to tell you which won't let you sleep again in a hurry. I brought up this here key of the house door for reasons of my own, which I'm sure you'll approve of; but I'm not come to that part of my story yet. I hope you were not disturbed by the noise in the house last night, ma'am.' 'I heard no noise.' 'I am surprised at that, though,' continued Mrs. Pomfret, and proceeded to give a most ample account of the fire, of her fears and her suspicions. 'To be sure, ma'am, what I say *is*, that without the spirit of prophecy one can nowadays account for what has passed. I'm quite clear in my own judgment that Mr. Corkscrew must have been out last night after I went to bed; for, besides the japanned candlestick, which of itself I'm sure is strong enough to hang a man, there's another circumstance, ma'am, that certifies it to me—though I have not mentioned it, ma'am, to no one yet,' lowering her voice— 'Franklin, when I questioned him, told me that he left the lantern in the outside porch in the court last night, and this morning it was on the kitchen table. Now, ma'am, that lantern could not come without hands; and I could not forget about that, you know; for Franklin says he's sure he left the lantern out.' 'And do you believe *him*?' inquired her mistress. 'To be sure, ma'am—how can I help believing him? I never found him out in the least symptom of a lie since ever he came into the house; so one can't help believing in him, like him or not.' 'Without meaning to tell a falsehood, however,' said the lady, 'he might make a mistake.' 'No, ma'am, he never makes mistakes; it is not his way to go gossiping and tattling; he never tells anything till he's asked, and then it's fit he should. About the sirloin of beef, and all, he was right in the end, I found, to do him justice; and I'm sure he's right now about the lantern—he's *always right*.'

Mrs. Churchill could not help smiling.

'If you had seen him, ma'am, last night in the midst of the fire—I'm sure we may thank him that we were not burned alive in our beds—and I shall never forget his coming to call me. Poor fellow! he that I was always scolding and scolding, enough to make him hate me. But he's too good to hate anybody; and I'll be bound I'll make it up to him now.' 'Take care that you don't go from one extreme into another, Pomfret; don't spoil the boy.' 'No, ma'am, there's no danger of that; but I'm sure if you had seen him last night yourself, you would think he deserved to be rewarded.' 'And so he shall be rewarded,' said Mrs. Churchill; 'but I will try him more fully yet.' 'There's no occasion, I think, for trying him any more, ma'am,' said Mrs. Pomfret, who was as violent in her likings as in her dislikes. 'Pray desire,' continued her mistress, 'that he will bring up breakfast this morning; and leave the key of the house door, Pomfret, with me.'

'You know this key? I shall trust it in your care.'

'You know this key? I shall trust it in your care.'

When Franklin brought the urn into the breakfast-parlour, his mistress was standing by the fire with the key in her hand. She spoke to him of his last night's exertions in terms of much approbation. 'How long have you lived with me?' said she, pausing; 'three weeks, I think?' 'Three weeks and four days, madam.' 'That is but a short time; yet you have conducted yourself so as to make me think I may depend upon you. You know this key?' 'I believe, madam, it is the key of the house door.' 'It is; I shall trust it in your care. It is a great trust for so young a person as you are.' Franklin stood silent, with a firm but modest look. 'If you take the charge of this key,' continued his mistress, 'remember it is upon condition that you never give it out of your own hands. In the daytime it must not be left in the door. You must not tell anybody where you keep it at night; and the hou door must not be unlocked after eleven o'clock at night, unless by my orders. Will you take charge of the key upon these conditions?' 'I will, madam, do anything you order me,' said Franklin, and received the key from her hands.

When Mrs. Churchill's orders were made known, they caused many secret marvellings and murmurings. Corkscrew and Felix were disconcerted, and dared not openly avow their discontent; and they treated Franklin with the greatest seeming kindness and cordiality.

Everything went on smoothly for three days. The butler never attempted his usual midnight visits to the alehouse, but went to bed in proper time, and paid particular court to Mrs. Pomfret, in order to dispel her suspicions. She had never had any idea of the real fact, that he and Felix were joined in a plot with housebreakers to rob the house, but thought he only went out at irregular hours to indulge himself in his passion for drinking.

Thus stood affairs the night before Mrs. Churchill's birthday. Corkscrew, by the housekeeper's means, ventured to present a petition that he might go to the play the next day, and his request was granted. Franklin came into the kitchen just when all the servants had gathered round the butler, who, with great importance, was reading aloud the play-bill. Everybody present soon began to speak at once, and with great enthusiasm talked of the playhouse, the actors and actresses; and then Felix, in the first pause, turned to Franklin and said, 'Lord, you know nothing of all this! *you* never went to a play, did you?' 'Never,' said Franklin, and felt, he did not know why, a little ashamed; and he longed extremely to go to one. 'How should you like to go to the play with me to-morrow?' said Corkscrew. 'Oh,' exclaimed Franklin, 'I should like it exceedingly.' 'And do you think mistress would let you if I asked?' 'I think—maybe she would, if Mrs. Pomfret asked her.' 'But then you have no money, have you?' 'No,' said Franklin, sighing. 'But stay,' said Corkscrew, 'what I'm thinking of is, that if mistress will let you go, I'll treat you myself, rather than that you should be disappointed.'

Delight, surprise, and gratitude appeared in Franklin's face at these words. Corkscrew rejoiced to see that now, at least, he had found a most powerful temptation. 'Well, then, I'll go just now and ask her. In the meantime, lend me the key of the house door for a minute or two.' 'The key!' answered Franklin, starting; 'I'm sorry, but I can't do that, for I've promised my mistress never to let it out of my own hands.' 'But how will she know anything of the matter? Run, run, and get it for us.' 'No, I *cannot*,' replied Franklin, resisting the push which the butler gave his shoulder. 'You can't?' cried Corkscrew, changing his tone; 'then, sir, I can't take you to the play.' 'Very well, sir,' said Franklin, sorrowfully, but with steadiness. 'Very well, sir,' said Felix, mimicking him, 'you need not look so important, nor fancy yourself such a great man, because you're master of a key.'

'Say no more to him,' interrupted Corkscrew; 'let him alone to take his own way. Felix, you would have no objection, I suppose, to going to the play with me?' 'Oh, I should like it of all things, if I did not come between anybody else. But come, come!' added the hypocrite, assuming a tone of friendly persuasion, 'you won't be such a blockhead, Franklin, as to lose going to the play for nothing; it's only just obstinacy. What harm can it do to lend Mr. Corkscrew the key for five minutes? he'll give it you back again safe and sound.' 'I don't doubt *that*,' answered Franklin. 'Then it must be all because you don't wish to oblige Mr. Corkscrew.' 'No, but I can't oblige him in this; for, as I told you before, my mistress trusted me. I promised never to let the key out of my own hands, and you would not have me break my trust. Mr. Spencer told me *that* was worse than *robbing*.'

At the word *robbing* both Corkscrew and Felix involuntarily cast down their eyes, and turned the conversation immediately, saying that he did very right, that they did not really want the key, and had only asked for it just to try if he would keep his word. 'Shake hands,' said Corkscrew, 'I am glad to find you out to be an honest fellow!' 'I am sorry you did not think me an honest fellow before, Mr. Corkscrew,' said Franklin giving his hand rather proudly, and he walked away.

'We shall make no hand of this prig,' said Corkscrew. 'But we'll have the key from him in spite of all his obstinacy,' said Felix; 'and let him make his story good as he can afterwards. He shall repent of these airs. To-night I'll watch him, and find out where he hides the key; and when he's asleep we'll get it without thanking him.'

This plan Felix put into execution. They discovered the place where Franklin kept the key at night, stole it whilst he slept, took off the impression in wax, and carefully replaced it in Franklin's trunk, exactly where they found it.

Probably our young readers cannot guess what use they could mean to make of this impression of the key in wax. Knowing how to do mischief is very different from wishing to do it, and the most innocent persons are generally the least ignorant. By means of the impression which they had thus obtained, Corkscrew and Felix proposed to get a false key made by Picklock, a smith who belonged to their gang of housebreakers; and with this false key knew they could open the door whenever they pleased.

Little suspecting what had happened, Franklin, the next morning, went to unlock the house door as usual; but finding the key entangled in the lock, he took it out to examine it, and perceived a lump of wax sticking in one of the wards. Struck with this circumstance, it brought to his mind all that had passed the preceding evening, and, being sure that he had no wax near the key, he began to suspect what had happened; and he could not help recollecting what he had once heard Felix say, that 'give him but a halfpenny worth of wax, and he could open the strongest lock that ever was made by hands.'

All these things considered, Franklin resolved to take the key just as it was, with the wax sticking to it, to his mistress.

'I was not mistaken when I thought I might trust *you* with this key,' said Mrs. Churchill, after she had heard his story. 'My brother will be here to-day, and I shall consult him. In the meantime, say nothing of what has passed.'

Evening came, and after tea Mr. Spencer sent for Franklin upstairs. 'So, Mr. Franklin,' said he, 'I'm glad to find you are in such high *trust* in this family.' Franklin bowed. 'But you have lost, I understand, the pleasure of going to the play to-night.' 'I don't think anything—much, I mean, of that, sir,' answered Franklin, smiling. 'Are Corkscrew and Felix *gone* to the play?' 'Yes; half an hour ago, sir.' 'Then I shall look into his room and examine the pantry and the plate that is under his care.'

When Mr. Spencer came to examine the pantry, he found the large salvers and cups in a basket behind the door, and the other things placed so as to be easily carried off. Nothing at first appeared in Corkscrew's bedchamber to strengthen their suspicions, till, just as they were going to leave the room, Mrs. Pomfret exclaimed, 'Why, if there is not Mr. Corkscrew's dress coat hanging up there! and if here isn't Felix's fine cravat that he wanted in such a hurry to go to the play! Why, sir, they can't be gone to the play. Look at the cravat. Ah! upon my word I am afraid they are not at the play. No, sir, you may be sure that they are plotting with their barbarous gang at the alehouse; and they'll certainly break into the house to-night. We shall all be murdered in our beds, as sure as I'm a living woman, sir; but if you'll only take my advice——' 'Pray, good Mrs. Pomfret,' Mr. Spencer observed, 'don't be alarmed.' 'Nay, sir, but I won't pretend to sleep in the house, if Franklin isn't to have a blunderbuss, and I a *baggonet*.' 'You shall have both, indeed, Mrs. Pomfret; but don't make such a noise, for everybody will hear you.'

The love of mystery was the only thing which could have conquered Mrs. Pomfret's love of talking. She was silent; and contented herself the rest of the evening with making signs, looking *ominous*, and stalking about the house like one possessed with a secret.

Escaped from Mrs. Pomfret's fears and advice, Mr. Spencer went to a shop within a few doors of the alehouse which he heard Corkscrew frequented, and sent to beg to speak to the landlord. He came; and, when Mr. Spencer questioned him, confessed that Corkscrew and Felix were actually drinking in his house, with two men of suspicious appearance; that, as he passed through the passage, he heard them disputing about a key; and that one of them said, 'Since we've got the key, we'll go about it to-night.' This was sufficient information. Mr. Spencer, lest the landlord should give them information of what was going forwards, took him along with him to Bow Street.

A constable and proper assistance was sent to Mrs. Churchill's. They stationed themselves in a back parlour which opened on a passage leading to the butler's pantry, where the plate was kept. A little after midnight they heard the hall door open. Corkscrew and his accomplices went directly to the pantry; and there Mr. Spencer and the constable immediately secured them, as they were carrying off their booty.

Mrs. Churchill and Pomfret had spent the night at the house of an acquaintance in the same street. 'Well, ma'am,' said Mrs. Pomfret, who had heard all the news in the morning, 'the villains are all safe, thank God. I was afraid to go to the window this morning; but it was my luck to see them all go by to gaol. They looked so shocking! I am sure I never shall forget Felix's look to my dying day! But poor Franklin! ma'am; that boy has the best heart in the world. I could not get him to give a second look at them as they passed. Poor fellow! I thought he would have dropped; and he was so modest, ma'am, when Mr. Spencer spoke to him, and told him he had done his duty.' 'And did my brother tell him what reward I intend for him?' 'No, ma'am, and I'm sure Franklin thinks no more of *reward* than I do.' 'I intend,' continued Mrs. Churchill, 'to sell some of my old useless plate, and to lay it out in an annuity for Franklin's life.' 'La, ma'am!' exclaimed Mrs. Pomfret, with unfeigned joy, 'I'm sure you are very good; and I'm very glad of it.' 'And,' continued Mrs. Churchill, 'here are some tickets for the play, which I shall beg you, Pomfret, to give him, and to take him with you.'

'I am very much obliged to you, indeed, ma'am; and I'll go with him with all my heart, and choose such plays as won't do no prejudice to his morality. And, ma'am,' continued Mrs. Pomfret, 'the night after the fire I left him my great Bible and my watch, in my will; for I never was more mistaken at the first in any boy in my born days; but he has won me by his own *deserts*, and I shall from this time forth love all the *Villaintropic* folks for his sake.'

SIMPLE SUSAN

CHAPTER I

Waked, as her custom was, before the day,
To do the observance due to sprightly May.
    Dryden.

In a retired hamlet on the borders of Wales, between Oswestry and Shrewsbury, it is still the custom to celebrate the 1st of May.

The children of the village, who look forward to this rural festival with joyful eagerness, usually meet on the last day of April to make up their nosegays for the morning and to choose their queen. Their customary place of meeting is at a hawthorn which stands in a little green nook, open on one side to a shady lane, and separated on the other side by a thick sweet-brier and hawthorn hedge from the garden of an attorney.

This attorney began the world with nothing, but he contrived to scrape together a good deal of money, everybody knew how. He built a new house at the entrance of the village, and had a large well-fenced garden, yet, notwithstanding his fences, he never felt himself secure. Such were his litigious habits and his suspicious temper that he was constantly at variance with his simple and peaceable neighbours. Some pig, or dog, or goat, or goose was for ever trespassing. His complaints and his extortions wearied and alarmed the whole hamlet. The paths in his fields were at length unfrequented, his stiles were blocked up with stones, or stuffed with brambles and briers, so that not a gosling could creep under, or a giant get over them. Indeed, so careful were even the village children of giving offence to this irritable man of the law, that they would not venture to fly a kite near his fields lest it should entangle in his trees or fall upon his meadow.

Mr. Case, for this was the name of our attorney, had a son and a daughter, to whose education he had not time to attend, as his whole soul was intent upon accumulating for them a fortune. For several years he suffered his children to run wild in the village; but suddenly, on his being appointed to a considerable agency, he began to think of making his children a little genteel. He sent his son to learn Latin; he hired a maid to wait upon his daughter Barbara, and he strictly forbade her *thenceforward* to keep company with any of the poor children who had hitherto been her playfellows. They were not sorry for this prohibition, because she had been their tyrant rather than their companion. She was vexed to observe that her absence was not regretted, and she was mortified to perceive that she could not humble them by any display of airs and finery.

There was one poor girl, amongst her former associates, to whom she had a peculiar dislike,—Susan Price, a sweet-tempered, modest, sprightly, industrious lass, who was the pride and delight of the village. Her father rented a small farm, and, unfortunately for him, he lived near Attorney Case.

Barbara used often to sit at her window, watching Susan at work. Sometimes she saw her in the neat garden raking the beds or weeding the borders; sometimes she was kneeling at her beehive with fresh flowers for her bees; sometimes she was in the poultry yard, scattering corn from her sieve amongst the eager chickens; and in the evening she was often seated in a little honeysuckle arbour, with a clean, light, three-legged deal table before her, upon which she put her plain work.

Susan had been taught to work neatly by her good mother, who was very fond of her, and to whom she was most gratefully attached.

Mrs. Price was an intelligent, active, domestic woman; but her health was not robust. She earned money, however, by taking in plain work; and she was famous for baking excellent bread and breakfast cakes. She was respected in the village, for her conduct as a wife and as a mother, and all were eager to show her attention. At her door the first branch of hawthorn was always placed on May morning, and her Susan was usually Queen of the May.

It was now time to choose the Queen. The setting sun shone full upon the pink blossoms of the hawthorn, when the merry group assembled upon their little green. Barbara was now walking in sullen state in her father's garden. She heard the busy voices in the lane, and she concealed herself behind the high hedge, that she might listen to their conversation.

'Where's Susan?' were the first unwelcome words which she overheard. 'Ay, where's Susan?' repeated Philip, stopping short in the middle of a new tune that he was playing on his pipe. 'I wish Susan would come! I want her to sing me this same tune over again; I have not it yet.'

'And I wish Susan would come, I'm sure,' cried a little girl, whose lap was full of primroses. 'Susan will give me some thread to tie up my nosegays, and she'll show me where the fresh violets grow; and she has promised to give me a great bunch of her double cowslips to wear to-morrow. I wish she would come.'

'Nothing can be done without Susan! She always shows us where the nicest flowers are to be found in the lanes and meadows,' said they. 'She must make up the garlands; and she shall be Queen of the May!' exclaimed a multitude of little voices.

'But she does not come!' said Philip.

Rose, who was her particular friend, now came forward to assure the impatient assembly 'that she would answer for it Susan would come as soon as she possibly could, and that she probably was detained by business at home.'

The little electors thought that all business should give way to theirs, and Rose was despatched to summon her friend immediately.

'Tell her to make haste,' cried Philip. 'Attorney Case dined at the Abbey to-day—luckily for us. If he comes home and finds us here, maybe he'll drive us away; for he says this bit of ground belongs to his garden: though that is not true, I'm sure; for Farmer Price knows, and says, it was always open to the road. The Attorney wants to get our playground, so he does. I wish he and his daughter Bab, or Miss Barbara, as she must now be called, were a hundred miles off, out of our way, I know. No later than yesterday she threw down my ninepins in one of her ill-humours, as she was walking by with her gown all trailing in the dust.'

'Yes,' cried Mary, the little primrose-girl, 'her gown is always trailing. She does not hold it up nicely, like Susan; and with all her fine clothes she never looks half so neat. Mamma says she wishes I may be like Susan, when I grow up to be a great girl, and so do I. I should not like to look conceited as Barbara does, if I was ever so rich.'

'Rich or poor,' said Philip, 'it does not become a girl to look conceited, much less *bold*, as Barbara did the other day, when she was at her father's door without a hat upon her head, staring at the strange gentleman who stopped hereabout to let his horse drink. I know what he thought of Bab by his looks, and of Susan too; for Susan was in her garden, bending down a branch of the laburnum tree, looking at its yellow flowers, which were just come out; and when the gentleman asked her how many miles it was from Shrewsbury, she answered him so modest!—not bashful, like as if she had never seen nobody before—but just right: and then she pulled on her straw hat, which was fallen back with her looking up at the laburnum, and she went her ways home; and the gentleman says to me, after she was gone, "Pray, who is that neat modest girl——?" But I wish Susan would come,' cried Philip, interrupting himself.

Susan was all this time, as her friend Rose rightly guessed, busy at home. She was detained by her father's returning later than usual. His supper was ready for him nearly an hour before he came home; and Susan swept up the ashes twice, and twice put on wood to make a cheerful blaze for him; but at last, when he did come in, he took no notice of the blaze or of Susan; and when his wife asked him how he did, he made no answer, but stood with his back to the fire, looking very gloomy. Susan put his supper upon the table, and set his own chair for him; but he pushed away the chair and turned from the table, saying—'I shall eat nothing, child! Why have you such a fire to roast me at this time of the year?'

'You said yesterday, father, I thought, that you liked a little cheerful wood fire in the evening; and there was a great shower of hail; your coat is quite wet, we must dry it.'

'Take it, then, child,' said he, pulling it off—'I shall soon have no coat to dry—and take my hat too,' said he, throwing it upon the ground.

Susan hung up his hat, put his coat over the back of a chair to dry, and then stood anxiously looking at her mother, who was not well; she had this day fatigued herself with baking; and now, alarmed by her husband's moody behaviour, she sat down pale and trembling. He threw himself into a chair, folded his arms, and fixed his eyes upon the fire.

Susan was the first who ventured to break silence. Happy the father who has such a daughter as Susan!—her unaltered sweetness of temper, and her playful, affectionate caresses, at last somewhat dissipated her father's melancholy.

He could not be prevailed upon to eat any of the supper which had been prepared for him; however, with a faint smile, he told Susan that he thought he could eat one of her guinea-hen's eggs. She thanked him, and with that nimble alacrity which marks the desire to please, she ran to her neat chicken-yard; but, alas! her guinea-hen was not there—it had strayed into the attorney's garden. She saw it through the paling, and timidly opening the little gate, she asked Miss Barbara, who was walking slowly by, to let her come in and take her guinea-hen. Barbara, who was at this instant reflecting, with no agreeable feelings, upon the conversation of the village children, to which she had recently listened, started when she heard Susan's voice, and with a proud, ill-humoured look and voice, refused her request.

'Shut the gate,' said Barbara, 'you have no business in *our* garden; and as for your hen, I shall keep it; it is always flying in here and plaguing us, and my father says it is a trespasser; and he told me I might catch it and keep it the next time it got in, and it is in now.' Then Barbara called to her maid, Betty, and bid her catch the mischievous hen.

30

'Oh, my guinea-hen! my pretty guinea-hen!' cried Susan, as they hunted the frightened, screaming creature from corner to corner.

'Here we have got it!' said Betty, holding it fast by the legs.

'Now pay damages, Queen Susan, or good-bye to your pretty guinea-hen,' said Barbara, in an insulting tone.

'Damages! what damages?' said Susan; 'tell me what I must pay.' 'A shilling,' said Barbara. 'Oh, if sixpence would do!' said Susan; 'I have but sixpence of my own in the world, and here it is.' 'It won't do,' said Barbara, turning her back. 'Nay, but hear me,' cried Susan; 'let me at least come in to look for its eggs. I only want *one* for my father's supper; you shall have all the rest.' 'What's your father, or his supper to us? is he so nice that he can eat none but guinea-hen's eggs?' said Barbara. 'If you want your hen and your eggs, pay for them, and you'll have them.' 'I have but sixpence, and you say that won't do,' said Susan, with a sigh, as she looked at her favourite, which was in the maid's grasping hands, struggling and screaming in vain.

Susan retired disconsolate. At the door of her father's cottage she saw her friend Rose, who was just come to summon her to the hawthorn bush.

'They are all at the hawthorn, and I am come for you. We can do nothing without *you*, dear Susan,' cried Rose, running to meet her, at the moment she saw her. 'You are chosen Queen of the May—come, make haste. But what is the matter? why do you look so sad?'

'Ah!' said Susan, 'don't wait for me; I can't come to you, but,' added she, pointing to the tuft of double cowslips in the garden, 'gather those for poor little Mary; I promised them to her, and tell her the violets are under a hedge just opposite the turnstile, on the right as we go to church. Good-bye! never mind me; I can't come—I can't stay, for my father wants me.'

'But don't turn away your face; I won't keep you a moment; only tell me what's the matter,' said her friend, following her into the cottage.

'Oh, nothing, not much,' said Susan; 'only that I wanted the egg in a great hurry for father, it would not have vexed me—to be sure I should have clipped my guinea-hen's wings, and then she could not have flown over the hedge; but let us think no more about it, now,' added she, twinkling away a tear.

When Rose, however, learnt that her friend's guinea-hen was detained prisoner by the attorney's daughter, she exclaimed, with all the honest warmth of indignation, and instantly ran back to tell the story to her companions.

'It won't do,' said Barbara, turning her back.

'It won't do,' said Barbara, turning her back.

'Barbara! ay; like father, like daughter,' cried Farmer Price, starting from the thoughtful attitude in which he had been fixed, and drawing his chair closer to his wife.

'You see something is amiss with me, wife—I'll tell you what it is.' As he lowered his voice, Susan, who was not sure that he wished she should hear what he was going to say, retired from behind his chair. 'Susan, don't go; sit you down here, my sweet Susan,' said he, making room for her upon his chair; 'I believe I was a little cross when I came in first to-night; but I had something to vex me, as you shall hear.

'About a fortnight ago, you know, wife,' continued he, 'there was a balloting in our town for the militia; now at that time I wanted but ten days of forty years of age; and the attorney told me I was a fool for not calling myself plump forty. But the truth is the truth, and it is what I think fittest to be spoken at all times come what will of it. So I was drawn for a militiaman; but when I thought how loth you and I would be to part, I was main glad to hear that I could get off by paying eight or nine guineas for a substitute—only I had not the nine guineas—for, you know, we had bad luck with our sheep this year, and they died away one after another—but that was no excuse, so I went to Attorney Case, and, with a power of difficulty, I got him to lend me the money; for which, to be sure, I gave him something, and left my lease of our farm with him, as he insisted upon it, by way of security for the loan. Attorney Case is too many for me. He has found what he calls a *flaw* in my lease; and the lease, he tells me, is not worth a farthing, and that he can turn us all out of our farm to-morrow if he pleases; and sure enough he will please; for I have thwarted him this day, and he swears he'll be revenged of me. Indeed, he has begun with me badly enough already. I'm not come to the worst part of my story yet——'

Here Farmer Price made a dead stop; and his wife and Susan looked up in his face, breathless with anxiety.

'It must come out,' said he, with a short sigh; 'I must leave you in three days, wife.'

'Must you?' said his wife, in a faint, resigned voice. 'Susan, love, open the window.' Susan ran to open the window, and then returned to support her mother's head. When she came a little to herself she sat up, begged that her husband would go on, and that nothing might be concealed from her. Her husband had no wish indeed to conceal anything from a wife he loved so well; but, firm as he was, and steady to his maxim, that the truth was the thing the fittest to be spoken at all times, his voice faltered, and it was with great difficulty that he brought himself to speak the whole truth at this moment.

The fact was this. Case met Farmer Price as he was coming home, whistling, from a new-ploughed field. The attorney had just dined at *The Abbey*. The Abbey was the family seat of an opulent baronet in the neighbourhood, to whom Mr. Case had been agent. The baronet died suddenly, and his estate and title devolved to a younger brother, who was now just arrived in the country, and to whom Mr. Case was eager to pay his court, in hopes of obtaining his favour. Of the agency he flattered himself that he was pretty secure; and he thought that he might assume a tone of command towards the tenants, especially towards one who was some guineas in debt, and in whose lease there was a flaw.

Accosting the farmer in a haughty manner, the attorney began with, 'So, Farmer Price, a word with you, if you please. Walk on here, man, beside my horse, and you'll hear me. You have changed your opinion, I hope, about that bit of land—that corner at the end of my garden?' 'As how, Mr. Case?' said the farmer. 'As how, man! Why, you said something about it's not belonging to me, when you heard me talk of enclosing it the other day.' 'So I did,' said Price, 'and so I do.'

Provoked and astonished at the firm tone in which these words were pronounced, the attorney was upon the point of swearing that he would have his revenge; but, as his passions were habitually attentive to the *letter* of the law, he refrained from any hasty expression, which might, he was aware, in a court of justice, be hereafter brought against him.

'My good friend, Mr. Price,' said he, in a soft voice, and pale with suppressed rage. He forced a smile. 'I'm under the necessity of calling in the money I lent you some time ago, and you will please to take notice that it must be paid to-morrow morning. I wish you a good evening. You have the money ready for me, I daresay.'

'No,' said the farmer, 'not a guinea of it; but John Simpson, who was my substitute, has not left our village yet. I'll get the money back from him, and go myself, if so be it must be so, into the militia—so I will.'

The attorney did not expect such a determination, and he represented, in a friendly, hypocritical tone to Price, that he had no wish to drive him to such an extremity; that it would be the height of folly in him *to run his head against a wall for no purpose*. 'You don't mean to take the corner into your own garden, do you, Price?' said he. 'I,' said the farmer, 'God forbid! it's none of mine; I never take what does not belong to me.' 'True, right, very proper, of course,' said Mr. Case; 'but then you have no interest in life in the land in question?' 'None.' 'Then why so stiff about it, Price? All I want of you to say——' 'To say that black is white, which I won't do, Mr. Case. The ground is a thing not worth talking of; but it's neither yours nor mine. In my memory, since the *new* lane was made, it has always been open to the parish; and no man shall enclose it with my good-will. Truth is truth, and must be spoken; justice is justice, and should be done, Mr. Attorney.'

'And law is law, Mr. Farmer, and shall have its course, to your cost,' cried the attorney, exasperated by the dauntless spirit of this village Hampden.

Here they parted. The glow of enthusiasm, the pride of virtue, which made our hero brave, could not render him insensible. As he drew nearer home, many melancholy thoughts pressed upon his heart. He passed the door of his own cottage with resolute steps, however, and went through the village in search of the man who had engaged to be his substitute. He found him, told him how the matter stood; and luckily the man, who had not yet spent the money, was willing to return it; as there were many others drawn for the militia, who, he observed, would be glad to give him the same price, or more, for his services.

The moment Price got the money, he hastened to Mr. Case's house, walked straight forward into his room, and laying the money down upon his desk, 'There, Mr. Attorney, are your nine guineas; count them; now I have done with you.'

'Not yet,' said the attorney, jingling the money triumphantly in his hand. 'We'll give you a taste of the law, my good sir, or I'm mistaken. You forgot the flaw in your lease, which I have safe in this desk.'

'Ah, my lease,' said the farmer, who had almost forgot to ask for it till he was thus put in mind of it by the attorney's imprudent threat.

'Give me my lease, Mr. Case. I've paid my money; you have no right to keep the lease any longer, whether it is a bad one or a good one.'

'Pardon me,' said the attorney, locking his desk and putting the key into his pocket, 'possession, my honest friend,' cried he, striking his hand upon the desk, 'is nine points of the law. Good-night to you. I cannot in conscience return a lease to a tenant in which I know there is a capital flaw. It is my duty to show it to my employer; or, in other words, to your new landlord, whose agent I have good reasons to expect I shall be. You will live to repent your obstinacy, Mr. Price. Your servant, sir.'

Price retired with melancholy feelings, but not intimidated. Many a man returns home with a gloomy countenance, who has not quite so much cause for vexation.

When Susan heard her father's story, she quite forgot her guinea-hen, and her whole soul was intent upon her poor mother, who, notwithstanding her utmost exertion, could not support herself under this sudden stroke of misfortune.

In the middle of the night Susan was called up; her mother's fever ran high for some hours; but towards morning it abated, and she fell into a soft sleep with Susan's hand locked fast in hers.

Susan sat motionless, and breathed softly, lest she should disturb her. The rushlight, which stood beside the bed, was now burnt low; the long shadow of the tall wicker chair flitted, faded, appeared, and vanished, as the flame rose and sank in the socket. Susan was afraid that the disagreeable smell might waken her mother; and, gently disengaging her hand, she went on tiptoe to extinguish the candle. All was silent: the gray light of the morning was now spreading over every object; the sun rose slowly, and Susan stood at the lattice window, looking through the small leaded, crossbarred panes at the splendid spectacle. A few birds began to chirp; but, as Susan was listening to

33

them, her mother started in her sleep, and spoke unintelligibly. Susan hung up a white apron before the window to keep out the light, and just then she heard the sound of music at a distance in the village. As it approached nearer, she knew that it was Philip playing upon his pipe and tabor. She distinguished the merry voices of her companions 'carolling in honour of the May,' and soon she saw them coming towards her father's cottage, with branches and garlands in their hands. She opened quick, but gently, the latch of the door, and ran out to meet them.

'Here she is!—here's Susan!' they exclaimed joyfully. 'Here's the Queen of the May.' 'And here's her crown!' cried Rose, pressing forward; but Susan put her finger upon her lips, and pointed to her mother's window. Philip's pipe stopped instantly.

'Thank you,' said Susan, 'my mother is ill; I can't leave her, you know.' Then gently putting aside the crown, her companions bid her say who should wear it for her.

'Will you, dear Rose?' said she, placing the garland upon her friend's head. 'It's a charming May morning,' added she, with a smile; 'good-bye. We shan't hear your voices or the pipe when you have turned the corner into the village; so you need only stop till then, Philip.'

'I shall stop for all day,' said Philip; 'I've no mind to play any more.'

'Good-bye, poor Susan. It is a pity you can't come with us,' said all the children; and little Mary ran after Susan to the cottage door.

'I forgot to thank you,' said she, 'for the double cowslips; look how pretty they are, and smell how sweet the violets are in my bosom, and kiss me quick, for I shall be left behind.' Susan kissed the little breathless girl, and returned softly to the side of her mother's bed.

'How grateful that child is to me for a cowslip only! How can I be grateful enough to such a mother as this?' said Susan to herself, as she bent over her sleeping mother's pale countenance.

Her mother's unfinished knitting lay upon a table near the bed, and Susan sat down in her wicker arm-chair, and went on with the row, in the middle of which her hand stopped the preceding evening. 'She taught me to knit, she taught me everything that I know,' thought Susan, 'and the best of all, she taught me to love her, to wish to be like her.'

Her mother, when she awakened, felt much refreshed by her tranquil sleep, and observing that it was a delightful morning, said 'that she had been dreaming she heard music; but that the drum frightened her, because she thought it was the signal for her husband to be carried away by a whole regiment of soldiers, who had pointed their bayonets at him. But that was but a dream, Susan; I awoke, and knew it was a dream, and I then fell asleep, and have slept soundly ever since.'

How painful it is to awake to the remembrance of misfortune. Gradually as this poor woman collected her scattered thoughts, she recalled the circumstances of the preceding evening. She was too certain that she had heard from her husband's own lips the words, '*I must leave you in three days*'; and she wished that she could sleep again, and think it all a dream.

'But he'll want, he'll want a hundred things,' said she, starting up. 'I must get his linen ready for him. I'm afraid it's very late. Susan, why did you let me lie so long?'

'Everything shall be ready, dear mother; only don't hurry yourself,' said Susan. And indeed her mother was ill able to bear any hurry, or to do any work this day. Susan's affectionate, dexterous, sensible activity was never more wanted, or more effectual. She understood so readily, she obeyed so exactly; and when she was left to her own discretion, judged so prudently, that her mother had little trouble and no anxiety in directing her. She said that Susan never did too little, or too much.

Susan was mending her father's linen, when Rose tapped softly at the window, and beckoned to her to come out. She went out. 'How does your mother do, in the first place?' said Rose. 'Better, thank you.' 'That's well, and I have a little bit of good news for you besides—here,' said she, pulling out a glove, in which there was money, 'we'll get the guinea-hen back again—we have all agreed about it. This is the money that has been given to us in the village this May morning. At every door they gave silver. See how generous they have been—twelve shillings, I assure you. Now we are a match for Miss Barbara. You won't like to leave home; I'll go to Barbara, and you shall see your guinea-hen in ten minutes.'

Rose hurried away, pleased with her commission, and eager to accomplish her business. Miss Barbara's maid, Betty, was the first person that was visible at the attorney's house. Rose insisted upon seeing Miss Barbara herself, and she was shown into a parlour to the young lady, who was reading a dirty novel, which she put under a heap of law papers as they entered.

'Dear, how you *startled* me! Is it only you?' said she to her maid; but as soon as she saw Rose behind the maid, she put on a scornful air. 'Could not ye say I was not at home, Betty? Well, my good girl, what brings you here? Something to borrow or beg, I suppose.'

May every ambassador—every ambassador in as good a cause—answer with as much dignity and moderation as Rose replied to Barbara upon the present occasion. She assured her that the person from whom she came did not send her either to beg or borrow; that she was able to pay the full value of that for which she came to ask; and, producing her well-filled purse, 'I believe that this is a very good shilling,' said she. 'If you don't like it, I will change it, and now you will be so good as to give me Susan's guinea-hen. It is in her name I ask for it.'

'No matter in whose name you ask for it,' replied Barbara, 'you will not have it. Take up your shilling, if you please. I would have taken a shilling yesterday, if it had been paid at the time properly; but I told Susan, that if it was not paid then, I should keep the hen, and so I shall, I promise her. You may go back, and tell her so.'

The attorney's daughter had, whilst Rose opened her negotiation, measured the depth of her purse with a keen eye; and her penetration discovered that it contained at least ten shillings. With proper management she had some hopes that the guinea-hen might be made to bring in at least half the money.

Rose, who was of a warm temper, not quite so fit a match as she had thought herself for the wily Barbara, incautiously exclaimed, 'Whatever it costs us, we are determined to have Susan's favourite hen; so, if one shilling won't do, take two; and if two won't do, why, take three.'

The shillings sounded provoking upon the table, as she threw them down one after another, and Barbara coolly replied, 'Three won't do.' 'Have you no conscience, Miss Barbara? Then take four.' Barbara shook her head. A fifth shilling was instantly proffered; but Bab, who now saw plainly that she had the game in her own hands, preserved a cold, cruel silence. Rose went on rapidly, bidding shilling after shilling, till she had completely emptied her purse. The twelve shillings were spread upon the table. Barbara's avarice was moved; she consented for this ransom to liberate her prisoner.

Rose pushed the money towards her; but just then, recollecting that she was acting for others more than for herself, and doubting whether she had full powers to conclude such an extravagant bargain, she gathered up the public treasure, and with newly-recovered prudence observed that she must go back to consult her friends. Her generous little friends were amazed at Barbara's meanness, but with one accord declared that they were most willing, for their parts, to give up every farthing of the money. They all went to Susan in a body, and told her so. 'There's our purse,' said they; 'do what you please with it.' They would not wait for one word of thanks, but ran away, leaving only Rose with her to settle the treaty for the guinea-hen.

There is a certain manner of accepting a favour, which shows true generosity of mind. Many know how to give, but few know how to accept a gift properly. Susan was touched, but not astonished, by the kindness of her young friends, and she received the purse with as much simplicity as she would have given it.

'Well,' said Rose, 'shall I go back for the guinea-hen?' 'The guinea-hen!' said Susan, starting from a reverie into which she had fallen, as she contemplated the purse. 'Certainly I *do* long to see my pretty guinea-hen once more; but I was not thinking of her just then—I was thinking of my father.'

Now Susan had heard her mother often, in the course of this day, wish that she had but money enough in the world to pay John Simpson for going to serve in the militia instead of her husband. 'This, to be sure, will go but a little way,' thought Susan; 'but still it may be of some use to my father.' She told her mind to Rose, and concluded by saying, decidedly, that 'if the money was given to her to dispose of as she pleased, she would give it to her father.'

'It is all yours, my dear good Susan,' cried Rose, with a look of warm approbation. 'This is so like you!—but I'm sorry that Miss Bab must keep your guinea-hen. I would not be her for all the guinea-hens, or guineas either, in the whole world. Why, I'll answer for it, the guinea-hen won't make her happy, and you'll be happy *even* without; because you are good. Let me come and help you to-morrow,' continued she, looking at Susan's work, 'if you have any more mending work to do—I never liked work till I worked with you. I won't forget my thimble or my scissors,' added she, laughing—'though I used to forget them when I was a giddy girl. I assure you I am a great hand at my needle, now—try me.'

Susan assured her friend that she did not doubt the powers of her needle, and that she would most willingly accept of her services, but that *unluckily* she had finished all her needlework that was immediately wanted.

'But do you know,' said she, 'I shall have a great deal of business to-morrow; but I won't tell you what it is that I have to do, for I am afraid I shall not succeed; but if I do succeed, I'll come and tell you directly, because you will be so glad of it.'

Susan, who had always been attentive to what her mother taught her, and who had often assisted her when she was baking bread and cakes for the family at the Abbey, had now formed the courageous, but not presumptuous, idea that she could herself undertake to bake a batch of bread. One of the servants from the Abbey had been sent all round the village in the morning in search of bread, and had not been able to procure any that was tolerable. Mrs. Price's last baking failed for want of good barm. She was not now strong enough to attempt another herself; and when the brewer's boy came with eagerness to tell her that he had some fine fresh yeast, she thanked him, but sighed, and said it would be of no use to her. Accordingly she went to work with much prudent care, and when her bread the next morning came out of the oven, it was excellent; at least her mother said so, and she was a good judge. It was sent to the Abbey; and as the family there had not tasted any good bread since their arrival in the country, they also were earnest and warm in its praise. Inquiries were made from the housekeeper, and they heard, with some surprise, that this excellent bread was made by a young girl only twelve years old.

The housekeeper, who had known Susan from a child, was pleased to have an opportunity in speaking in her favour. 'She is the most industrious little creature, ma'am, in the world,' said she to her mistress. 'Little I can't so well call her now, since she's grown tall and slender to look at; and glad I am she is grown up likely to look at; for handsome is that handsome does; she thinks no more of her being handsome than I do myself; yet she has as proper a respect for herself, ma'am, as you have; and I always see her neat, and with her mother, ma'am, or fit people, as a girl should be. As for her mother, she dotes upon her, as well she may; for I should myself if I had half such a daughter; and then she has two little brothers; and she's as good to them, and, my boy Philip says, taught 'em to read more than the schoolmistress, all with tenderness and good nature; but I beg your pardon, ma'am, I cannot stop myself when I once begin to talk of Susan.'

'You have really said enough to excite my curiosity,' said her mistress; 'pray send for her immediately; we can see her before we go out to walk.'

The benevolent housekeeper despatched her boy Philip for Susan, who never happened to be in such an *untidy* state as to be unable to obey a summons without a long preparation. She had, it is true, been very busy; but orderly people can be busy and neat at the same time. She put on her usual straw hat, and accompanied Rose's mother, who was going with a basket of cleared muslin to the Abbey.

The modest simplicity of Susan's appearance, and the artless good sense and propriety of the answers she gave to all the questions that were asked her, pleased the ladies at the Abbey, who were good judges of character and manners.

Sir Arthur Somers had two sisters, sensible, benevolent women. They were not of that race of fine ladies who are miserable the moment they come to *the country*; nor yet were they of that bustling sort, who quack and direct all their poor neighbours, for the mere love of managing, or the want of something to do. They were judiciously generous; and whilst they wished to diffuse happiness, they were not peremptory in requiring that people should be happy precisely their own way. With these dispositions, and with a well-informed brother, who, though he never wished to direct, was always willing to assist in their efforts to do good, there were reasonable hopes that these ladies would be a blessing to the poor villagers amongst whom they were now settled.

As soon as Miss Somers had spoken to Susan, she inquired for her brother; but Sir Arthur was in his study, and a gentleman was with him on business.

Susan was desirous of returning to her mother, and the ladies therefore would not detain her. Miss Somers told her, with a smile, when she took leave, that she would call upon her in the evening at six o'clock.

It was impossible that such a grand event as Susan's visit to the Abbey could long remain unknown to Barbara Case and her gossiping maid. They watched eagerly for the moment of her return, that they might satisfy their curiosity. 'There she is, I declare, just come into her garden,' cried Bab; 'I'll run in and get it all out of her in a minute.'

Bab could descend, without shame, whenever it suited her purposes, from the height of insolent pride to the lowest meanness of fawning familiarity.

Susan was gathering some marigolds and some parsley for her mother's broth.

'So, Susan,' said Bab, who came close up to her before she perceived it, 'how goes the world with you to-day?' 'My mother is rather better to-day, she says, ma'am—thank you,' replies Susan, coldly but civilly. '*Ma'am!* dear, how polite we are grown of a sudden!' cried Bab, winking at her maid. 'One may see you've been in good company this morning—hey, Susan? Come, let's hear about it.' 'Did you see the ladies themselves, or was it only the housekeeper sent for you?' said the maid. 'What room did you go into?' continued Bab. 'Did you see Miss Somers, or Sir Arthur?' 'Miss Somers.' 'La! she saw Miss Somers! Betty, I must hear about it. Can't you stop gathering those things for a minute and chat a bit with us, Susan?' 'I can't stay, indeed, Miss Barbara; for my mother's broth is just wanted, and I'm in a hurry.' Susan ran home.

'Lord, her head is full of broth now,' said Bab to her maid; 'and she has not a word for herself, though she has been abroad. My papa may well call her *Simple Susan*; for simple she is, and simple she will be, all the world over. For my part, I think she's little better than a downright simpleton. But, however, simple or not, I'll get what I want out of her. She'll be able to speak, maybe, when she has settled the grand matter of the broth. I'll step in and ask to see her mother, that will put her in a good humour in a trice.'

Barbara followed Susan into the cottage, and found her occupied with the grand affair of the broth. 'Is it ready?' said Bab, peeping into the pot that was over the fire. 'Dear, how savoury it smells! I'll wait till you go in with it to your mother; for I must ask her how she does myself.' 'Will you please to sit down then, miss?' said Simple Susan, with a smile; for at this instant she forgot the guinea-hen; 'I have but just put the parsley into the broth; but it soon will be ready.'

During this interval Bab employed herself, much to her own satisfaction, in cross-questioning Susan. She was rather provoked indeed that she could not learn exactly how each of the ladies was dressed, and what there was to be for dinner at the Abbey; and she was curious beyond measure to find out what Miss Somers meant by saying that she would call at Mr. Price's cottage at six o'clock in the evening. 'What do you think she could mean?' 'I thought she meant what she said,' replied Susan, 'that she would come here at six o'clock.' 'Ay, that's as plain as a pike-staff,' said Barbara; 'but what else did she mean, think you? People, you know, don't always mean exactly, downright, neither more nor less than what they say.' 'Not always,' said Susan, with an arch smile, which convinced Barbara that she was not quite a simpleton. '*Not always*,' repeated Barbara colouring,—'oh, then I suppose you have some guess at what Miss Somers meant.' 'No,' said Susan, 'I was not thinking about Miss Somers, when I said not always.' 'How nice that broth does look,' resumed Barbara, after a pause.

Susan had now poured the broth into a basin, and as she strewed over it the bright orange marigolds, it looked very tempting. She tasted it, and added now a little salt, and now a little more, till she thought it was just to her mother's taste. 'Oh, *I* must taste it,' said Bab, taking the basin up greedily. 'Won't you take a spoon?' said Susan, trembling at the large mouthfuls which Barbara sucked up with a terrible noise. 'Take a spoonful, indeed!' exclaimed Barbara, setting down the basin in high anger. 'The next time I taste your broth you shall affront me, if you dare! The next time I set my foot in this house, you shall be as saucy to me as you please.' And she flounced out of the house, repeating '*Take a spoon, pig*, was what you meant to say.'

Susan stood in amazement at the beginning of this speech; but the concluding words explained to her the mystery.

Some years before this time, when Susan was a very little girl, and could scarcely speak plain, as she was eating a basin of bread and milk for her supper at the cottage door, a great pig came up and put his nose into the basin. Susan was willing that the pig should have some share of the bread and milk; but as she ate with a spoon and he with his large mouth, she presently discovered that he was likely to have more than his share; and in a simple tone of expostulation she said to him, 'Take a *poon*, pig.'[7] The saying became proverbial in the village. Susan's little companions repeated it, and applied it upon many occasions, whenever any one claimed more than his share of anything good. Barbara, who was then not Miss Barbara, but plain Bab, and who had played with all the poor children in the neighbourhood, was often reproved in her unjust methods of division by Susan's proverb. Susan, as she grew up, forgot the childish saying; but the remembrance of it rankled in Barbara's mind, and it was to this that she suspected Susan had alluded, when she recommended a spoon to her, whilst she was swallowing the basin of broth.

'La, miss,' said Barbara's maid, when she found her mistress in a passion upon her return from Susan's, 'I only wondered you did her the honour to set your foot within her doors. What need have you to trouble her for news about the Abbey folks, when your own papa has been there all the morning, and is just come in, and can tell you everything?'

Barbara did not know that her father meant to go to the Abbey that morning, for Attorney Case was mysterious even to his own family about his morning rides. He never chose to be asked where he was going, or where he had been; and this made his servants more than commonly inquisitive to trace him.

Barbara, against whose apparent childishness and real cunning he was not sufficiently on his guard, had often the art of drawing him into conversation about his visits. She ran into her father's parlour; but she knew, the moment she saw his face, that it was no time to ask questions; his pen was across his mouth, and his brown wig pushed oblique upon his contracted forehead. The wig was always pushed crooked whenever he was in a brown, or rather a black, study. Barbara, who did not, like Susan, bear with her father's testy humour from affection and gentleness of disposition, but who always humoured him from artifice, tried all her skill to fathom his thoughts, and when she found that *it* would not do, she went to tell her maid so, and to complain that her father was so cross there was no bearing him.

It is true that Attorney Case was not in the happiest mood possible; for he was by no means satisfied with his morning's work at the Abbey. Sir Arthur Somers, the *new man*, did not suit him, and he began to be rather apprehensive that he should not suit Sir Arthur. He had sound reasons for his doubts.

Sir Arthur Somers was an excellent lawyer, and a perfectly honest man. This seemed to our attorney a contradiction in terms; in the course of his practice the case had not occurred; and he had no precedents ready to direct his proceedings. Sir Arthur was also a man of wit and eloquence, yet of plain dealing and humanity. The attorney could not persuade himself to believe that his benevolence was anything but enlightened cunning, and his plain dealing he one minute dreaded as the masterpiece of art, and the next despised as the characteristic of folly. In short, he had not yet decided whether he was an honest man or a knave. He had settled accounts with him for his late agency, and had talked about sundry matters of business. He constantly perceived, however, that he could not impose upon Sir Arthur; but the idea that he could know all the mazes of the law, and yet prefer the straight road, was incomprehensible.

Mr. Case having paid Sir Arthur some compliments on his great legal abilities, and his high reputation at the bar, he coolly replied, 'I have left the bar.' The attorney looked in unfeigned astonishment that a man who was actually making £3000 per annum at the bar should leave it.

Tried all her skill to fathom his thoughts.

Tried all her skill to fathom his thoughts.

'I am come,' said Sir Arthur, 'to enjoy that kind of domestic life in the country which I prefer to all others, and amongst people whose happiness I hope to increase.' At this speech the attorney changed his ground, flattering himself that he should find his man averse to business, and ignorant of country affairs. He talked of the value of land, and of new leases.

The Parent's Assistant; Or, Stories for Children

Sir Arthur wished to enlarge his domain, and to make a ride round it. A map of it was lying upon the table, and Farmer Price's garden came exactly across the new road for the ride. Sir Arthur looked disappointed; and the keen attorney seized the moment to inform him that 'Price's whole land was at his disposal.'

'At my disposal! how so?' cried Sir Arthur, eagerly; 'it will not be out of lease, I believe, these ten years. I'll look into the rent-roll again; perhaps I am mistaken.'

'You are mistaken, my good sir, and you are not mistaken,' said Mr. Case, with a shrewd smile. 'In one sense, the land will not be out of lease these ten years, and in another it is out of lease at this present time. To come to the point at once, the lease is, *ab origine*, null and void. I have detected a capital flaw in the body of it. I pledge my credit upon it, sir, it can't stand a single term in law or equity.'

The attorney observed that at these words Sir Arthur's eye was fixed with a look of earnest attention. 'Now I have him,' said the cunning tempter to himself.

'Neither in law nor equity,' repeated Sir Arthur, with apparent incredulity. 'Are you sure of that, Mr. Case?' 'Sure! As I told you before, sir, I'd pledge my whole credit upon the thing—I'd stake my existence.' '*That's something*,' said Sir Arthur, as if he was pondering upon the matter.

The attorney went on with all the eagerness of a keen man, who sees a chance at one stroke of winning a rich friend and of ruining a poor enemy. He explained, with legal volubility and technical amplification, the nature of the mistake in Mr. Price's lease. 'It was, sir,' said he, 'a lease for the life of Peter Price, Susanna his wife, and to the survivor or survivors of them, or for the full time and term of twenty years, to be computed from the first day of May then next ensuing. Now, sir, this, you see, is a lease in reversion, which the late Sir Benjamin Somers had not, by his settlement, a right to make. This is a curious mistake, you see, Sir Arthur; and in filling up those printed leases there's always a good chance of some flaw. I find it perpetually; but I never found a better than this in the whole course of my practice.'

Sir Arthur stood in silence.

'My dear sir,' said the attorney, taking him by the button, 'you have no scruple of stirring in this business?'

'A little,' said Sir Arthur.

'Why, then, that can be done away in a moment. Your name shall not appear in it at all. You have nothing to do but to make over the lease to me. I make all safe to you with my bond. Now, being in possession, I come forward in my own proper person. *Shall I proceed?*'

'No—you have said enough,' replied Sir Arthur.

'The case, indeed, lies in a nutshell,' said the attorney, who had by this time worked himself up to such a pitch of professional enthusiasm that, intent upon his vision of a lawsuit, he totally forgot to observe the impression his words made upon Sir Arthur.

'There's only one thing we have forgotten all this time,' said Sir Arthur. 'What can that be, sir?' 'That we shall ruin this poor man.'

Case was thunderstruck at these words, or rather, by the look which accompanied them. He recollected that he had laid himself open before he was sure of Sir Arthur's *real* character. He softened, and said he should have had certainly more *consideration* in the case of any but a litigious, pig-headed fellow, as he knew Price to be.

'If he be litigious,' said Sir Arthur, 'I shall certainly be glad to get him fairly out of the parish as soon as possible. When you go home, you will be so good, sir, as to send me his lease, that I may satisfy myself before we stir in this business.'

The attorney, brightening up, prepared to take leave; but he could not persuade himself to take his departure without making one push at Sir Arthur about the agency.

'I will not trouble *you*, Sir Arthur, with this lease of Price's,' said Case; 'I'll leave it with your agent. Whom shall I apply to?' '*To myself*, sir, if you please,' replied Sir Arthur.

The courtiers of Louis the Fourteenth could not have looked more astounded than our attorney, when they received from their monarch a similar answer. It was this unexpected reply of Sir Arthur's which had deranged the temper of Mr. Case, and caused his wig to stand so crooked upon his forehead, and which had rendered him impenetrably silent to his inquisitive daughter Barbara.

After having walked up and down his room, conversing with himself, for some time, the attorney concluded that the agency must be given to somebody when Sir Arthur should have to attend his duty in Parliament; that the agency, even for the winter season, was not a thing to be neglected; and that, if he managed well, he might yet secure it for himself. He had often found that small timely presents worked wonderfully upon his own mind, and he judged of others by himself. The tenants had been in the reluctant but constant practice of making him continual petty offerings; and he resolved to try the same course with Sir Arthur, whose resolution to be his own agent, he thought, argued a close, saving, avaricious disposition. He had heard the housekeeper at the Abbey inquiring, as he passed through the servants, whether there was any lamb to be gotten. She said that Sir Arthur was remarkably fond of lamb, and that she wished she could get a quarter for him. Immediately he sallied into his kitchen, as soon as the idea struck him, and asked a shepherd, who was waiting there, whether he knew of a nice fat lamb to be had anywhere in the neighbourhood.

'I know of one,' cried Barbara. 'Susan Price has a pet lamb that's as fat as fat could be.' The attorney easily caught at these words, and speedily devised a scheme for obtaining Susan's lamb for nothing.

It would be something strange if an attorney of his talents and standing was not an over-match for Simple Susan. He prowled forth in search of his prey. He found Susan packing up her father's little wardrobe; and when she looked up as she knelt, he saw that she had been in tears.

'How is your mother to-day, Susan?' inquired the attorney. 'Worse, sir. My father goes to-morrow.' 'That's a pity.' 'It can't be helped,' said Susan, with a sigh. 'It can't be helped—how do you know that?' said Case. 'Sir, *dear* sir!' cried she, looking up at him, and a sudden ray of hope beamed in her ingenuous countenance. 'And if *you* could help it, Susan?' said he. Susan clasped her hands in silence, more expressive than words. 'You *can* help it, Susan.' She started up in an ecstasy. 'What would you give now to have your father at home for a whole week longer?' 'Anything!—but I have nothing.' 'Yes, but you have, a lamb,' said the hard-hearted attorney. 'My poor little lamb!' said Susan; 'but what can that do?' 'What good can any lamb do? Is not lamb good to eat? Why do you look so pale, girl? Are not sheep killed every day,

38

and don't you eat mutton? Is your lamb better than anybody else's, think you?' 'I don't know,' said Susan, 'but I love it better.' 'More fool you,' said he. 'It feeds out of hand, it follows me about; I have always taken care of it; my mother gave it to me.' 'Well, say no more about it, then,' he cynically observed; 'if you love your lamb better than both your father and your mother, keep it, and good morning to you.'

'Stay, oh stay!' cried Susan, catching the skirt of his coat with an eager, trembling hand;—'a whole week, did you say? My mother may get better in that time. No, I do not love my lamb half so well.' The struggle of her mind ceased, and with a placid countenance and calm voice, 'Take the lamb,' said she. 'Where is it?' said the attorney. 'Grazing in the meadow, by the river-side.' 'It must be brought up before nightfall for the butcher, remember.' 'I shall not forget it,' said Susan, steadily.

As soon, however, as her persecutor turned his back and quitted the house, Susan sat down and hid her face in her hands. She was soon aroused by the sound of her mother's feeble voice, who was calling *Susan* from the inner room where she lay. Susan went in, but did not undraw the curtain as she stood beside the bed.

'Are you there, love? Undraw the curtain, that I may see you, and tell me;—I thought I heard some strange voice just now talking to my child. Something's amiss, Susan,' said her mother, raising herself as well as she was able in the bed, to examine her daughter's countenance.

'Would you think it amiss, then, my dear mother,' said Susan, stooping to kiss her—'would you think it amiss, if my father was to stay with us a week longer?' 'Susan! you don't say so?' 'He is, indeed, a whole week;—but how burning hot your hand is still.' 'Are you sure he will stay?' inquired her mother. 'How do you know? Who told you so? Tell me all quick.' 'Attorney Case told me so; he can get him a week's longer leave of absence, and he has promised he will.' 'God bless him for it, for ever and ever!' said the poor woman, joining her hands. 'May the blessing of heaven be with him!'

Susan closed the curtains, and was silent. She *could not say Amen*. She was called out of the room at this moment, for a messenger was come from the Abbey for the bread-bills. It was she who always made out the bills, for though she had not a great number of lessons from the writing-master, she had taken so much pains to learn that she could write a very neat, legible hand, and she found this very useful. She was not, to be sure, particularly inclined to draw out a long bill at this instant, but business must be done. She set to work, ruled her lines for the pounds, shillings, and pence, made out the bill for the Abbey, and despatched the impatient messenger. She then resolved to make out all the bills for the neighbours, who had many of them taken a few loaves and rolls of her baking. 'I had better get all my business finished,' said she to herself, 'before I go down to the meadow to take leave of my poor lamb.'

This was sooner said than done, for she found that she had a great number of bills to write, and the slate on which she had entered the account was not immediately to be found, and when it was found the figures were almost rubbed out. Barbara had sat down upon it. Susan pored over the number of loaves, and the names of the persons who took them; and she wrote and cast up sums, and corrected and re-corrected them, till her head grew quite puzzled.

The table was covered with little square bits of paper, on which she had been writing bills over and over again, when her father came in with a bill in his hand. 'How's this, Susan?' said he. 'How can ye be so careless, child? What is your head running upon? Here, look at the bill you were sending up to the Abbey? I met the messenger, and luckily asked to see how much it was. Look at it.'

Susan looked and blushed; it was written, 'Sir Arthur Somers, to John Price, debtor, six dozen *lambs*, so much.' She altered it, and returned it to her father; but he had taken up some of the papers which lay upon the table. 'What are all these, child?' 'Some of them are wrong, and I've written them out again,' said Susan. 'Some of them! All of them, I think, seem to be wrong, if I can read,' said her father, rather angrily, and he pointed out to her sundry strange mistakes. Her head, indeed, had been running upon her poor lamb. She corrected all the mistakes with so much patience, and bore to be blamed with so much good humour, that her father at last said that it was impossible ever to scold Susan, without being in the wrong at the last.

As soon as all was set right, Price took the bills, and said he would go round to the neighbours and collect the money himself; for that he should be very proud to have it to say to them that it was all earned by his own little daughter.

Susan resolved to keep the pleasure of telling him of his week's reprieve till he should come home to sup, as he had promised to do, in her mother's room. She was not sorry to hear him sigh as he passed the knapsack, which she had been packing up for his journey. 'How delighted he will be when he hears the good news!' said she to herself; 'but I know he will be a little sorry too for my poor lamb.'

As Susan had now settled all her business, she thought she could have time to go down to the meadow by the river-side to see her favourite; but just as she had tied on her straw hat the village clock struck four, and this was the hour at which she always went to fetch her little brothers home from a dame-school near the village. She knew that they would be disappointed if she was later than usual, and she did not like to keep them waiting, because they were very patient, good boys; so she put off the visit to her lamb, and went immediately for her brothers.

CHAPTER II

Evn in the spring and playtime of the year,
That calls th' unwonted villager abroad,
With all her little ones, a sportive train,
To gather kingcups in the yellow mead,
And prink their heads with daisies.

Cowper.

The dame-school, which was about a mile from the hamlet, was not a showy edifice: but it was reverenced as much by the young race of village scholars as if it had been the most stately mansion in the land; it was a low-roofed, long, thatched tenement, sheltered by a few reverend oaks, under which many generations of hopeful children had gambolled in their turn.

The close-shaven green, which sloped down from the hatch-door of the schoolroom, was paled round with a rude paling, which, though decayed in some parts by time, was not in any place broken by violence.

The place bespoke order and peace. The dame who governed was well obeyed, because she was just and well beloved, and because she was ever glad to give well-earned praise and pleasure to her little subjects.

Susan had once been under her gentle dominion, and had been deservedly her favourite scholar. The dame often cited her as the best example to the succeeding tribe of emulous youngsters. She had scarcely opened the wicket which separated the green before the schoolroom door from the lane, when she heard the merry voices of the children, and saw the little troup issuing from the hatchway and spreading over the green.

'Oh, there's Susan!' cried her two little brothers, running, leaping, and bounding up to her; and many of the other rosy girls and boys crowded round her, to talk of their plays; for Susan was easily interested in all that made others happy; but she could not make them comprehend that, if they all spoke at once, it was not possible that she could hear what was said.

The voices were still raised one above another, all eager to establish some important observation about ninepins, or marbles, or tops, or bows and arrows, when suddenly music was heard and the crowd was silenced. The music seemed to be near the spot where the children were standing, and they looked round to see whence it could come. Susan pointed to the great oak tree, and they beheld, seated under its shade, an old man playing upon his harp. The children all approached—at first timidly, for the sounds were solemn; but as the harper heard their little footsteps coming towards him, he changed his hand and played one of his most lively tunes. The circle closed, and pressed nearer and nearer to him; some who were in the foremost row whispered to each other, 'He is blind!' 'What a pity!' and 'He looks very poor,—what a ragged coat he wears!' said others. 'He must be very old, for all his hair is white: and he must have travelled a great way, for his shoes are quite worn out,' observed another.

All these remarks were made whilst he was tuning his harp, for when he once more began to play, not a word was uttered. He seemed pleased by their simple exclamations of wonder and delight, and, eager to amuse his young audience, he played now a gay and now a pathetic air, to suit their several humours.

Susan's voice, which was soft and sweet, expressive of gentleness and good nature, caught his ear the moment she spoke. He turned his face eagerly to the place where she stood; and it was observed that, whenever she said that she liked any tune particularly, he played it over again.

'I am blind,' said the old man, 'and cannot see your faces; but I know you all asunder by your voices, and I can guess pretty well at all your humours and characters by your voices.'

'Can you so, indeed?' cried Susan's little brother William, who had stationed himself between the old man's knees. 'Then you heard *my* sister Susan speak just now. Can you tell us what sort of person she is?' 'That I can, I think, without being a conjurer,' said the old man, lifting the boy up on his knee; '*your* sister Susan is good-natured.' The boy clapped his hands. 'And good-tempered.' '*Right*,' said little William, with a louder clap of applause. 'And very fond of the little boy who sits upon my knee.' 'O right! right! quite right!' exclaimed the child, and 'quite right' echoed on all sides.

'But how came you to know so much, when you are blind?' said William, examining the old man attentively.

'Hush,' said John, who was a year older than his brother, and very sage, 'you should not put him in mind of his being blind.'

'Though I am blind,' said the harper, 'I can hear, you know, and I heard from your sister herself all that I told you of her, that she was good-tempered and good-natured and fond of you.' 'Oh, that's wrong—you did not hear all that from herself, I'm sure,' said John, 'for nobody ever hears her praising herself.' 'Did not I hear her tell you,' said the harper, 'when you first came round me, that she was in a great hurry to go home, but that she would stay a little while, since you wished it so much? Was not that good-natured? And when you said you did not like the tune she liked best, she was not angry with you, but said, "Then play William's first, if you please,"—was not that good-tempered?' 'Oh,' interrupted William, 'it's all true; but how did you find out that she was fond of me?' 'That is such a difficult question,' said the harper, 'that I must take time to consider.' The harper tuned his instrument, as he pondered, or seemed to ponder; and at this instant two boys who had been searching for birds' nests in the hedges, and who had heard the sound of the harp, came blustering up, and pushing their way through the circle, one of them exclaimed, 'What's going on here? Who are you, my old fellow? A blind harper! Well, play us a tune, if you can play ever a good one—play me—let's see, what shall he play, Bob?' added he, turning to his companion. 'Bumper Squire Jones.'

The old man, though he did not seem quite pleased with the peremptory manner of the request, played, as he was desired, 'Bumper Squire Jones'; and several other tunes were afterwards bespoke by the same rough and tyrannical voice.

The little children shrank back in timid silence, and eyed the brutal boy with dislike. This boy was the son of Attorney Case; and as his father had neglected to correct his temper when he was a child, as he grew up it became insufferable. All who were younger and weaker than himself dreaded his approach, and detested him as a tyrant.

When the old harper was so tired that he could play no more, a lad, who usually carried his harp for him, and who was within call, came up, and held his master's hat to the company, saying, 'Will you be pleased to remember us?' The children readily produced their halfpence, and thought their wealth well bestowed upon this poor, good-natured man, who had taken so much pains to entertain them, better even than upon the gingerbread woman, whose stall they loved to frequent. The hat was held some time to the attorney's son before he chose to see it. At last he put his hand surlily into his waistcoat pocket and pulled out a shilling. There were sixpennyworth of halfpence in the hat. 'I'll take these halfpence,' said he, 'and here's a shilling for you.'

'God bless you, sir,' said the lad; but as he took the shilling, which the young gentleman had slily put *into the blind man's hand*, he saw that it was not worth one farthing. 'I am afraid it is not good, sir,' said the lad, whose business it was to examine the money for his master. 'I am afraid, then, you'll get no other,' said young Case, with an insulting laugh. 'It never will do, sir,' persisted the lad; 'look at it yourself; the edges are all yellow! you can see the copper through it quite plain. Sir, nobody will take it from us.' 'That's your affair,' said the brutal boy, pushing away his hand. 'You may pass it, you know, as well as I do, if you look sharp. You have taken it from me, and I shan't take it back again, I promise you.'

A whisper of 'that's very unjust,' was heard. The little assembly, though under evident constraint, could no longer suppress their indignation.

'Who says it's unjust?' cried the tyrant sternly, looking down upon his judges.

Susan's little brothers had held her gown fast, to prevent her from moving at the beginning of this contest, and she was now so much interested to see the end of it, that she stood still, without making any resistance.

'Is any one here amongst yourselves a judge of silver?' said the old man. 'Yes, here's the butcher's boy,' said the attorney's son; 'show it to him.' He was a sickly-looking boy, and of a remarkably peaceful disposition. Young Case fancied that he would be afraid to give judgment against him. However, after some moments' hesitation, and after turning the shilling round several times, he pronounced, 'that, as far as his judgment went, but he did not pretend to be a downright *certain sure* of it, the shilling was not over and above good.' Then turning to Susan, to screen himself from manifest danger, for the attorney's son looked upon him with a vengeful mien, 'But here's Susan here, who understands silver a great deal better than I do; she takes a power of it for bread, you know.'

'I'll leave it to her,' said the old harper; 'if she says the shilling is good, keep it, Jack.' The shilling was handed to Susan, who, though she had with becoming modesty forborne all interference, did not hesitate, when she was called upon, to speak the truth: 'I think that this shilling is a bad one,' said she; and the gentle but firm tone in which she pronounced the words for a moment awed and silenced the angry and brutal boy. 'There's another, then,' cried he; 'I have sixpences and shillings too in plenty, thank my stars.'

Susan now walked away with her two little brothers, and all the other children separated to go to their several homes. The old harper called to Susan, and begged that, if she was going towards the village, she would be so kind as to show him the way. His lad took up his harp, and little William took the old man by the hand. 'I'll lead him, I can lead him,' said he; and John ran on before them, to gather kingcups in the meadow.

There was a small rivulet which they had to cross, and as a plank which served for a bridge over it was rather narrow, Susan was afraid to trust the old blind man to his little conductor; she therefore went on the tottering plank first herself, and then led the old harper carefully over. They were now come to a gate, which opened upon the highroad to the village. 'There is the highroad straight before you,' said Susan to the lad, who was carrying his master's harp; 'you can't miss it. Now I must bid you a good evening; for I'm in a great hurry to get home, and must go the short way across the fields here, which would not be so pleasant for you, because of the stiles. Good-bye.' The old harper thanked her, and went along the highroad, whilst she and her brothers tripped on as fast as they could by the short way across the fields.

'Miss Somers, I am afraid, will be waiting for us,' said Susan. 'You know she said she would call at six; and by the length of our shadows I'm sure it is late.'

When they came to their own cottage door, they heard many voices, and they saw, when they entered, several ladies standing in the kitchen. 'Come in, Susan; we thought you had quite forsaken us,' said Miss Somers to Susan, who advanced timidly. 'I fancy you forgot that we promised to pay you a visit this evening; but you need not blush so much about the matter; there is no great harm done; we have only been here about five minutes; and we have been well employed in admiring your neat garden and your orderly shelves. Is it you, Susan, who keep these things in such nice order?' continued Miss Somers, looking round the kitchen.

Before Susan could reply, little William pushed forward and answered, 'Yes, ma'am, it is *my* sister Susan that keeps everything neat; and she always comes to school for us, too, which was what caused her to be so late.' 'Because as how,' continued John, 'she was loth to refuse us the hearing a blind man play on the harp. It was we kept her, and we hopes, ma'am, as you *are*—as you *seem* so good, you won't take it amiss.'

Miss Somers and her sister smiled at the affectionate simplicity with which Susan's little brothers undertook her defence, and they were, from this slight circumstance, disposed to think yet more favourably of a family which seemed so well united. They took Susan along with them through the village. Many neighbours came to their doors, and far from envying, they all secretly wished Susan well as she passed.

'I fancy we shall find what we want here,' said Miss Somers, stopping before a shop, where unfolded sheets of pins and glass buttons glistened in the window, and where rolls of many coloured ribbons appeared ranged in tempting order. She went in, and was rejoiced to see the shelves at the back of the counter well furnished with glossy tiers of stuffs, and gay, neat printed linens and calicoes.

'Now, Susan, choose yourself a gown,' said Miss Somers; 'you set an example of industry and good conduct, of which we wish to take public notice, for the benefit of others.'

The shopkeeper, who was father to Susan's friend Rose, looked much satisfied by this speech, and as if a compliment had been paid to himself, bowed low to Miss Somers, and then with alertness, which a London linendraper might have admired, produced piece after piece of his best goods to his young customer—unrolled, unfolded, held the bright stuffs and calendered calicoes in various lights. Now stretched his arm to the highest shelves, and brought down in a trice what seemed to be beyond the reach of any but a giant's arm; now dived into some hidden recess beneath the counter, and brought to light fresh beauties and fresh temptations.

Susan looked on with more indifference than most of the spectators. She was thinking much of her lamb, and more of her father.

Miss Somers had put a bright guinea into her hand, and had bid her pay for her own gown; but Susan, as she looked at the guinea, thought it was a great deal of money to lay out upon herself, and she wished, but did not know how to ask, that she might keep it for a better purpose.

Some people are wholly inattentive to the lesser feelings, and incapable of reading the countenances of those on whom they bestow their bounty. Miss Somers and her sister were not of this roughly charitable class.

'She does not like any of these things,' whispered Miss Somers to her sister. Her sister observed that Susan looked as if her thoughts were far distant from gowns.

'If you don't fancy any of these things,' said the civil shopkeeper to Susan, 'we shall have a new assortment of calicoes for the spring season soon from town.' 'Oh,' interrupted Susan, with a smile and a blush, 'these are all pretty, and too good for me, but——' '*But* what, Susan?' said Miss Somers. 'Tell us what is passing in your little mind.' Susan hesitated. 'Well then, we will not press you, you are scarcely acquainted with us yet; when you are, you will not be afraid, I hope, to speak your mind. Put this shining yellow counter,' continued she, pointing to the guinea, 'in your pocket, and make what use of it you please. From what we know, and from what we have heard of you, we are persuaded that you will make a good use of it.'

41

'I think, madam,' said the master of the shop, with a shrewd, good-natured look, 'I could give a pretty good guess myself what will become of that guinea; but I say nothing.'

'No, that is right,' said Miss Somers; 'we leave Susan entirely at liberty; and now we will not detain her any longer. Good night, Susan, we shall soon come again to your neat cottage.' Susan curtsied, with an expressive look of gratitude, and with a modest frankness in her countenance which seemed to say, 'I would tell you, and welcome, what I want to do with the guinea; but I am not used to speak before so many people. When you come to our cottage again you shall know all.'

When Susan had departed, Miss Somers turned to the obliging shopkeeper, who was folding up all the things he had opened. 'You have had a great deal of trouble with us, sir,' said she; 'and since Susan will not choose a gown for herself, I must.' She selected the prettiest; and whilst the man was rolling it in paper, she asked him several questions about Susan and her family, which he was delighted to answer, because he had now an opportunity of saying as much as he wished in her praise.

'No later back, ma'am, than last May morning,' said he, 'as my daughter Rose was telling us, Susan did a turn, in her quiet way, by her mother, that would not displease you if you were to hear it. She was to have been Queen of the May, which in our little village, amongst the younger tribe, is a thing that is thought of a good deal; but Susan's mother was ill, and Susan, after sitting up with her all night, would not leave her in the morning, even when they brought the crown to her. She put the crown upon my daughter Rose's head with her own hands; and, to be sure, Rose loves her as well as if she was her own sister. But I don't speak from partiality; for I am no relation whatever to the Prices—only a well-wisher, as every one, I believe, who knows them is. I'll send the parcel up to the Abbey, shall I, ma'am?'

'If you please,' said Miss Somers, 'and, as soon as you receive your new things from town, let us know. You will, I hope, find us good customers and well-wishers,' added she, with a smile; 'for those who wish well to their neighbours surely deserve to have well-wishers themselves.'

A few words may encourage the benevolent passions, and may dispose people to live in peace and happiness; a few words may set them at variance, and may lead to misery and lawsuits. Attorney Case and Miss Somers were both equally convinced of this, and their practice was uniformly consistent with their principles.

But now to return to Susan. She put the bright guinea carefully into the glove with the twelve shillings which she had received from her companions on May day. Besides this treasure, she calculated that the amount of the bills for bread could not be less than eight or nine and thirty shillings; and as her father was now sure of a week's reprieve, she had great hopes that, by some means or other, it would be possible to make up the whole sum necessary to pay for a substitute. 'If that could but be done,' said she to herself, 'how happy would my mother be. She would be quite stout again, for she certainly is a great deal better since I told her that father would stay a week longer. Ah! but she would not have blessed Attorney Case, though, if she had known about my poor Daisy.'

Susan took the path that led to the meadow by the water-side, resolved to go by herself and take leave of her innocent favourite. But she did not pass by unperceived. Her little brothers were watching for her return, and as soon as they saw her they ran after her, and overtook her as she reached the meadow.

'What did that good lady want with you?' cried William; but looking up in his sister's face he saw tears in her eyes, and he was silent, and walked on quietly. Susan saw her lamb by the water-side. 'Who are those two men?' said William. 'What are they going to do with *Daisy*?' The two men were Attorney Case and the butcher. The butcher was feeling whether the lamb was fat.

Susan sat down upon the bank in silent sorrow; her little brothers ran up to the butcher, and demanded whether he was going to *do any harm* to the lamb. The butcher did not answer, but the attorney replied, 'It is not your sister's lamb any longer; it's mine—mine to all intents and purposes.' 'Yours!' cried the children, with terror; 'and will you kill it?' 'That's the butcher's business.'

The little boys now burst into piercing lamentations. They pushed away the butcher's hand; they threw their arms round the neck of the lamb; they kissed its forehead—it bleated. 'It will not bleat to-morrow!' said William, and he wept bitterly. The butcher looked aside, and hastily rubbed his eyes with the corner of his blue apron. The attorney stood unmoved; he pulled up the head of the lamb, which had just stooped to crop a mouthful of clover. 'I have no time to waste,' said he; 'butcher, you'll account with me. If it's fat—the sooner the better. I've no more to say.' And he walked off, deaf to the prayers of the poor children.

Let it eat out of her hand for the last time.

Let it eat out of her hand for the last time.

As soon as the attorney was out of sight, Susan rose from the bank where she was seated, came up to her lamb, and stooped to gather some of the fresh dewy trefoil, to let it eat out of her hand for the last time. Poor Daisy licked her well-known hand.

'Now, let us go,' said Susan. 'I'll wait as long as you please,' said the butcher. Susan thanked him, but walked away quickly, without looking again at her lamb. Her little brothers begged the man to stay a few minutes, for they had gathered a handful of blue speedwell and yellow crowsfoot, and they were decking the poor animal. As it followed the boys through the village, the children collected as they passed, and the butcher's own son was amongst the number. Susan's steadiness about the bad shilling was full in this boy's memory; it had saved him a beating. He went directly to his father to beg the life of Susan's lamb.

'I was thinking about it, boy, myself,' said the butcher; 'it's a sin to kill a *pet lamb*, I'm thinking—any way, it's what I'm not used to, and don't fancy doing, and I'll go and say as much to Attorney Case; but he's a hard man; there's but one way to deal with him, and that's the way I must take, though so be I shall be the loser thereby; but we'll say nothing to the boys, for fear it might be the thing would not take; and then it would be worse again to poor Susan, who is a good girl, and always was, as well she may, being of a good breed, and well reared from the first.'

'Come, lads, don't keep a crowd and a scandal about my door,' continued he, aloud, to the children; 'turn the lamb in here, John, in the paddock, for to-night, and go your ways home.'

The crowd dispersed, but murmured, and the butcher went to the attorney. 'Seeing that all you want is a good, fat, tender lamb, for a present for Sir Arthur, as you told me,' said the butcher, 'I could let you have what's as good or better for your purpose.' 'Better—if it's better, I'm ready to hear reason.' The butcher had choice, tender lamb, he said, fit to eat the next day; and as Mr. Case was impatient to make his offering to Sir Arthur, he accepted the butcher's proposal, though with such seeming reluctance, that he actually squeezed out of him, before he would complete the bargain, a bribe of a fine sweetbread.

In the meantime Susan's brothers ran home to tell her that her lamb was put into the paddock for the night; this was all they knew, and even this was some comfort to her. Rose, her good friend, was with her, and she had before her the pleasure of telling her father of his week's reprieve. Her mother was better, and even said she was determined to sit up to supper in her wicker armchair.

Susan was getting things ready for supper, when little William, who was standing at the house door, watching in the dusk for his father's return, suddenly exclaimed, 'Susan! if here is not our old man!'

'Yes,' said the old harper, 'I have found my way to you. The neighbours were kind enough to show me whereabouts you lived; for, though I didn't know your name, they guessed who I meant by what I said of you all.' Susan came to the door, and the old man was delighted to hear her speak again. 'If it would not be too bold,' said he, 'I'm a stranger in this part of the country, and come from afar off. My boy has got a bed for himself here in the village, but I have no place. Could you be so charitable as to give an old blind man a night's lodging?' Susan said she would step in and ask her mother; and she soon returned with an answer that he was heartily welcome, if he could sleep upon the children's bed, which was but small.

The old man thankfully entered the hospitable cottage. He struck his head against the low roof, as he stepped over the door-sill. 'Many roofs that are twice as high are not half so good,' said he. Of this he had just had experience at the house of the Attorney Case, while he had asked, but had been roughly refused all assistance by Miss Barbara, who was, according to her usual custom, standing staring at the hall door.

The old man's harp was set down in Farmer Price's kitchen, and he promised to play a tune for the boys before they went to bed; their mother giving them leave to sit up to supper with their father. He came home with a sorrowful countenance; but how soon did it brighten when Susan, with a smile, said to him, 'Father, we've good news for you! good news for us all!—You have a whole week longer to stay with us; and perhaps,' continued she, putting her little purse into his hands, 'perhaps with what's here and the bread bills, and what may somehow be got together before a week's at an end, we may make up the nine guineas for the substitute, as they call him. Who knows, dearest mother, but we may keep him with us for ever!' As she spoke, she threw her arms round her father, who pressed her to his bosom without speaking, for his heart was full. He was some little time before he could perfectly believe that what he heard was true; but the revived smiles of his wife, the noisy joy of his little boys, and the satisfaction that shone in Susan's countenance, convinced him that he was not in a dream.

As they sat down to supper, the old harper was made welcome to his share of the cheerful though frugal meal.

Susan's father, as soon as supper was finished, even before he would let the harper play a tune for his boys, opened the little purse which Susan had given him. He was surprised at the sight of the twelve shillings, and still more, when he came to the bottom of the purse, to see the bright golden guinea.

'How did you come by all this money, Susan?' said he. 'Honestly and handsomely, that I'm sure of beforehand,' said her proud mother; 'but how I can't make out, except by the baking. Hey, Susan, is this your first baking?' 'Oh no, no,' said her father, 'I have her first baking snug here, besides, in my pocket. I kept it for a surprise, to do your mother's heart good, Susan. Here's twenty-nine shillings, and the Abbey bill, which is not paid yet, comes to ten more. What think you of this, wife? Have we not a right to be proud of our Susan? Why,' continued he, turning to the harper, 'I ask your pardon for speaking out so free before strangers in praise of my own, which I know is not mannerly; but the truth is the fittest thing to be spoken, as I think, at all times; therefore, here's your good health, Susan; why, by-and-by she'll be worth her weight in gold—in silver at least. But tell us, child, how came you by all this riches? and how comes it that I don't go to-morrow? All this happy news makes me so gay in myself, I'm afraid I shall hardly understand it rightly. But speak on, child—first bringing us a bottle of the good mead you made last year from your own honey.'

Susan did not much like to tell the history of her guinea-hen—of the gown and of her poor lamb. Part of this would seem as if she was vaunting of her own generosity, and part of it she did not like to recollect. But her mother pressed to know the whole, and she related it as simply as she could. When she came to the story of her lamb, her voice faltered, and everybody present was touched. The old harper sighed once, and cleared his throat several times. He then asked for his harp, and, after tuning it for a considerable time, he recollected—for he had often fits of absence—that he had sent for it to play the tune he had promised to the boys.

This harper came from a great distance, from the mountains of Wales, to contend with several other competitors for a prize, which had been advertised by a musical society about a year before this time. There was to be a splendid ball given upon the occasion at Shrewsbury, which was about five miles from our village. The prize was ten guineas for the best performer on the harp, and the prize was now to be decided in a few days.

All this intelligence Barbara had long since gained from her maid, who often paid visits to the town of Shrewsbury, and she had long had her imagination inflamed with the idea of this splendid music-meeting and ball. Often had she sighed to be there, and often had she revolved in her mind schemes for introducing herself to some *genteel* neighbours, who might take her to the ball *in their carriage*. How rejoiced, how triumphant was she when this very evening, just about the time when the butcher was bargaining with her father about Susan's lamb, a *livery* servant from the Abbey rapped at the door, and left a card for Mr. and Miss Barbara Case.

'There,' cried Bab, '*I* and *papa* are to dine and drink tea at the Abbey to-morrow. Who knows? I daresay, when they see that I'm not a vulgar-looking person, and all that, and if I go cunningly to work with Miss Somers, as I shall, to be sure—I daresay she'll take me to the ball with her.'

'To be sure,' said the maid; 'it's the least one may expect from a lady who *demeans* herself to visit Susan Price, and goes about a-shopping for her. The least she can do for you is to take you in her carriage, *which* costs nothing, but is just a common civility, to a ball.'

'Then pray, Betty,' continued Miss Barbara, 'don't forget to-morrow, the first thing you do, to send off to Shrewsbury for my new bonnet. I must have it *to dine in*, at the Abbey, or the ladies will think nothing of me; and, Betty, remember the mantua-maker too. I must see and coax papa to buy me a new gown against the ball. I can see, you know, something of the fashions to-morrow at the Abbey. I shall *look the ladies well over*, I promise you. And, Betty, I have thought of the most charming present for Miss Somers, as papa says it's good never to go empty-handed to a great house, I'll make Miss Somers, who is fond, as her maid told you, of such things—I'll make Miss Somers a present of that guinea-hen of Susan's; it's of no use to me, so do you carry it up early in the morning to the Abbey, with my compliments. That's the thing.'

In full confidence that her present and her bonnet would operate effectually in her favour, Miss Barbara paid her first visit at the Abbey. She expected to see wonders. She was dressed in all the finery which she had heard from her maid, who had heard from the 'prentice of a Shrewsbury milliner, was *the thing* in London; and she was much surprised and disappointed, when she was shown into the room where the Miss Somerses and the ladies of the Abbey were sitting, to see that they did not, in any one part of their dress, agree with the picture her imagination had formed of fashionable ladies. She was embarrassed when she saw books and work and drawings upon the table, and she began to think that some affront was meant to her, because *the company* did not sit with their hands before them.

When Miss Somers endeavoured to find out conversation that would interest her, and spoke of walks and flowers and gardening, of which she was herself fond, Miss Barbara still thought herself undervalued, and soon contrived to expose her ignorance most completely, by talking of things which she did not understand.

Those who never attempt to appear what they are not—those who do not in their manners pretend to anything unsuited to their habits and situation in life, never are in danger of being laughed at by sensible, well-bred people of any rank; but affectation is the constant and just object of ridicule.

Miss Barbara Case, with her mistaken airs of gentility, aiming to be thought a woman and a fine lady, whilst she was, in reality, a child and a vulgar attorney's daughter, rendered herself so thoroughly ridiculous, that the good-natured, yet discerning spectators were painfully divided between their sense of comic absurdity and a feeling of shame for one who could feel nothing for herself.

One by one the ladies dropped off. Miss Somers went out of the room for a few minutes to alter her dress, as it was the custom of the family, before dinner. She left a portfolio of pretty drawings and good prints for Miss Barbara's amusement; but Miss Barbara's thoughts were so intent upon the harpers' ball, that she could not be entertained with such *trifles*. How unhappy are those who spend their time in expectation! They can never enjoy the present moment. Whilst Barbara was contriving means of interesting Miss Somers in her favour, she recollected, with surprise, that not one word had yet been said of her present of the guinea-hen. Mrs. Betty, in the hurry of her dressing her young lady in the morning, had forgotten it; but it came just whilst Miss Somers was dressing; and the housekeeper came into her mistress's room to announce its arrival.

'Ma'am,' said she, 'here's a beautiful guinea-hen just come, *with* Miss Barbara Case's compliments to you.'

Miss Somers knew, by the tone in which the housekeeper delivered this message, that there was something in the business which did not perfectly please her. She made no answer, in expectation that the housekeeper, who was a woman of a very open temper, would explain her cause of dissatisfaction. In this she was not mistaken. The housekeeper came close up to the dressing-table, and continued, 'I never like to speak till I'm sure, ma'am, and I'm not quite sure, to say certain, in this case, ma'am, but still I think it right to tell you, which can't wrong anybody, what came across my mind about this same guinea-hen, ma'am; and you can inquire into it, and do as you please afterwards, ma'am. Some time ago we had fine guinea-fowls of our own, and I made bold, not thinking, to be sure, that all our own would die away from us, as they have done, to give a fine couple last Christmas to Susan Price, and very fond and pleased she was at the time, and I'm sure would never have parted with the hen with her good-will; but if my eyes don't strangely mistake, this hen, that comes from Miss Barbara, is the self-same identical guinea-hen that I gave to Susan. And how Miss Bab came by it is the thing that puzzles me. If my boy Philip was at home, maybe, as he's often at Mrs. Price's (which I don't disapprove), he might know the history of the guinea-hen. I expect him home this night, and if you have no objection, I will sift the affair.'

'The shortest way, I think,' said Henrietta, 'would be to ask Miss Case herself about it, which I will do this evening.' 'If you please, ma'am,' said the housekeeper, coldly; for she knew that Miss Barbara was not famous in the village for speaking truth.

Dinner was now served. Attorney Case expected to smell mint sauce, and, as the covers were taken from off the dishes, looked around for lamb; but no lamb appeared. He had a dexterous knack of twisting the conversation to his point. Sir Arthur was speaking, when they sat down to dinner, of a new carving knife, which he lately had had made for his sister. The Attorney immediately went from carving-knives to poultry; thence to butchers meat. Some joints, he observed, were much more difficult to carve than others. He never saw a man carve better than the gentleman opposite him, who was the curate of the parish. 'But, sir,' said the vulgar attorney, 'I must make bold to differ with you in one point, and I'll appeal to Sir Arthur. Sir Arthur, pray may I ask, when you carve a forequarter of lamb, do you, when you raise the shoulder, throw in salt, or not?' This well-prepared question was not lost upon Sir Arthur. The attorney was thanked for his intended present; but mortified and surprised to hear Sir Arthur say that it was a constant rule of his never to accept of any presents from his neighbours. 'If we were to accept a lamb from a rich neighbour on my estate,' said he, 'I am afraid we should mortify many of our poor tenants, who can have little to offer, though, perhaps, they may bear us thorough good-will notwithstanding.'

After the ladies left the dining-room, as they were walking up and down the large hall, Miss Barbara had a fair opportunity of imitating her keen father's method of conversing. One of the ladies observed that this hall would be a charming place for music. Bab brought in harps and harpers, and the harpers' ball, in a breath. 'I know so much about it,—about the ball I mean,' said she, 'because a lady in Shrewsbury, a friend of papa's, offered to take me with her; but papa did not like to give her the trouble of sending so far for me, though she has a coach of her own.' Barbara fixed her eyes upon Miss Somers as she spoke; but she could not read her countenance as distinctly as she wished, because Miss Somers was at this moment letting down the veil of her hat.

'Shall we walk out before tea?' said Miss Somers to her companions; 'I have a pretty guinea-hen to show you.' Barbara, secretly drawing propitious omens from the guinea-hen, followed with a confidential step. The pheasantry was well filled with pheasants, peacocks, etc.; and Susan's pretty little guinea-hen appeared well, even in this high company. It was much admired. Barbara was in glory; but her glory was of short duration.

Just as Miss Somers was going to inquire into the guinea-hen's history, Philip came up, to ask permission to have a bit of sycamore, to turn a nutmeg box for his mother. He was an ingenious lad, and a good turner for his age. Sir Arthur had put by a bit of sycamore on purpose for him; and Miss Somers told him where it was to be found. He thanked her; but in the midst of his bow of thanks his eye was struck by the sight of the guinea-hen, and he involuntarily exclaimed, 'Susan's guinea-hen, I declare!' 'No, it's not Susan's guinea-hen,' said Miss Barbara, colouring furiously; 'it is mine, and I have made a present of it to Miss Somers.'

At the sound of Bab's voice, Philip turned—saw her—and indignation, unrestrained by the presence of all the amazed spectators, flashed in his countenance.

'What is the matter, Philip?' said Miss Somers, in a pacifying tone; but Philip was not inclined to be pacified. 'Why, ma'am,' said he, 'may I speak out?' and, without waiting for permission, he spoke out, and gave a full, true, and warm account of Rose's embassy, and of Miss Barbara's cruel and avaricious proceedings.

Barbara denied, prevaricated, stammered, and at last was overcome with confusion; for which even the most indulgent spectators could scarcely pity her.

Miss Somers, however, mindful of what was due to her guest, was anxious to despatch Philip for his piece of sycamore. Bab recovered herself as soon as he was out of sight; but she further exposed herself by exclaiming, 'I'm sure I wish this pitiful guinea-hen had never come into my possession. I wish Susan had kept it at home, as she should have done!'

'Perhaps she will be more careful now that she has received so strong a lesson,' said Miss Somers. 'Shall we try her?' continued she. 'Philip will, I daresay, take the guinea-hen back to Susan, if we desire it.' 'If you please, ma'am,' said Barbara, sullenly; 'I have nothing more to do with it.'

So the guinea-hen was delivered to Philip, who set off joyfully with his prize, and was soon in sight of Farmer Price's cottage. He stopped when he came to the door. He recollected Rose and her generous friendship for Susan. He was determined that she should have the pleasure of restoring the guinea-hen. He ran into the village. All the children who had given up their little purse on May-day were assembled on the play-green. They were delighted to see the guinea-hen once more. Philip took his pipe and tabor, and they marched in innocent triumph towards the white washed cottage.

'Let me come with you—let me come with you,' said the butcher's boy to Philip. 'Stop one minute! my father has something to say to you.' He darted into his father's house. The little procession stopped, and in a few minutes the bleating of a lamb was heard. Through a back passage, which led into the paddock behind the house, they saw the butcher leading a lamb.

'It is Daisy!' exclaimed Rose. 'It's Daisy!' repeated all her companions. 'Susan's lamb! Susan's lamb!' and there was a universal shout of joy.

'Well, for my part,' said the good butcher, as soon as he could be heard,—'for my part, I would not be so cruel as Attorney Case for the whole world. These poor brute beasts don't know aforehand what's going to happen to them; and as for dying, it's what we must all do some time or another; but to keep wringing the hearts of the living, that have as much sense as one's self, is what I call cruel; and is not this what Attorney Case has been doing by poor Susan and her whole family, ever since he took a spite against them? But, at any rate, here's Susan's lamb safe and sound. I'd have taken it back sooner, but I was off before day to the fair, and am but just come back. Daisy, however, has been as well off in my paddock as he would have been in the field by the water-side.'

The obliging shopkeeper, who showed the pretty calicoes to Susan, was now at his door, and when he saw the lamb, and heard that it was Susan's, and learned its history, he said that he would add his mite; and he gave the children some ends of narrow riband, with which Rose decorated her friend's lamb.

The pipe and tabor now once more began to play, and the procession moved on in joyful order, after giving the humane butcher three cheers; three cheers which were better deserved than 'loud huzzas' usually are.

Susan was working in her arbour, with her little deal table before her. When she heard the sound of the music, she put down her work and listened. She saw the crowd of children coming nearer and nearer. They had closed round Daisy, so that she did not see it; but as they came up to the garden gate she saw that Rose beckoned to her. Philip played as loud as he could, that she might not hear, till the proper moment, the bleating of the lamb. Susan opened the garden-wicket, and at this signal the crowd divided, and the first thing that Susan saw, in the midst of her taller friends, was little smiling Mary, with the guinea-hen in her arms.

'Come on! Come on!' cried Mary, as Susan started with joyful surprise; 'you have more to see.'

At this instant the music paused, Susan heard the bleating of a lamb, and scarcely daring to believe her senses, she pressed eagerly forward, and beheld poor Daisy!—she burst into tears. 'I did not shed one tear when I parted with you, my dear little Daisy!' said she. 'It was for my father and mother. I would not have parted with you for anything else in the whole world. Thank you, thank you all,' added she, to her companions, who sympathised in her joy, even more than they had sympathised in her sorrow. 'Now, if my father was not to go away from us next week, and if my mother was quite stout, I should be the happiest person in the world!'

As Susan pronounced these words, a voice behind the little listening crowd cried, in a brutal tone, 'Let us pass, if you please; you have no right to stop up the public road!' This was the voice of Attorney Case, who was returning with his daughter Barbara from his visit to the Abbey. He saw the lamb, and tried to whistle as he went on. Barbara also saw the guinea-hen, and turned her head another way, that she might avoid the contemptuous, reproachful looks of those whom she only affected to despise. Even her new bonnet, in which she had expected to be so much admired, was now only serviceable to hide her face and conceal her mortification.

'I am glad she saw the guinea-hen,' cried Rose, who now held it in her hands. 'Yes,' said Philip, 'she'll not forget May-day in a hurry.' 'Nor I neither, I hope,' said Susan, looking round upon her companions with a most affectionate smile: 'I hope, whilst I live, I shall never forget your goodness to me last May-day. Now I've my pretty guinea-hen safe once more, I should think of returning your money.' 'No! no! no!' was the general cry. 'We don't want the money—keep it, keep it—you want it for your father.' 'Well,' said Susan, 'I am not too proud to be obliged. I *will* keep your money for my father. Perhaps some time or other I may be able to earn——' 'Oh,' interrupted Philip, 'don't let us talk of earning; don't let us talk to her of money now; she has not had time hardly to look at poor Daisy and her guinea-hen. Come, we had best go about our business, and let her have them all to herself.'

The crowd moved away in consequence of Philip's considerate advice; but it was observed that he was the very last to stir from the garden-wicket himself. He stayed, first, to inform Susan that it was Rose who tied the ribands on Daisy's head. Then he stayed a little longer to let her into the history of the guinea-hen, and to tell her who it was that brought the hen home from the Abbey.

Rose held the sieve, and Susan was feeding her long-lost favourite, whilst Philip leaned over the wicket, prolonging his narration. 'Now, my pretty guinea-hen,' said Susan—'my naughty guinea-hen, that flew away from me, you shall never serve me so again. I must cut your nice wings; but I won't hurt you.' 'Take care,' cried Philip; 'you'd better, indeed you'd better let me hold her whilst you cut her wings.'

When this operation was successfully performed, which it certainly could never have been if Philip had not held the hen for Susan, he recollected that his mother had sent him with a message to Mrs. Price. This message led to another quarter of an hour's delay; for he had the whole history of the guinea-hen to tell over again to Mrs. Price, and the farmer himself luckily came in whilst it was going on, so it was but civil to begin it afresh; and then the farmer was so rejoiced to see his Susan so happy again with her two little favourites, that he declared he must see Daisy fed himself; and Philip found that he was wanted to hold the jugful of milk, out of which Farmer Price filled the pan for Daisy. Happy Daisy! who lapped at his ease whilst Susan caressed him, and thanked her fond father and her pleased mother.

'But, Philip,' said Mrs. Price, 'I'll hold the jug—you'll be late with your message to your mother; we'll not detain you any longer.'

Philip departed, and as he went out of the garden-wicket he looked up, and saw Bab and her maid Betty staring out of the window, as usual. On this, he immediately turned back to try whether he had shut the gate fast, lest the guinea-hen might stray, out and fall again into the hands of the enemy.

Miss Barbara, in the course of this day, felt considerable mortification, but no contrition. She was vexed that her meanness was discovered, but she felt no desire to cure herself of any of her faults. The ball was still uppermost in her vain, selfish soul. 'Well,' said she to her *confidante*, Betty, 'you hear how things have turned out; but if Miss Somers won't think of asking me to go out with her, I've a notion I know who will. As papa says, it's a good thing to have two strings to one's bow.'

Now some officers, who were quartered at Shrewsbury, had become acquainted with Mr. Case. They had gotten into some quarrel with a tradesman of the town, and Attorney Case had promised to bring them through the affair, as the man threatened to take the law of them. Upon the faith of this promise, and with the vain hope that, by civility, they might dispose him to bring in a *reasonable* bill of costs, these officers sometimes invited Mr. Case to the mess; and one of them, who had lately been married, prevailed upon his bride *sometimes* to take a little notice of Miss Barbara. It was with this lady that Miss Barbara now hoped to go to the harpers' ball.

'The officers and Mrs. Strathspey, or, more properly, Mrs. Strathspey and the officers, are to breakfast here, to-morrow, do you know?' said Bab to Betty. 'One of them dined at the Abbey to-day, and told papa they'd all come. They are going out on a party, somewhere into the country, and breakfast here on their way. Pray, Betty, don't forget that Mrs. Strathspey can't breakfast without honey. I heard her say so myself.' 'Then, indeed,' said Betty, 'I'm afraid Mrs. Strathspey will be likely to go without her breakfast here; for not a spoonful of honey have we, let her long for it ever so much.' 'But, surely,' said Bab, 'we can contrive to get some honey in the neighbourhood.' 'There's none to be bought, as I know of,' said Betty. 'But is there none to be begged or borrowed?' said Bab, laughing. 'Do you forget Susan's beehive? Step over to her in the morning with *my compliments*, and see what you can do. Tell her it's for Mrs. Strathspey.'

In the morning Betty went with Miss Barbara's compliments to Susan, to beg some honey for Mrs. Strathspey who could not breakfast without it. Susan did not like to part with her honey, because her mother loved it, and she therefore gave Betty but a small quantity. When Barbara saw how little Susan sent, she called her a *miser*, and she said she *must* have some more for Mrs. Strathspey. 'I'll go myself and speak to her. Come with me, Betty,' said the young lady, who found it at present convenient to forget her having declared, the day that she sucked up the broth, that she never would honour Susan with another visit. 'Susan,' said she, accosting the poor girl, whom she had done everything in her power to injure, 'I must beg a little more honey from you for Mrs. Strathspey's breakfast. You know, on a particular occasion such as this, neighbours must help one another.' 'To be sure they should,' added Betty.

Susan, though she was generous, was not weak; she was willing to give to those she loved, but not disposed to let anything be taken from her, or coaxed out of her, by those she had reason to despise. She civilly answered that she was sorry she had no more honey to spare.

Barbara grew angry, and lost all command of herself, when she saw that Susan, without regarding her reproaches, went on looking through the glass pane in the beehive. 'I'll tell you what, Susan Price,' said she, in a high tone, 'the honey I *will* have, so you may as well give it to me by fair means. Yes or no? Speak! Will you give it me or not? Will you give me that piece of the honeycomb that lies there?' 'That bit of honeycomb is for my mother's breakfast,' said Susan; 'I cannot give it you.' 'Can't you?' said Bab, 'then see if I don't take it!' She stretched across Susan for the honeycomb, which was lying by some rosemary leaves that Susan had freshly gathered for her mother's tea. Bab grasped, but at her first effort she only reached the rosemary. She made a second dart at the honeycomb, and, in her struggle to obtain it, she overset the beehive. The bees swarmed about her. Her maid Betty screamed and ran away. Susan, who was sheltered by a laburnum tree, called to Barbara, upon whom the black clusters of bees were now settling, and begged her to stand still, and not to beat them away. 'If you stand quietly you won't be stung, perhaps.' But instead of standing quietly, Bab buffeted and stamped and roared, and the bees stung her terribly. Her arms and her face swelled in a frightful manner. She was helped home by poor Susan and treacherous Mrs. Betty, who, now the mischief was done, thought only of exculpating herself to her master.

'Indeed, Miss Barbara,' said she, 'this was quite wrong of you to go and get yourself into such a scrape. I shall be turned away for it, you'll see.'

'I don't care whether you are turned away or not,' said Barbara; 'I never felt such pain in my life. Can't you do something for me? I don't mind the pain either so much as being such a fright. Pray, how am I to be fit to be seen at breakfast by Mrs. Strathspey; and I suppose I can't go to the ball either to-morrow, after all!'

'No, that you can't expect to do, indeed,' said Betty, the comforter. 'You need not think of balls; for those lumps and swellings won't go off your face this week. That's not what pains me; but I'm thinking of what your papa will say to me when he sees you, miss.'

Whilst this amiable mistress and maid were in their adversity reviling one another, Susan, when she saw that she could be of no further use, was preparing to depart, but at the house-door she was met by Mr. Case. Mr. Case had revolved things in his mind; for his second visit at the Abbey pleased him as little as his first, owing to a few words which Sir Arthur and Miss Somers dropped in speaking of Susan and Farmer Price. Mr. Case began to fear that he had mistaken his game in quarrelling with this family. The refusal of his present dwelt upon the attorney's mind; and he was aware that, if the history of Susan's lamb ever reached the Abbey, he was undone. He now thought that the most prudent course he could possibly follow would be to *hush up* matters with the *Prices* with all convenient speed. Consequently, when he met Susan at his door, he forced a gracious smile. 'How is your mother, Susan?' said he. 'Is there anything in our house can be of service to her?' On hearing his daughter he cried out, 'Barbara, Barbara—Bab! come downstairs, child, and speak to Susan Price.' But as no Barbara answered, her father stalked upstairs directly, opened the door, and stood amazed at the spectacle of her swelled visage.

Betty instantly began to tell the story of Barbara's mishap her own way. Bab contradicted her as fast as she spoke. The attorney turned the maid away on the spot; and partly with real anger, and partly with feigned affectation of anger, he demanded from his daughter how she dared to treat Susan Price so ill, 'when,' as he said, 'she was so neighbourly and obliging as to give you some of her honey? Couldn't you be content, without seizing upon the honeycomb by force? This is scandalous behaviour, and what, I assure you, I can't countenance.'

Susan now interceded for Barbara; and the attorney, softening his voice, said that 'Susan was a great deal too good to her; as you are, indeed,' added he, 'to everybody. I forgive her for your sake.' Susan curtsied, in great surprise; but her lamb could not be forgotten, and she left the attorney's house as soon as she could, to make her mother's rosemary tea breakfast.

Mr. Case saw that Susan was not so simple as to be taken in by a few fair words. His next attempt was to conciliate Farmer Price. The farmer was a blunt, honest man, and his countenance remained inflexibly contemptuous, when the attorney addressed him in his softest tone.

So stood matters the day of the long-expected harpers' ball. Miss Barbara Case, stung by Susan's bees, could not, after all her manœuvres, go with Mrs. Strathspey to the ball. The ballroom was filled early in the evening. There was a numerous assembly. The harpers, who contended for the prize, were placed under the music-gallery at the lower end of the room. Amongst them was our old blind friend, who, as he was not so well clad as his competitors, seemed to be disdained by many of the spectators. Six ladies and six gentlemen were now appointed to be judges of the performance. They were seated in a semicircle, opposite to the harpers. The Miss Somerses, who were fond of music, were amongst the ladies in the semicircle; and the prize was lodged in the hands of Sir Arthur. There was now silence. The first harp sounded, and as each musician tried his skill, the audience seemed to think that each deserved the prize. The old blind man was the last. He tuned his instrument; and such a simple pathetic strain was heard as touched every heart. All were fixed in delighted attention; and when the music ceased, the silence for some moments continued.

The silence was followed by a universal buzz of applause. The judges were unanimous in their opinions, and it was declared that the old blind harper, who played the last, deserved the prize.

The simple pathetic air which won the suffrages of the whole assembly, was his own composition. He was pressed to give the words belonging to the music; and at last he modestly offered to repeat them, as he could not see to write. Miss Somers' ready pencil was instantly produced; and the old harper dictated the words of his ballad, which he called—*Susan's Lamentation for her Lamb*.

Miss Somers looked at her brother from time to time, as she wrote; and Sir Arthur, as soon as the old man had finished, took him aside, and asked him some questions, which brought the whole history of Susan's lamb and of Attorney Case's cruelty to light.

The attorney himself was present when the harper began to dictate his ballad. His colour, as Sir Arthur steadily looked at him, varied continually; till at length, when he heard the words 'Susan's Lamentation for her Lamb,' he suddenly shrank back, skulked through the crowd, and disappeared. We shall not follow him; we had rather follow our old friend, the victorious harper.

No sooner had he received the ten guineas, his well-merited prize, than he retired to a small room belonging to the people of the house, asked for pen, ink, and paper, and dictated, in a low voice, to his boy, who was a tolerably good scribe, a letter, which he ordered him to put directly into the Shrewsbury post-office. The boy ran with the letter to the post-office. He was but just in time, for the postman's horn was sounding.

The next morning, when Farmer Price, his wife, and Susan, were sitting together, reflecting that his week's leave of absence was nearly at an end, and that the money was not yet made up for John Simpson, the substitute, a knock was heard at the door, and the person who usually delivered the letters in the village put a letter into Susan's hand, saying, 'A penny, if you please—here's a letter for your father.'

'For me!' said Farmer Price; 'here's the penny then; but who can it be from, I wonder? Who can think of writing to me, in this world?' He tore open the letter; but the hard name at the bottom of the page puzzled him—'*your obliged friend*, Llewellyn.'

'And what's this?' said he, opening a paper that was enclosed in the letter. 'It's a song, seemingly; it must be somebody that has a mind to make an April fool of me.' 'But it is not April, it is May, father,' said Susan. 'Well, let us read the letter, and we shall come to the truth all in good time.'

Farmer Price sat down in his own chair, for he could not read entirely to his satisfaction in any other, and read as follows:—

'My worthy Friend—I am sure you will be glad to hear that I have had good success this night. I have won the ten guinea prize, and for that I am in a great measure indebted to your sweet daughter Susan; as you will see by a little ballad I enclose for her. Your hospitality to me has afforded to me an opportunity of learning some of your family history. You do not, I hope, forget that I was present when you were counting the treasure in Susan's little purse, and that I heard for what purpose it was all destined. You have not, I know, yet made up the full sum for your substitute, John Simpson; therefore do me the favour to use the five guinea banknote which you will find within the ballad. You shall not find me as hard a creditor as Attorney Case. Pay me the money at your own convenience. If it is never convenient to you to pay it, I shall never ask it. I shall go my rounds again through this country, I believe, about this time next year, and will call to see how you do, and to play the new tune for Susan and the dear little boys.

'I should just add, to set you hearts at rest about the money, that it does not distress me at all to lend it to you. I am not quite so poor as I appear to be. But it is my humour to go about as I do. I see more of the world under my tattered garb than, perhaps, I should ever see in a better dress. There are many of my profession who are of the same mind as myself in this respect; and we are glad, when it lies in our way, to do any kindness to such a worthy family as yours. So, fare ye well.—Your obliged Friend, Llewellyn.'

Susan now, by her father's desire, opened the ballad. He picked up the five-guinea banknote, whilst she read, with surprise, 'Susan's Lamentation for her Lamb.' Her mother leaned over her shoulder to read the words; but they were interrupted, before they had finished the first stanza, by another knock at the door. It was not the postman with another letter. It was Sir Arthur and his sisters.

They came with an intention, which they were much disappointed to find that the old harper had rendered vain—they came to lend the farmer and his good family the money to pay for his substitute.

'But, since we are here,' said Sir Arthur, 'let me do my own business, which I had like to have forgotten. Mr. Price, will you come out with me, and let me show you a piece of your land, through which I want to make a road? Look there,' said Sir Arthur, pointing to the spot; 'I am laying out a ride round my estate, and that bit of land of yours stops me.'

'Why, sir,' said Price, 'the land's mine, to be sure, for that matter; but I hope you don't look upon me to be that sort of person that would be stiff about a trifle or so.'

'The fact is,' said Sir Arthur, 'I had heard you were a litigious, pig-headed fellow; but you do not seem to deserve this character.'

'Hope not, sir,' said the farmer; 'but about the matter of the land, I don't want to take any advantage of your wishing for it. You are welcome to it; and I leave it to you to find me out another bit of land convenient to me that will be worth neither more nor less; or else to make up the value to me some way or other. I need say no more about it.'

'I hear something,' continued Sir Arthur, after a short silence—'I hear something, Mr. Price, of a *flaw* in your lease. I would not speak to you about it whilst we were bargaining about your land, lest I should overawe you; but, tell me, what is this *flaw*?'

'In truth, and the truth is the fittest thing to be spoken at all times,' said the farmer, 'I didn't know myself what a *flaw*, as they call it, meant, till I heard of the word from Attorney Case; and, I take it, a *flaw* is neither more nor less than a mistake, as one should say. Now, by reason a man does not make a mistake on purpose, it seems to me to be the fair thing that if a man finds out his mistake, he might set it right; but Attorney Case says this is not law; and I've no more to say. The man who drew up my lease made a mistake; and if I must suffer for it, I must,' said the farmer. 'However, I can show you, Sir Arthur, just for my own satisfaction and yours, a few lines of a memorandum on a slip of paper, which was given me by your relation, the gentleman who lived here before, and let me my farm. You'll see, by that bit of paper, what was meant; but the attorney says the paper's not worth a button in a court of justice, and I don't understand these things. All I understand is the common honesty of the matter. I've no more to say.'

'This attorney, whom you speak of so often,' said Sir Arthur, 'you seem to have some quarrel with. Now, would you tell me frankly what is the matter between——?'

'The matter between us, then,' said Price, 'is a little bit of ground, not worth much, that is there open to the lane at the end of Mr. Case's garden, and he wanted to take it in. Now I told him my mind, that it belonged to the parish, and that I never would willingly give my consent to his cribbing it in that way. Sir, I was the more loth to see it shut into his garden, which, moreover, is large enough of all conscience without it, because you must know, Sir Arthur, the children in our village are fond of making a little play-green of it; and they have a custom of meeting on May-day at a hawthorn that stands in the middle of it, and altogether I was very loth to see 'em turned out of it by those who have no right.'

'Let us go and see this nook,' said Sir Arthur. 'It is not far off, is it?'

'Oh no, sir, just hard by here.'

When they got to the ground, Mr. Case, who saw them walking together, was in a hurry to join them, that he might put a stop to any explanations. Explanations were things of which he had a great dread; but, fortunately, he was upon this occasion a little too late.

'Is this the nook in dispute?' said Sir Arthur. 'Yes; this is the whole thing,' said Price. 'Why, Sir Arthur,' interposed the politic attorney, with an assumed air of generosity, 'don't let us talk any more about it. Let it belong to whom it will, I give it up to you.'

'So great a lawyer, Mr. Case, as you are,' replied Sir Arthur, 'must know that a man cannot give up that to which he has no legal title; and in this case it is impossible that, with the best intentions to oblige me in the world, you can give up this bit of land to me, because it is mine already, as I can convince you effectually by a map of the adjoining land, which I have fortunately safe amongst my papers. This piece of ground belonged to the farm on the opposite side of the road, and it was cut off when the lane was made.'

'Very possibly. I daresay you are quite correct; you must know best,' said the attorney, trembling for the agency.

'Then,' said Sir Arthur, 'Mr. Price, you will observe that I now promise this little green to the children for a playground; and I hope they may gather hawthorn many a May-day at this their favourite bush.' Mr. Price bowed low, which he seldom did, even when he received a favour himself. 'And now, Mr. Case,' said Sir Arthur, turning to the attorney, who did not know which way to look, 'you sent me a lease to look over.'

'Ye—ye—yes,' stammered Mr. Case. 'I thought it my duty to do so; not out of any malice or ill-will to this good man.'

'You have done him no injury,' said Sir Arthur coolly. 'I am ready to make him a new lease, whenever he pleases, of his farm, and I shall be guided by a memorandum of the original bargain, which he has in his possession. I hope I never shall take an unfair advantage of any one.'

'Heaven forbid, sir,' said the attorney, sanctifying his face, 'that I should suggest the taking an *unfair* advantage of any man, rich or poor; but to break a bad lease is not taking an unfair advantage.'

'You really think so?' said Sir Arthur. 'Certainly I do, and I hope I have not hazarded your good opinion by speaking my mind concerning the flaw so plainly. I always understood that there could be nothing ungentlemanlike, in the way of business, in taking advantage of the flaw in a lease.'

'Now,' said Sir Arthur, 'you have pronounced judgment *undesignedly* in your own case. You intended to send me this poor man's lease; but your son, by some mistake, brought me your own, and I have discovered a fatal error in it.' 'A fatal error!' said the alarmed attorney. 'Yes, sir,' said Sir Arthur, pulling the lease out of his pocket. 'Here it is. You will observe that it is neither signed nor sealed by the grantor.' 'But you won't take advantage of me, surely, Sir Arthur?' said Mr. Case, forgetting his own principles. 'I shall not take advantage of you, as you would have taken of this honest man. In both cases I shall be guided by memoranda which I have in my possession. I shall not, Mr. Case, defraud you of one shilling of your property. I am ready, at a fair valuation, to pay the exact value of your house and land; but upon this condition—that you quit the parish within one month!'

Attorney Case was thus compelled to submit to the hard necessity of the case, for he knew that he could not legally resist. Indeed he was glad to be let off so easily; and he bowed and sneaked away, secretly comforting himself with the hope that when they came to the valuation of the house and land he should be the gainer, perhaps, of a few guineas. His reputation he justly held very cheap.

'You are a scholar; you write a good hand; you can keep accounts, cannot you?' said Sir Arthur to Mr. Price, as they walked home towards the cottage. 'I think I saw a bill of your little daughter's drawing out the other day, which was very neatly written. Did you teach her to write?'

'No, sir,' said Price, 'I can't say I did *that*; for she mostly taught it herself; but I taught her a little arithmetic, as far as I knew, on our winter nights, when I had nothing better to do.'

'Your daughter shows that she has been well taught,' said Sir Arthur; 'and her good conduct and good character speak strongly in favour of her parents.'

'You are very good, very good indeed, sir, to speak in this sort of way,' said the delighted father.

'But I mean to do more than *pay you with words*,' said Sir Arthur. 'You are attached to your own family, perhaps you may become attached to me, when you come to know me, and we shall have frequent opportunities of judging of one another. I want no agent to squeeze my tenants, or do my dirty work. I only want a steady, intelligent, honest man, like you, to collect my rents, and I hope, Mr. Price, you will have no objection to the employment.' 'I hope, sir,' said Price, with joy and gratitude glowing in his honest countenance, 'that you'll never have cause to repent your goodness.'

'And what are my sisters about here?' said Sir Arthur, entering the cottage, and going behind his sisters, who were busily engaged in measuring an extremely pretty coloured calico.

'It is for Susan, my dear brother,' said they. 'I knew she did not keep that guinea for herself,' said Miss Somers. 'I have just prevailed upon her mother to tell me what became of it. Susan gave it to her father; but she must not refuse a gown of our choosing this time; and I am sure she will not, because her mother, I see, likes it. And, Susan, I hear that instead of becoming Queen of the May this year, you were sitting in your sick mother's room. Your mother has a little colour in her cheeks now.'

'Oh, ma'am,' interrupted Mrs. Price, 'I'm quite well. Joy, I think, has made me quite well.'

'Then,' said Miss Somers, 'I hope you will be able to come out on your daughter's birthday, which, I hear, is the 25th of this month. Make haste and get quite well before that day; for my brother intends that all the lads and lassies of the village shall have a dance on Susan's birthday.'

'Yes,' said Sir Arthur, 'and I hope on that day, Susan, you will be very happy with your little friends upon their play-green. I shall tell them that it is your good conduct which has obtained it for them; and if you have anything to ask, any little favour for any of your companions, which we can grant, now ask, Susan. These ladies look as if they would not refuse you anything that is reasonable; and, I think, you look as if you would not ask anything unreasonable.'

'Sir,' said Susan, after consulting her mother's eyes, 'there is, to be sure, a favour I should like to ask; it is for Rose.'

'Well, I don't know who Rose is,' said Sir Arthur, smiling; 'but go on.'

'Ma'am, you have seen her, I believe; she is a very good girl, indeed,' said Mrs. Price. 'And works very neatly, indeed,' continued Susan, eagerly, to Miss Somers; 'and she and her mother heard you were looking out for some one to wait upon you.'

'Say no more,' said Miss Somers; 'your wish is granted. Tell Rose to come to the Abbey to-morrow morning, or, rather, come with her yourself; for our housekeeper, I know, wants to talk to you about a certain cake. She wishes, Susan, that you should be the maker of the cake for the dance; and she has good things ready looked out for it already, I know. It must be large enough for everybody to have a slice, and the housekeeper will ice it for you. I only hope your cake will be as good as your bread. Fare ye well.'

How happy are those who bid farewell to a whole family, silent with gratitude, who will bless them aloud when they are far out of hearing!

'How do I wish, now,' said Farmer Price, 'and it's almost a sin for one who has had such a power of favours done him to wish for anything more; but how I *do* wish, wife, that our good friend, the harper, was only here at this time. It would do his old warm heart good. Well, the best of it is, we shall be able next year, when he comes his rounds, to pay him his money with thanks, being all the time, and for ever, as much obliged to him as if we kept it. I long, so I do, to see him in this house again, drinking, as he did, just in this spot, a glass of Susan's mead, to her very good health.'

'Yes,' said Susan, 'and the next time he comes, I can give him one of my guinea-hen's eggs, and I shall show my lamb, Daisy.'

'True, love,' said her mother, 'and he will play that tune and sing that pretty ballad. Where is it? for I have not finished it.'

'Rose ran away with it, mother, but I'll step after her, and bring it back to you this minute,' said Susan.

Susan found her friend Rose at the hawthorn, in the midst of a crowded circle of her companions, to whom she was reading 'Susan's Lamentation for her Lamb.'

'The words are something, but the tune—the tune—I must have the tune,' cried Philip. 'I'll ask my mother to ask Sir Arthur to try and find out which way that good old man went after the ball; and if he's above ground, we'll have him back by Susan's birthday, and he shall sit here—just exactly here—by this, our bush, and he shall play—I mean, if he pleases—that same tune for us, and I shall learn it—I mean, if I can—in a minute.'

The good news that Farmer Price was to be employed to collect the rents, and that Attorney Case was to leave the parish in a month, soon spread over the village. Many came out of their houses to have the pleasure of hearing the joyful tidings confirmed by Susan herself. The crowd on the play-green increased every minute.

'Yes,' cried the triumphant Philip, 'I tell you it's all true, every word of it. Susan's too modest to say it herself; but I tell ye all, Sir Arthur gave us this play-green for ever, on account of her being so good.'

You see, at last Attorney Case, with all his cunning, has not proved a match for 'Simple Susan.'

THE WHITE PIGEON

The little town of Somerville, in Ireland, has, within these few years, assumed the neat and cheerful appearance of an English village. Mr. Somerville, to whom this town belongs, wished to inspire his tenantry with a taste for order and domestic happiness, and took every means in his power to encourage industrious, well-behaved people to settle in his neighbourhood. When he had finished building a row of good slated houses in his town, he declared that he would let them to the best tenants he could find, and proposals were publicly sent to him from all parts of the country.

By the best tenants, Mr. Somerville did not, however, mean the best bidders; and many, who had offered an extravagant price for the houses, were surprised to find their proposals rejected. Amongst these was Mr. Cox, an alehouse-keeper, who did not bear a very good character.

'Please your honour, sir,' said he to Mr. Somerville, 'I *expected*, since I bid as fair and fairer for it than any other, that you would have let me the house next the apothecary's. Was not it fifteen guineas I mentioned in my proposal? and did not your honour give it against me for thirteen?' 'My honour did just so,' replied Mr. Somerville calmly. 'And please your honour, but I don't know what it is I or mine have done to offend you. I'm sure there is not a gentleman in all Ireland I'd go further to sarve. Would not I go to Cork to-morrow for the least word from your honour?' 'I am much obliged to you, Mr. Cox, but I have no business at Cork at present,' answered Mr. Somerville drily. 'It is all I wish,' exclaimed Mr. Cox, 'that I could find out and light upon the man that has belied me to your honour.' 'No man has belied you, Mr. Cox, but your nose belies you much, if you do not love drinking a little, and your black eye and cut chin belie you much if you do not love quarrelling a little.'

'Quarrel! I quarrel, please your honour! I defy any man, or set of men, ten mile round, to prove such a thing, and I am ready to fight him that dares to say the like of me. I'd fight him here in your honour's presence, if he'd only come out this minute and meet me like a man.'

Here Mr. Cox put himself into a boxing attitude, but observing that Mr. Somerville looked at his threatening gesture with a smile, and that several people, who had gathered round him as he stood in the street, laughed at the proof he gave of his peaceable disposition, he changed his attitude, and went on to vindicate himself against the charge of drinking.

'And as to drink, please your honour, there's no truth in it. Not a drop of whisky, good or bad, have I touched these six months, except what I took with Jemmy M'Doole the night I had the misfortune to meet your honour coming home from the fair of Ballynagrish.'

To this speech Mr. Somerville made no answer, but turned away to look at the bow-window of a handsome new inn, which the glazier was at this instant glazing. 'Please your honour, that new inn is not let, I hear, as yet,' resumed Mr. Cox; 'if your honour recollects, you promised to make me a compliment of it last Seraphtide was twelvemonth.'

'Impossible!' cried Mr. Somerville, 'for I had no thoughts of building an inn at that time.' 'Oh, I beg your honour's pardon, but if you'd be just pleased to recollect, it was coming through the gap in the bog meadows, *forenent* Thady O'Connor, you made me the promise—I'll leave it to him, so I will.' 'But I will not leave it to him, I assure you,' cried Mr. Somerville; 'I never made any such promise. I never thought of letting this inn to you.' 'Then your honour won't let me have it?' 'No; you have told me a dozen falsehoods. I do not wish to have you for a tenant.'

'Well, God bless your honour; I've no more to say, but God bless your honour,' said Mr. Cox; and he walked away, muttering to himself, as he slouched his hat over his face, 'I hope I'll live to be revenged on him!'

Mr. Somerville the next morning went with his family to look at the new inn, which he expected to see perfectly finished; but he was met by the carpenter, who, with a rueful face, informed him that six panes of glass in the large bow-window had been broken during the night.

'Ha! perhaps Mr. Cox has broken my windows, in revenge for my refusing to let him my house,' said Mr. Somerville; and many of the neighbours, who knew the malicious character of this Mr. Cox, observed that this was like one of his tricks. A boy of about twelve years old, however, stepped forward and said, 'I don't like Mr. Cox, I'm sure; for once he beat me when he was drunk; but, for all that, no one should be accused wrongfully. He *could* not be the person that broke these windows last night, for he was six miles off. He slept at his cousin's last night, and he has not returned home yet. So I think he knows nothing of the matter.'

Mr. Somerville was pleased with the honest simplicity of this boy, and observing that he looked in eagerly at the staircase, when the house door was opened, he asked him whether he would like to go in and see the new house. 'Yes, sir,' said the boy, 'I should like to go up those stairs, and to see what I should come to.' 'Up with you, then!' said Mr. Somerville; and the boy ran up the stairs. He went from room to room with great expressions of admiration and delight. At length, as he was examining one of the garrets, he was startled by a fluttering noise over his head; and looking up he saw a white pigeon, who, frightened at his appearance, began to fly round and round the room, till it found its way out of the door, and flew into the staircase.

The carpenter was speaking to Mr. Somerville upon the landing-place of the stairs; but, the moment he spied the white pigeon, he broke off in the midst of a speech about *the nose* of the stairs, and exclaimed, 'There he is, please your honour! There's he that has done all the damage to our bow-window—that's the very same wicked white pigeon that broke the church windows last Sunday was se'nnight; but he's down for it now; we have him safe, and I'll chop his head off, as he deserves, this minute.'

'Stay! oh stay! don't chop his head off.'

'Stay! oh stay! don't chop his head off.'

'Stay! oh stay! don't chop his head off: he does not deserve it,' cried the boy, who came running out of the garret with the greatest eagerness—'*I* broke your window, sir,' said he to Mr. Somerville. 'I broke your window with this ball; but I did not know that I had done it, till this moment, I assure you, or I should have told you before. Don't chop his head off,' added the boy to the carpenter, who had now the white pigeon in his hands. 'No,' said Mr. Somerville, 'the pigeon's head shall not be chopped off, nor yours either, my good boy, for breaking a window. I am persuaded by your open, honest countenance, that you are speaking the truth; but pray explain this matter to us; for you have not made it quite clear. How happened it that you could break my windows without knowing it? and how came you to find it out at last?' 'Sir,' said the boy, 'if you'll come up here, I'll show you all I know, and how I came to know it.'

Mr. Somerville followed the boy into the garret, who pointed to a pane of glass that was broken in a small window that looked out upon a piece of waste ground behind the house. Upon this piece of waste ground the children of the village often used to play. 'We were playing there at ball yesterday evening,' continued the boy, addressing himself to Mr. Somerville, 'and one of the lads challenged me to hit a mark in the wall, which I did; but he said I did not hit it, and bade me give him up my ball as the forfeit. This I would not do; and when he began to wrestle with me for it, I threw the ball, as I thought, over the house. He ran to look for it in the street, but could not find it, which I was very glad of; but I was very sorry just now to find it myself lying upon this heap of shavings, sir, under this broken window; for, as soon as I saw it lying there, I knew I must have been the person that broke the window; and through this window came the white pigeon. Here's one of his white feathers sticking in the gap.'

52

'Yes,' said the carpenter, 'and in the bow-window room below there's plenty of his feathers to be seen; for I've just been down to look. It was the pigeon broke *them* windows, sure enough.' 'But he could not have got in had I not broke this little window,' said the boy eagerly; 'and I am able to earn sixpence a day, and I'll pay for all the mischief, and welcome. The white pigeon belongs to a poor neighbour, a friend of ours, who is very fond of him, and I would not have him killed for twice as much money.'

'Take the pigeon, my honest, generous lad,' said Mr. Somerville, 'and carry him back to your neighbour. I forgive him all the mischief he has done me, tell your friend, for your sake. As to the rest, we can have the windows mended; and do you keep all the sixpences you earn for yourself.'

'That's what he never did yet,' said the carpenter. 'Many's the sixpence he earns, but not a halfpenny goes into his own pocket: it goes every farthing to his poor father and mother. Happy for them to have such a son!'

'More happy for him to have such a father and mother,' exclaimed the boy. 'Their good days they took all the best care of me that was to be had for love or money, and would, if I would let them, go on paying for my schooling now, falling as they be in the world; but I must learn to mind the shop now. Good morning to you, sir; and thank you kindly,' said he to Mr. Somerville.

'And where does this boy live, and who are his father and mother? They cannot live in town,' said Mr. Somerville, 'or I should have heard of them.'

'They are but just come into the town, please your honour,' said the carpenter. 'They lived formerly upon Counsellor O'Donnel's estate; but they were ruined, please your honour, by taking a joint lease with a man who fell afterwards into bad company, ran out all he had, so could not pay the landlord; and these poor people were forced to pay his share and their own too, which almost ruined them. They were obliged to give up the land; and now they have furnished a little shop in this town with what goods they could afford to buy with the money they got by the sale of their cattle and stock. They have the goodwill of all who know them; and I am sure I hope they will do well. The boy is very ready in the shop, though he said only that he could earn sixpence a day. He writes a good hand, and is quick at casting up accounts, for his age. Besides, he is likely to do well in the world, because he is never in idle company, and I've known him since he was two foot high, and never heard of his telling a lie.'

'This is an excellent character of the boy, indeed,' said Mr. Somerville, 'and from his behaviour this morning I am inclined to think that he deserves all your praises.'

Mr. Somerville resolved to inquire more fully concerning this poor family, and to attend to their conduct himself, fully determined to assist them if he should find them such as they had been represented.

In the meantime, this boy, whose name was Brian O'Neill, went to return the white pigeon to its owner. 'You have saved its life,' said the woman to whom it belonged, 'and I'll make you a present of it.' Brian thanked her; and he from that day began to grow fond of the pigeon. He always took care to scatter some oats for it in his father's yard; and the pigeon grew so tame at last that it would hop about the kitchen, and eat off the same trencher with the dog.

Brian, after the shop was shut up at night, used to amuse himself with reading some little books which the schoolmaster who formerly taught him arithmetic was so good as to lend him. Amongst these he one evening met with a little book full of the history of birds and beasts; he looked immediately to see whether the pigeon was mentioned amongst the birds, and, to his great joy, he found a full description and history of his favourite bird.

'So, Brian, I see your schooling has not been thrown away upon you; you like your book, I see, when you have no master over you to bid you read,' said his father, when he came in and saw Brian reading his book very attentively.

'Thank you for having me taught to read, father,' said Brian. 'Here I've made a great discovery: I've found out in this book, little as it looks, father, a most curious way of making a fortune; and I hope it will make your fortune, father, and if you'll sit down, I'll tell it to you.'

Mr. O'Neill, in hopes of pleasing his son rather than in the expectation of having his fortune made, immediately sat down to listen; and his son explained to him that he had found in his book an account of pigeons who carried notes and letters: 'and, father,' continued Brian, 'I find my pigeon is of this sort; and I intend to make my pigeon carry messages. Why should not he? If other pigeons have done so before him, I think he is as good, and, I daresay, will be as easy to teach as any pigeon in the world. I shall begin to teach him to-morrow morning; and then, father, you know people often pay a great deal for sending messengers: and no boy can run, no horse can gallop, so fast as a bird can fly; therefore the bird must be the best messenger, and I should be paid the best price. Hey, father?'

'To be sure, to be sure, my boy,' said his father, laughing; 'I wish you may make the best messenger in Ireland of your pigeon; but all I beg, my dear boy, is that you won't neglect our shop for your pigeon; for I've a notion we have a better chance of making a fortune by the shop than by the white pigeon.'

Brian never neglected the shop: but in his leisure hours he amused himself with training his pigeon; and after much patience he at last succeeded so well, that one day he went to his father and offered to send him word by his pigeon what beef was a pound in the market of Ballynagrish, where he was going. 'The pigeon will be home long before me, father; and he will come in at the kitchen window and light upon the dresser; then you must untie the little note which I shall have tied under his left wing, and you'll know the price of beef directly.'

The pigeon carried his message well; and Brian was much delighted with his success. He soon was employed by the neighbours, who were aroused by Brian's fondness of his swift messenger; and soon the fame of the white pigeon was spread amongst all who frequented the markets and fairs of Somerville.

At one of these fairs a set of men of desperate fortunes met to drink, and to concert plans of robberies. Their place of meeting was at the alehouse of Mr. Cox, the man who, as our readers may remember, was offended by Mr. Somerville's hinting that he was fond of drinking and of quarrelling, and who threatened vengeance for having been refused the new inn.

Whilst these men were talking over their schemes, one of them observed that one of their companions was not arrived. Another said, 'No.' 'He's six miles off,' said another; and a third wished that he could make him hear at that distance. This turned the discourse upon the difficulties of sending messages secretly and quickly. Cox's son, a lad of about nineteen, who was one of this gang, mentioned the white carrier pigeon, and he was desired to try all means to get it into his possession. Accordingly, the next day young Cox went to Brian O'Neill, and tried, at first by persuasion and afterwards by threats, to prevail upon him to give up the pigeon. Brian was resolute in his refusal, more especially when the petitioner began to bully him.

'If we can't have it by fair means, we will by foul,' said Cox; and a few days afterwards the pigeon was gone. Brian searched for it in vain—inquired from all the neighbours if they had seen it, and applied, but to no purpose, to Cox. He swore that he knew nothing about the matter. But this was false, for it was he who during the night-time had stolen the white pigeon. He conveyed it to his employers, and they rejoiced that they had gotten it into their possession, as they thought it would serve them for a useful messenger.

Nothing can be more short-sighted than cunning. The very means which these people took to secure secrecy were the means of bringing their plots to light. They endeavoured to teach the pigeon, which they had stolen, to carry messages for them in a part of the country at some distance from Somerville; and when they fancied that it had forgotten its former habits and its old master, they thought that they might venture to employ him nearer home. The pigeon, however, had a better memory than they imagined. They loosed him from a bag near the town of Ballynagrish, in hopes that he would stop at the house of Cox's cousin, which was on its road between Ballynagrish and Somerville. But the pigeon, though he had been purposely fed at this house for a week before this trial, did not stop there, but flew on to his old master's house in Somerville, and pecked at the kitchen window, as he had formerly been taught to do. His father, fortunately, was within hearing, and poor Brian ran with the greatest joy to open the window and to let him in.

'Oh, father, here's my white pigeon come back of his own accord,' exclaimed Brian; 'I must run and show him to my mother.' At this instant the pigeon spread his wings, and Brian discovered under one of its wings a small and very dirty-looking billet. He opened it in his father's presence. The scrawl was scarcely legible; but these words were at length deciphered:—

'Thare are eight of uz sworn: I send yo at botom thare names. We meat at tin this nite at my faders, and have harms and all in radiness to brak into the grate 'ouse. Mr. Summervill is to lye out to nite—kip the pigeon untill to-morrow. For ever yours, Murtagh Cox, Jun.'

Scarcely had they finished reading this note, than both father and son exclaimed, 'Let us go and show it to Mr. Somerville.' Before they set out, they had, however, the prudence to secure the pigeon, so that he should not be seen by any one but themselves.

Mr. Somerville, in consequence of this fortunate discovery, took proper measures for the apprehension of the eight men who had sworn to rob his house. When they were all safely lodged in the county gaol, he sent for Brian O'Neill and his father; and after thanking them for the service they had done him, he counted out ten bright guineas upon a table, and pushed them towards Brian, saying, 'I suppose you know that a reward of ten guineas was offered some weeks ago for the discovery of John MacDermod, one of the eight men whom we have just taken up?'

'No, sir,' said Brian; 'I did not know it, and I did not bring that note to you to get ten guineas, but because I thought it was right. I don't want to be paid for doing it.' 'That's my own boy,' said his father. 'We thank you, sir; but we'll not take the money; *I don't like to take the price of blood.*'

'I know the difference, my good friends,' said Mr. Somerville, 'between vile informers and courageous, honest men.' 'Why, as to that, please your honour, though we are poor, I hope we are honest.' 'And, what is more,' said Mr. Somerville, 'I have a notion that you would continue to be honest, even if you were rich.

'Will you, my good lad,' continued Mr. Somerville, after a moment's pause—'will you trust me with your pigeon a few days?' 'Oh, and welcome, sir,' said the boy, with a smile; and he brought the pigeon to Mr. Somerville when it was dark, and nobody saw him.

A few days afterwards, Mr. Somerville called at O'Neill's house, and bid him and his son follow him. They followed till he stopped opposite to the bow-window of the new inn. The carpenter had just put up a sign, which was covered over with a bit of carpeting.

'Go up the ladder, will you?' said Mr. Somerville to Brian, 'and pull that sign straight, for it hangs quite crooked. There, now it is straight. Now pull off the carpet, and let us see the new sign.'

The boy pulled off the cover, and saw a white pigeon painted upon the sign, and the name of O'Neill in large letters underneath.

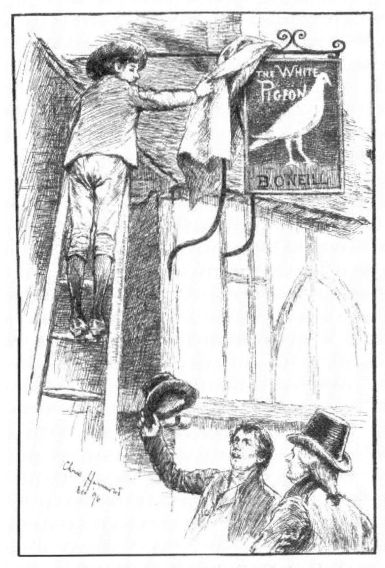

The boy pulled off the cover, and saw a white pigeon painted upon the sign.

The boy pulled off the cover, and saw a white pigeon painted upon the sign.

'Take care you do not tumble down and break your neck upon this joyful occasion,' said Mr. Somerville, who saw that Brian's surprise was too great for his situation. 'Come down from the ladder, and wish your father joy of being master of the new inn called the "White Pigeon." And I wish him joy of having such a son as you are. Those who bring up their children well, will certainly be rewarded for it, be they poor or rich.'

THE BIRTHDAY PRESENT

'Mamma,' said Rosamond, after a long silence, 'do you know what I have been thinking of all this time?' 'No, my dear—What?' 'Why, mamma, about my cousin Bell's birthday; do you know what day it is?' 'No, I don't remember.' 'Dear mother! don't you remember it's the 22nd of December; and her birthday is the day after to-morrow? Don't you recollect now? But you never remember about birthdays, mamma. That was just what I was thinking of, that you never remember my sister Laura's birthday, or—or—or *mine*, mamma.'

'What do you mean, my dear? I remember your birthday perfectly well.' 'Indeed! but you never *keep* it, though.' 'What do you mean by keeping your birthday?' 'Oh, mamma, you know very well—as Bell's birthday is kept. In the first place, there is a great dinner.' 'And can Bell eat more upon her birthday than upon any other day?' 'No; nor I should not mind about the dinner, except the mince-pies. But Bell has

55

a great many nice things—I don't mean nice eatable things, but nice new playthings, given to her always on her birthday; and everybody drinks her health, and she's so happy.'

'But stay, Rosamond, how you jumble things together! Is it everybody's drinking her health that makes her so happy? or the new playthings, or the nice mince-pies? I can easily believe that she is happy whilst she is eating a mince-pie, or whilst she is playing; but how does everybody's drinking her health at dinner make her happy?'

Rosamond paused, and then said she did not know. 'But,' added she, 'the *nice new* playthings, mother!' 'But why the nice new playthings? Do you like them only because they are *new*?' 'Not *only*—*I* do not like playthings *only* because they are new: but Bell *does*, I believe—for that puts me in mind—Do you know, mother, she had a great drawer full of *old* playthings that she never used, and she said that they were good for nothing, because they were *old*; but I thought many of them were good for a great deal more than the new ones. Now you shall be judge, mamma; I'll tell you all that was in the drawer.'

'Nay, Rosamond, thank you, not just now; I have not time to listen to you.'

'Well then, mamma, the day after to-morrow I can show you the drawer. I want you to judge very much, because I am sure I was in the right. And, mother,' added Rosamond, stopping her as she was going out of the room, 'will you—not now, but when you've time—will you tell me why you never keep my birthday—why you never make any difference between that day and any other day?' 'And will you, Rosamond—not now, but when you have time to think about it—tell me why I should make any difference between your birthday and any other day?'

Rosamond thought, but she could not find out any reason; besides, she suddenly recollected that she had not time to think any longer; for there was a certain work-basket to be finished, which she was making for her cousin Bell, as a present upon her birthday. The work was at a stand for want of some filigree-paper, and, as her mother was going out, she asked her to take her with her, that she might buy some. Her sister Laura went with them.

'Sister,' said Rosamond, as they were walking along, 'what have you done with your half-guinea?' 'I have it in my pocket.' 'Dear! you will keep it for ever in your pocket. You know, my godmother when she gave it to you said you would keep it longer than I should keep mine; and I know what she thought by her look at the time. I heard her say something to my mother.' 'Yes,' said Laura, smiling; 'she whispered so loud that I could not help hearing her too. She said I was a little miser.' 'But did not you hear her say that I was very *generous*? and she'll see that she was not mistaken. I hope she'll be by when I give my basket to Bell—won't it be beautiful? There is to be a wreath of myrtle, you know, round the handle, and a frost ground, and then the medallions——'

'Stay,' interrupted her sister, for Rosamond, anticipating the glories of her work-basket, talked and walked so fast that she had passed, without perceiving it, the shop where the filigree-paper was to be bought. They turned back. Now it happened that the shop was the corner house of a street, and one of the windows looked out into a narrow lane. A coach full of ladies stopped at the door, just before they went in, so that no one had time immediately to think of Rosamond and her filigree-paper, and she went to the window where she saw her sister Laura looking earnestly at something that was passing in the lane.

Opposite to the window, at the door of a poor-looking house, there was sitting a little girl weaving lace. Her bobbins moved as quick as lightning, and she never once looked up from her work. 'Is not she very industrious?' said Laura; 'and very honest, too?' added she in a minute afterwards; for just then a baker with a basket of rolls on his head passed, and by accident one of the rolls fell close to the little girl. She took it up eagerly, looked at it as if she was very hungry, then put aside her work, and ran after the baker to return it to him. Whilst she was gone, a footman in a livery laced with silver, who belonged to the coach that stood at the shop door, as he was lounging with one of his companions, chanced to spy the weaving pillow, which she had left upon a stone before the door. To divert himself (for idle people do mischief often to divert themselves) he took up the pillow, and entangled all the bobbins. The little girl came back out of breath to her work; but what was her surprise and sorrow to find it spoiled. She twisted and untwisted, placed and replaced, the bobbins, while the footman stood laughing at her distress. She got up gently, and was retiring into the house, when the silver-laced footman stopped her, saying, insolently, 'Sit still, child.' 'I must go to my mother, sir,' said the child; 'besides, you have spoiled all my lace. I can't stay.' 'Can't you?' said the brutal footman, snatching her weaving-pillow again, 'I'll teach you to complain of me.' And he broke off, one after another, all the bobbins, put them into his pocket, rolled her weaving-pillow down the dirty lane, then jumped up behind his mistress's coach, and was out of sight in an instant.

'Poor girl!' exclaimed Rosamond, no longer able to restrain her indignation at this injustice; 'poor little girl!'

She twisted and untwisted, placed and replaced, the bobbins, while the footman stood laughing at her distress.

She twisted and untwisted, placed and replaced, the bobbins, while the footman stood laughing at her distress.

At this instant her mother said to Rosamond—'Come, now, my dear, if you want this filigree-paper, buy it.' 'Yes, madam,' said Rosamond; and the idea of what her godmother and her cousin Bell would think of her generosity rushed again upon her imagination. All her feelings of pity were immediately suppressed. Satisfied with bestowing another exclamation upon the '*poor little girl*!' she went to spend her half-guinea upon her filigree basket. In the meantime, she that was called the '*little miser*' beckoned to the poor girl, and, opening the window, said, pointing to the cushion, 'Is it quite spoiled?' 'Quite! quite spoiled! and I can't, nor mother neither, buy another; and I can't do anything else for my bread.' A few, but very few, tears fell as she said this.

'How much would another cost?' said Laura. 'Oh, a great—*great* deal.' 'More than that?' said Laura, holding up her half-guinea. 'Oh no.' 'Then you can buy another with that,' said Laura, dropping the half-guinea into her hand; and she shut the window before the child could find words to thank her, but not before she saw a look of joy and gratitude, which gave Laura more pleasure probably than all the praise which could have been bestowed upon her generosity.

Late on the morning of her cousin's birthday, Rosamond finished her work-basket. The carriage was at the door—Laura came running to call her; her father's voice was heard at the same instant; so she was obliged to go down with her basket but half wrapped up in silver paper—a circumstance at which she was a good deal disconcerted; for the pleasure of surprising Bell would be utterly lost if one bit of the filigree should peep out before the proper time. As the carriage went on, Rosamond pulled the paper to one side and to the other, and by each of the four corners.

'It will never do, my dear,' said her father, who had been watching her operations. 'I am afraid you will never make a sheet of paper cover a box which is twice as large as itself.'

'It is not a box, father,' said Rosamond, a little peevishly; 'it's a basket.'

'Let us look at this basket,' said he, taking it out of her unwilling hands, for she knew of what frail materials it was made, and she dreaded its coming to pieces under her father's examination. He took hold of the handle rather roughly; when, starting off the coach seat, she cried, 'Oh, sir! father! sir! you will spoil it indeed!' said she, with increased vehemence, when, after drawing aside the veil of silver paper, she saw him grasp the myrtle-wreathed handle. 'Indeed, sir, you will spoil the poor handle.'

'But what is the use of *the poor handle*,' said her father, 'if we are not to take hold of it? And pray,' continued he, turning the basket round with his finger and thumb, rather in a disrespectful manner, 'pray, is this the thing you have been about all this week? I have seen you all this week dabbling with paste and rags; I could not conceive what you were about. Is this the thing?' 'Yes, sir. You think, then, that I have wasted my time, because the basket is of no use; but then it is for a present for my cousin Bell.' 'Your cousin Bell will be very much obliged to you for a present that is of no use. You had better have given her the purple jar.'

'Oh, father! I thought you had forgotten that—it was two years ago; I'm not so silly now. But Bell will like the basket, I know, though it is of no use.'

'Then you think Bell is sillier *now* than you were two years ago,—well, perhaps that is true; but how comes it, Rosamond, now that you are so wise, that you are fond of such a silly person?' '*I*, father?' said Rosamond, hesitating; 'I don't think I am *very* fond of her.' 'I did not say *very* fond.' 'Well, but I don't think I am at all fond of her.' 'But you have spent a whole week in making this thing for her.' 'Yes, and all my half-guinea besides.'

'Yet you think her silly, and you are not fond of her at all; and you say you know this thing will be of no use to her.'

'But it is her birthday, sir; and I am sure she will *expect* something, and everybody else will give her something.'

'Then your reason for giving is because she expects you to give her something. And will you, or can you, or should you, always give, merely because others *expect*, or because somebody else gives?' 'Always?—no, not always.' 'Oh, only on birthdays.'

Rosamond, laughing: 'Now you are making a joke of me, papa, I see; but I thought you liked that people should be generous,—my godmother said that she did.' 'So do I, full as well as your godmother; but we have not yet quite settled what it is to be generous.' 'Why, is it not generous to make presents?' said Rosamond. 'That is the question which it would take up a great deal of time to answer. But, for instance, to make a present of a thing that you know can be of no use to a person you neither love nor esteem, because it is her birthday, and because everybody gives her something, and because she expects something, and because your godmother says she likes that people should be generous, seems to me, my dear Rosamond, to be, since I must say it, rather more like folly than generosity.'

Rosamond looked down upon the basket, and was silent. 'Then I am a fool, am I?' said she, looking up at last. 'Because you have made *one* mistake? No. If you have sense enough to see your own mistakes, and can afterwards avoid them, you will never be a fool.'

Here the carriage stopped, and Rosamond recollected that the basket was uncovered.

Now we must observe that Rosamond's father had not been too severe upon Bell when he called her a silly girl. From her infancy she had been humoured; and at eight years old she had the misfortune to be a spoiled child. She was idle, fretful, and selfish; so that nothing could make her happy. On her birthday she expected, however, to be perfectly happy. Everybody in the house tried to please her, and they succeeded so well that between breakfast and dinner she had only six fits of crying. The cause of five of these fits no one could discover: but the last, and most lamentable, was occasioned by a disappointment about a worked muslin frock; and accordingly, at dressing time, her maid brought it to her, exclaiming, 'See here, miss, what your mamma has sent you on your birthday. Here's a frock fit for a queen—if it had but lace round the cuffs.' 'And why has not it lace around the cuffs? mamma said it should.' 'Yes, but mistress was disappointed about the lace; it is not come home.' 'Not come home, indeed! and didn't they know it was my birthday? But then I say I won't wear it without the lace—I can't wear it without the lace, and I won't.'

The lace, however, could not be had; and Bell at length submitted to let the frock be put on. 'Come, Miss Bell, dry your eyes,' said the maid who *educated* her; 'dry your eyes, and I'll tell you something that will please you.'

'What, then?' said the child, pouting and sobbing. 'Why——but you must not tell that I told you.' 'No,—but if I am asked?' 'Why, if you are asked, you must tell the truth, to be sure. So I'll hold my tongue, miss.' 'Nay, tell me, though, and I'll never tell—if I *am* asked.' 'Well, then,' said the maid, 'your cousin Rosamond is come, and has brought you the most *beautifullest* thing you ever saw in your life; but you are not to know anything about it till after dinner, because she wants to surprise you; and mistress has put it into her wardrobe till after dinner.' 'Till after dinner!' repeated Bell impatiently; 'I can't wait till then; I must see it this minute.' The maid refused her several times, till Bell burst into another fit of crying, and the maid, fearing that her mistress would be angry with *her*, if Bell's eyes were red at dinner time, consented to show her the basket.

'How pretty!—but let me have it in my own hands,' said Bell, as the maid held the basket up out of her reach. 'Oh, no, you must not touch it; for if you should spoil it, what would become of me?' 'Become of you, indeed!' exclaimed the spoiled child, who never considered anything but her own immediate gratification—'Become of *you*, indeed! what signifies that?—I shan't spoil it; and I will have it in my own hands. If you don't hold it down for me directly, I'll tell that you showed it to me.' 'Then you won't snatch it?' 'No, no, I won't indeed,' said Bell; but she had learned from her maid a total disregard of truth. She snatched the basket the moment it was within her reach. A struggle ensued, in which the handle and lid were torn off, and one of the medallions crushed inwards, before the little fury returned to her senses.

Calmed at this sight, the next question was, how she should conceal the mischief which she had done. After many attempts, the handle and lid were replaced; the basket was put exactly in the same spot in which it had stood before, and the maid charged the child '*to look as if nothing was the matter*.'

We hope that both children and parents will here pause for a moment to reflect. The habits of tyranny, meanness, and falsehood, which children acquire from living with bad servants, are scarcely ever conquered in the whole course of their future lives.

'I shan't spoil it; and I will have it in my own hands.'

'I shan't spoil it; and I will have it in my own hands.'

After shutting up the basket they left the room, and in the adjoining passage they found a poor girl waiting with a small parcel in her hand. 'What's your business?' said the maid. 'I have brought home the lace, madam, that was bespoke for the young lady.' 'Oh, you have, have you, at last?' said Bell; 'and pray why didn't you bring it sooner?' The girl was going to answer, but the maid interrupted her, saying, 'Come, come, none of your excuses; you are a little idle, good-for-nothing thing, to disappoint Miss Bell upon her birthday. But now you have brought it, let us look at it!'

The little girl gave the lace without reply, and the maid desired her to go about her business, and not to expect to be paid; for that her mistress could not see anybody, *because* she was in a room full of company.

'May I call again, madam, this afternoon?' said the child, timidly.

'Lord bless my stars!' replied the maid, 'what makes people so poor, I *wonders*! I wish mistress would buy her lace at the warehouse, as I told her, and not of these folks. Call again! yes, to be sure. I believe you'd call, call, call twenty times for twopence.'

However ungraciously the permission to call again was granted, it was received with gratitude. The little girl departed with a cheerful countenance, and Bell teased her maid till she got her to sew the long-wished-for lace upon her cuffs.

Unfortunate Bell!—All dinner time passed, and people were so hungry, so busy, or so stupid, that not an eye observed her favourite piece of finery. Till at length she was no longer able to conceal her impatience, and turning to Laura, who sat next to her, she said, 'You have no lace upon your cuffs. Look how beautiful mine is!—is not it? Don't you wish your mamma could afford to give some like it? But you can't get any if she would, for this was made on purpose for me on my birthday, and nobody can get a bit more anywhere, if they would give the world for it.' 'But cannot the person who made it,' said Laura, 'make any more like it?' 'No, no, no!' cried Bell; for she had already learned, either from her maid or her mother, the mean pride which values things not for being really pretty or useful, but for being such as nobody

59

else can procure. 'Nobody can get any like it, I say,' repeated Bell; 'nobody in all London can make it but one person, and that person will never make a bit for anybody but me, I am sure. Mamma won't let her, if I ask her not.' 'Very well,' said Laura coolly, 'I do not want any of it; you need not be so violent: I assure you that I don't want any of it.' 'Yes, but you do, though,' said Bell, more angrily. 'No, indeed,' said Laura, smiling. 'You do, in the bottom of your heart; but you say you don't to plague me, I know,' cried Bell, swelling with disappointed vanity. 'It is pretty for all that, and it cost a great deal of money too, and nobody shall have any like it, if they cried their eyes out.'

Laura received this declaration in silence—Rosamond smiled; and at her smile the ill-suppressed rage of the spoiled child burst forth into the seventh and loudest fit of crying which had yet been heard on her birthday.

'What's the matter, my pet?' cried her mother; 'come to me and tell me what's the matter.' Bell ran roaring to her mother; but no otherwise explained the cause of her sorrow than by tearing the fine lace with frantic gestures from her cuffs, and throwing the fragments into her mother's lap. 'Oh! the lace, child!—are you mad?' said her mother, catching hold of both her hands. 'Your beautiful lace, my dear love—do you know how much it cost?' 'I don't care how much it cost—it is not beautiful, and I'll have none of it,' replied Bell, sobbing; 'for it is not beautiful.' 'But it is beautiful,' retorted her mother; 'I chose the pattern myself. Who has put it into your head, child, to dislike it? Was it Nancy?' 'No, not Nancy, but *them*, mamma,' said Bell, pointing to Laura and Rosamond. 'Oh, fie! don't *point*,' said her mother, putting down her stubborn finger; 'nor say *them*, like Nancy; I am sure you misunderstood. Miss Laura, I am sure, did not mean any such thing.' 'No, madam; and I did not say any such thing, that I recollect,' said Laura, gently. 'Oh no, indeed!' cried Rosamond, warmly, rising in her sister's defence.

No defence or explanation, however, was to be heard, for everybody had now gathered round Bell, to dry her tears, and to comfort her for the mischief she had done to her own cuffs. They succeeded so well, that in about a quarter of an hour the young lady's eyes and the reddened arches over her eyebrows came to their natural colour; and the business being thus happily hushed up, the mother, as a reward to her daughter for her good humour, begged that Rosamond would now be so good as to produce her 'charming present.'

Rosamond, followed by all the company, amongst whom, to her great joy, was her godmother, proceeded to the dressing-room. 'Now I am sure,' thought she, 'Bell will be surprised, and my godmother will see she was right about my generosity.'

The doors of the wardrobe were opened with due ceremony, and the filigree basket appeared in all its glory. 'Well, this is a charming present, indeed!' said the godmother, who was one of the company; '*my* Rosamond knows how to make presents.' And as she spoke, she took hold of the basket, to lift it down to the admiring audience. Scarcely had she touched it, when, lo! the basket fell to the ground, and only the handle remained in her hand. All eyes were fixed upon the wreck. Exclamations of sorrow were heard in various tones; and 'Who can have done this?' was all that Rosamond could say. Bell stood in sullen silence, which she obstinately preserved in the midst of the inquiries that were made about the disaster.

At length the servants were summoned, and amongst them Nancy, Miss Bell's maid and governess. She affected much surprise when she saw what had befallen the basket, and declared that she knew nothing of the matter, but that she had seen her mistress in the morning put it quite safe into the wardrobe; and that, for her part, she had never touched it, or thought of touching it, in her born days. 'Nor Miss Bell, neither, ma'am,—I can answer for her; for she never knew of its being there, because I never so much as mentioned it to her, that there was such a thing in the house, because I knew Miss Rosamond wanted to surprise her with the secret; so I never mentioned a sentence of it—did I, Miss Bell?'

Bell, putting on the deceitful look which her maid had taught her, answered boldly, '*No*'; but she had hold of Rosamond's hand, and at the instant she uttered this falsehood she squeezed it terribly. 'Why do you squeeze my hand so?' said Rosamond, in a low voice; 'what are you afraid of?' 'Afraid of!' cried Bell, turning angrily; 'I'm not afraid of anything—I've nothing to be afraid about.' 'Nay, I did not say you had,' whispered Rosamond; 'but only if you did by accident—you know what I mean—I should not be angry if you did—only say so.' 'I say I did not!' cried Bell furiously. 'Mamma, mamma! Nancy! my cousin Rosamond won't believe me! That's very hard. It's very rude, and I won't bear it—I won't.' 'Don't be angry, love. Don't,' said the maid. 'Nobody suspects you, darling,' said her mother; 'but she has too much sensibility. Don't cry, love; nobody suspected you.' 'But you know,' continued she, turning to the maid, 'somebody must have done this, and I must know how it was done. Miss Rosamond's charming present must not be spoiled in this way, in my house, without my taking proper notice of it. I assure you I am very angry about it, Rosamond.'

Rosamond did not rejoice in her anger, and had nearly made a sad mistake by speaking aloud her thoughts—'*I was very foolish*——' she began and stopped.

'Ma'am,' cried the maid, suddenly, 'I'll venture to say I know who did it.' 'Who?' said every one, eagerly. 'Who?' said Bell, trembling. 'Why, miss, don't you recollect that little girl with the lace, that we saw peeping about in the passage? I'm sure she must have done it; for here she was by herself half an hour or more, and not another creature has been in mistress's dressing-room, to my certain knowledge, since morning. Those sort of people have so much curiosity. I'm sure she must have been meddling with it,' added the maid.

'Oh yes, that's the thing,' said the mistress, decidedly. 'Well, Miss Rosamond, for your comfort she shall never come into my house again.' 'Oh, that would not comfort me at all,' said Rosamond; 'besides, we are not sure that she did it, and if——' A single knock at the door was heard at this instant. It was the little girl, who came to be paid for her lace. 'Call her in,' said the lady of the house; 'let us see her directly.'

The maid, who was afraid that the girl's innocence would appear if she were produced, hesitated; but upon her mistress repeating her commands, she was forced to obey. The girl came in with a look of simplicity; but when she saw a room full of company she was a little abashed. Rosamond and Laura looked at her and one another with surprise, for it was the same little girl whom they had seen weaving lace. 'Is not it she?' whispered Rosamond to her sister. 'Yes, it is; but hush,' said Laura, 'she does not know us. Don't say a word, let us hear what she will say.'

Laura got behind the rest of the company as she spoke, so that the little girl could not see her.

'Vastly well!' said Bell's mother; 'I am waiting to see how long you will have the assurance to stand there with that innocent look. Did you ever see that basket before?' 'Yes, ma'am,' said the girl. '*Yes, ma'am!*' cried the maid; 'and what else do you know about it? You had better confess it at once, and mistress, perhaps, will say no more about it.' 'Yes, do confess it,' added Bell, earnestly. 'Confess what, madam?' said the little girl; 'I never touched the basket, madam.' 'You never *touched* it; but you confess,' interrupted Bell's mother, 'that you *did see* it before. And, pray, how came you to see it? You must have opened my wardrobe.' 'No, indeed, ma'am,' said the little girl; 'but I was waiting in the passage, ma'am, and this door was partly open; and looking at the maid, you know, I could not help seeing it.' 'Why, how could you see through the doors of my wardrobe?' rejoined the lady.

The maid, frightened, pulled the little girl by the sleeve.

'Answer me,' said the lady, 'where did you see this basket?' Another stronger pull. 'I saw it, madam, in her hands,' looking at the maid; 'and——' 'Well, and what became of it afterwards?' 'Ma'am'—hesitating—'miss pulled, and by accident—I believe, I saw, ma'am—miss, you know what I saw.' 'I do not know—I do not know; and if I did, you had no business there; and mamma won't believe you, I am sure.' Everybody else, however, did believe; and their eyes were fixed upon Bell in a manner which made her feel rather ashamed. 'What do you all look at me so for? Why do you all look so? And am I to be put to shame on my birthday?' cried she, bursting into a roar of passion; 'and all for this nasty thing!' added she, pushing away the remains of the basket, and looking angrily at Rosamond. 'Bell! Bell! oh, fie! fie!— Now I *am* ashamed of you; that's quite rude to your cousin,' said her mother, who was more shocked at her daughter's want of politeness than at her falsehood. 'Take her away, Nancy, till she has done crying,' added she to the maid, who accordingly carried off her pupil.

Rosamond, during this scene, especially at the moment when her present was pushed away with such disdain, had been making reflections upon the nature of true generosity. A smile from her father, who stood by, a silent spectator of the catastrophe of the filigree basket, gave rise to these reflections; nor were they entirely dissipated by the condolence of the rest of the company, nor even by the praises of her godmother, who, for the purpose of condoling with her, said, 'Well, my dear Rosamond, I admire your generous spirit. You know I prophesied that your half-guinea would be gone the soonest. Did I not, Laura?' said she, appealing, in a sarcastic tone, to where she thought Laura was. 'Where is Laura? I don't see her.' Laura came forward. 'You are too *prudent* to throw away your money like your sister. Your half-guinea, I'll answer for it, is snug in your pocket—is it not?' 'No, madam,' answered she, in a low voice.

But low as the voice of Laura was, the poor little lace-girl heard it; and now, for the first time, fixing her eyes upon Laura, recollected her benefactress. 'Oh, that's the young lady!' she exclaimed, in a tone of joyful gratitude, 'the good, good young lady who gave me the half-guinea, and would not stay to be thanked for it; but I *will* thank her now.'

'The half-guinea, Laura!' said her godmother. 'What is all this?' 'I'll tell you, madam, if you please,' said the little girl.

It was not in expectation of being praised for it that Laura had been generous, and therefore everybody was really touched with the history of the weaving-pillow; and whilst they praised, felt a certain degree of respect, which is not always felt by those who pour forth eulogiums. *Respect* is not an improper word, even applied to a child of Laura's age; for let the age or situation of the person be what it may, they command respect who deserve it.

'Ah, madam!' said Rosamond to her godmother, 'now you see—you see she is *not* a little miser. I'm sure that's better than wasting half a guinea upon a filigree basket; is it not, ma'am?' said she, with an eagerness which showed that she had forgotten all her own misfortunes in sympathy with her sister. 'This is being *really generous*, father, is it not?'

'Yes, Rosamond,' said her father, and he kissed her; 'this *is* being really generous. It is not only by giving away money that we can show generosity; it is by giving up to others anything that we like ourselves; and therefore,' added he, smiling, 'it is really generous of you to give your sister the thing you like best of all others.'

'The thing I like the best of all others, father,' said Rosamond, half pleased, half vexed. 'What is that, I wonder? You don't mean *praise*, do you, sir?' 'Nay, you must decide that yourself, Rosamond.' 'Why, sir,' said she, ingenuously, 'perhaps it *was* once the thing I liked best; but the pleasure I have just felt makes me like something else much better.'

ETON MONTEM

'Yesterday this triennial ceremony took place, with which the public are too well acquainted to require a particular description. A collection, called *Salt*, is taken from the public, which forms a purse, to support the Captain of the School in his studies at Cambridge. This collection is made by the Scholars, dressed in fancy dresses, all round the country.

'At eleven o'clock, the youths being assembled in their habiliments at the College, the Royal Family set off from the Castle to see them, and, after walking round the Courtyard, they proceeded to Salt Hill in the following order:—

'His Majesty, his Royal Highness the Prince of Wales, and the Earl of Uxbridge.

'Their Royal Highnesses the Dukes of Kent and Cumberland, Earl Morton, and General Gwynne, all on horseback, dressed in the Windsor uniform, except the Prince of Wales, who wore a suit of dark blue, and a brown surtout over.

'Then followed the Scholars, preceded by the Marechal Serjeant, the Musicians of the Staffordshire Band, and Mr. Ford, Captain of the Seminary, the Serjeant-Major, Serjeants, Colonels, Corporals, Musicians, Ensign, Lieutenant, Steward, Salt-Bearers, Polemen, and Runners.

'The cavalcade was brought up by Her Majesty and her amiable daughters in two carriages, and a numerous company of equestrians and pedestrians, all eager to behold their Sovereign and his family. Among the former, Lady Lade was foremost in the throng; only two others dared venture their persons on horseback in such a multitude.

'The King and Royal Family were stopped on Eton Bridge by Messrs. Young and Mansfield, the Salt-Bearers, to whom their Majesties delivered their customary donation of fifty guineas each.

'At Salt Hill, His Majesty, with his usual affability, took upon himself to arrange the procession round the Royal carriages; and even when the horses were taken off, with the assistance of the Duke of Kent, fastened the traces round the pole of the coaches, to prevent any inconvenience.

'An exceeding heavy shower of rain coming on, the Prince took leave, and went to the "Windmill Inn" till it subsided. The King and his attendants weathered it out in their greatcoats.

'After the young gentlemen walked round the carriage, Ensign Vince and the Salt-Bearers proceeded to the summit of the hill; but the wind being boisterous, he could not exhibit his dexterity in displaying his flag, and the space being too small before the carriages, from the concourse of spectators, the King kindly acquiesced in not having it displayed under such inconvenience.

'Their Majesties and the Princesses then returned home, the King occasionally stopping to converse with the Dean of Windsor, the Earl of Harrington, and other noblemen.

'The Scholars partook of an elegant dinner at the "Windmill Inn," and in the evening walked on Windsor Terrace.

'Their Royal Highnesses the Prince of Wales and Duke of Cumberland, after taking leave of their Majesties, set off for town, and honoured the Opera House with their presence in the evening.

'The profit arising from the Salt collected, according to account, amounted to £800.

'The Stadtholder, the Duke of Gordon, Lord and Lady Melbourne, Viscount Brome, and a numerous train of fashionable nobility were present.

'The following is an account of their dresses, made as usual, very handsomely, by Mrs. Snow, milliner, of Windsor:—

'Mr. Ford, Captain, with eight Gentlemen to attend him as servitors.
'Mr. Sarjeant, Marechal.
'Mr. Bradith, Colonel.
'Mr. Plumtree, Lieutenant.
'Mr. Vince, Ensign.
'Mr. Young, College Salt-Bearer; white and gold dress, rich satin bag, covered with gold netting.
'Mr. Mansfield, Oppidin, white, purple, and orange dress, trimmed with silver; rich satin bag, purple and silver: each carrying elegant poles, with gold and silver cord.
'Mr. Keity, yellow and black velvet; helmet trimmed with silver.
'Mr. Bartelot, plain mantle and sandals, Scotch bonnet, a very Douglas.
'Mr. Knapp, flesh-colour and blue; Spanish hat and feathers.
'Mr. Ripley, rose-colour; helmet.
'Mr. Islip (being in mourning), a scarf; helmet, black velvet; and white satin.
'Mr. Tomkins, violet and silver; helmet.
'Mr. Thackery, lilac and silver; Roman cap.
'Mr. Drury, mazarin blue; fancy cap.
'Mr. Davis, slate-colour and straw.
'Mr. Routh, pink and silver; Spanish hat.
'Mr. Curtis, purple; fancy cap.
'Mr. Lloyd, blue; ditto.

'At the conclusion of the ceremony the Royal Family returned to Windsor, and the boys were all sumptuously entertained at the tavern at Salt Hill. About six in the evening all the boys returned in the order of procession, and, marching round the great square of Eton, were dismissed. The Captain then paid his respects to the Royal Family, at the Queen's Lodge, Windsor, previously to his departure for King's College, Cambridge, to defray which expense the produce of the Montem was presented to him.

'The day concluded by a brilliant promenade of beauty, rank, and fashion on Windsor Terrace, enlivened by the performance of several bands of music.

'The origin of the procession is from the custom by which the Manor was held.

'The custom of hunting the Ram belonged to Eton College, as well as the custom of Salt; but it was discontinued by Dr. Cook, late Dean of Ely. Now this custom we know to have been entered on the register of the Royal Abbey of Bee, in Normandy, as one belonging to the Manor of East or Great Wrotham, in Norfolk, given by Ralph de Toni to the Abbey of Bee, and was as follows:—When the harvest was finished, the tenants were to have half an acre of barley, and a ram let loose; and if they caught him he was their own to make merry with, but if he escaped from them he was the Lord's. The Etonians, in order to secure the ram, houghed him in the Irish fashion, and then attacked him with great clubs. The cruelty of this proceeding brought it into disuse, and now it exists no longer.—*See Register of the Royal Abbey of Bee*, folio 58.

'After the dissolution of the alien priories, in 1414, by the Parliament of Leicester, they remained in the Crown till Henry VI., who gave Wrotham Manor to Eton College; and if the Eton Fellows would search, they would perhaps find the Manor in their possession, that was held by the custom of Salt.'

Men
Alderman Bursal, Father of young Bursal.
Lord   }

John,

> Talbot,   }
>
> Wheeler,   } Young Gentlemen of Eton, from 17 to 19 years of age.
>
> Bursal,   }
>
> Rory
> O'Ryan   }

Mr. Newington, Landlord of the Inn at Salt Hill.

Farmer Hearty.

A Waiter and crowd of Eton Lads.

Women

The Marchioness of Piercefield, Mother of Lord John.

Lady Violetta—her Daughter, a Child of six or seven years old.

Mrs. Talbot.

Louisa Talbot, her Daughter.

Miss Bursal, Daughter to the Alderman.

Mrs. Newington, Landlady of the Inn at Salt Hill.

Sally, a Chambermaid.

Patty, a Country Girl.

Pipe and Tabor, and Dance of Peasants.

ACT THE FIRST

SCENE I

The Bar of the 'Windmill Inn' at Salt Hill

Mr. *and* Mrs. Newington, *the Landlord and Landlady*

Landlady. 'Tis an unpossibility, Mr. Newington; and that's enough. Say no more about it; 'tis an unpossibility in the *natur* of things. (*She ranges jellies, etc., in the Bar.*) And pray, do you take your great old-fashioned tankard, Mr. Newington, from among my jellies and confectioneries.

Landlord (*takes his tankard and drinks*). Anything for a quiet life. If it is an unpossibility, I've no more to say; only, for the soul of me, I can't see the great unpossibility, wife.

Landlady. Wife, indeed!—wife!—wife! wife every minute.

Landlord. Heyday! Why, what a plague would you have me call you? The other day you quarrelled with me for calling you Mrs. Landlady.

Landlady. To be sure I did, and very proper in me I should. I've turned off three waiters and five chambermaids already, for screaming after me *Mrs. Landlady! Mrs. Landlady!* But 'tis all your ill manners.

Landlord. Ill manners! Why, if I may be so bold, if you are not Mrs. Landlady, in the name of wonder what are you?

Landlady. Mrs. Newington, Mr. Newington.

Landlord (*drinks*). Mrs. Newington, Mr. Newington drinks your health; for I suppose I must not be landlord any more in my own house (*shrugs*).

Landlady. Oh, as to that, I have no objections nor impediments to your being called *Landlord.* You look it, and become it very proper.

Landlord. Why, yes, indeed, thank my tankard, I do look it, and become it, and am nowise ashamed of it; but every one to their mind, as you, wife, don't fancy the being called Mrs. Landlady.

Landlady. To be sure I don't. Why, when folks hear the old-fashioned cry of Mrs. Landlady! Mrs. Landlady! who do they expect, think you, to see, but an overgrown, fat, featherbed of a woman coming waddling along with her thumbs sticking on each side of her apron, o' this fashion? Now, to see me coming, nobody would take me to be a landlady.

Landlord. Very true, indeed, wife—Mrs. Newington, I mean—I ask pardon; but now to go on with what we were saying about the unpossibility of letting that old lady and the civil-spoken young lady there above have them there rooms for another day.

Landlady. Now, Mr. Newington, let me hear no more about that old gentlewoman and that civil-spoken young lady. Fair words cost nothing; and I've a notion that's the cause they are so plenty with the young lady. Neither o' them, I take it, by what they've ordered since their coming into the house, are such grand folk that one need be so *petticular* about them.

Landlord. Why, they came only in a chaise and pair, to be sure; I can't deny that.

Landlady. But, bless my stars! what signifies talking? Don't you know, as well as I do, Mr. Newington, that to-morrow is Eton Montem, and that if we had twenty times as many rooms and as many more to the back of them, it would not be one too many for all the company we've a right to expect, and those the highest quality of the land? Nay, what do I talk of to-morrow? isn't my Lady Piercefield and suite expected? and, moreover, Mr. and Miss Bursal's to be here, and will call for as much in an hour as your civil-spoken young lady in a twelvemonth, I reckon. So, Mr. Newington, if you don't think proper to go up and inform the ladies above that the Dolphin rooms are not for them, I must *speak* myself, though 'tis a thing I never do when I can help it.

Landlord (*aside*). She not like to speak! (*Aloud.*) My dear, you can speak a power better than I can; so take it all upon yourself, if you please; for, old-fashioned as I and my tankard here be, I can't make a speech that borders on the uncivil order, to a lady like, for the life and lungs of me. So, in the name of goodness, do you go up, Mrs. Newington.

Landlady. And so I will, Mr. Newington. Help ye! Civilities and rarities are out o' season for them that can't pay for them in this world; and very proper.

(*Exit Landlady.*)

Landlord. And very proper! Ha! who comes yonder? The Eton chap who wheedled me into lending him my best hunter last year, and was the ruination of him; but that must be paid for, wheedle or no wheedle; and, for the matter of wheedling, I'd stake this here Mr. Wheeler, that is making up to me, do you see, against e'er a boy, or hobbledehoy, in all Eton, London, or Christendom, let the other be who he will.

Enter Wheeler.

Wheeler. A fine day, Mr. Newington.

Landlord. A fine day, Mr. Wheeler.

Wheel. And I hope, for *your* sake, we may have as fine a day for the Montem to-morrow. It will be a pretty penny in your pocket! Why, all the world will be here; and (*looking round at the jellies, etc.*) so much the better for them; for here are good things enough, and enough for them. And here's the best thing of all, the good old tankard still; not empty, I hope.

Landlord. Not empty, I hope. Here's to you, Mr. Wheeler.

Wheel. Mr. Wheeler!—*Captain* Wheeler, if you please.

Landlord. You, Captain Wheeler!—Why, I thought in former times it was always the oldest scholar at Eton that was Captain at the Montems; and didn't Mr. Talbot come afore you?

Wheel. Not at all; we came on the same day. Some say I came first; some say Talbot. So the choice of which of us is to be captain is to be put to the vote amongst the lads—most votes carry it; and I have most votes, I fancy; so I shall be captain, to-morrow, and a pretty deal of *salt*8 I reckon I shall pocket. Why, the collection at the last Montem, they say, came to a plump thousand! No bad thing for a young fellow to set out with for Oxford or Cambridge—hey?

Landlord. And no bad thing, before he sets out for Cambridge or Oxford, 'twould be for a young gentleman to pay his debts.

Wheel. Debts! Oh, time enough for that. I've a little account with you in horses, I know; but that's between you and me, you know—mum.

Landlord. Mum me no mums, Mr. Wheeler. Between you and me, my best hunter has been ruinationed; and I can't afford to be mum. So you'll take no offence if I speak; and as you'll set off to-morrow, as soon as the Montem's over, you'll be pleased to settle with me some way or other to-day, as we've no other time.

Wheel. No time so proper, certainly. Where's the little account?—I have money sent me for my Montem dress, and I can squeeze that much out of it. I came home from Eton on purpose to settle with you. But as to the hunter, you must call upon Talbot—do you understand? to pay for him; for though Talbot and I had him the same day, 'twas Talbot did for him, and Talbot must pay. I spoke to him about it, and charged him to remember you; for I never forget to speak a good word for my friends.

Landlord. So I perceive.

Wheel. I'll make bold just to give you my opinion of these jellies whilst you are getting my account, Mr. Newington.

(*He swallows down a jelly or two—Landlord is going.*)

Enter Talbot.

Talbot. Hallo, Landlord! where are you making off so fast? Here, your jellies are all going as fast as yourself.

Wheel. (*aside*). Talbot!—I wish I was a hundred miles off.

Landlord. You are heartily welcome, Mr. Talbot. A good morning to you, sir; I'm glad to see you—very glad to see you, Mr. Talbot.

Talb. Then shake hands, my honest landlord.

(*Talbot, in shaking hands with him, puts a purse into the Landlord's hands.*)

Landlord. What's here? Guineas?

Talb. The hunter, you know; since Wheeler won't pay, I must—that's all. Good morning.

Wheel. (*aside.*) What a fool!

(*Landlord, as Talbot is going catches hold of his coat.*)

'Then shake hands, my honest landlord.'

'Then shake hands, my honest landlord.'

Landlord. Hold, Mr. Talbot, this won't do!

Talb. Won't it? Well, then, my watch must go.

Landlord. Nay, nay! but you are in such a hurry to pay—you won't hear a man. Half this is enough for your share o' the mischief, in all conscience. Mr. Wheeler, there, had the horse on the same day.

Wheel. But Bursal's my witness——

Talb. Oh, say no more about witnesses; a man's conscience is always his best witness, or his worst. Landlord, take your money, and no more words.

Wheel. This is very genteel of you, Talbot. I always thought you would do the genteel thing, as I knew you to be so generous and considerate.

Talb. Don't waste your fine speeches, Wheeler, I advise you, this election time. Keep them for Bursal or Lord John, or some of those who like them. They won't go down with *me*. Good morning to you. I give you notice, I'm going back to Eton as fast as I can gallop; and who knows what plain speaking may do with the Eton lads? I may be captain yet, Wheeler. Have a care! Is my horse ready there?

Landlord. Mr. Talbot's horse, there! Mr. Talbot's horse, I say.

Talbot sings.

He carries weight—he rides a race—
'Tis for a thousand pound!

(*Exit Talbot.*)

Wheel. And, dear me! I shall be left behind. A horse for me, pray; a horse for Mr. Wheeler!

(*Exit Wheeler.*)

Landlord (*calls very loud*). Mr. Talbot's horse! Hang the hostler! I'll saddle him myself.

(*Exit Landlord.*)

SCENE II

A Dining-room in the Inn at Salt Hill

Mrs. Talbot *and* Louisa

Louisa (*laughing*). With what an air Mrs. Landlady made her exit!

Mrs. Talbot. When I was young, they say, I was proud; but I am humble enough now: these petty mortifications do not vex me.

Louisa. It is well my brother was gone before Mrs. Landlady made her *entrée*; for if he had heard her rude speech, he would at least have given her the retort courteous.

Mrs. Talb. Now tell me honestly, my Louisa——You were, a few days ago, at Bursal House. Since you have left it and have felt something of the difference that is made in this world between splendour and no splendour, you have never regretted that you did not stay there, and that you did not bear more patiently with Miss Bursal's little airs?

Louisa. Never for a moment. At first Miss Bursal paid me a vast deal of attention; but, for what reason I know not, she suddenly changed her manner, grew first strangely cold, then condescendingly familiar, and at last downright rude. I could not guess the cause of these variations.

Mrs. Talb. (*aside*). I guess the cause too well.

Louisa. But as I perceived the lady was out of tune, I was in haste to leave her. I should make a very bad, and, I am sure, a miserable toad eater. I had much rather, if I were obliged to choose, earn my own bread, than live as toad eater with anybody.

Mrs. Talb. Fine talking, dear Louisa!

Louisa. Don't you believe me to be in earnest, mother? To be sure, you cannot know what I would do, unless I were put to the trial.

Mrs. Talb. Nor you either, my dear.

(*She sighs, and is silent.*)

Louisa (*takes her mother's hand*). What is the matter, dear mother? You used to say that seeing my brother always made you feel ten years younger; yet even while he was here, you had, in spite of all your efforts to conceal them, those sudden fits of sadness.

Mrs. Talb. The Montem—is not it to-morrow? Ay, but my boy is not sure of being captain.

Louisa. No; there is one Wheeler, who, as he says, is most likely to be chosen captain. He has taken prodigious pains to flatter and win over many to his interest. My brother does not so much care about it; he is not avaricious.

Mrs. Talb. I love your generous spirit and his! but, alas! my dear, people may live to want, and wish for money, without being avaricious. I would not say a word to Talbot; full of spirits as he was this morning, I would not say a word to him, till after the Montem, of what has happened.

Louisa. And what has happened, dear mother? Sit down,—you tremble.

Mrs. Talb. (*sits down and puts a letter into Louisa's hand*). Read that, love. A messenger brought me that from town a few hours ago.

Louisa (*reads*). 'By an express from Portsmouth, we hear the *Bombay Castle* East Indiaman is lost, with all your fortune on board.' *All!* I hope there is something left for you to live upon.

Mrs. Talb. About £150 a year for us all.

Louisa. That is enough, is it not, for you?

Mrs. Talb. For me, love? I am an old woman, and want but little in this world, and shall be soon out of it.

Louisa (*kneels down beside her*). Do not speak so, dearest mother.

Mrs. Talb. Enough for me, love! Yes, enough, and too much for me. I am not thinking of myself.

Louisa. Then, as to my brother, he has such abilities, and such industry, he will make a fortune at the bar for himself, most certainly.

Mrs. Talb. But his education is not completed. How shall we provide him with money at Cambridge?

Louisa. This Montem. The last time the captain had eight hundred, the time before a thousand, pounds. Oh, I hope—I fear! Now, indeed, I know that, without being avaricious, we may want, and wish for money.

(*Landlady's voice heard behind the scenes.*)

Landlady. Waiter!—Miss Bursal's curricle, and Mr. Bursal's *vis-à-vis*. Run! see that the Dolphin's empty. I say run!—run!

Mrs. Talb. I will rest for a few moments upon the sofa, in this bedchamber, before we set off.

Louisa (*goes to open the door*). They have bolted or locked it. How unlucky!

(*She turns the key, and tries to unlock the door.*)

Enter Waiter.

Waiter. Ladies, I'm sorry—Miss Bursal and Mr. Bursal are come—just coming upstairs.

Mrs. Talb. Then, will you be so good, sir, as to unlock this door?

(*Waiter tries to unlock the door.*)

Waiter. It must be bolted on the inside. Chambermaid! Sally! Are you within there? Unbolt this door.

Mr. Bursal's voice behind the scenes. Let me have a basin of good soup directly.

Waiter. I'll go round and have the door unbolted immediately, ladies.

(*Exit Waiter.*)

Enter Miss Bursal, *in a riding dress, and with a long whip.*

Miss Bursal. Those creatures, the ponies, have a'most pulled my '*and* off. Who '*ave* we '*ere*? Ha! Mrs. Talbot! Louisa, '*ow* are ye? I'm so vastly glad to see you; but I'm so shocked to '*ear* of the loss of the *Bombay Castle*. Mrs. Talbot, you look but poorly; but this Montem will put everybody in spirits. I '*ear* everybody's to be '*ere*; and my brother tells me, 'twill be the finest ever seen at *H* Eton. Louisa, my dear, I'm sorry I've not a seat for you in my curricle for to-morrow; but I've promised Lady Betty; so, you know, 'tis impossible for me.

Louisa. Certainly; and it would be impossible for me to leave my mother at present.

Chambermaid (*opens the bedchamber door*). The room's ready now, ladies.

Mrs. Talb. Miss Bursal, we intrude upon you no longer.

Miss Burs. Nay, why do you decamp, Mrs. Talbot? I '*ad* a thousand things to say to you, Louisa; but am so tired and so annoyed——

(*Seats herself. Exeunt Mrs. Talbot, Louisa, and Chambermaid.*)

Enter Miss Bursal, in a riding dress.

Enter Miss Bursal, in a riding dress.

Enter Mr. Bursal, *with a basin of soup in his hand.*

Mr. Burs. Well, thank my stars the *Airly Castle* is safe in the Downs.

Miss Burs. Mr. Bursal, can you inform me why Joe, my groom, does not make his appearance?

Mr. Burs. (eating and speaking). Yes, that I can, child; because he is with his *'orses*, where he ought to be. 'Tis fit they should be looked after well; for they cost me a pretty penny—more than their heads are worth, and yours into the bargain; but I was resolved, as we were to come to this Montem, to come in style.

Miss Burs. In style, to be sure; for all the world's to be here—the King, the Prince of W*h*ales, and Duke o' York, and all the first people; and we shall cut a dash! Dash! dash! will be the word to-morrow!—*(playing with her whip).*

Mr. Burs. (aside). Dash! dash! ay, just like her brother. He'll pay away finely, I warrant, by the time he's her age. Well, well, he can afford it; and I do love to see my children make a figure for their money. As Jack Bursal says, what's money for, if it e'nt to make a figure? *(Aloud.)* There's your brother Jack, now. The extravagant dog! he'll have such a dress as never was seen, I suppose, at this here Montem. Why, now, Jack Bursal spends more money at Eton, and has more to spend, than my Lord John, though my Lord John's the son of a marchioness.

Miss Burs. Oh, that makes no difference nowadays. I wonder whether her ladyship is to be at this Montem. The only good I ever got out of these stupid Talbots was an introduction to their friend Lady Piercefield. What she could find to like in the Talbots, heaven knows. I've a notion she'll drop them, when she hears of the loss of the *Bombay Castle.*

Enter a Waiter, *with a note.*

Waiter. A note from my Lady Piercefield, sir.

Miss B. Charming woman! Is she here, pray, sir?

Waiter. Just come. Yes, ma'am.

(*Exit Waiter.*)

Miss B. Well, Mr. Bursal, what is it?

Mr. B. (*reads*). 'Business of importance to communicate——' Hum! what can it be?—(*going*).

Miss B. (*aside*). Perhaps some match to propose for me! (*Aloud.*) Mr. Bursal, pray before you go to her ladyship, do send my *ooman* to me to make me *presentable.*

(*Exit Miss Bursal at one door.*)

Mr. B. (*at the opposite door*). 'Business of importance!' Hum! I'm glad I'm prepared with a good basin of soup. There's no doing business well upon an empty stomach. Perhaps the business is to lend cash; and I've no great stomach for that. But it will be an honour, to be sure.

(*Exit.*)

SCENE III

Landlady's Parlour

Landlady—Mr. Finsbury, *a man-milliner, with bandboxes—a fancy cap, or helmet, with feathers, in the Landlady's hand—a satin bag, covered with gold netting, in the man-milliner's hand—a mantle hanging over his arm. A rough-looking Farmer is sitting with his back towards them, eating bread and cheese, and reading a newspaper.*

Landlady. Well, this, to be sure, will be the best-dressed Montem that ever was seen at Eton; and you Lon'on gentlemen have the most fashionablest notions; and this is the most elegantest fancy cap——

Finsbury. Why, as you observe, ma'm, that is the most elegant fancy cap of them all. That is Mr. Hector Hogmorton's fancy cap, ma'm; and here, ma'm, is Mr. Saul's rich satin bag, covered with gold net. He is college salt-bearer, I understand, and has a prodigious superb white and gold dress. But, in my humble opinion, ma'm, the marshal's white and purple and orange fancy-dress, trimmed with silver, will bear the bell; though, indeed, I shouldn't say that,—for the colonel's and lieutenant's, and ensign's, are beautiful in the extreme. And, to be sure, nothing could be better imagined than Mr. Marlborough's lilac and silver, with a Roman cap. And it must be allowed that nothing in nature can have a better effect than Mr. Drake's flesh-colour and blue, with this Spanish hat, ma'm, you see.

(*The Farmer looks over his shoulder from time to time during this speech, with contempt.*)

Farmer (*reads the newspaper*). French fleet at sea—Hum!

Landlady. O gemini: Mr. Drake's Spanish hat is the sweetest, tastiest thing! Mr. Finsbury, I protest——

Finsb. Why, *ma'm*, I knew a lady of your taste couldn't but approve of it. My own invention entirely, ma'm. But it's nothing to the captain's cap, ma'm. Indeed, ma'm, Mr. Wheeler, the captain that is to be, has the prettiest taste in dress. To be sure, his sandals were my suggestion; but the mantle he has the entire credit of, to do him justice; and when you see it, ma'm, you will be really surprised; for (for contrast and elegance, and richness, and lightness, and propriety, and effect, and costume) you've never yet seen anything at all to be compared to Captain Wheeler's mantle, ma'm.

Farmer (*to the Landlady*). Why, now, pray, Mrs. Landlady, how long may it have been the fashion for milliners to go about in men's clothes?

Landlady (*aside to Farmer*). Lord, Mr. Hearty, hush! This is Mr. Finsbury, the great man-milliner.

Farm. The great man-milliner! This is a sight I never thought to see in Old England.

Finsb. (*packing up bandboxes*). Well, ma'm, I'm glad I have your approbation. It has ever been my study to please the ladies.

Farm. (*throws a fancy mantle over his frieze coat*). And is this the way to please the ladies, Mrs. Landlady, nowadays?

Finsb. (*taking off the mantle*). Sir, with your leave—I ask pardon—but the least thing detriments these tender colours; and as you have just been eating cheese with your hands——

Farm. 'Tis my way to eat cheese with my mouth, man.

Finsb. Man!

Farm. I ask pardon—man-milliner, I mean.

Enter Landlord.

Landlord. Why, wife!

Landlady. Wife!

Landlord. I ask pardon—Mrs. Newington I mean. Do you know who them ladies are that you have been and turned out of the Dolphin?

Landlady (alarmed). Not I, indeed. Who are they, pray? Why, if they are quality it's no fault of mine. It is their own fault for coming, like scrubs, without four horses. Why, if quality will travel the road this way, incognito, how can they expect to be known and treated as quality? 'Tis no fault of mine. Why didn't you find out sooner who they were, Mr. Newington? What else in the 'versal world have you to do, but to go basking about in the yards and places with your tankard in your hand, from morning till night? What have you else to ruminate, all day long, but to find out who's who, I say?

Farm. Clapper! clapper! clapper! like my mill in a high wind, landlord. Clapper! clapper! clapper!—enough to stun a body.

Landlord. That is not used to it; but use is all, they say.

Landlady. Will you answer me, Mr. Newington? Who are the grandees that were in the Dolphin?—and what's become *on* them?

Landlord. Grandees was your own word, wife. They be not to call grandees; but I reckon you'd be sorry not to treat 'em civil, when I tell you their name is Talbot, mother and sister to our young Talbot of Eton; he that paid me so handsome for the hunter this very morning.

Landlady. Mercy! is that all? What a combustion for nothing in life!

Finsb. For nothing in life, as you say, ma'm; that is, nothing in high life, I'm sure, ma'm; nay, I dare a'most venture to swear. Would you believe it, Mr. Talbot is one of the few young gentlemen of Eton that has not bespoke from me a fancy-dress for this grand Montem?

Landlady. There, Mr. Newington; there's your Talbot for you! and there's your grandees! Oh, trust me, I know your scrubs at first sight.

Landlord. Scrubs, I don't, nor can't, nor won't call them that pay their debts honestly. Scrubs, I don't, nor won't, nor can't call them that behave as handsome as young Mr. Talbot did here to me this morning about the hunter. A scrub he is not, wife. Fancy-dress or no fancy-dress, Mr. Finsbury, this young gentleman is no scrub.

Finsb. Dear me! 'Twas not I said *scrub.* Did I say scrub?

Farm. No matter if you did.

Finsb. No matter, certainly; and yet it is a matter; for I'm confident I wouldn't for the world leave it in any one's power to say that I said—that I called—any young gentleman of Eton a *scrub*! Why, you know, sir, it might breed a riot!

Farm. And a pretty figure you'd make in a riot!

Landlady. Pray let me hear nothing about riots in my house.

Farm. Nor about scrubs.

Finsb. But I beg leave to explain, gentlemen. All I ventured to remark or suggest was, that as there was some talk of Mr. Talbot's being captain to-morrow, I didn't conceive how he could well appear without any dress. That was all, upon my word and honour. A good morning to you, gentlemen; it is time for me to be off. Mrs. Newington, you were so obliging as to promise to accommodate me with a return chaise as far as Eton.

(*Finsbury bows and exit.*)

Farm. A good day to you and your bandboxes. There's a fellow for you now! Ha! ha! ha!—A man-milliner, forsooth!

Landlord. Mrs. Talbot's coming—stand back.

Landlady. Lord! why does Bob show them through this way?

Enter Mrs. Talbot, *leaning on* Louisa; *Waiter showing the way.*

Landlady. You are going on, I suppose, ma'am?

Waiter (aside to Landlord). Not if she could help it; but there's no beds, since Mr. Bursal and Miss Bursal's come.

Landlord. I say nothing, for it is vain to say more. But isn't it a pity she can't stay for the Montem, poor old lady! Her son—as good and fine a lad as ever you saw—they say, has a chance, too, of being captain. She may never live to see another such a sight.

(*As Mrs. Talbot walks slowly on, the Farmer puts himself across her way, so as to stop her short.*)

Farm. No offence, madam, I hope; but I have a good snug farmhouse, not far off hand; and if so be you'd be so good to take a night's lodging, you and the young lady with you, you'd have a hearty welcome. That's all I can say; and you'd make my wife very happy; for she's a good woman, to say nothing of myself.

Landlord. If I may be so bold to put in my word, madam, you'd have as good beds, and be as well lodged, with Farmer Hearty, as in e'er a house at Salt Hill.

Mrs. Talb. I am very much obliged——

Farm. Oh, say nothing o' that, madam. I am sure I shall be as much obliged if you do come. Do, miss, speak for me.

Louisa. Pray, dear mother——

Farm. She will. (*Calls behind the scenes.*) Here, waiter! hostler! driver! what's your name? drive the chaise up here to the door, smart, close. Lean on my arm, madam, and we'll have you in and home in a whiff.

(*Exeunt Mrs. Talbot, Louisa, Farmer, Landlord, and Waiter.*)

Landlady (sola). What a noise and a rout this farmer man makes! and my husband, with his great broad face, bowing, as great a nincompoop as t'other. The folks are all bewitched with the old woman, I verily believe. (*Aloud.*) A good morning to you, ladies.

ACT THE SECOND

SCENE I

A field near Eton College;—several boys crossing backwards and forwards in the background. In front, Talbot, Wheeler, Lord John *and* Bursal.

Talbot. Fair play, Wheeler! Have at 'em, my boy! There they stand, fair game! There's Bursal there, with his *dead* forty-five votes at command; and Lord John with his—how many live friends?

Lord John (coolly). Sir, I have fifty-six friends, I believe.

Talb. Fifty-six friends, his lordship believes—Wheeler inclusive no doubt.

Lord J. That's as hereafter may be.

Wheeler. Hereafter! Oh, fie, my *lud*! You know your own Wheeler has, from the first minute he ever saw you, been your fast friend.

Talb. Your fast friend from the first minute he ever saw you, my lord! That's well hit, Wheeler; stick to that; stick fast. Fifty-six friends, Wheeler *in*clusive, hey, my lord! hey, my *lud*!

Lord J. Talbot *ex*clusive, I find, contrary to my expectations.

Talb. Ay, contrary to your expectations, you find that Talbot is not a dog that will lick the dust: but then there's enough of the true spaniel breed to be had for whistling for; hey, Wheeler?

Bursal (aside to Wheeler). A pretty electioneerer. So much the better for you, Wheeler. Why, unless he bought a vote, he'd never win one, if he talked from this to the day of judgment.

Wheeler (aside to Bursal). And as he has no money to buy votes—he! he! he!—we are safe enough.

Talb. That's well done, Wheeler; fight the by-battle there with Bursal, now you are sure of the main with Lord John.

Lord J. Sure! I never made Mr. Wheeler any promise yet.

Wheel. Oh, I ask no promise from his lordship; we are upon honour: I trust entirely to his lordship's good nature and generosity, and to his regard for his own family; I having the honour, though distantly, to be related.

Lord J. Related! How, Wheeler?

Wheel. Connected, I mean, which is next door, as I may say, to being related. Related slipped out by mistake; I beg pardon, my Lord John.

Lord J. Related!—a strange mistake, Wheeler.

Talb. Overshot yourself, Wheeler; overshot yourself, by all that's awkward. And yet, till now, I always took you for '*a dead-shot at a yellow-hammer.*'9

Wheel. (taking Bursal by the arm). Bursal, a word with you. (*Aside to Bursal.*) What a lump of family pride that Lord John is.

Talb. Keep out of my hearing, Wheeler, lest I should spoil sport. But never fear: you'll please Bursal sooner than I shall. I can't, for the soul of me, bring myself to say that Bursal's not purse-proud, and you can. Give you joy.

Burs. A choice electioneerer!—ha! ha! ha!

Wheel. (faintly). He! he! he!—a choice electioneerer, as you say.

(*Exeunt Wheeler and Bursal; manent Lord J. and Talbot.*)

Lord J. There was a time, Talbot——

Talb. There was a time, my lord—to save trouble and a long explanation—there was a time when you liked Talbots better than spaniels; you understand me?

Lord J. I have found it very difficult to understand you of late, Mr. Talbot.

Talb. Yes, because you have used other people's understandings instead of your own. Be yourself, my lord. See with your own eyes, and hear with your own ears, and then you'll find me still, what I've been these seven years; not your under-strapper, your hanger-on, your flatterer, but your friend! If you choose to have me for a friend, here's my hand. I am your friend, and you'll not find a better.

Lord J. (giving his hand). You are a strange fellow, Talbot; I thought I never could have forgiven you for what you said last night.

Talb. What? for I don't keep a register of my sayings. Oh, it was something about gaming—Wheeler was flattering your taste for it, and he put me into a passion—I forget what I said. But, whatever it was, I'm sure it was well meant, and I believe it was well said.

Lord J. But you laugh at me sometimes to my face.

Talb. Would you rather I should laugh at you behind your back?

Lord J. But of all things in the world I hate to be laughed at. Listen to me, and don't fumble in your pockets while I'm talking to you.

Talb. I'm fumbling for—oh, here it is. Now, Lord John, I once did laugh at you behind your back, and what's droll enough, it was *at* your back I laughed. Here's a caricature I drew of you—I really am sorry I did it; but 'tis best to show it to you myself.

Lord J. (aside). It is all I can do to forgive this. (*After a pause, he tears the paper.*) I have heard of this caricature before; but I did not expect, Talbot, that you would come and show it to me yourself, Talbot, so handsomely, especially at such a time as this. Wheeler might well say you are a bad electioneerer.

Talb. Oh, hang it! I forgot my election, and your fifty-six friends.

71

Enter Rory O'Ryan.

Rory (*claps Talbot on the back*). Fifty-six friends, have you, Talbot? Say seven—fifty-seven, I mean; for I'll lay you a wager, you've forgot me; and that's a shame for you, too; for out of the whole posse-comitatus entirely now, you have not a stauncher friend than poor little Rory O'Ryan. And a good right he has to befriend you; for you stood by him when many who ought to have known better were hunting him down for a wild Irishman. Now that same wild Irishman has as much gratitude in him as any tame Englishman of them all. But don't let's be talking *sintimint*; for, for my share I'd not give a bogberry a bushel for *sintimint*, when I could get anything better.

Lord J. And pray, sir, what may a bogberry be?

Rory. Phoo! don't be playing the innocent, now. Where have you lived all your life (I ask pardon, my *lard*) not to know a bogberry when you see or hear of it? (*Turns to Talbot.*) But what are ye standing idling here for? Sure, there's Wheeler, and Bursal along with him, canvassing out yonder at a terrible fine rate. And haven't I been huzzaing for you there till I'm hoarse? So I am, and just stepped away to suck an orange for my voice—(*sucks an orange*). I am a *thoroughgoing* friend, at any rate.

Talb. Now, Rory, you are the best fellow in the world, and a *thoroughgoing* friend; but have a care, or you'll get yourself and me into some scrape, before you have done with this violent *thoroughgoing* work.

Rory. Never fear! never fear, man!—a warm *frind* and a bitter enemy, that's my maxim.

Talb. Yes, but too warm a friend is as bad as a bitter enemy.

Rory. Oh, never fear me! I'm as cool as a cucumber all the time; and whilst they *tink* I'm *tinking* of nothing in life but making a noise, I make my own snug little remarks in prose and verse, as—now my voice is after coming back to me, you shall hear, if you *plase*.

Talb. I do please.

Rory. I call it Rory's song. Now, mind, I have a verse for everybody—o' the leading lads, I mean; and I shall put 'em in or *lave* 'em out, according to their inclinations and deserts, *wise-a-wee* to you, my little *frind*. So you comprehend it will be Rory's song, with variations.

Talbot and Lord John. Let's have it; let's have it without further preface.

Rory sings.
I'm true game to the last, and no *Wheeler* for me.

Rory. There's a stroke, in the first place, for Wheeler,—you take it?

Talb. Oh yes, yes, we take it; go on.

Rory sings.
I'm true game to the last, and no Wheeler for me.
Of all birds, beasts, or fishes, that swim in the sea,
Webb'd or finn'd, black or white, man or child, Whig or Tory,
None but Talbot, O Talbot's the dog for Rory.

Talb. 'Talbot the dog' is much obliged to you.

Lord J. But if I have any ear, one of your lines is a foot too long, Mr. O'Ryan.

Rory. Phoo, put the best foot foremost for a *frind*. Slur it in the singing, and don't be quarrelling, anyhow, for a foot more or less. The more feet the better it will stand, you know. Only let me go on, and you'll come to something that will *plase* you.

Rory sings.
Then there's he with the purse that's as long as my arm.

Rory. That's Bursal, mind now, whom I mean to allude to in this verse.

Lord J. If the allusion's good, we shall probably find out your meaning.

Talb. On with you, Rory, and don't read us notes on a song.

Lord J. Go on, and let us hear what you say of Bursal.

Rory sings.
Then there's he with the purse that's as long as my arm;
His father's a tanner,—but then where's the harm?
Heir to houses, and hunters, and horseponds in fee,
Won't his skins sure soon buy him a pedigree?

Lord J. Encore! encore! Why, Rory, I did not think you could make so good a song.

Rory. Sure 'twas none of I made it—'twas Talbot here.

Talb. I!

Rory (*aside*). Not a word: I'll make you a present of it: sure, then, it's your own.

72

Talb. I never wrote a word of it.

Rory (*to Lord J.*) Phoo, phoo! he's only denying it out of false modesty.

Lord J. Well, no matter who wrote it,—sing it again.

Rory. Be easy; so I will, and as many more verses as you will to the back of it. (*Winking at Talbot aside.*) You shall have the credit of all. (*Aloud.*) Put me in when I'm out, Talbot, and you (*to Lord John*) join—join.

Rory sings, and Lord John sings with him.

Then there's he with the purse that's as long as my arm;
His father's a tanner,—but then where's the harm?
Heir to houses, and hunters, and horseponds in fee,
Won't his skins sure soon buy him a pedigree?
There's my lord with the back that never was bent——

(*Lord John stops singing; Talbot makes signs to Rory to stop; but Rory does not see him, and sings on.*)

There's my lord with the back that never was bent;
Let him live with his ancestors, I am content.

(*Rory pushes Lord J. and Talbot with his elbows.*)

Rory. Join, join, both of ye—why don't you join? (*Sings.*)

Who'll buy my Lord John? the arch fishwoman cried,
A nice oyster shut up in a choice shell of pride.

Rory. But join or ye spoil all.

Talb. You have spoiled all, indeed.

Lord J. (*making a formal low bow*). Mr. Talbot, Lord John thanks you.

Rory. Lord John! blood and thunder! I forgot you were by—quite and clean.

Lord J. (*puts him aside and continues speaking to Talbot*). Lord John thanks you, Mr. Talbot: this is the second part of the caricature. Lord John thanks you for these proofs of friendship—Lord John has reason to thank you, Mr. Talbot.

Rory. No reason in life now. Don't be thanking so much for nothing in life; or if you must be thanking of somebody, it's me you ought to thank.

Lord J. I ought and do, sir, for unmasking one who——

Talb. (*warmly*). Unmasking, my lord——

Rory (*holding them asunder*). Phoo! phoo! phoo! be easy, can't ye?—there's no unmasking at all in the case. My Lord John, Talbot's writing the song was all a mistake.

Lord J. As much a mistake as your singing it, sir, I presume——

Rory. Just as much. 'Twas all a mistake. So now don't you go and make a mistake into a misunderstanding. It was I made every word of the song *out o' the face*10—that about the back that never was bent, and the ancestors of the oyster, and all. He did not waste a word of it; upon my conscience, I wrote it all—though I'll engage you didn't think I could write such a good thing. (*Lord John turns away.*) I'm telling you the truth, and not a word of a lie, and yet you won't believe me.

Lord J. You will excuse me, sir, if I cannot believe two contradictory assertions within two minutes. Mr. Talbot, I thank you (*going*).

(*Rory tries to stop Lord John from going, but cannot.—Exit Lord John.*)

Rory. Well, if he *will* go, let him go then, and much good may it do him. Nay, but don't you go too.

Talb. O Rory, what have you done?—(*Talbot runs after Lord J.*) Hear me, my lord.

(*Exit Talbot.*)

Rory. Hear him! hear him! hear him!—Well, I'm point blank mad with myself for making this blunder; but how could I help it? As sure as ever I am meaning to do the best thing on earth, it turns out the worst.

Enter a party of lads, huzzaing.

Rory (*joins*). Huzza! huzza!—Who, pray, are ye huzzaing for?

1st Boy. Wheeler! Wheeler for ever! huzza!

Rory. Talbot! Talbot for ever! huzza! Captain Talbot for ever! huzza!

2nd Boy. Captain he'll never be,—at least not to-morrow; for Lord John has just declared for Wheeler.

1st Boy. And that turns the scale.

Rory. Oh, the scale may turn back again.

3rd Boy. Impossible! Lord John has just given his *promise* to Wheeler. I heard him with my own ears.

(*Several speak at once.*) And I heard him; and I! and I! and I!—Huzza! Wheeler for ever!

Rory. Oh, murder! murder! murder! (*Aside.*) This goes to my heart! it's all my doing. O, my poor Talbot! murder! murder! murder! But I won't let them see me cast down, and it is good to be huzzaing at all events. Huzza for Talbot! Talbot for ever! huzza!

(*Exit.*)

Enter Wheeler *and* Bursal.

Wheel. Who was that huzzaing for Talbot?

(*Rory behind the scenes*, 'Huzza for Talbot! Talbot for ever! huzza!')

Burs. Pooh, it is only Rory O'Ryan, or the roaring lion, as I call him. Ha! ha! ha! Rory O'Ryan, *alias* O'Ryan, the roaring lion; that's a good one; put it about—Rory O'Ryan, the roaring lion, ha! ha! ha! but you don't take it—you don't laugh, Wheeler.

Wheeler. Ha! ha! ha! Oh, upon my honour I do laugh; ha! ha! ha! (*It is the hardest work to laugh at his wit—aside.*) (*Aloud.*) Rory O'Ryan, the roaring lion—ha! ha! ha! You know I always laugh, Bursal, at your jokes—he! he! he!—ready to kill myself.

Burs. (*sullenly*). You are easily killed, then, if that much laughing will do the business.

Wheel. (*coughing*). Just then—something stuck in my throat; I beg your pardon.

Burs. (*still sullen*). Oh, you need not beg my pardon about the matter; I don't care whether you laugh or no—not I. Now you have got Lord John to declare for you, you are above laughing at my jokes, I suppose.

Wheel. No, upon my word and honour, *I did* laugh.

Burs. (*aside*). A fig for your word and honour. (*Aloud.*) I know I'm of no consequence now; but you'll remember that, if his lordship has the honour of making you captain, he must have the honour to pay for your captain's accoutrements; for I shan't pay the piper, I promise you, since I'm of no consequence.

Wheel. Of no consequence! But, my dear Bursal, what could put that into your head? that's the strangest, oddest fancy. Of no consequence! Bursal, of no consequence! Why, everybody that knows anything—everybody that has seen Bursal House—knows that you are of the greatest consequence, my dear Bursal.

Burs. (*taking out his watch, and opening it, looks at it*). No, I'm of no consequence. I wonder that rascal Finsbury is not come yet with the dresses (*still looking at his watch*).

Wheel. (*aside*). If Bursal takes it into his head not to lend me the money to pay for my captain's dress, what will become of me? for I have not a shilling—and Lord John won't pay for me—and Finsbury has orders not to leave the house till he is paid by everybody. What will become of me?—(*bites his nails*).

Burs. (*aside*). How I love to make him bite his nails! (*Aloud.*) I know I'm of no consequence. (*Strikes his repeater.*)

Wheel. What a fine repeater that is of yours, Bursal! It is the best I ever heard.

Burs. So it well may be; for it cost a mint of money.

Wheel. No matter to you what anything costs. Happy dog as you are! You roll in money; and yet you talk of being of no consequence.

Burs. But I am not of half so much consequence as Lord John—am I?

Wheel. Are you? Why, aren't you twice as rich as he!

Burs. Very true, but I'm not purse-proud.

Wheel. You purse-proud! I should never have thought of such a thing.

Burs. Nor I, if Talbot had not used the word.

Wheel. But Talbot thinks everybody purse-proud that has a purse.

Burs. (*aside*). Well, this Wheeler does put one into a good humour with one's self in spite of one's teeth. (*Aloud.*) Talbot says blunt things; but I don't think he's what you can call clever—hey, Wheeler?

Wheel. Clever! Oh, not he.

Burs. I think I could walk round him.

Wheel. To be sure you could. Why, do you know, I've *quizzed* him famously myself within this quarter of an hour?

Burs. Indeed! I wish I had been by.

Wheel. So do I, 'faith! It was the best thing. I wanted, you see, to get him out of my way, that I might have the field clear for electioneering to-day. So I bowls up to him with a long face—such a face as this. 'Mr. Talbot, do you know—I'm sorry to tell you, here's Jack Smith has just brought the news from Salt Hill. Your mother, in getting into the carriage, slipped, and has *broke* her leg, and there she's lying at a farmhouse, two miles off. Is not it true, Jack?' said I. 'I saw the farmer helping her in with my own eyes,' cries Jack. Off goes Talbot like an arrow. '*Quizzed* him, *quizzed* him!' said I.

Burs. Ha! ha! ha! quizzed him indeed, with all his cleverness; that was famously done.

Wheel. Ha! ha! ha! With all his cleverness he will be all the evening hunting for the farmhouse and the mother that has *broke* her leg; so he is out of our way.

Burs. But what need have you to want him out of your way, now Lord John has come over to your side? You have the thing at a dead beat.

Wheel. Not so dead either; for there's a great independent party, you know; and if *you* don't help me, Bursal, to canvass them, I shall be no captain. It is you I depend upon after all. Will you come and canvass them with me? Dear Bursal, pray—all depends upon you.

(*Pulls him by the arm—Bursal follows.*)

Burs. Well, if all depends upon me, I'll see what I can do for you. (*Aside.*) Then I am of some consequence! Money makes a man of some consequence, I see; at least with some folks.

SCENE II

In the back scene a flock of sheep are seen penned. In front, a party of country lads and lasses, gaily dressed, as in sheep-shearing time, with ribands and garlands of flowers, etc., are dancing and singing.

Enter Patty, *dressed as the Queen of the Festival, with a lamb in her arms. The dancers break off when she comes in, and direct their attention towards her.*

1st Peasant. Oh, here comes Patty! Here comes the Queen o' the day. What has kept you from us so long, Patty?

2nd Peasant. '*Please your Majesty*,' you should say.

Patty. This poor little lamb of mine was what kept me so long. It strayed away from the rest; and I should have lost him, so I should, for ever, if it had not been for a good young gentleman. Yonder he is, talking to Farmer Hearty. That's the young gentleman who pulled my lamb out of the ditch for me, into which he had fallen—pretty creature!

1st Peasant. Pretty creature—or, your Majesty, whichever you choose to be called—come and dance with them, and I'll carry your lamb.

(*Exeunt, singing and dancing.*)

Enter Farmer Hearty *and* Talbot.

Farmer. Why, young gentleman, I'm glad I happened to light upon you here, and so to hinder you from going farther astray, and set your heart at ease like.

Talb. Thanks, good farmer, you have set my heart at ease, indeed. But the truth is, they did frighten me confoundedly—more fool I.

Farm. No fool at all, to my notion. I should, at your age, ay, or at my age, just the self-same way have been frightened myself, if so be that mention had been made to me, that way, of my own mother's having broke her leg or so. And greater, by a great deal, the shame for them that frighted you, than for you to be frighted. How young gentlemen, now, can bring themselves for to tell such lies, is to me, now, a matter of amazement, like, that I can't noways get over.

Talb. Oh, farmer, such lies are very witty, though you and I don't just now like the wit of them. This is fun, this is *quizzing*; but you don't know what we young gentlemen mean by *quizzing*.

Farm. Ay, but I do though, to my cost, ever since last year. Look you, now, at yon fine field of wheat. Well, it was just as fine, and finer, last year, till a young Eton jackanapes——

Talb. Take care what you say, farmer; for I am a young Eton jackanapes.

Farm. No; but you be not the young Eton jackanapes that I'm a-thinking on. I tell you it was this time last year, man; he was a-horseback, I tell ye, mounted upon a fine bay hunter, out o' hunting, like.

Talb. I tell you 'it was this time last year, man, that I was mounted upon a fine bay hunter, out a-hunting.

Farm. Zooks! would you argufy a man out of his wits? You won't go for to tell me that you are that impertinent little jackanapes!

Talb. No! no! I'll not tell you that I am an impertinent little jackanapes!

Farm. (*wiping his forehead*). Well, don't then, for I can't believe it; and you put me out. Where was I?

Talb. Mounted upon a fine bay hunter.

Farm. Ay, so he was. 'Here, *you*,' says he, meaning me—'open this gate for me.' Now, if he had but a-spoke me fair, I would not have gainsaid him; but he falls to swearing, so I bid him open the gate for himself. 'There's a bull behind you, farmer,' says he. I turns. '*Quizzed* him!' cries my jackanapes, and off he gallops him, through the very thick of my corn; but he got a fall, leaping the ditch out yonder, which pacified me, like, at the minute. So I goes up to see whether he was killed; but he was not a whit the worse for his tumble. So I should ha' fell into a passion with him then, to be sure, about my corn; but his horse had got such a terrible sprain, I couldn't say anything to him; for I was a-pitying the poor animal. As fine a hunter as ever you saw! I am sartain sure he could never come to good after.

Talb. (*aside*). I do think, from the description, that this was Wheeler; and I have paid for the horse which he spoiled! (*Aloud.*) Should you know either the man or the horse again, if you were to see them?

Farm. Ay, that I should, to my dying day.

Talb. Will you come with me, then, and you'll do me some guineas' worth of service?

Farm. Ay, that I will, with a deal of pleasure; for you be a civil-spoken young gentleman; and, besides, I don't think the worse *on* you for being *frighted* a little about your mother; being what I might ha' been, at your age, myself; for I had a mother myself once. So lead on, master.

(*Exeunt.*)

ACT THE THIRD

SCENE I

The Garden of the 'Windmill Inn' at Salt Hill

Miss Bursal, Mrs. Newington, Sally *the Chambermaid*

(*Miss Bursal, in a fainting state, is sitting on a garden stool, and leaning her head against the Landlady. Sally is holding a glass of water and a smelling bottle.*)

Miss Bursal. Where am I? Where am I?

Landlady. At the 'Windmill,' at Salt Hill, young lady; and ill or well, you can't be better.

Sally. Do you find yourself better since coming into the air, miss?

Miss B. Better! Oh, I shall never be better!

(*Leans her head on hand, and rocks herself backwards and forwards.*)

Landlady. My dear young lady, don't take on so. (*Aside.*) Now would I give something to know what it was my Lady Piercefield said to the father, and what the father said to this one, and what's the matter at the bottom of affairs. Sally, did you hear anything at the doors?

Sally (*aside*). No, indeed, ma'am; I never *be's* at the doors.

Landlady (*aside*). Simpleton! (*Aloud.*) But, my dear Miss Bursal, if I may be so bold—if you'd only disembosom your mind of what's on it——

Miss B. Disembosom my mind! Nonsense! I've nothing on my mind. Pray leave me, madam.

Landlady (*aside*). Madam, indeed! madam, forsooth! Oh, I'll make her pay for that! That *madam* shall go down in the bill as sure as my name's Newington. (*In a higher tone.*) Well, I wish you better, ma'am. I suppose I'd best send your own servant?

Miss B. (*sullenly*). Yes, I suppose so. (*To Sally.*) You need not wait, child, nor look so curious.

Sally. Cur'ous! Indeed, miss, if I look a little *cur'ous*, or so (*looking at her dress*), 'tis only because I was *frighted* to see you take on, which made me forget my clean apron when I came out; and this apron——

Miss B. Hush! hush! child. Don't tell me about clean aprons, nor run on with your vulgar talk. Is there ever a seat one can set on in that *h*arbour yonder?

Sally. O dear *'art*, yes, miss; 'tis the pleasantest *h*arbour on *h*earth. Be pleased to lean on my *h*arm, and you'll soon be there.

Miss B. (*going*). Then tell my woman she need not come to me, and let nobody *interude* on me—do you *'ear*? (*Aside.*) Oh, what will become of me? and the Talbots will soon know it! And the ponies, and the curricle, and the *vis-à-vis*—what will become of them? and how shall I make my appearance at the Montem, or any *ware* else?

SCENE II

Lord John—Wheeler—Bursal

Wheeler. Well, but, my lord—Well, but, Bursal—though my Lady Piercefield—though Miss Bursal is come to Salt Hill, you won't leave us all at sixes and sevens. What can we do without you?

Lord J. You can do very well without *me*.

Bursal. You can do very well without *me*.

Wheel. (*to Burs.*). Impossible!—impossible! You know Mr. Finsbury will be here just now, with the dresses; and we have to try them on.

Burs. And to pay for them.

Wheel. And to settle about the procession. And then, my lord, the election is to come on this evening. You won't go till that's over, as your lordship has *promised* me your lordship's vote and interest.

Lord J. My vote I promised you, Mr. Wheeler; but I said not a syllable about my *interest*. My friends, perhaps, have not been offended, though I have, by Mr. Talbot. I shall leave them to their own inclinations.

Burs. (*whistling*). Wheugh! wheugh! wheugh! Wheeler, the principal's nothing without the interest.

Wheel. Oh, the interest will go along with the principal, of course; for I'm persuaded, if my lord leaves his friends to their inclinations, it will be the inclination of my lord's friends to vote as he does, if he says nothing to them to the contrary.

Lord J. I told you, Mr. Wheeler, that I should leave them to themselves.

Burs. (*still whistling*). Well, I'll do my best to make that father of mine send me off to Oxford. I'm sure I'm fit to go—along with Wheeler. Why, you'd best be my tutor, Wheeler!—a devilish good thought.

Wheel. An excellent thought.

Burs. And a cursed fine dust we should kick up at Oxford, with your Montem money and all!—Money's *the go* after all. I wish it was come to my making you my last bow, 'ye distant spires, ye *antic* towers!'

Wheel. (*aside to Lord J.*). Ye *antic* towers!—fit for Oxford, my lord!

Lord J. *Antique* towers, I suppose Mr. Bursal means.

Burs. Antique, to be sure!—I said antique, did not I, Wheeler?

Wheel. Oh yes.

Lord J. (*aside*). What a mean animal is this!

Enter Rory O'Ryan.

Rory. Why, now, what's become of Talbot, I want to know? There he is not to be found anywhere in the wide world; and there's a hullabaloo amongst his friends for him.

(*Wheeler and Bursal wink at one another.*)

Wheel. We know nothing of him.

Lord J. I have not the honour, sir, to be one of Mr. Talbot's friends. It is his own fault, and I am sorry for it.

Rory. 'Faith, so am I, especially as it is mine—fault I mean; and especially as the election is just going to come on.

Enter a party of boys, who cry, Finsbury's come!—Finsbury's come with the dresses!

Wheel. Finsbury's come? Oh, let us see the dresses, and let us try 'em on to-night.

Burs. (*pushing the crowd*). On with ye—on with ye, there!—Let's try 'em on!—Try 'em on—I'm to be colonel.

1st Boy. And I lieutenant.

2nd Boy. And I ensign.

3rd Boy. And I college salt-bearer.

4th Boy. And I oppidan.

5th Boy. Oh, what a pity I'm in mourning.

(*Several speak at once.*) And we are servitors. We are to be the eight servitors.

Wheel. And I am to be your Captain, I hope. Come on, my Colonel (*to Bursal*). My lord, you are coming?

Rory. By-and-by—I've a word in his ear, by your *lave* and his.

Burs. Why, what the devil stops the way, there?—Push on—on with them.

6th Boy. I'm marshal.

Burs. On with you—on with you—who cares what you are?

Wheel. (*to Bursal, aside*). You'll pay Finsbury for me, you rich Jew? (*To Lord John.*) Your lordship will remember your lordship's promise?

Lord J. I do not usually forget my promises, sir; and therefore need not to be reminded of them.

Wheel. I beg pardon—I beg ten thousand pardons, my lord.

Burs. (*taking him by the arm*). Come on, man, and don't stand begging pardon there, or I'll leave you.

Wheel. (*to Burs.*). I beg pardon, Bursal—I beg pardon, ten thousand times.

(*Exeunt.*)

Manent Lord John and Rory O'Ryan.

Rory. Wheugh!—Now put the case. If I was going to be hanged, for the life of me I couldn't be after begging so many pardons for nothing at all. But many men, many minds—(*Hums.*) True game to the last! No Wheeler for me. Oh, murder! I forgot, I was nigh letting the cat out o' the bag again.

Lord J. You had something to say to me, sir? I wait till your recollection returns.

Rory. 'Faith, and that's very kind of you; and if you had always done so, you would never have been offended with me, my lord.

Lord J. You are mistaken, Mr. O'Ryan, if you think that you did or could offend me.

Rory. Mistaken was I, then, sure enough; but we are all liable to mistakes, and should forget and forgive one another; that's the way to go through.

Lord J. You will go through the world your own way, Mr. O'Ryan, and allow me to go through it my way.

Rory. Very fair—fair enough—then we shan't cross. But now, to come to the point. I don't like to be making disagreeable retrospects, if I could any way avoid it; nor to be going about the bush, especially at this time o' day; when, as Mr. Finsbury's come, we've not so much time to lose as we had. Is there any truth, then, my lord, in the report that is going about this hour past, that you have gone in a huff and given your promise there to that sneaking Wheeler to vote for him now?

Lord J. In answer to your question, sir, I am to inform you that I *have* promised Mr. Wheeler to vote for him.

Rory. In a huff?—Ay, now, there it is!—Well, when a man's *mad*, to be sure, he's mad—and that's all that can be said about it. And I know, if I had been *mad* myself, I might have done a foolish thing as well as another. But now, my lord, that you are not mad——

Lord J. I protest, sir, I cannot understand you. In one word, sir, I'm neither mad nor a fool!—Your most obedient (*going, angrily*).

Rory (*holding him*). Take care, now; you are going mad with me again. But phoo! I like you the better for being mad. I'm very often mad myself, and I would not give a potato for one that had never been mad in his life.

Lord J. (*aside*). He'll not be quiet till he makes me knock him down.

Rory. Agh! agh! agh!—I begin to guess whereabouts I am at last. *Mad*, in your country, I take it, means fit for Bedlam; but with us in Ireland, now, 'tis no such thing; it means nothing in life but the being in a passion. Well, one comfort is, my lord, as you're a bit of a scholar, we have the Latin proverb in our favour—'*Ira furor brevis est*' (Anger is short madness). The shorter the better, I think. So, my lord, to put an end to whatever of the kind you may have felt against poor Talbot, I'll assure you he's as innocent o' that unfortunate song as the babe unborn.

Lord J. It is rather late for Mr. Talbot to make apologies to me.

Rory. He make apologies! Not he, 'faith; he'd send me to Coventry, or maybe to a worse place, did he but know I was condescending to make this bit of explanation, unknown to him. But, upon my conscience, I've a regard for you both, and don't like to see you go together by the ears. Now, look you, my lord. By this book, and all the books that were ever shut and opened, he never saw or heard of that unlucky song of mine till I came out with it this morning.

Lord J. But you told me this morning that it was he who wrote it.

Rory. For that I take shame to myself, as it turned out; but it was only a *white* lie to sarve a friend, and make him cut a dash with a new song at election time. But I've done for ever with white lies.

Lord J. (*walking about as if agitated*). I wish you had never begun with them, Mr. O'Ryan. This may be a good joke to you, but it is none to me or Talbot. So Talbot never wrote a word of the song?

Rory. Not a word or syllable, good or bad.

Lord J. And I have given my promise to vote against him. He'll lose his election.

Rory. Not if you'll give me leave to speak to your friends in your name.

Lord J. I have promised to leave them to themselves; and Wheeler, I am sure, has engaged them by this time.

Rory. Bless my body! I'll not stay prating here then.

(*Exit Rory.*)

Lord J. (*follows*). But what can have become of Talbot? I have been too hasty for once in my life. Well, I shall suffer for it more than anybody else; for I love Talbot, since he did not make the song, of which I hate to think.

(*Exit.*)

SCENE III

A large hall in Eton College—A staircase at the end—Eton lads, dressed in their Montem Dresses, in the Scene—In front, Wheeler (*dressed as Captain*), Bursal, *and* Finsbury.

Fins. I give you infinite credit, Mr. Wheeler, for this dress.

Burs. Infinite credit! Why, he'll have no objection to that—hey, Wheeler? But I thought Finsbury knew you too well to give you credit for anything.

Fins. You are pleased to be pleasant, sir. Mr. Wheeler knows, in that sense of the word, it is out of my power to give him credit, and I'm sure he would not ask it.

Wheel. (*aside*). O, Bursal, pay him, and I'll pay you to-morrow.

Burs. Now, if you weren't to be captain after all, Wheeler, what a pretty figure you'd cut. Ha! ha! ha!—Hey?

Wheel. Oh, I am as sure of being captain as of being alive. (*Aside.*) Do pay for me, now, there's a good, dear fellow, before *they* (*looking back*) come up.

Burs. (*aside*). I love to make him lick the dust. (*Aloud.*) Hollo! here's Finsbury waiting to be paid, lads. (*To the lads who are in the back scene.*) Who has paid, and who has not paid? I say.

(*The lads come forward, and several exclaim at once,*) I've paid! I've paid!

Enter Lord John *and* Rory O'Ryan.

Rory. Oh, King of Fashion, how fine we are! Why, now, to look at ye all one might fancy one's self at the playhouse at once, or at a fancy ball in dear little Dublin. Come, strike up a dance.

Burs. Pshaw! Wherever you come, Rory O'Ryan, no one else can be heard. Who has paid, and who has not paid? I say.

Several boys exclaim, We've all paid.

1st Boy. I've not paid, but here's my money.

Several Boys. We have not paid, but here's our money.

6th Boy. Order there, I am marshal. All that have paid march off to the staircase, and take your seats there, one by one. March!

(*As they march by, one by one, so as to display their dresses, Mr. Finsbury bows, and says,*)

A thousand thanks, gentlemen. Thank you, gentlemen. Thanks, gentlemen. The finest sight ever I saw out of Lon'on.

Rory, as each lad passes, catches his arm, Are you a Talbo*tite*, or a Wheele*rite*? *To each who answers* 'A Wheelerite,' *Rory replies,* 'Phoo! dance off, then. Go to the devil and shake yourself.'11 *Each who answers* 'A Talbotite,' *Rory shakes by the hand violently, singing,*

Talbot, oh, Talbot's the dog for Rory.

When they have almost all passed, Lord John says, But where can Mr. Talbot be all this time?

Burs. Who knows? Who cares?

Wheel. A pretty electioneerer! (*Aside to Bursal.*) Finsbury's waiting to be paid.

Lord J. You don't wait for me, Mr. Finsbury. You know, I have settled with you.

Fins. Yes, my lord—yes. Many thanks; and I have left your lordship's dress here, and everybody's dress, I believe, as bespoke.

Burs. Here, Finsbury, is the money for Wheeler, who, between you and me, is as poor as a rat.

Wheeler (*affecting to laugh*). Well, I hope I shall be as rich as a Jew to-morrow.

(*Bursal counts money, in an ostentatious manner, into Finsbury's hand.*)

Fins. A thousand thanks for all favours.

Rory. You will be kind enough to *lave* Mr. Talbot's dress with me, Mr. Finsbury, for I'm a friend.

Fins. Indubitably, sir; but the misfortune is—he! he! he!—Mr. Talbot, sir, has bespoke no dress. Your servant, gentlemen.

(*Exit Finsbury.*)

Burs. So your friend Mr. Talbot could not afford to bespeak a dress—(*Bursal and Wheeler laugh insolently*). How comes that, I wonder?

Lord J. If I'm not mistaken, here comes Talbot to answer for himself.

Rory. But who, in the name of St. Patrick, has he along with him?

Enter Talbot *and* Landlord.

Talb. Come in along with us, Farmer Hearty—come in.

(*Whilst the Farmer comes in, the boys who were sitting on the stairs rise and exclaim,*)

Whom have we here? What now? Come down, lads; here's more fun.

Rory. What's here, Talbot?

Talb. An honest farmer and a good-natured landlord, who *would* come here along with me to speak——

Farm. (*interrupting*). To speak the truth—(*strikes his stick on the ground*).

Landlord (*unbuttoning his waistcoat*). But I am so hot—so short-winded, that (*panting and puffing*)—that for the soul and body of me, I cannot say what I have got for to say.

Rory. 'Faith, now, the more short-winded a story, the better, to my fancy.

Burs. Wheeler, what's the matter, man? you look as if your under jaw was broke.

Farm. The matter is, young gentlemen, that there was once upon a time a fine bay hunter.

Wheel. (*squeezing up to Talbot, aside*). Don't expose me, don't let him tell. (*To the Farmer.*) I'll pay for the corn I spoiled. (*To the Landlord.*) I'll pay for the horse.

Farm. I does not want to be paid for my corn. The short of it is, young gentlemen, this 'un here, in the fine thing-em-bobs (*pointing to Wheeler*), is a shabby fellow; he went and spoiled Master Newington's best hunter.

Land. (*panting*). Ruinationed him! ruinationed him!

Rory. But was that all the shabbiness? Now I might, or any of us might, have had such an accident as that. I suppose he paid the gentleman for the horse, or will do so, in good time.

Land. (*holding his sides*). Oh, that I had but a little breath in this body o' mine to speak all—speak on, Farmer.

Farm. (*striking his stick on the floor*). Oons, sir, when a man's put out, he can't go on with his story.

Omnes. Be quiet, Rory—hush!

(*Rory puts his finger on his lips.*)

Farm. Why, sir, I was a-going to tell you the shabbiness—why, sir, he did not pay the landlord, here, for the horse; but he goes and says to the landlord, here—'Mr. Talbot had your horse on the self-same day; 'twas he did the damage; 'tis from he you must get your money.' So Mr. Talbot, here, who is another sort of a gentleman (though he has not so fine a coat), would not see a man at a loss, that could not afford it; and not knowing which of 'em it was that spoiled the horse, goes, when he finds the other would not pay a farthing, and pays all.

Rory (*rubbing his hands*). There's Talbot for ye. And now, gentlemen (*to Wheeler and Bursal*), you guess the *rason*, as I do, I suppose, why he bespoke no dress; he had not money enough to be fine—and honest, too. You are very fine, Mr. Wheeler, to do you justice.

Lord J. Pray, Mr. O'Ryan, let the farmer go on; he has more to say. How did you find out, pray, my good friend, that it was not Talbot who spoiled the horse? Speak loud enough to be heard by everybody.

Farm. Ay, that I will—I say (*very loudly*) I say I saw *him* there (*pointing to Wheeler*) take the jump which strained the horse; and I'm ready to swear to it. Yet he let another pay; there's the shabbiness.

(*A general groan from all the lads.* 'Oh, shabby Wheeler, shabby! I'll not vote for shabby Wheeler!')

Lord J. (*aside*). Alas! I must vote for him.

Rory sings.

True game to the last; no Wheeler for me;
Talbot, oh, Talbot's the dog for me.

79

(*Several voices join the chorus.*)

Burs. Wheeler, if you are not chosen Captain, you must see and pay me for the dress.

Wheel. I am as poor as a rat.

Rory. Oh yes! oh yes! hear ye! hear ye, all manner of men—the election is now going to begin forthwith in the big field, and Rory O'Ryan holds the poll for Talbot. Talbot for ever!—huzza!

(*Exit Rory followed by the Boys, who exclaim,* Talbot for ever!—huzza! *The Landlord and Farmer join them.*)

Lord J. Talbot, I am glad you *are* what I always thought you—I'm glad you did not write that odious song. I would not lose such a friend for all the songs in the world. Forgive me for my hastiness this morning. I've punished myself—I've promised to vote for Wheeler.

Talb. Oh, no matter whom you vote for, my lord, if you are still my friend, and if you know me to be yours.

(*They shake hands.*)

Lord J. I must not say, '*Huzza for Talbot!*'

(*Exeunt.*)

'*I say I saw* him *there take the jump which strained the horse.*'

SCENE IV

Windsor Terrace

Lady Piercefield, Mrs. Talbot, Louisa, *and a little girl of six years old*, Lady Violetta, *daughter to* Lady Piercefield.

Violetta (looking at a paper which Louisa holds). I like it *very* much.

Lady P. What is it you like *very* much, Violetta?

Violet. You are not to know *yet*, mamma; it is—I may tell her that—it is a little drawing that Louisa is doing for me. Louisa, I wish you would let me show it to mamma.

Louisa. And welcome, my dear; it is only a sketch of 'The Little Merchants,' a story which Violetta was reading, and she asked me to try to draw the pictures of the little merchants for her.

(Whilst Lady P. looks at the drawing, Violetta says to Louisa)

But are you in earnest, Louisa, about what you were saying to me just now,—quite in earnest?

Louisa. Yes, in earnest,—quite in earnest, my dear.

Violet. And may I ask mamma *now*?

Louisa. If you please, my dear.

Violet. (runs to her mother). Stoop down to me, mamma; I've something to whisper to you.

(Lady Piercefield stoops down; Violetta throws her arms round her mother's neck.)

Violet. (aside to her mother). Mamma, do you know—you know you want a governess for me.

Lady P. Yes, if I could find a good one.

Violet. (aloud). Stoop again, mamma, I've more to whisper. *(Aside to her mother.) She* says she will be my governess, if you please.

Lady P. She!—who is *she*?

Violet. Louisa.

Lady P. (patting Violetta's cheek). You are a little fool. Miss Talbot is only playing with you.

Violet. No, indeed, mamma; she is in earnest; are not you, Louisa?—Oh, say yes!

Louisa. Yes.

Violet. (claps her hands). *Yes*, mamma; do you hear *yes*?

Louisa. If Lady Piercefield will trust you to my care, I am persuaded that I should be much happier as your governess, my good little Violetta, than as an humble dependent of Miss Bursal's. *(Aside to her mother.)* You see that, now I am put to the trial, I keep to my resolution, dear mother.

Mrs. T. Your ladyship would not be surprised at this offer of my Louisa, if you had heard, as we have done within these few hours, of the loss of the East India ship in which almost our whole property was embarked.

Louisa. The *Bombay Castle* is wrecked.

Lady P. The *Bombay Castle*! I have the pleasure to tell you that you are misinformed—it was the *Airly Castle* that was wrecked.

Louisa and Mrs. T. Indeed!

Lady P. Yes; you may depend upon it—it was the *Airly Castle* that was lost. You know I am just come from Portsmouth, where I went to meet my brother, Governor Morton, who came home with the last India fleet, and from whom I had the intelligence.

(Here Violetta interrupts, to ask her mother for her nosegay—Lady P. gives it to her,—then goes on speaking.)

Lady P. They were in such haste, foolish people! to carry their news to London, that they mistook one castle for another. But do you know that Mr. Bursal loses fifty thousand pounds, it is said, by the *Airly Castle*? When I told him she was lost, I thought he would have dropped down. However, I found he comforted himself afterwards with a bottle of Burgundy; but poor Miss Bursal has been in hysterics ever since.

Mrs. T. Poor girl! My Louisa, *you* did not fall into hysterics, when I told you of the loss of our whole fortune.

(Violetta, during this dialogue, has been seated on the ground making up a nosegay.)

Violet. (aside). Fall into hysterics! What are hysterics, I wonder.

Louisa. Miss Bursal is much to be pitied; for the loss of wealth will be the loss of happiness to her.

Lady P. It is to be hoped that the loss may at least check the foolish pride and extravagance of young Bursal, who, as my son tells me—

——

(A cry of 'Huzza! huzza!' *behind the scenes.)*

' Talbot and truth for ever! Huzza.'

'*Talbot and truth for ever! Huzza.*'

Enter Lord John.

Lord J. (*hastily*). How d'ye do, mother? Miss Talbot, I give you joy.
Lady P. Take breath—take breath.
Louisa. It is my brother.
Mrs. T. Here he is!—Hark! hark!
(*A cry behind the scenes of* 'Talbot and truth for ever! Huzza!')
Louisa. They are chairing him.
Lord J. Yes, they are chairing him; and he has been chosen for his honourable conduct, not for his electioneering skill; for, to do him justice, Coriolanus himself was not a worse electioneerer.

Enter Rory O'Ryan *and another Eton lad, carrying* Talbot *in a chair, followed by a crowd of Eton lads.*

Rory. By your *lave*, my lord—by your *lave*, ladies.

Omnes. Huzza! Talbot and truth for ever! Huzza!

Talb. Set me down! There's my mother! There's my sister!

Rory. Easy, easy. Set him down! No such *ting*! give him t'other huzza! There's nothing like a good loud huzza in this world. Yes, there is! for, as my Lord John said just now, out of some book or out of his own head—

One self-approving hour whole years outweighs
Of stupid starers and of loud huzzas.

CURTAIN FALLS

FORGIVE AND FORGET

In the neighbourhood of a seaport town in the west of England there lived a gardener, who had one son, called Maurice, to whom he was very partial. One day his father sent him to the neighbouring town to purchase some garden seeds for him. When Maurice got to the seed-shop, it was full of people, who were all impatient to be served: first a great tall man, and next a great fat woman pushed before him; and he stood quietly beside the counter, waiting till somebody should be at leisure to attend to him. At length, when all the other people who were in the shop had got what they wanted, the shopman turned to Maurice—'And what do you want, my patient little fellow?' said he.

'I want all these seeds for my father,' said Maurice, putting a list of seeds into the shopman's hand; 'and I have brought money to pay for them all.'

The seedsman looked out all the seeds that Maurice wanted, and packed them up in paper: he was folding up some painted lady-peas, when, from a door at the back of the shop, there came in a square, rough-faced man, who exclaimed, the moment he came in, 'Are the seeds I ordered ready?—The wind's fair—they ought to have been aboard yesterday. And my china jar, is it packed up and directed? where is it?'

'It is up there on the shelf over your head, sir,' answered the seedsman. 'It is very safe, you see; but we have not had time to pack it yet. It shall be done to-day; and we will get the seeds ready for you, sir, immediately.'

'Immediately! then stir about it. The seeds will not pack themselves up. Make haste, pray.' 'Immediately, sir, as soon as I have done up the parcel for this little boy.' 'What signifies the parcel for this little boy? He can wait, and I cannot—wind and tide wait for no man. Here, my good lad, take your parcel and sheer off,' said the impatient man; and, as he spoke, he took up the parcel of seeds from the counter, as the shopman stooped to look for a sheet of thick brown paper and packthread to tie it up.

The parcel was but loosely folded up, and as the impatient man lifted it, the weight of the peas which were withinside of it burst the paper, and all the seeds fell out upon the floor, whilst Maurice in vain held his hands to catch them. The peas rolled to all parts of the shop; the impatient man swore at them, but Maurice, without being out of humour, set about collecting them as fast as possible.

Whilst the boy was busied in this manner, the man got what seeds he wanted; and as he was talking about them, a sailor came into the shop, and said, 'Captain, the wind has changed within these five minutes, and it looks as if we should have ugly weather.'

'Well, I'm glad of it,' replied the rough-faced man, who was the captain of a ship. 'I am glad to have a day longer to stay ashore, and I've business enough on my hands.' The captain pushed forward towards the shop door. Maurice, who was kneeling on the floor, picking up his seeds, saw that the captain's foot was entangled in some packthread which hung down from the shelf on which the china jar stood. Maurice saw that, if the captain took one more step forward, he must pull the string, so that it would throw down the jar, round the bottom of which the packthread was entangled. He immediately caught hold of the captain's leg, and stopped him, 'Stay! Stand still, sir!' said he, 'or you will break your china jar.'

'Stay! Stand still, sir! or you will break your china jar.'

'Stay! Stand still, sir! or you will break your china jar.'

The man stood still, looked, and saw how the packthread had caught in his shoe buckle, and how it was near dragging down his beautiful china jar. 'I am really very much obliged to you, my little fellow,' said he. 'You have saved my jar, which I would not have broken for ten guineas, for it is for my wife, and I've brought it safe from abroad many a league. It would have been a pity if I had broken it just when it was safe landed. I am really much obliged to you, my little fellow, this was returning good for evil. I am sorry I threw down your seeds, as you are such a good-natured, forgiving boy. Be so kind,' continued he, turning to the shopman, 'as to reach down that china jar for me.'

The shopman lifted down the jar very carefully, and the captain took off the cover, and pulled out some tulip-roots. 'You seem, by the quantity of seeds you have got, to belong to a gardener. Are you fond of gardening?' said he to Maurice.

'Yes, sir,' replied Maurice, 'very fond of it; for my father is a gardener, and he lets me help him at his work, and he has given me a little garden of my own.'

'Then here are a couple of tulip-roots for you; and if you take care of them, I'll promise you that you will have the finest tulips in England in your little garden. These tulips were given to me by a Dutch merchant, who told me that they were some of the rarest and finest in Holland. They will prosper with you, I'm sure, wind and weather permitting.'

Maurice thanked the gentleman, and returned home, eager to show his precious tulip-roots to his father, and to a companion of his, the son of a nurseryman, who lived near him. Arthur was the name of the nurseryman's son.

The first thing Maurice did, after showing his tulip-roots to his father, was to run to Arthur's garden in search of him. Their gardens were separated only by a low wall of loose stones:—'Arthur! Arthur! where are you? Are you in your garden? I want you.' But Arthur made no answer, and did not, as usual, come running to meet his friend. 'I know where you are,' continued Maurice, 'and I'm coming to you as fast as the raspberry-bushes will let me. I have good news for you—something you'll be delighted to see, Arthur!—Ha!—but here is something that I am not delighted to see, I am sure,' said poor Maurice, who, when he had got through the raspberry-bushes, and had come in sight of his own garden, beheld his bell-glass—his beloved bell-glass, under which his cucumbers were grown so finely—his only bell-glass, broken to pieces!

'I am sorry for it,' said Arthur, who stood leaning upon his spade in his own garden; 'I am afraid you will be very angry with me.' 'Why, was it you, Arthur, broke my bell-glass? Oh, how could you do so?' 'I was throwing weeds and rubbish over the wall, and by accident a great lump of couch-grass, with stones hanging to the roots, fell upon your bell-glass, and broke it, as you see.'

Maurice lifted up the lump of couch-grass, which had fallen through the broken glass upon his cucumbers, and he looked at his cucumbers for a moment in silence—'Oh, my poor cucumbers! you must all die now. I shall see all your yellow flowers withered to-morrow; but it is done, and it cannot be helped; so, Arthur, let us say no more about it.'

'You are very good; I thought you would have been angry. I am sure I should have been exceedingly angry if you had broken the glass, if it had been mine.'

'Oh, forgive and forget, as my father always says; that's the best way. Look what I have got for you.' Then he told Arthur the story of the captain of the ship, and the china jar; the seeds having been thrown down, and of the fine tulip-roots which had been given to him; and Maurice concluded by offering one of the precious roots to Arthur, who thanked him with great joy, and repeatedly said, 'How good you were not to be angry with me for breaking your bell-glass! I am much more sorry for it than if you had been in a passion with me!'

Arthur now went to plant his tulip-root; and Maurice looked at the beds which his companion had been digging, and at all the things which were coming up in his garden.

'I don't know how it is,' said Arthur, 'but you always seem as glad to see the things in my garden coming up, and doing well, as if they were all your own. I am much happier since my father came to live here, and since you and I have been allowed to work and to play together, than I ever was before; for you must know, before we came to live here, I had a cousin in the house with me, who used to plague me. He was not nearly so good-natured as you are. He never took pleasure in looking at my garden, or at anything that I did that was well done; and he never gave me a share of anything that he had; and so I did not like him; how could I? But, I believe that hating people makes us unhappy; for I know I never was happy when I was quarrelling with him; and I am always happy with you, Maurice. You know we never quarrel.'

It would be well for all the world if they could be convinced, like Arthur, that to live in friendship is better than to quarrel. It would be well for all the world if they followed Maurice's maxim of 'Forgive and Forget,' when they receive, or when they imagine that they receive, an injury.

Arthur's father, Mr. Oakly, the nurseryman, was apt to take offence at trifles; and when he thought that any of his neighbours disobliged him, he was too proud to ask them to explain their conduct; therefore he was often mistaken in his judgment of them. He thought that it showed *spirit*, to remember and to resent an injury; and, therefore, though he was not an ill-natured man, he was sometimes led, by this mistaken idea of *spirit*, to do ill-natured things: 'A warm friend and a bitter enemy,' was one of his maxims, and he had many more enemies than friends. He was not very rich, but he was proud; and his favourite proverb was, 'Better live in spite than in pity.'

When first he settled near Mr. Grant, the gardener, he felt inclined to dislike him, because he was told that Mr. Grant was a Scotchman, and he had a prejudice against Scotchmen; all of whom he believed to be cunning and avaricious, because he had once been overreached by a Scotch peddler. Grant's friendly manners in some degree conquered this prepossession; but still he secretly suspected that *this civility*, as he said, '*was all show*, and *that he was not, nor could not, being a Scotchman, be such a hearty friend as a true-born Englishman.*'

Grant had some remarkably fine raspberries. The fruit was so large as to be quite a curiosity. When it was in season, many strangers came from the neighbouring town, which was a sea-bathing place, to look at these raspberries, which obtained the name of *Brobdingnag* raspberries.

'How came you, pray, neighbour Grant, if a man may ask, by these wonderful fine raspberries?' said Mr. Oakly, one evening, to the gardener. 'That's a secret,' replied Grant, with an arch smile.

'Oh, in case it's a secret, I've no more to say; for I never meddle with any man's secrets that he does not choose to trust me with. But I wish, neighbour Grant, you would put down that book. You are always poring over some book or another when a man comes to see you, which is not, according to my notions (being a plain, *unlarned* Englishman bred and born), so civil and neighbourly as might be.'

Mr. Grant hastily shut his book, but remarked, with a shrewd glance at his son, that it was in that book he found his Brobdingnag raspberries.

'You are pleased to be pleasant upon them that have not the luck to be as book-*larned* as yourself, Mr. Grant; but I take it, being only a plain-spoken Englishman, as I observed afore, that one is to the full as like to find a raspberry in one's garden as in one's book, Mr. Grant.'

Grant, observing that his neighbour spoke rather in a surly tone, did not contradict him; being well versed in the Bible, he knew that 'A soft word turneth away wrath,' and he answered, in a good-humoured voice, 'I hear, neighbour Oakly, you are likely to make a great deal of money of your nursery this year. Here's to the health of you and yours, not forgetting the seedling larches, which I see are coming on finely.'

'Thank ye, neighbour, kindly; the larches are coming on tolerably well, that's certain; and here's to your good health, Mr. Grant—you and yours, not forgetting your, what d'ye call 'em raspberries'—(*drinks*)—and, after a pause, resumes, 'I'm not apt to be a beggar, neighbour, but if you could give me——'

Here Mr. Oakly was interrupted by the entrance of some strangers, and he did not finish making his request—Mr. Oakly was not, as he said of himself, apt to ask favours, and nothing but Grant's cordiality could have conquered his prejudices so far as to tempt him to ask a favour from a Scotchman. He was going to have asked for some of the Brobdingnag raspberry-plants. The next day the thought of the raspberry-plants recurred to his memory, but, being a bashful man, he did not like to go himself on purpose to make his request, and he desired his wife, who was just setting out to market, to call at Grant's gate, and, if he was at work in his garden, to ask him for a few plants of his raspberries.

The answer which Oakly's wife brought to him was that Mr. Grant had not a raspberry-plant in the world to give him, and that if he had ever so many, he would not give one away, except to his own son.

Oakly flew into a passion when he received such a message, declared it was just such a mean, shabby trick as might have been expected from a Scotchman—called himself a booby, a dupe, and a blockhead, for ever having trusted to the civil speeches of a Scotchman—swore that he would die in the parish workhouse before he would ever ask another favour, be it ever so small, from a Scotchman; related to his wife, for the hundredth time, the way in which he had been taken in by the Scotch peddler ten years ago, and concluded by forswearing all further intercourse with Mr. Grant, and all belonging to him.

'Son Arthur,' said he, addressing himself to the boy, who just then came in from work—'Son Arthur, do you hear me? let me never again see you with Grant's son.' 'With Maurice, father?' 'With Maurice Grant, I say; I forbid you from this day and hour forward to have anything to do with him.' 'Oh, why, dear father?' 'Ask me no questions, but do as I bid you.'

Arthur burst out a-crying, and only said, 'Yes, father, I'll do as you bid me, to be sure.'

'Why now, what does the boy cry for? Is there no other boy, simpleton, think you, to play with, but this Scotchman's son? I'll find out another playfellow for ye, child, if that be all.' 'That's not all, father,' said Arthur, trying to stop himself from sobbing; 'but the thing is, I shall never have such another playfellow,—I shall never have such another friend as Maurice Grant.'

'Like father like son—you may think yourself well off to have done with him.' 'Done with him! Oh, father, and shall I never go again to work in his garden, and may not he come to mine?' 'No,' replied Oakly sturdily; 'his father has used me uncivil, and no man shall use me uncivil twice. I say no. Wife, sweep up this hearth. Boy, don't take on like a fool; but eat thy bacon and greens, and let's hear no more of Maurice Grant.'

Arthur promised to obey his father. He only begged that he might once more speak to Maurice, and tell him that it was by his father's orders he acted. This request was granted; but when Arthur further begged to know what reason he might give for this separation, his father refused to tell his reasons. The two friends took leave of one another very sorrowfully.

Mr. Grant, when he heard of all this, endeavoured to discover what could have offended his neighbour; but all explanation was prevented by the obstinate silence of Oakly.

Now, the message which Grant really sent about the Brobdingnag raspberries was somewhat different from that which Mr. Oakly received. The message was, that the raspberries were not Mr. Grant's; that therefore he had no right to give them away; that they belonged to his son Maurice, and that this was not the right time of year for planting them. This message had been unluckily misunderstood. Grant gave his answer to his wife; she to a Welsh servant-girl, who did not perfectly comprehend her mistress's broad Scotch; and she in her turn could not make herself intelligible to Mrs. Oakly, who hated the Welsh accent, and whose attention, when the servant-girl delivered the message, was principally engrossed by the management of her own horse. The horse on which Mrs. Oakly rode this day, being ill-broken, would not stand still quietly at the gate, and she was extremely impatient to receive her answer, and to ride on to market.

Oakly, when he had once resolved to dislike his neighbour Grant, could not long remain without finding out fresh causes of complaint. There was in Grant's garden a plum-tree, which was planted close to the loose stone wall that divided the garden from the nursery. The soil in which the plum-tree was planted happened not to be quite so good as that which was on the opposite side of the wall, and the plum-tree had forced its way through the wall, and gradually had taken possession of the ground which it liked best.

Oakly thought the plum-tree, as it belonged to Mr. Grant, had no right to make its appearance on his ground: an attorney told him that he might oblige Grant to cut it down; but Mr. Grant refused to cut down his plum-tree at the attorney's desire, and the attorney persuaded Oakly to go to law about the business, and the lawsuit went on for some months.

The attorney, at the end of this time, came to Oakly with a demand for money to carry on his suit, assuring him that, in a short time, it would be determined in his favour. Oakly paid his attorney ten golden guineas, remarked that it was a great sum for him to pay, and that nothing but the love of justice could make him persevere in this lawsuit about a bit of ground, 'which, after all,' said he, 'is not worth twopence. The plum-tree does me little or no damage, but I don't like to be imposed upon by a Scotchman.'

The attorney saw and took advantage of Oakly's prejudice against the natives of Scotland; and he persuaded him, that to show the *spirit* of a true-born Englishman it was necessary, whatever it might cost him, to persist in this lawsuit.

It was soon after this conversation with the attorney that Mr. Oakly walked with resolute steps towards the plum-tree, saying to himself, 'If it cost me a hundred pounds I will not let this cunning Scotchman get the better of me.'

Arthur interrupted his father's reverie by pointing to a book and some young plants which lay upon the wall. 'I fancy, father,' said he, 'those things are for you, for there is a little note directed to you in Maurice's handwriting. Shall I bring it to you?' 'Yes, let me read it, child, since I must.' It contained these words:

'Dear Mr. Oakly—I don't know why you have quarrelled with us; I am very sorry for it. But though you are angry with me, I am not angry with you. I hope you will not refuse some of my Brobdingnag raspberry-plants, which you asked for a great while ago, when we were all good friends. It was not the right time of the year to plant them, which was the reason they were not sent to you; but it is just the right time to plant them now; and I send you the book, in which you will find the reason why we always put seaweed ashes about their roots; and I have got some seaweed ashes for you. You will find the ashes in the flower-pot upon the wall. I have never spoken to Arthur, nor he to me, since you bid us not. So, wishing your Brobdingnag raspberries may turn out as well as ours, and longing to be all friends again, I am, with love to dear Arthur and self, your affectionate neighbour's son, Maurice Grant.

'P.S.—It is now about four months since the quarrel began, and that is a very long while.'

A great part of the effect of this letter was lost upon Oakly, because he was not very expert in reading writing, and it cost him much trouble to spell it and put it together. However, he seemed affected by it, and said, 'I believe this Maurice loves you well enough, Arthur, and he seems a good sort of boy; but as to the raspberries, I believe all that he says about them is but an excuse; and, at any rate, as I could not get 'em when I asked for them, I'll not have 'em now. Do you hear me, I say, Arthur? What are you reading there?'

Arthur was reading the page that was doubled down in the book which Maurice had left along with the raspberry-plants upon the wall. Arthur read aloud as follows:—

(*Monthly Magazine*, Dec. '98, p. 421.)

'There is a sort of strawberry cultivated at Jersey which is almost covered with seaweed in the winter, in like manner as many plants in England are with litter from the stable. These strawberries are usually of the largeness of a middle-sized apricot, and the flavour is particularly grateful. In Jersey and Guernsey, situate scarcely one degree farther south than Cornwall, all kinds of fruit, pulse, and vegetables are produced in their seasons a fortnight or three weeks sooner than in England, even on the southern shores; and snow will scarcely remain twenty-four hours on the earth. Although this may be attributed to these islands being surrounded with a salt, and consequently a moist atmosphere, yet the ashes (seaweed ashes) made use of as manure may also have their portion of influence.'12

'And here,' continued Arthur, 'is something written with a pencil, on a slip of paper, and it is Maurice's writing. I will read it to you.

'When I read in this book what is said about the strawberries growing as large as apricots, after they had been covered over with seaweed, I thought that perhaps seaweed ashes might be good for my father's raspberries; and I asked him if he would give me leave to try them. He gave me leave, and I went directly and gathered together some seaweed that had been cast on shore; and I dried it, and burned it, and then I manured the raspberries with it, and the year afterwards the raspberries grew to the size that you have seen. Now, the reason I tell you this is, first, that you may know how to manage your raspberries, and next, because I remember you looked very grave, as if you were not pleased with my father, Mr. Grant, when he told you that the way by which he came by his Brobdingnag raspberries was a secret. Perhaps this was the thing that has made you so angry with us all; for you never have come to see father since that evening. Now I have told you all I know; and so I hope you will not be angry with us any longer.'

Mr. Oakly was much pleased by this openness, and said, 'Why now, Arthur, this is something like, this is telling one the thing one wants to know, without fine speeches. This is like an Englishman more than a Scotchman. Pray, Arthur, do you know whether your friend Maurice was born in England or in Scotland?'

'No, indeed, sir, I don't know—I never asked—I did not think it signified. All I know is that, wherever he was born, he is *very* good. Look, papa, my tulip is blowing.' 'Upon my word,' said his father, 'this will be a beautiful tulip!' 'It was given to me by Maurice.' 'And did you give him nothing for it?' was the father's inquiry. 'Nothing in the world; and he gave it to me just at the time when he had good cause to be angry with me, just when I had broken his bell-glass.'

'I have a great mind to let you play together again,' said Arthur's father. 'Oh, if you would,' cried Arthur, clapping his hands, 'how happy we should be! Do you know, father, I have often sat for an hour at a time up in that crab-tree, looking at Maurice at work in his garden, and wishing that I was at work with him.'

Here Arthur was interrupted by the attorney, who came to ask Mr. Oakly some question about the lawsuit concerning the plum-tree. Oakly showed him Maurice's letter; and to Arthur's extreme astonishment, the attorney had no sooner read it than he exclaimed, 'What an artful little gentleman this is! I never, in the course of all my practice, met with anything better. Why, this is the most cunning letter I ever read.' 'Where's the cunning?' said Oakly, and he put on his spectacles. 'My good sir, don't you see that all this stuff about Brobdingnag raspberries is to ward off your suit about the plum-tree? They know—that is, Mr. Grant, who is sharp enough, knows—that he will be worsted in that suit; that he must, in short, pay you a good round sum for damages, if it goes on——'

'Damages!' said Oakly, staring round him at the plum-tree; 'but I don't know what you mean. I mean nothing but what's honest. I don't mean to ask for any good round sum; for the plum-tree has done me no great harm by coming into my garden; but only I don't choose it should come there without my leave.'

'Well, well,' said the attorney, 'I understand all that; but what I want to make you, Mr. Oakly, understand is, that this Grant and his son only want to make up matters with you, and prevent the thing's coming to a fair trial, by sending you, in this underhand sort of way, a bribe of a few raspberries.'

'A bribe!' exclaimed Oakly, 'I never took a bribe, and I never will'; and, with sudden indignation, he pulled the raspberry plants from the ground in which Arthur was planting them; and he threw them over the wall into Grant's garden.

Maurice had put his tulip, which was beginning to blow, in a flower-pot, on the top of the wall, in hopes that his friend Arthur would see it from day to day. Alas! he knew not in what a dangerous situation he had placed it. One of his own Brobdingnag raspberry-plants, swung by the angry arm of Oakly, struck off the head of his precious tulip! Arthur, who was full of the thought of convincing his father that the attorney was mistaken in his judgment of poor Maurice, did not observe the fall of the tulip.

The next day, when Maurice saw his raspberry-plants scattered upon the ground, and his favourite tulip broken, he was in much astonishment, and, for some moments, angry; but anger, with him, never lasted long. He was convinced that all this must be owing to some accident or mistake. He could not believe that any one could be so malicious as to injure him on purpose—'And even if they did all this on purpose to vex me,' said he to himself, 'the best thing I can do is not to let it vex me. Forgive and forget.' This temper of mind Maurice was more happy in enjoying than he could have been made, without it, by the possession of all the tulips in Holland.

Tulips were, at this time, things of great consequence in the estimation of the country several miles round where Maurice and Arthur lived. There was a florist's feast to be held at the neighbouring town, at which a prize of a handsome set of gardening tools was to be given to the person who could produce the finest flower of its kind. A tulip was the flower which was thought the finest the preceding year, and consequently numbers of people afterwards endeavoured to procure tulip-roots, in hopes of obtaining the prize this year. Arthur's tulip was beautiful. As he examined it from day to day, and every day thought it improving, he longed to thank his friend Maurice for it; and he often mounted into his crab-tree, to look into Maurice's garden, in hopes of seeing his tulip also in full bloom and beauty. He never could see it.

When Maurice saw his raspberry-plants scattered upon the ground, and his favourite tulip broken, he was in much astonishment.

When Maurice saw his raspberry-plants scattered upon the ground, and his favourite tulip broken, he was in much astonishment.

The day of the florist's feast arrived, and Oakly went with his son and the fine tulip to the place of meeting. It was on a spacious bowling-green. All the flowers of various sorts were ranged upon a terrace at the upper end of the bowling-green; and, amongst all this gay variety, the tulip which Maurice had given to Arthur appeared conspicuously beautiful. To the owner of this tulip the prize was adjudged; and, as the handsome garden-tools were delivered to Arthur, he heard a well-known voice wish him joy. He turned, looked about him, and saw his friend Maurice.

'But, Maurice, where is your own tulip?' said Mr. Oakly; 'I thought, Arthur, you told me that he kept one for himself.' 'So I did,' said Maurice; 'but somebody (I suppose by accident) broke it.' 'Somebody! who?' cried Arthur and Mr. Oakly at once. 'Somebody who threw the raspberry-plants back again over the wall,' replied Maurice. 'That was me—that somebody was me,' said Oakly. 'I scorn to deny it; but I did not intend to break your tulip, Maurice.'

'Dear Maurice,' said Arthur—'you know I may call him dear Maurice—now you are by, papa; here are all the garden-tools; take them, and welcome.' 'Not one of them,' said Maurice, drawing back. 'Offer them to the father—offer them to Mr. Grant,' whispered Oakly; 'he'll take them, I'll answer for it.'

Mr. Oakly was mistaken: the father would not accept of the tools. Mr. Oakly stood surprised—'Certainly,' said he to himself, 'this cannot be such a miser as I took him for'; and he walked immediately up to Grant, and bluntly said to him, 'Mr. Grant, your son has behaved very handsomely to my son, and you seem to be glad of it.' 'To be sure I am,' said Grant. 'Which,' continued Oakly, 'gives me a better opinion of you than ever I had before—I mean, than ever I had since the day you sent me the shabby answer about those foolish, what d'ye call 'em, cursed raspberries.'

'What shabby answer?' said Grant, with surprise; and Oakly repeated exactly the message which he received; and Grant declared that he never sent any such message. He repeated exactly the answer which he really sent, and Oakly immediately stretched out his hand to him, saying, 'I believe you; no more need be said. I'm only sorry I did not ask you about this four months ago; and so I should have done if you had not been a Scotchman. Till now, I never rightly liked a Scotchman. We may thank this good little fellow,' continued he, turning to Maurice, 'for our coming at last to a right understanding. There was no holding out against his good nature. I'm sure, from the bottom of my heart, I'm sorry I broke his tulip. Shake hands, boys; I'm glad to see you, Arthur, look so happy again, and hope Mr. Grant will forgive——' 'Oh, forgive and forget,' said Grant and his son at the same moment. And from this time forward the two families lived in friendship with each other.

Oakly laughed at his own folly, in having been persuaded to go to law about the plum-tree; and he, in process of time, so completely conquered his early prejudice against Scotchmen, that he and Grant became partners in business. Mr. Grant's book-*larning* and knowledge of arithmetic he found highly useful to him; and he, on his side, possessed a great many active, good qualities, which became serviceable to his partner.

The two boys rejoiced in this family union; and Arthur often declared that they owed all their happiness to Maurice's favourite maxim, 'Forgive and Forget.'

WASTE NOT, WANT NOT;
OR,
TWO STRINGS TO YOUR BOW

Mr. Gresham, a Bristol merchant, who had, by honourable industry and economy, accumulated a considerable fortune, retired from business to a new house which he had built upon the Downs, near Clifton. Mr. Gresham, however, did not imagine that a new house alone could make him happy. He did not propose to live in idleness and extravagance; for such a life would have been equally incompatible with his habits and his principles. He was fond of children; and as he had no sons, he determined to adopt one of his relations. He had two nephews, and he invited both of them to his house, that he might have an opportunity of judging of their dispositions, and of the habits which they had acquired.

Hal and Benjamin, Mr. Gresham's nephews, were about ten years old. They had been educated very differently. Hal was the son of the elder branch of the family. His father was a gentleman, who spent rather more than he could afford; and Hal, from the example of the servants in his father's family, with whom he had passed the first years of his childhood, learned to waste more of everything than he used. He had been told that 'gentlemen should be above being careful and saving'; and he had unfortunately imbibed a notion that extravagance was the sign of a generous disposition, and economy of an avaricious one.

Benjamin, on the contrary, had been taught habits of care and foresight. His father had but a very small fortune, and was anxious that his son should early learn that economy ensures independence, and sometimes puts it in the power of those who are not very rich to be very generous.

The morning after these two boys arrived at their uncle's they were eager to see all the rooms in the house. Mr. Gresham accompanied them, and attended to their remarks and exclamations.

'Oh! what an excellent motto!' exclaimed Ben, when he read the following words, which were written in large characters over the chimneypiece in his uncle's spacious kitchen—

'WASTE NOT, WANT NOT.'

'"Waste not, want not!"' repeated his cousin Hal, in rather a contemptuous tone; 'I think it looks stingy to servants; and no gentleman's servants, cooks especially, would like to have such a mean motto always staring them in the face.' Ben, who was not so conversant as his cousin in the ways of cooks and gentlemen's servants, made no reply to these observations.

Mr. Gresham was called away whilst his nephews were looking at the other rooms in the house. Some time afterwards, he heard their voices in the hall.

'Boys,' said he, 'what are you doing there?' 'Nothing, sir,' said Hal; 'you were called away from us and we did not know which way to go.' 'And have you nothing to do?' said Mr. Gresham. 'No, sir, nothing,' answered Hal, in a careless tone, like one who was well content with the state of habitual idleness. 'No, sir, nothing!' replied Ben, in a voice of lamentation. 'Come,' said Mr. Gresham, 'if you have nothing to do, lads, will you unpack those two parcels for me?'

The two parcels were exactly alike, both of them well tied up with good whipcord. Ben took his parcel to a table, and, after breaking off the sealing-wax, began carefully to examine the knot, and then to untie it. Hal stood still, exactly in the spot where the parcel was put into his hands, and tried, first at one corner and then at another, to pull the string off by force. 'I wish these people wouldn't tie up their parcels so tight, as if they were never to be undone,' cried he, as he tugged at the cord; and he pulled the knot closer instead of loosening it.

'Ben! why, how did you get yours undone, man? what's in your parcel?—I wonder what is in mine! I wish I could get this string off—I must cut it.'

'Oh no,' said Ben, who now had undone the last knot of his parcel, and who drew out the length of string with exultation, 'don't cut it, Hal,—look what a nice cord this is, and yours is the same; it's a pity to cut it; "*Waste not, want not!*" you know.'

'Pooh!' said Hal, 'what signifies a bit of packthread?' 'It is whipcord,' said Ben. 'Well, whipcord! what signifies a bit of whipcord! you can get a bit of whipcord twice as long as that for twopence; and who cares for twopence? Not I, for one! so here it goes,' cried Hal, drawing out his knife; and he cut the cord, precipitately, in sundry places.

'Lads, have you undone the parcels for me?' said Mr. Gresham, opening the parlour door as he spoke. 'Yes, sir,' cried Hal; and he dragged off his half-cut, half-entangled string—'here's the parcel.' 'And here's my parcel, uncle; and here's the string,' said Ben. 'You may keep the string for your pains,' said Mr. Gresham. 'Thank you, sir,' said Ben; 'what an excellent whipcord it is!' 'And you, Hal,' continued Mr. Gresham, 'you may keep your string too, if it will be of any use to you.' 'It will be of no use to me, thank you, sir,' said Hal. 'No, I am afraid not, if this be it,' said his uncle, taking up the jagged knotted remains of Hal's cord.

A few days after this, Mr. Gresham gave to each of his nephews a new top.

'But how's this?' said Hal; 'these tops have no strings; what shall we do for strings?' 'I have a string that will do very well for mine,' said Ben; and he pulled out of his pocket the fine, long, smooth string which had tied up the parcel. With this he soon set up his top, which spun admirably well.

'Oh, how I wish I had but a string,' said Hal. 'What shall I do for a string? I'll tell you what, I can use the string that goes round my hat!' 'But then,' said Ben, 'what will you do for a hat-band?' 'I'll manage to do without one,' said Hal, and he took the string off his hat for his top. It soon was worn through; and he split his top by driving the peg too tightly into it. His cousin Ben let him set up his the next day; but Hal was not more fortunate or more careful when he meddled with other people's things than when he managed his own. He had scarcely played half an hour before he split it, by driving the peg too violently.

Ben bore this misfortune with good humour. 'Come,' said he, 'it can't be helped; but give me the string, because *that* may still be of use for something else.'

It happened some time afterwards that a lady, who had been intimately acquainted with Hal's mother at Bath—that is to say, who had frequently met her at the card-table during the winter—now arrived at Clifton. She was informed by his mother that Hal was at Mr. Gresham's, and her sons, who were *friends* of his, came to see him, and invited him to spend the next day with them.

Hal joyfully accepted the invitation. He was always glad to go out to dine, because it gave him something to do, something to think of, or at least something to say. Besides this, he had been educated to think it was a fine thing to visit fine people; and Lady Diana Sweepstakes (for that was the name of his mother's acquaintance) was a very fine lady, and her two sons intended to be very *great* gentlemen. He was in a prodigious hurry when these young gentlemen knocked at his uncle's door the next day; but just as he got to the hall door, little Patty called to him from the top of the stairs, and told him that he had dropped his pocket-handkerchief.

'Pick it up, then, and bring it to me, quick, can't you, child?' cried Hal, 'for Lady Di's sons are waiting for me.'

Little Patty did not know anything about Lady Di's sons; but as she was very good-natured, and saw that her cousin Hal was, for some reason or other, in a desperate hurry, she ran downstairs as fast as she possibly could towards the landing-place, where the handkerchief lay; but, alas! before she reached the handkerchief, she fell, rolling down a whole flight of stairs, and when her fall was at last stopped by the landing-place, she did not cry out, she writhed, as if she was in great pain.

'Where are you hurt, my love?' said Mr. Gresham, who came instantly, on hearing the noise of some one falling downstairs. 'Where are you hurt, my dear?'

'Here, papa,' said the little girl, touching her ankle, which she had decently covered with her gown. 'I believe I am hurt here, but not much,' added she, trying to rise; 'only it hurts me when I move.' 'I'll carry you; don't move then,' said her father, and he took her up in his arms. 'My shoe! I've lost one of my shoes,' said she.

Ben looked for it upon the stairs, and he found it sticking in a loop of whipcord, which was entangled round one of the banisters. When this cord was drawn forth, it appeared that it was the very same jagged, entangled piece which Hal had pulled off his parcel. He had diverted himself with running up and down stairs, whipping the banisters with it, as he thought he could convert it to no better use; and, with his usual carelessness, he at last left it hanging just where he happened to throw it when the dinner bell rang. Poor little Patty's ankle was terribly strained, and Hal reproached himself for his folly, and would have reproached himself longer, perhaps, if Lady Di Sweepstakes' sons had not hurried him away.

In the evening, Patty could not run about as she used to do; but she sat upon the sofa, and she said that she did not feel the pain of her ankle *so much* whilst Ben was so good as to play at *jack straws* with her.

'That's right, Ben; never be ashamed of being good-natured to those who are younger and weaker than yourself,' said his uncle, smiling at seeing him produce his whipcord, to indulge his little cousin with a game at her favourite cat's cradle. 'I shall not think you one bit less manly, because I see you playing at cat's cradle with a little child of six years old.'

Hal, however, was not precisely of his uncle's opinion; for when he returned in the evening, and saw Ben playing with his little cousin, he could not help smiling contemptuously, and asked if he had been playing at cat's cradle all night. In a heedless manner he made some inquiries after Patty's sprained ankle, and then he ran on to tell all the news he had heard at Lady Diana Sweepstakes'—news which he thought would make him appear a person of vast importance.

'Do you know, uncle—do you know, Ben,' said he, 'there's to be the most *famous* doings that ever were heard of upon the Downs here, the first day of next month, which will be in a fortnight, thank my stars! I wish the fortnight was over; I shall think of nothing else, I know, till that happy day comes!'

Mr. Gresham inquired why the first of September was to be so much happier than any other day in the year. 'Why,' replied Hal, 'Lady Diana Sweepstakes, you know, is a *famous* rider, and archer, and *all that*——' 'Very likely,' said Mr. Gresham, soberly; 'but what then?'

Playing at cat's cradle.

Playing at cat's cradle.

'Dear uncle!' cried Hal, 'but you shall hear. There's to be a race upon the Downs on the first of September, and after the race, there's to be an archery meeting for the ladies, and Lady Diana Sweepstakes is to be one of *them*. And after the ladies have done shooting—now, Ben, comes the best part of it!—we boys are to have our turn, and Lady Di is to give a prize to the best marksman amongst us, of a very handsome bow and arrow. Do you know, I've been practising already, and I'll show you, to-morrow, as soon as it comes home, the *famous* bow and arrow that Lady Diana has given me; but, perhaps,' added he, with a scornful laugh, 'you like a cat's cradle better than a bow and arrow.'

Ben made no reply to this taunt at the moment; but the next day, when Hal's new bow and arrow came home, he convinced him that he knew how to use it very well.

'Ben,' said his uncle, 'you seem to be a good marksman, though you have not boasted of yourself. I'll give you a bow and arrow, and, perhaps, if you practise, you may make yourself an archer before the first of September; and, in the meantime, you will not wish the fortnight to be over, for you will have something to do.'

'Oh, sir,' interrupted Hal, 'but if you mean that Ben should put in for the prize, he must have a uniform.' 'Why *must* he?' said Mr. Gresham. 'Why, sir, because everybody has—I mean everybody that's anybody; and Lady Diana was talking about the uniform all dinner time, and it's settled, all about it, except the buttons: the young Sweepstakes are to get theirs made first for patterns—they are to be white, faced with green, and they'll look very handsome, I'm sure; and I shall write to mamma to-night, as Lady Diana bid me, about mine; and I shall tell her to be sure to answer my letter, without fail, by return of post; and then, if mamma makes no objection, which I know she won't, because she never thinks much about expense, and *all that*—then I shall bespeak my uniform, and get it made by the same tailor that makes for Lady Diana and the young Sweepstakes.'

91

'Mercy upon us!' said Mr. Gresham, who was almost stunned by the rapid vociferation with which this long speech about a uniform was pronounced. 'I don't pretend to understand these things,' added he, with an air of simplicity; 'but we will inquire, Ben, into the necessity of the case; and if it is necessary—or, if you think it necessary, that you shall have a uniform—why, I'll give you one.'

'*You*, uncle? Will you, *indeed*?' exclaimed Hal, with amazement painted in his countenance. 'Well that's the last thing in the world I should have expected! You are not at all the sort of person I should have thought would care about a uniform; and now I should have supposed you'd have thought it extravagant to have a coat on purpose only for one day; and I'm sure Lady Diana Sweepstakes thought as I do; for when I told her of that motto over your kitchen chimney, 'WASTE NOT, WANT NOT,' she laughed, and said that I had better not talk to you about uniforms, and that my mother was the proper person to write to about my uniform; but I'll tell Lady Diana, uncle, how good you are, and how much she was mistaken.'

'Take care how you do that,' said Mr. Gresham; 'for perhaps the lady was not mistaken.' 'Nay, did not you say, just now, you would give poor Ben a uniform?' 'I said I would, if he thought it necessary to have one.' 'Oh, I'll answer for it, he'll think it necessary,' said Hal, laughing, 'because it is necessary.' 'Allow him, at least, to judge for himself,' said Mr. Gresham. 'My dear uncle, but I assure you,' said Hal, earnestly, 'there's no judging about the matter, because really, upon my word, Lady Diana said distinctly that her sons were to have uniforms, white faced with green, and a green and white cockade in their hats.' 'May be so,' said Mr. Gresham, still with the same look of calm simplicity; 'put on your hats, boys, and come with me. I know a gentleman whose sons are to be at this archery meeting, and we will inquire into all the particulars from him. Then, after we have seen him (it is not eleven o'clock yet), we shall have time enough to walk on to Bristol, and choose the cloth for Ben's uniform, if it is necessary.'

'I cannot tell what to make of all he says,' whispered Hal, as he reached down his hat; 'do you think, Ben, he means to give you this uniform, or not?' 'I think,' said Ben, 'that he means to give me one, if it is necessary; or, as he said, if I think it is necessary.'

'And that to be sure you will; won't you? or else you'll be a great fool, I know, after all I've told you. How can any one in the world know so much about the matter as I, who have dined with Lady Diana Sweepstakes but yesterday, and heard all about it from beginning to end? And as for this gentleman that we are going to, I'm sure, if he knows anything about the matter, he'll say exactly the same as I do.' 'We shall hear,' said Ben, with a degree of composure which Hal could by no means comprehend when a uniform was in question.

The gentleman upon whom Mr. Gresham called had three sons, who were all to be at this archery meeting; and they unanimously assured him, in the presence of Hal and Ben, that they had never thought of buying uniforms for this grand occasion, and that, amongst the number of their acquaintance, they knew of but three boys whose friends intended to be at such an *unnecessary* expense. Hal stood amazed.

'Such are the varieties of opinion upon all the grand affairs of life,' said Mr. Gresham, looking at his nephews. 'What amongst one set of people you hear asserted to be absolutely necessary, you will hear from another set of people is quite unnecessary. All that can be done, my dear boys, in these difficult cases, is to judge for yourselves which opinions and which people are the most reasonable.'

Hal, who had been more accustomed to think of what was fashionable than of what was reasonable, without at all considering the good sense of what his uncle said to him, replied, with childish petulance, 'Indeed, sir, I don't know what other people think; but I only know what Lady Diana Sweepstakes said.' The name of Lady Diana Sweepstakes, Hal thought, must impress all present with respect; he was highly astonished when, as he looked round, he saw a smile of contempt upon every one's countenance; and he was yet further bewildered when he heard her spoken of as a very silly, extravagant, ridiculous woman, whose opinion no prudent person would ask upon any subject, and whose example was to be shunned instead of being imitated.

'Ay, my dear Hal,' said his uncle, smiling at his look of amazement, 'these are some of the things that young people must learn from experience. All the world do not agree in opinion about characters: you will hear the same person admired in one company and blamed in another; so that we must still come round to the same point, *Judge for yourself*.'

Hal's thoughts were, however, at present too full of the uniform to allow his judgment to act with perfect impartiality. As soon as their visit was over, and all the time they walked down the hill from Prince's Buildings towards Bristol, he continued to repeat nearly the same arguments which he had formerly used respecting necessity, the uniform, and Lady Diana Sweepstakes. To all this Mr. Gresham made no reply, and longer had the young gentleman expatiated upon the subject, which had so strongly seized upon his imagination, had not his senses been forcibly assailed at this instant by the delicious odours and tempting sight of certain cakes and jellies in a pastrycook's shop. 'Oh, uncle,' said he, as his uncle was going to turn the corner to pursue the road to Bristol, 'look at those jellies!' pointing to a confectioner's shop. 'I must buy some of those good things, for I have got some halfpence in my pocket.' 'Your having halfpence in your pocket is an excellent reason for eating,' said Mr. Gresham, smiling. 'But I really am hungry,' said Hal; 'you know, uncle, it is a good while since breakfast.'

His uncle, who was desirous to see his nephews act without restraint, that he might judge their characters, bid them do as they pleased.

'Come, then, Ben, if you've any halfpence in your pocket.' 'I'm not hungry,' said Ben. 'I suppose *that* means that you've no halfpence,' said Hal, laughing, with the look of superiority which he had been taught to think *the rich* might assume towards those who were convicted either of poverty or economy. 'Waste not, want not,' said Ben to himself. Contrary to his cousin's surmise, he happened to have two pennyworth of halfpence actually in his pocket.

At the very moment Hal stepped into the pastrycook's shop, a poor, industrious man, with a wooden leg, who usually sweeps the dirty corner of the walk which turns at this spot to the Wells, held his hat to Ben, who, after glancing his eye at the petitioner's well-worn broom, instantly produced his twopence. 'I wish I had more halfpence for you, my good man,' said he; 'but I've only twopence.'

Hal came out of Mr. Millar's, the confectioner's shop, with a hatful of cakes in his hand. Mr. Millar's dog was sitting on the flags before the door, and he looked up with a wistful, begging eye at Hal, who was eating a queen-cake. Hal, who was wasteful even in his good-nature, threw a whole queen-cake to the dog, who swallowed it for a single mouthful.

'There goes twopence in the form of a queen-cake,' said Mr. Gresham.

Hal next offered some of his cakes to his uncle and cousin; but they thanked him, and refused to eat any, because, they said, they were not hungry; so he ate and ate as he walked along, till at last he stopped and said, 'This bun tastes so bad after the queen-cakes, I can't bear it!' and he was going to fling it from him into the river. 'Oh, it is a pity to waste that good bun; we may be glad of it yet,' said Ben; 'give it me rather than throw it away.' 'Why, I thought you said you were not hungry,' said Hal. 'True, I am not hungry now; but that is no reason why I should never be hungry again.' 'Well, there is the cake for you. Take it; for it has made me sick, and I don't care what becomes of it.'

Ben folded the refuse bit of his cousin's bun in a piece of paper, and put it into his pocket.

'I'm beginning to be exceeding tired or sick or something,' said Hal; 'and as there is a stand of coaches somewhere hereabouts, had we not better take a coach, instead of walking all the way to Bristol?'

'For a stout archer,' said Mr. Gresham, 'you are more easily tired than one might have expected. However, with all my heart, let us take a coach, for Ben asked me to show him the cathedral yesterday; and I believe I should find it rather too much for me to walk so far, though I am not sick with eating good things.'

The cathedral!' said Hal, after he had been seated in the coach about a quarter of an hour, and had somewhat recovered from his sickness—'the cathedral! Why, are we only going to Bristol to see the cathedral? I thought we came out to see about a uniform.'

There was a dulness and melancholy kind of stupidity in Hal's countenance as he pronounced these words, like one wakening from a dream, which made both his uncle and his cousin burst out a-laughing.

'Why,' said Hal, who was now piqued, 'I'm sure you *did* say, uncle, you would go to Mr. Hall's to choose the cloth for the uniform.' 'Very true, and so I will,' said Mr. Gresham; 'but we need not make a whole morning's work, need we, of looking at a piece of cloth? Cannot we see a uniform and a cathedral both in one morning?'

They went first to the cathedral. Hal's head was too full of the uniform to take any notice of the painted window, which immediately caught Ben's embarrassed attention. He looked at the large stained figures on the Gothic window, and he observed their coloured shadows on the floor and walls.

Mr. Gresham, who perceived that he was eager on all subjects to gain information, took this opportunity of telling him several things about the lost art of painting on glass, Gothic arches, etc., which Hal thought extremely tiresome.

'Come! come! we shall be late indeed,' said Hal; 'surely you've looked long enough, Ben, at this blue and red window.' 'I'm only thinking about these coloured shadows,' said Ben. 'I can show you when we go home, Ben,' said his uncle, 'an entertaining paper upon such shadows.'13 'Hark!' cried Ben, 'did you hear that noise?' They all listened; and they heard a bird singing in the cathedral. 'It's our old robin, sir,' said the lad who had opened the cathedral door for them.

'Yes,' said Mr. Gresham, 'there he is, boys—look—perched upon the organ; he often sits there, and sings, whilst the organ is playing.' 'And,' continued the lad who showed the cathedral, 'he has lived here these many, many winters. They say he is fifteen years old; and he is so tame, poor fellow! that if I had a bit of bread he'd come down and feed in my hand.' 'I've a bit of bun here,' cried Ben joyfully, producing the remains of the bun which Hal but an hour before would have thrown away. 'Pray, let us see the poor robin eat out of your hand.'

The lad crumbled the bun, and called to the robin, who fluttered and chirped, and seemed rejoiced at the sight of the bread; but yet he did not come down from his pinnacle on the organ.

'He is afraid of *us*,' said Ben; 'he is not used to eat before strangers, I suppose.'

'Ah, no, sir,' said the young man, with a deep sigh, 'that is not the thing. He is used enough to eat afore company. Time was he'd have come down for me before ever so many fine folks, and have eat his crumbs out of my hand, at my first call; but, poor fellow! it's not his fault now. He does not know me now, sir, since my accident, because of this great black patch.' The young man put his hand to his right eye, which was covered with a huge black patch. Ben asked what *accident* he meant; and the lad told him that, but a few weeks ago, he had lost the sight of his eye by the stroke of a stone, which reached him as he was passing under the rocks at Clifton, unluckily when the workmen were blasting. 'I don't mind so much for myself, sir,' said the lad; 'but I can't work so well now, as I used to do before my accident, for my old mother, who has had a *stroke* of the palsy; and I've a many little brothers and sisters not well able yet to get their own livelihood, though they be as willing as willing can be.'

'Where does your mother live?' said Mr. Gresham. 'Hard by, sir, just close to the church here: it was *her* that always had the showing of it to strangers, till she lost the use of her poor limbs.'

'Shall we, may we, uncle, go that way? This is the house; is not it?' said Ben, when they went out of the cathedral.

They went into the house; it was rather a hovel than a house; but, poor as it was, it was as neat as misery could make it. The old woman was sitting up in her wretched bed, winding worsted; four meagre, ill-clothed, pale children, were all busy, some of them sticking pins in paper for the pin-maker, and others sorting rags for the paper-maker.

'What a horrid place it is!' said Hal, sighing; 'I did not know there were such shocking places in the world. I've often seen terrible-looking, tumble-down places, as we drove through the town in mamma's carriage; but then I did not know who lived in them; and I never saw the inside of any of them. It is very dreadful, indeed, to think that people are forced to live in this way. I wish mamma would send me some more pocket-money, that I might do something for them. I had half a crown; but,' continued he, feeling in his pockets, 'I'm afraid I spent the last shilling of it this morning upon those cakes that made me sick. I wish I had my shilling now, I'd give it to *these poor people*.'

Ben, though he was all this time silent, was as sorry as his talkative cousin for all these poor people. But there was some difference between the sorrow of these two boys.

Hal, after he was again seated in the hackney-coach, and had rattled through the busy streets of Bristol for a few minutes, quite forgot the spectacle of misery which he had seen; and the gay shops in Wine Street and the idea of his green and white uniform wholly occupied his imagination.

'Now for our uniforms!' cried he, as he jumped eagerly out of the coach, when his uncle stopped at the woollen-draper's door.

'Uncle,' said Ben, stopping Mr. Gresham before he got out of the carriage, 'I don't think a uniform is at all necessary for me. I'm very much obliged to you; but I would rather not have one. I have a very good coat, and I think it would be waste.'

'Well, let me get out of the carriage, and we will see about it,' said Mr. Gresham; 'perhaps the sight of the beautiful green and white cloth, and the epaulette (have you ever considered the epaulettes?) may tempt you to change your mind.' 'Oh no,' said Ben, laughing; 'I shall not change my mind.'

The green cloth, and the white cloth, and the epaulettes were produced, to Hal's infinite satisfaction. His uncle took up a pen, and calculated for a few minutes; then, showing the back of the letter, upon which he was writing, to his nephews, 'Cast up these sums, boys,' said he, 'and tell me whether I am right.' 'Ben, do you do it,' said Hal, a little embarrassed; 'I am not quick at figures.' Ben *was*, and he went over his uncle's calculation very expeditiously.

'It is right, is it?' said Mr. Gresham. 'Yes, sir, quite right.' 'Then, by this calculation, I find I could, for less than half the money your uniforms would cost, purchase for each of you boys a warm greatcoat, which you will want, I have a notion, this winter upon the Downs.'

'Oh, sir,' said Hal, with an alarmed look; 'but it is not winter *yet*; it is not cold weather *yet*. We shan't want greatcoats *yet*.'

'Don't you remember how cold we were, Hal, the day before yesterday, in that sharp wind, when we were flying our kite upon the Downs? and winter will come, though it is not come yet—I am sure, I should like to have a good warm greatcoat very much.'

Mr. Gresham took six guineas out of his purse; and he placed three of them before Hal, and three before Ben. 'Young gentlemen,' said he, 'I believe your uniforms would come to about three guineas apiece. Now I will lay out this money for you just as you please. Hal, what say you?' 'Why, sir,' said Hal, 'a greatcoat is a good thing, to be sure; and then, after the greatcoat, as you said it would only cost half as much as the uniform, there would be some money to spare, would not there?' 'Yes, my dear, about five-and-twenty shillings.' 'Five-and-twenty shillings?—I could buy and do a great many things, to be sure, with five-and-twenty shillings; but then, *the thing is*, I must go without the uniform, if I have the greatcoat.' 'Certainly,' said his uncle. 'Ah!' said Hal, sighing, as he looked at the epaulette, 'uncle, if you would not be displeased, if I choose the uniform——' 'I shall not be displeased at your choosing whatever you like best,' said Mr. Gresham.

'Well, then, thank you, sir,' said Hal; 'I think I had better have the uniform, because, if I have not the uniform, now, directly, it will be of no use to me, as the archery meeting is the week after next, you know; and, as to the greatcoat, perhaps between this time and the *very* cold weather, which, perhaps, won't be till Christmas, papa will buy a greatcoat for me; and I'll ask mamma to give me some pocket-money to give away, and she will, perhaps.' To all this conclusive, conditional reasoning, which depended upon the word *perhaps*, three times repeated, Mr. Gresham made no reply; but he immediately bought the uniform for Hal, and desired that it should be sent to Lady Diana Sweepstakes' son's tailor, to be made up. The measure of Hal's happiness was now complete.

'And how am I to lay out the three guineas for you, Ben?' said Mr. Gresham; 'speak, what do you wish for first?' 'A greatcoat, uncle, if you please.' Mr. Gresham bought the coat; and, after it was paid for, five-and-twenty shillings of Ben's three guineas remained. 'What next, my boy?' said his uncle. 'Arrows, uncle, if you please; three arrows.' 'My dear, I promised you a bow and arrows.' 'No, uncle, you only said a bow.' 'Well, I meant a bow and arrows. I'm glad you are so exact, however. It is better to claim less than more than what is promised. The three arrows you shall have. But go on; how shall I dispose of these five-and-twenty shillings for you?' 'In clothes, if you will be so good, uncle, for that poor boy who has the great black patch on his eye.'

'I always believed,' said Mr. Gresham, shaking hands with Ben, 'that economy and generosity were the best friends, instead of being enemies, as some silly, extravagant people would have us think them. Choose the poor, blind boy's coat, my dear nephew, and pay for it. There's no occasion for my praising you about the matter. Your best reward is in your own mind, child; and you want no other, or I'm mistaken. Now, jump into the coach, boys, and let's be off. We shall be late, I'm afraid,' continued he, as the coach drove on; 'but I must let you stop, Ben, with your goods, at the poor boy's door.'

When they came to the house, Mr. Gresham opened the coach door, and Ben jumped out with his parcel under his arm.

'Stay, stay! you must take me with you,' said his pleased uncle; 'I like to see people made happy as well as you do.' 'And so do I, too,' said Hal; 'let me come with you. I almost wish my uniform was not gone to the tailor's, so I do.' And when he saw the look of delight and gratitude with which the poor boy received the clothes which Ben gave him, and when he heard the mother and children thank him, Hal sighed, and said, 'Well, I hope mamma will give me some more pocket-money soon.'

Upon his return home, however, the sight of the *famous* bow and arrow, which Lady Diana Sweepstakes had sent him, recalled to his imagination all the joys of his green and white uniform; and he no longer wished that it had not been sent to the tailor's. 'But I don't understand, Cousin Hal,' said little Patty, 'why you call this bow a *famous* bow. You say *famous* very often; and I don't know exactly what it means; a *famous* uniform—*famous* doings. I remember you said there are to be *famous* doings, the first of September, upon the Downs. What does *famous* mean?' 'Oh, why, *famous* means—now, don't you know what *famous* means? It means—it is a word that people say—it is the fashion to say it—it means—it means *famous*.' Patty laughed, and said, '*This* does not explain it to me.'

'No,' said Hal, 'nor can it be explained: if you don't understand it, that's not my fault. Everybody but little children, I suppose, understands it; but there's no explaining *those sort* of words, if you don't *take them* at once. There's to be *famous* doings upon the Downs, the first of September; that is grand, fine. In short, what does it signify talking any longer, Patty, about the matter? Give me my bow, for I must go out upon the Downs and practise.'

Ben accompanied him with the bow and the three arrows which his uncle had now given to him; and, every day, these two boys went out upon the Downs and practised shooting with indefatigable perseverance. Where equal pains are taken, success is usually found to be pretty nearly equal. Our two archers, by constant practice, became expert marksmen; and before the day of trial, they were so exactly matched in point of dexterity, that it was scarcely possible to decide which was superior.

The long-expected 1st of September at length arrived. 'What sort of a day is it?' was the first question that was asked by Hal and Ben the moment that they wakened. The sun shone bright, but there was a sharp and high wind. 'Ha!' said Ben, 'I shall be glad of my good greatcoat to-day; for I've a notion it will be rather cold upon the Downs, especially when we are standing still, as we must, whilst all the people are shooting.' 'Oh, never mind! I don't think I shall feel it cold at all,' said Hal, as he dressed himself in his new green and white uniform; and he viewed himself with much complacency.

'Good morning to you, uncle; how do you do?' said he, in a voice of exultation, when he entered the breakfast-room. How do you do? seemed rather to mean 'How do you like me in my uniform?' And his uncle's cool 'Very well, I thank you, Hal,' disappointed him, as it seemed only to say, 'Your uniform makes no difference in my opinion of you.'

Even little Patty went on eating her breakfast much as usual, and talked of the pleasure of walking with her father to the Downs, and of all the little things which interested her; so that Hal's epaulettes were not the principal object in any one's imagination but his own.

'Papa,' said Patty, 'as we go up the hill where there is so much red mud, I must take care to pick my way nicely; and I must hold up my frock, as you desired me, and, perhaps, you will be so good, if I am not troublesome, to lift me over the very bad place where are no stepping-stones. My ankle is entirely well, and I'm glad of that, or else I should not be able to walk so far as the Downs. How good you were to me, Ben, when I was in pain the day I sprained my ankle! You played at jack straws and at cat's cradle with me. Oh, that puts me in mind—here are your gloves which I asked you that night to let me mend. I've been a great while about them; but are not they very neatly mended, papa? Look at the sewing.'

'I am not a very good judge of sewing, my dear little girl,' said Mr. Gresham, examining the work with a close and scrupulous eye; 'but, in my opinion, here is one stitch that is rather too long. The white teeth are not quite even.' 'Oh, papa, I'll take out that long tooth in a minute,' said Patty, laughing; 'I did not think that you would observe it so soon.'

'I would not have you trust to my blindness,' said her father, stroking her head fondly; 'I observe everything. I observe, for instance, that you are a grateful little girl, and that you are glad to be of use to those who have been kind to you; and for this I forgive you the long stitch.' 'But it's out, it's out, papa,' said Patty; 'and the next time your gloves want mending, Ben, I'll mend them better.'

'They are very nice, I think,' said Ben, drawing them on; 'and I am much obliged to you. I was just wishing I had a pair of gloves to keep my fingers warm to-day, for I never can shoot well when my hands are benumbed. Look, Hal; you know how ragged these gloves were; you said they were good for nothing but to throw away; now look, there's not a hole in them,' said he, spreading his fingers.

'Now, is it not very extraordinary,' said Hal to himself, 'that they should go on so long talking about an old pair of gloves, without saying scarcely a word about my new uniform? Well, the young Sweepstakes and Lady Diana will talk enough about it; that's one comfort. Is not it time to think of setting out, sir?' said Hal to his uncle. 'The company, you know, are to meet at the Ostrich at twelve, and the race to begin at one, and Lady Diana's horses, I know, were ordered to be at the door at ten.'

Mr. Stephen, the butler, here interrupted the hurrying young gentleman in his calculations. 'There's a poor lad, sir, below, with a great black patch on his right eye, who is come from Bristol, and wants to speak a word with the young gentlemen, if you please. I told him they were just going out with you; but he says he won't detain them more than half a minute.'

'Show him up, show him up,' said Mr. Gresham.

'But, I suppose,' said Hal, with a sigh, 'that Stephen mistook, when he said the young *gentlemen*; he only wants to see Ben, I daresay; I'm sure he has no reason to want to see me.'

'Here he comes—O Ben, he is dressed in the new coat you gave him,' whispered Hal, who was really a good-natured boy, though extravagant. 'How much better he looks than he did in the ragged coat! Ah! he looked at you first, Ben—and well he may!'

The boy bowed, without any cringing civility, but with an open, decent freedom in his manner, which expressed that he had been obliged, but that he knew his young benefactor was not thinking of the obligation. He made as little distinction as possible between his bows to the two cousins.

'As I was sent with a message, by the clerk of our parish, to Redland chapel out on the Downs, to-day, sir,' said he to Mr. Gresham, 'knowing your house lay in my way, my mother, sir, bid me call, and make bold to offer the young gentlemen two little worsted balls that she has worked for them,' continued the lad, pulling out of his pocket two worsted balls worked in green and orange-coloured stripes. 'They are but poor things, sir, she bid me say, to look at; but, considering she has but one hand to work with, and *that* her left hand, you'll not despise 'em, we hopes.' He held the balls to Ben and Hal. 'They are both alike, gentlemen,' said he. 'If you'll be pleased to take 'em, they're better than they look, for they bound higher than your head. I cut the cork round for the inside myself, which was all I could do.'

'They are nice balls, indeed: we are much obliged to you,' said the boys as they received them, and they proved them immediately. The balls struck the floor with a delightful sound, and rebounded higher than Mr. Gresham's head. Little Patty clapped her hands joyfully. But now a thundering double rap at the door was heard.

'The Master Sweepstakes, sir,' said Stephen, 'are come for Master Hal. They say that all the young gentlemen who have archery uniforms are to walk together, in a body, I think they say, sir; and they are to parade along the Well Walk, they desired me to say, sir, with a drum and fife, and so up the hill by Prince's Place, and all to go upon the Downs together, to the place of meeting. I am not sure I'm right, sir; for both the young gentlemen spoke at once, and the wind is very high at the street door; so that I could not well make out all they said; but I believe this is the sense of it.'

'Yes, yes,' said Hal eagerly, 'it's all right. I know that is just what was settled the day I dined at Lady Diana's; and Lady Diana and a great party of gentlemen are to ride——'

'Well, that is nothing to the purpose,' interrupted Mr. Gresham. 'Don't keep these Master Sweepstakes waiting. Decide—do you choose to go with them or with us?' 'Sir—uncle—sir, you know, since all the *uniforms* agreed to go together——' 'Off with you, then, Mr. Uniform, if you mean to go,' said Mr. Gresham.

Hal ran downstairs in such a hurry that he forgot his bow and arrows. Ben discovered this when he went to fetch his own; and the lad from Bristol, who had been ordered by Mr. Gresham to eat his breakfast before he proceeded to Redland Chapel, heard Ben talking about his cousin's bow and arrows. 'I know,' said Ben, 'he will be sorry not to have his bow with him, because here are the green knots tied to it, to match his cockade; and he said that the boys were all to carry their bows, as part of the show.'

'If you'll give me leave, sir,' said the poor Bristol lad, 'I shall have plenty of time; and I'll run down to the Well Walk after the young gentleman, and take him his bow and arrows.'

'Will you? I shall be much obliged to you,' said Ben; and away went the boy with the bow that was ornamented with green ribands.

The public walk leading to the Wells was full of company. The windows of all the houses in St. Vincent's Parade were crowded with well-dressed ladies, who were looking out in expectation of the archery procession. Parties of gentlemen and ladies, and a motley crowd of spectators, were seen moving backwards and forwards, under the rocks, on the opposite side of the water. A barge, with coloured streamers flying, was waiting to take up a party who were going upon the water. The bargemen rested upon their oars, and gazed with broad face of curiosity upon the busy scene that appeared upon the public walk.

The archers and archeresses were now drawn up on the flags under the semicircular piazza just before Mrs. Yearsley's library. A little band of children, who had been mustered by Lady Diana Sweepstakes' *spirited exertions*, closed the procession. They were now all in readiness. The drummer only waited for her ladyship's signal; and the archers' corps only waited for her ladyship's word of command to march.

'Where are your bow and arrows, my little man?' said her ladyship to Hal, as she reviewed her Lilliputian regiment. 'You can't march, man, without your arms?'

Hal had despatched a messenger for his forgotten bow, but the messenger returned not. He looked from side to side in great distress— 'Oh, there's my bow coming, I declare!' cried he; 'look, I see the bow and the ribands. Look now, between the trees, Charles Sweepstakes, on the Hotwell Walk; it is coming!' 'But you've kept us all waiting a confounded time,' said his impatient friend. 'It is that good-natured poor fellow from Bristol, I protest, that has brought it me; I'm sure I don't deserve it from him,' said Hal to himself, when he saw the lad with the black patch on his eye running, quite out of breath, towards him, with his bow and arrows.

'Fall back, my good friend—fall back,' said the military lady, as soon as he had delivered the bow to Hal; 'I mean, stand out of the way, for your great patch cuts no figure amongst us. Don't follow so close, now, as if you belonged to us, pray.'

The poor boy had no ambition to partake the triumph; he *fell back* as soon as he understood the meaning of the lady's words. The drum beat, the fife played, the archers marched, the spectators admired. Hal stepped proudly, and felt as if the eyes of the whole universe were upon his epaulettes, or upon the facings of his uniform; whilst all the time he was considered only as part of a show.

The walk appeared much shorter than usual, and he was extremely sorry that Lady Diana, when they were half-way up the hill leading to Prince's Place, mounted her horse, because the road was dirty, and all the gentlemen and ladies who accompanied her followed her example.

'We can leave the children to walk, you know,' said she to the gentleman who helped her to mount her horse. 'I must call to some of them, though, and leave orders where they are to *join*.'

She beckoned: and Hal, who was foremost, and proud to show his alacrity, ran on to receive her ladyship's orders. Now, as we have before observed, it was a sharp and windy day; and though Lady Diana Sweepstakes was actually speaking to him, and looking at him, he could not prevent his nose from wanting to be blowed: he pulled out his handkerchief and out rolled the new ball which had been given to him just before he left home, and which, according to his usual careless habits, he had stuffed into his pocket in his hurry. 'Oh, my new ball!' cried he, as he ran after it. As he stopped to pick it up, he let go his hat, which he had hitherto held on with anxious care; for the hat, though it had a fine green and white cockade, had no band or string round it. The string, as we may recollect, our wasteful hero had used in spinning his top. The hat was too large for his head without this band; a sudden gust of wind blew it off. Lady Diana's horse started and reared. She was a *famous* horsewoman, and sat him to the admiration of all beholders; but there was a puddle of red clay and water in this spot, and her ladyship's uniform habit was a sufferer by the accident. 'Careless brat!' said she, 'why can't he keep his hat upon his head?' In the meantime, the wind blew the hat down the hill, and Hal ran after it amidst the laughter of his kind friends, the young Sweepstakes, and the rest of the little regiment. The hat was lodged, at length, upon a bank. Hal pursued it: he thought this bank was hard, but, alas! the moment he set his foot upon it the foot sank. He tried to draw it back; his other foot slipped, and he fell prostrate, in his green and white uniform, into the treacherous bed of red mud. His companions, who had halted upon the top of the hill, stood laughing spectators of his misfortune.

It happened that the poor boy with the black patch upon his eye, who had been ordered by Lady Diana to '*fall back*,' and to '*keep at a distance*' was now coming up the hill; and the moment he saw our fallen hero, he hastened to his assistance. He dragged poor Hal, who was a deplorable spectacle, out of the red mud. The obliging mistress of a lodging-house, as soon as she understood that the young gentleman was nephew to Mr. Gresham, to whom she had formerly let her house, received Hal, covered as he was with dirt.

The poor Bristol lad hastened to Mr. Gresham's for clean stockings and shoes for Hal. He was willing to give up his uniform: it was rubbed and rubbed, and a spot here and there was washed out; and he kept continually repeating,—'When it's dry it will all brush off— when it's dry it will all brush off, won't it?' But soon the fear of being too late at the archery meeting began to balance the dread of appearing in his stained habiliments; and he now as anxiously repeated, whilst the woman held the wet coat to the fire, 'Oh, I shall be too late; indeed, I shall be too late; make haste; it will never dry; hold it nearer—nearer to the fire. I shall lose my turn to shoot; oh, give me the coat; I don't mind how it is, if I can but get it on.'

He dragged poor Hal out of the red mud.

He dragged poor Hal out of the red mud.

Holding it nearer and nearer to the fire dried it quickly, to be sure; but it shrank it also, so that it was no easy matter to get the coat on again. However, Hal, who did not see the red splashes, which, in spite of all these operations, were too visible upon his shoulders, and upon the skirts of his white coat behind, was pretty well satisfied to observe that there was not one spot upon the facings. 'Nobody,' said he, 'will take notice of my coat behind, I daresay. I think it looks as smart almost as ever!'—and under this persuasion our young archer resumed his bow—his bow with green ribands, now no more!—and he pursued his way to the Downs.

All his companions were far out of sight. 'I suppose,' said he to his friend with the black patch—'I suppose my uncle and Ben had left home before you went for the shoes and stockings for me?'

'Oh yes, sir; the butler said they had been gone to the Downs the matter of a good half-hour or more.'

Hal trudged on as fast as he possibly could. When he got upon the Downs, he saw numbers of carriages, and crowds of people, all going towards the place of meeting at the Ostrich. He pressed forwards. He was at first so much afraid of being late, that he did not take notice of the mirth his motley appearance excited in all beholders. At length he reached the appointed spot. There was a great crowd of people. In the midst he heard Lady Diana's loud voice betting upon some one who was just going to shoot at the mark.

'So then the shooting is begun, is it?' said Hal. 'Oh, let me in! pray let me into the circle! I'm one of the archers—I am, indeed; don't you see my green and white uniform?'

'Your red and white uniform, you mean,' said the man to whom he addressed himself; and the people, as they opened a passage for him, could not refrain laughing at the mixture of dirt and finery which it exhibited. In vain, when he got into the midst of the formidable circle, he looked to his friends, the young Sweepstakes, for their countenance and support. They were amongst the most unmerciful of the laughers. Lady Diana also seemed more to enjoy than to pity his confusion.

97

'Why could you not keep your hat upon your head, man?' said she, in her masculine tone. 'You have been almost the ruin of my poor uniform habit; but I've escaped rather better than you have. Don't stand there, in the middle of the circle, or you'll have an arrow in your eyes just now, I've a notion.'

Hal looked round in search of better friends. 'Oh, where's my uncle?—where's Ben?' said he. He was in such confusion, that, amongst the number of faces, he could scarcely distinguish one from another; but he felt somebody at this moment pull his elbow, and, to his great relief, he heard the friendly voice and saw the good-natured face of his cousin Ben.

'Come back—come behind these people,' said Ben, 'and put on my greatcoat; here it is for you.'

Right glad was Hal to cover his disgraced uniform with the rough greatcoat which he had formerly despised. He pulled the stained, drooping cockade out of his unfortunate hat; and he was now sufficiently recovered from his vexation to give an intelligible account of his accident to his uncle and Patty, who anxiously inquired what had detained him so long, and what had been the matter. In the midst of the history of his disaster, he was just proving to Patty that his taking the hatband to spin his top had nothing to do with his misfortune, and he was at the same time endeavouring to refute his uncle's opinion that the waste of the whipcord that tied the parcel was the original cause of all his evils, when he was summoned to try his skill with his *famous* bow.

'My hands are benumbed; I can scarcely feel,' said he, rubbing them, and blowing upon the ends of his fingers.

'Come, come,' cried young Sweepstakes, 'I'm within one inch of the mark; who'll go nearer? I shall like to see. Shoot away, Hal; but first understand our laws; we settled them before you came upon the green. You are to have three shots, with your own bow and your own arrows; and nobody's to borrow or lend under pretence of other's bows being better or worse, or under any pretence. Do you hear, Hal?'

This young gentleman had good reasons for being so strict in these laws, as he had observed that none of his companions had such an excellent bow as he had provided for himself. Some of the boys had forgotten to bring more than one arrow with them, and by his cunning regulation that each person should shoot with his own arrows, many had lost one or two of their shots.

'You are a lucky fellow; you have your three arrows,' said young Sweepstakes. 'Come, we can't wait whilst you rub your fingers, man—shoot away.'

Hal was rather surprised at the asperity with which his friend spoke. He little knew how easily acquaintance who call themselves friends can change when their interest comes in the slightest degree in competition with their friendship. Hurried by his impatient rival, and with his hands so much benumbed that he could scarcely feel how to fix the arrow in the string, he drew the bow. The arrow was within a quarter of an inch of Master Sweepstakes' mark, which was the nearest that had yet been hit. Hal seized his second arrow. 'If I have any luck——' said he. But just as he pronounced the word *luck*, and as he bent his bow, the string broke in two, and the bow fell from his hands.

'There, it's all over with you!' cried Master Sweepstakes, with a triumphant laugh.

'Here's my bow for him, and welcome,' said Ben. 'No, no, sir,' said Master Sweepstakes, 'that is not fair; that's against the regulation. You may shoot with your own bow, if you choose it, or you may not, just as you think proper; but you must not lend it, sir.'

It was now Ben's turn to make his trial. His first arrow was not successful. His second was exactly as near as Hal's first. 'You have but one more,' said Master Sweepstakes; 'now for it!' Ben, before he ventured his last arrow, prudently examined the string of his bow; and, as he pulled it to try its strength, it cracked. Master Sweepstakes clapped his hands, with loud exultations and insulting laughter. But his laughter ceased when our provident hero calmly drew from his pocket an excellent piece of whipcord.

'The everlasting whipcord, I declare!' exclaimed Hal, when he saw that it was the very same that had tied up the parcel. 'Yes,' said Ben, as he fastened it to his bow, 'I put it into my pocket to-day on purpose, because I thought I might happen to want it.' He drew his bow the third and last time.

'Oh, papa!' cried little Patty, as his arrow hit the mark, 'it's the nearest; is it not the nearest?'

Master Sweepstakes, with anxiety, examined the hit. There could be no doubt. Ben was victorious! The bow, the prize bow, was now delivered to him; and Hal, as he looked at the whipcord, exclaimed, 'How *lucky* this whipcord has been to you, Ben!'

'It is *lucky*, perhaps, you mean, that he took care of it,' said Mr. Gresham.

'Ay,' said Hal, 'very true; he might well say, "Waste not, want not." It is a good thing to have two strings to one's bow.'

OLD POZ

Lucy, *daughter to the Justice.*
Mrs. Bustle, *landlady of the 'Saracen's Head.'*
Justice Headstrong.
Old Man.
William, *a Servant.*

SCENE I

The House of Justice Headstrong—A hall—Lucy watering some myrtles—A servant behind the scenes is heard to say—

I tell you my master is not up. You can't see him, so go about your business, I say.

Lucy. To whom are you speaking, William? Who's that?

Will. Only an old man, miss, with a complaint for my master.

Lucy. Oh, then, don't send him away—don't send him away.

Will. But master has not had his chocolate, ma'am. He won't ever see anybody before he drinks his chocolate, you know, ma'am.

Lucy. But let the old man, then, come in here. Perhaps he can wait a little while. Call him.

(*Exit servant.*)

(*Lucy sings, and goes on watering her myrtles; the servant shows in the Old Man.*)

Will. You can't see my master this hour; but miss will let you stay here.

Lucy (*aside*). Poor old man! how he trembles as he walks. (*Aloud.*) Sit down, sit down. My father will see you soon; pray sit down.

(*He hesitates; she pushes a chair towards him.*)

Lucy. Pray sit down.

(*He sits down.*)

Old Man. You are very good, miss; very good.

(*Lucy goes to her myrtles again.*)

Lucy. Ah! I'm afraid this poor myrtle is quite dead—quite dead.

(*The Old Man sighs, and she turns round.*)

Lucy (*aside*). I wonder what can make him sigh so! (*Aloud.*) My father won't make you wait long.

Old M. Oh, ma'am, as long as he pleases. I'm in no haste—no haste. It's only a small matter.

Lucy. But does a small matter make you sigh so?

Old M. Ah, miss; because though it is a small matter in itself, it is not a small matter to me (*sighing again*); it was my all, and I've lost it.

Lucy. What do you mean? What have you lost?

Old M. Why, miss—but I won't trouble you about it.

Lucy. But it won't trouble me at all—I mean, I wish to hear it; so tell it me.

Old M. Why, miss, I slept last night at the inn here, in town—the 'Saracen's Head'——

Lucy (*interrupts him*). Hark! there is my father coming downstairs; follow me. You may tell me your story as we go along.

Old M. I slept at the 'Saracen's Head,' miss, and——

(*Exit talking.*)

SCENE II

Justice Headstrong's Study

(*He appears in his nightgown and cap, with his gouty foot upon a stool—a table and chocolate beside him—Lucy is leaning on the arm of his chair.*)

Just. Well, well, my darling, presently; I'll see him presently.

Lucy. Whilst you are drinking your chocolate, papa?

Just. No, no, no—I never see anybody till I have done my chocolate, darling. (*He tastes his chocolate.*) There's no sugar in this, child.

Lucy. Yes, indeed, papa.

Just. No, child—there's *no* sugar, I tell you; that's poz!

Lucy. Oh, but, papa, I assure you I put in two lumps myself.

Just. There's *no* sugar, I say; why will you contradict me, child, for ever? There's no sugar, I say.

(*Lucy leans over him playfully, and with his teaspoon pulls out two lumps of sugar.*)

Lucy. What's this, papa?

Just. Pshaw! pshaw! pshaw!—it is not melted, child—it is the same as no sugar.—Oh, my foot, girl, my foot!—you kill me. Go, go, I'm busy. I've business to do. Go and send William to me; do you hear, love?

Lucy. And the old man, papa?

Just. What old man? I tell you what, I've been plagued ever since I was awake, and before I was awake, about that old man. If he can't wait, let him go about his business. Don't you know, child, I never see anybody till I've drunk my chocolate; and I never will, if it were a duke—that's poz! Why, it has but just struck twelve; if he can't wait, he can go about his business, can't he?

Lucy. Oh, sir, he *can* wait. It was not he who was impatient. (*She comes back playfully.*) It was only I, papa; don't be angry.

Just. Well, well, well (*finishing his cup of chocolate, and pushing his dish away*); and at any rate there was not sugar enough. Send William, send William, child; and I'll finish my own business, and then——

(*Exit Lucy, dancing, 'And then!—and then!'*)

Justice, *alone.*

Just. Oh, this foot of mine!—(*twinges*)—Oh, this foot! Ay, if Dr. Sparerib could cure one of the gout, then, indeed, I should think something of him; but as to my leaving off my bottle of port, it's nonsense; it's all nonsense; I can't do it; I can't, and I won't for all the Dr. Spareribs in Christendom; that's poz!

Enter William.

Just. William—oh! ay! hey! what answer, pray, did you bring from the 'Saracen's Head'? Did you see Mrs. Bustle herself, as I bid you?

Will. Yes, sir, I saw the landlady herself; she said she would come up immediately, sir.

Just. Ah, that's well—immediately?

Will. Yes, sir, and I hear her voice below now.

Just. Oh, show her up; show Mrs. Bustle in.

Lucy. *What's this, papa?* Just. *Pshaw! pshaw! pshaw!—it is not melted, child—it is the same as no sugar.*

Lucy. *What's this, papa?* Just. *Pshaw! pshaw! pshaw!—it is not melted, child—it is the same as no sugar.*

Enter Mrs. Bustle, *the landlady of the 'Saracen's Head.'*

Land. Good-morrow to your worship! I'm glad to see your worship look so purely. I came up with all speed (*taking breath*). Our pie is in the oven; that was what you sent for me about, I take it.

Just. True, true; sit down, good Mrs. Bustle, pray——

Land. Oh, your worship's always very good (*settling her apron*). I came up just as I was—only threw my shawl over me. I thought your worship would excuse—I'm quite, as it were, rejoiced to see your worship look so purely, and to find you up so hearty——

Just. Oh, I'm very hearty (*coughing*), always hearty, and thankful for it. I hope to see many Christmas doings yet, Mrs. Bustle. And so our pie is in the oven, I think you say?

Land. In the oven it is. I put it in with my own hands; and if we have but good luck in the baking, it will be as pretty a goose-pie—though I say it that should not say it—as pretty a goose-pie as ever your worship set your eyes upon.

Just. Will you take a glass of anything this morning, Mrs. Bustle?—I have some nice usquebaugh.

Land. Oh, no, your worship!—I thank your worship, though, as much as if I took it; but I just took my luncheon before I came up; or more proper, *my sandwich*, I should say, for the fashion's sake, to be sure. A *luncheon* won't go down with nobody nowadays (*laughs*). I expect hostler and boots will be calling for their sandwiches just now (*laughs again*). I'm sure I beg your worship's pardon for mentioning a *luncheon.*

Just. Oh, Mrs. Bustle, the word's a good word, for it means a good thing—ha! ha! ha! (*pulls out his watch*); but pray, is it luncheon time? Why, it's past one, I declare; and I thought I was up in remarkably good time, too.

Land. Well, and to be sure so it was, remarkably good time for *your worship*; but folks in our way must be up betimes, you know. I've been up and about these seven hours.

Just. (*stretching*). Seven hours!

Land. Ay, indeed—eight, I might say, for I am an early little body; though I say it that should not say it—I *am* an early little body.

Just. An early little body, as you say, Mrs. Bustle—so I shall have my goose-pie for dinner, hey?

Land. For dinner, as sure as the clock strikes four—but I mustn't stay prating, for it may be spoiling if I'm away; so I must wish your worship a good morning.

(*She curtsies.*)

Just. No ceremony—no ceremony; good Mrs. Bustle, your servant.

Enter William, *to take away the chocolate. The Landlady is putting on her shawl.*

Just. You may let that man know, William, that I have dispatched my *own* business, and am at leisure for his now (*taking a pinch of snuff*). Hum! pray, William (*Justice leans back gravely*), what sort of a looking fellow is he, pray?

Will. Most like a sort of travelling man, in my opinion, sir—or something that way, I take it.

(*At these words the Landlady turns round inquisitively, and delays, that she may listen, while she is putting on and pinning her shawl.*)

Just. Hum! a sort of a travelling man. Hum! lay my books out open at the title Vagrant; and, William, tell the cook that Mrs. Bustle promises me the goose-pie for dinner. Four o'clock, do you hear? And show the old man in now.

(*The Landlady looks eagerly towards the door, as it opens, and exclaims,*)

Land. My old gentleman, as I hope to breathe!

Enter the Old Man.

(*Lucy follows the Old Man on tiptoe—The Justice leans back and looks consequential—The Landlady sets her arms akimbo—The Old Man starts as he sees her.*)

Just. What stops you, friend? Come forward, if you please.

Land. (*advancing*). So, sir, is it you, sir? Ay, you little thought, I warrant ye, to meet me here with his worship; but there you reckoned without your host—Out of the frying-pan into the fire.

Just. What is all this? What is this?

Land. (*running on*). None of your flummery stuff will go down with his worship no more than with me, I give you warning; so you may go further and far worse, and spare your breath to cool your porridge.

Just. (*waves his hand with dignity*). Mrs. Bustle, good Mrs. Bustle, remember where you are. Silence! silence! Come forward, sir, and let me hear what you have to say.

(*The Old Man comes forward.*)

Just. Who and what may you be, friend, and what is your business with me?

Land. Sir, if your worship will give me leave——

(*Justice makes a sign to her to be silent.*)

Old M. Please your worship, I am an old soldier.

Land. (*interrupting*). An old hypocrite, say.

101

Just. Mrs. Bustle, pray, I desire, let the man speak.

Old M. For these two years past—ever since, please your worship—I wasn't able to work any longer; for in my youth I did work as well as the best of them.

Land. (*eager to interrupt*). You work—you——

Just. Let him finish his story, I say.

Lucy. Ay, do, do, papa, speak for him. Pray, Mrs. Bustle——

Land. (*turning suddenly round to Lucy*). Miss, a good morrow to you, ma'am. I humbly beg your apologies for not seeing you sooner, Miss Lucy.

(*Justice nods to the Old Man, who goes on.*)

Old Man. But, please your worship, it pleased God to take away the use of my left arm; and since that I have never been able to work.

Land. Flummery! flummery!

Just. (*angrily*). Mrs. Bustle, I have desired silence, and I will have it, that's poz! You shall have your turn presently.

Old M. For these two years past (for why should I be ashamed to tell the truth?) I have lived upon charity, and I scraped together a guinea and a half and upwards, and I was travelling with it to my grandson, in the north, with him to end my days—*but* (*sighing*)——

Just. *But* what? Proceed, pray, to the point.

Old M. But last night I slept here in town, please your worship, at the 'Saracen's Head.'

Land. (*in a rage*). At the 'Saracen's Head!' Yes, forsooth! none such ever slept at the 'Saracen's Head' afore, or ever shall afterwards, as long as my name's Bustle and the 'Saracen's Head' is the 'Saracen's Head.'

Just. Again! again! Mrs. Landlady, this is downright—I have said you should speak presently. He *shall* speak first, since I've said it—that's poz! Speak on, friend. You slept last night at the 'Saracen's Head.'

' Five times have I commanded silence, and I won't command anything five times in vain—that's poz!'

'*Five times have I commanded silence, and I won't command anything five times in vain*—that's poz!'

Old M. Yes, please your worship, and I accuse nobody; but at night I had my little money safe, and in the morning it was gone.

Land. Gone!—gone, indeed, in my house! and this is the way I'm to be treated! Is it so? I couldn't but speak, your worship, to such an inhuman like, out o' the way, scandalous charge, if King George and all the Royal Family were sitting in your worship's chair, beside you, to silence me (*turning to the Old Man*). And this is your gratitude, forsooth! Didn't you tell me that any hole in my house was good enough for you, wheedling hypocrite? And the thanks I receive is to call me and mine a pack of thieves.

Old M. Oh, no, no, no, *No*—a pack of thieves, by no means.

Land. Ay, I thought when *I* came to speak we should have you upon your marrow-bones in——

Just. (*imperiously*). Silence! Five times have I commanded silence, and five times in vain; and I won't command anything five times in vain—*that's poz!*

Land. (*in a pet, aside*). Old Poz! (*Aloud.*) Then, your worship, I don't see any business I have to be waiting here; the folks want me at home (*returning and whispering*). Shall I send the goose-pie up, your worship, if it's ready?

Just. (*with magnanimity*). I care not for the goose-pie, Mrs. Bustle. Do not talk to me of goose-pies; this is no place to talk of pies.

Land. Oh, for that matter, your worship knows best, to be sure.

(*Exit Landlady, angry.*)

SCENE III

Justice Headstrong, Old Man, *and* Lucy

Lucy. Ah, now, I'm glad he can speak; now tell papa; and you need not be afraid to speak to him, for he is very good-natured. Don't contradict him, though, because he told *me* not.

Just. Oh, darling, *you* shall contradict me as often as you please—only not before I've drunk my chocolate, child—hey? Go on, my good friend; you see what it is to live in Old England, where, thank Heaven, the poorest of His Majesty's subjects may have justice, and speak his mind before the first in the land. Now speak on; and you hear she tells you that you need not be afraid of me. Speak on.

Old M. I thank your worship, I'm sure.

Just. Thank me! for what, sir? I won't be thanked for doing justice, sir; so—but explain this matter. You lost your money, hey, at the 'Saracen's Head'? You had it safe last night, hey?—and you missed it this morning? Are you sure you had it safe at night?

Old M. Oh, please your worship, quite sure; for I took it out and looked at it just before I said my prayers.

Just. You did—did ye so?—hum! Pray, my good friend, where might you put your money when you went to bed?

Old M. Please, your worship, where I always put it—always—in my tobacco-box.

Just. Your tobacco-box! I never heard of such a thing—to make a *strong box* of a tobacco-box. Ha! ha! ha! hum!—and you say the box and all were gone in the morning?

Old M. No, please your worship, no; not the box—the box was never stirred from the place where I put it. They left me the box.

Just. Tut, tut, tut, man!—took the money and left the box? I'll never believe *that*! I'll never believe that any one could be such a fool. Tut, tut! the thing's impossible! It's well you are not upon oath.

Old M. If I were, please your worship, I should say the same; for it is the truth.

Just. Don't tell me, don't tell me; I say the thing is impossible.

Old M. Please your worship, here's the box.

Just. (*goes on without looking at it*). Nonsense! nonsense! it's no such thing; it's no such thing, I say—no man would take the money and leave the tobacco-box. I won't believe it. Nothing shall make me believe it—that's poz.

Lucy (*takes the box and holds it up before her father's eyes*). You did not see the box, did you, papa?

Just. Yes, yes, yes, child—nonsense! it's all a lie from beginning to end. A man who tells one lie will tell a hundred. All a lie!—all a lie!

Old M. If your worship would give me leave——

Just. Sir, it does not signify—it does not signify! I've said it, I've said it, and that's enough to convince me, and I'll tell you more; if my Lord Chief Justice of England told it to me, I would not believe it—that's poz!

Lucy (*still playing with the box*). But how comes the box here, I wonder?

Just. Pshaw! pshaw! pshaw! darling. Go to your dolls, darling, and don't be positive—go to your dolls, and don't talk of what you don't understand. What can you understand, I want to know, of the law?

Lucy. No, papa, I didn't mean about the law, but about the box; because, if the man had taken it, how could it be here, you know, papa?

Just. Hey, hey, what? Why, what I say is this, that I don't dispute that that box, that you hold in your hands, is a box; nay, for aught I know, it may be a tobacco-box—but it's clear to me that if they left the box they did not take the money; and how do you dare, sir, to come before Justice Headstrong with a lie in your mouth? recollect yourself, I'll give you time to recollect yourself.

(*A pause.*)

Just. Well, sir; and what do you say now about the box?

Old M. Please your worship, with submission, I *can* say nothing but what I said before.

Just. What, contradict me again, after I gave you time to recollect yourself! I've done with you; I have done. Contradict me as often as you please, but you cannot impose upon me; I defy you to impose upon me!

Old M. Impose!

Just. I know the law!—I know the law!—and I'll make you know it, too. One hour I'll give you to recollect yourself, and if you don't give up this idle story, I'll—I'll commit you as a vagrant—that's poz! Go, go, for the present. William, take him into the servants' hall, do you hear?—What, take the money, and leave the box? I'll never do it—that's poz!

(*Lucy speaks to the Old Man as he is going off.*)

Lucy. Don't be frightened! don't be frightened!—I mean, if you tell the truth, never be frightened.

Old M. If I tell the truth—(*turning up his eyes*).

(*Old Man is still held back by the young lady.*)

Lucy. One moment—answer me one question—because of something that just came into my head. Was the box shut fast when you left it?

Old M. No, miss, no!—open—it was open; for I could not find the lid in the dark—my candle went out. If I tell the truth—oh!

(*Exit.*)

SCENE IV

Justice's Study—the Justice is writing

Old M. Well!—I shall have but few days' more misery in this world!

Just. (*looks up*). Why! why—why then, why will you be so positive to persist in a lie? Take the money and leave the box! Obstinate blockhead! Here, William (*showing the committal*), take this old gentleman to Holdfast, the constable, and give him this warrant.

Enter Lucy, *running, out of breath.*

Lucy. I've found it! I've found it! Here, old man; here's your money—here it is all—a guinea and a half, and a shilling and a sixpence, just as he said, papa.

Enter Landlady.

Land. Oh la! your worship, did you ever hear the like?

Just. I've heard nothing yet that I can understand. First, have you secured the thief, I say?

Lucy (*makes signs to the landlady to be silent*). Yes, yes, yes! we have him safe—we have him prisoner. Shall he come in, papa?

Just. Yes, child, by all means; and now I shall hear what possessed him to leave the box. I don't understand—there's something deep in all this; I don't understand it. Now I do desire, Mrs. Landlady, nobody may speak a single word whilst I am cross-examining the thief.

(*Landlady puts her finger upon her lips—Everybody looks eagerly towards the door.*)

Re-enter Lucy, *with a huge wicker cage in her hand, containing a magpie—The Justice drops the committal out of his hand.*

Just. Hey!—what, Mrs. Landlady—the old magpie? hey?

Land. Ay, your worship, my old magpie. Who'd have thought it? Miss was very clever—it was she caught the thief. Miss was very clever.

Old M. Very good! very good!

Just. Ay, darling, her father's own child! How was it, child? Caught the thief, *with the mainour*, hey? Tell us all; I will hear all—that's poz.

Lucy. Oh! then first I must tell you how I came to suspect Mr. Magpie. Do you remember, papa, that day last summer when I went with you to the bowling-green at the 'Saracen's Head'?

Land. Oh, of all days in the year! but I ask pardon, miss.

Lucy. Well, that day I heard my uncle and another gentleman telling stories of magpies hiding money; and they laid a wager about this old magpie and they tried him—they put a shilling upon the table, and he ran away with it and hid it; so I thought that he might do so again, you know, this time.

Just. Right, right. It's a pity, child, you are not upon the Bench—ha! ha! ha!

Lucy. And when I went to his old hiding-place, there it was; but you see, papa, he did not take the box.

Just. No, no, no! because the thief was a magpie. No *man* would have taken the money and left the box. You see I was right; no *man* would have left the box, hey?

Lucy. Certainly not, I suppose; but I'm so very glad, old man, that you have obtained your money.

Just. Well then, child, here—take my purse, and add that to it. We were a little too hasty with the committal—hey?

Land. Ay, and I fear I was, too; but when one is touched about the credit of one's house, one's apt to speak warmly.

Old M. Oh, I'm the happiest old man alive! You are all convinced that I told you no lies. Say no more—say no more. I am the happiest man! Miss, you have made me the happiest man alive! Bless you for it!

Land. Well, now, I'll tell you what. I know what I think—you must keep that there magpie, and make a show of him, and I warrant he'll bring you many an honest penny; for it's a *true story*, and folks would like to hear it, I hopes——

Just. (*eagerly*). And, friend, do you hear? You'll dine here to-day, you'll dine here. We have some excellent ale. I will have you drink my health—that's poz!—hey? You'll drink my health, won't you—hey?

'And Mr. Smack, the curate, and Squire Solid, and the doctor, sir, are come, and dinner is upon the table.'

'And Mr. Smack, the curate, and Squire Solid, and the doctor, sir, are come, and dinner is upon the table.'

Old M. (*bows*). Oh! and the young lady's, if you please.

Just. Ay, ay, drink her health—she deserves it. Ay, drink my darling's health.

Land. And please your worship, it's the right time, I believe, to speak of the goose-pie now; and a charming pie it is, and it's on the table.

Will. And Mr. Smack, the curate, and Squire Solid, and the doctor, sir, are come, and dinner is upon the table.

Just. Then let us say no more, but do justice immediately to the goose-pie; and, darling, put me in mind to tell this story after dinner.

(*After they go out, the Justice stops.*)

'Tell this story'—I don't know whether it tells well for me; but I'll never be positive any more—*that's poz*!

THE MIMIC

CHAPTER I

Mr. and Mrs. Montague spent the summer of the year 1795 at Clifton with their son Frederick, and their two daughters Sophia and Marianne. They had taken much care of the education of their children; nor were they ever tempted, by any motive of personal convenience or temporary amusement, to hazard the permanent happiness of their pupils.

Sensible of the extreme importance of early impressions, and of the powerful influence of external circumstances in forming the characters and the manners, they were now anxious that the variety of new ideas and new objects which would strike the minds of their children should appear in a just point of view.

'Let children see and judge for themselves,' is often inconsiderately said. Where children see only a part they cannot judge of the whole; and from the superficial view which they can have in short visits and desultory conversation, they can form only a false estimate of the objects of human happiness, a false notion of the nature of society, and false opinions of characters.

For the above reasons, Mr. and Mrs. Montague were particularly cautious in the choice of their acquaintances, as they were well aware that whatever passed in conversation before their children became part of their education.

When they came to Clifton, they wished to have a house entirely to themselves; but, as they came late in the season, almost all the lodging-houses were full, and for a few weeks they were obliged to remain in a house where some of the apartments were already occupied.

During the first fortnight they scarcely saw or heard anything of one of the families who lodged on the same floor with them. An elderly Quaker and his sister Bertha were their silent neighbours. The blooming complexion of the lady had indeed attracted the attention of the children, as they caught a glimpse of her face when she was getting into her carriage to go out upon the Downs. They could scarcely believe that she came to the Wells on account of her health.

Besides her blooming complexion, the delicate white of her garments had struck them with admiration; and they observed that her brother carefully guarded her dress from the wheel of the carriage, as he handed her in. From this circumstance, and from the benevolent countenance of the old gentleman, they concluded that he was very fond of his sister, and that they were certainly very happy, except that they never spoke, and could be seen only for a moment.

Not so the maiden lady who occupied the ground-floor. On the stairs, in the passages, at her window, she was continually visible; and she appeared to possess the art of being present in all these places at once. Her voice was eternally to be heard, and it was not particularly melodious. The very first day she met Mrs. Montague's children on the stairs, she stopped to tell Marianne that she was a charming dear, and a charming little dear; to kiss her, to inquire her name, and to inform her that her own name was 'Mrs. Theresa Tattle,' a circumstance of which there was little danger of their long remaining in ignorance; for, in the course of one morning, at least twenty single and as many double raps at the door were succeeded by vociferations of 'Mrs. Theresa Tattle's servant!' 'Mrs. Theresa Tattle at home?' 'Mrs. Theresa Tattle not at home!'

No person at the Wells was oftener at home and abroad than Mrs. Tattle. She had, as she deemed it, the happiness to have a most extensive acquaintance residing at Clifton. She had for years kept a register of arrivals. She regularly consulted the subscriptions to the circulating libraries, and the lists at the Ball and the Pump rooms; so that, with a memory unencumbered with literature and free from all domestic cares, she contrived to retain a most astonishing and correct list of births, deaths, and marriages, together with all the anecdotes, amusing, instructive, or scandalous, which are necessary to the conversation of a water-drinking place, and essential to the character of a 'very pleasant woman.'

'A very pleasant woman' Mrs. Tattle was usually called; and, conscious of her accomplishments, she was eager to introduce herself to the acquaintance of her new neighbours; having, with her ordinary expedition, collected from their servants, by means of her own, all that could be known, or rather all that could be told about them. The name of Montague, at all events, she knew was a good name, and justified in courting the acquaintance. She courted it first by nods and becks and smiles at Marianne whenever she met her; and Marianne, who was a very little girl, began presently to nod and smile in return, persuaded that a lady who smiled so much could not be ill-natured. Besides, Mrs. Theresa's parlour door was sometimes left more than half open, to afford a view of a green parrot. Marianne sometimes passed very slowly by this door. One morning it was left quite wide open, when she stopped to say 'Pretty Poll'; and immediately Mrs. Tattle begged she would do her the honour to walk in and see 'Pretty Poll,' at the same time taking the liberty to offer her a piece of iced plum-cake.

The next day Mrs. Theresa Tattle did herself the honour to wait upon Mrs. Montague.

The next day Mrs. Theresa Tattle did herself the honour to wait upon Mrs. Montague.

The next day Mrs. Theresa Tattle did herself the honour to wait upon Mrs. Montague, 'to apologise for the liberty she had taken in inviting Mrs. Montague's charming Miss Marianne into her apartment to see Pretty Poll, and for the still greater liberty she had taken in offering her a piece of plum-cake—inconsiderate creature that she was!—which might possibly have disagreed with her, and which certainly were liberties she never should have been induced to take, if she had not been unaccountably bewitched by Miss Marianne's striking though highly flattering resemblance to a young gentleman (an officer) with whom she had danced, now nearly twelve years ago, of the name of Montague, a most respectable young man, and of a most respectable family, with which, in a remote degree, she might presume to say, she herself was someway connected, having the honour to be nearly related to the Joneses of Merionethshire, who were cousins to the Mainwarings of Bedfordshire, who married into the family of the Griffiths, the eldest branch of which, she understood, had the honour to be cousin-german to Mr. Montague; on which account she had been impatient to pay a visit, so likely to be productive of most agreeable consequences, by the acquisition of an acquaintance whose society must do her infinite honour.'

Having thus happily accomplished her first visit, there seemed little probability of escaping Mrs. Tattle's further acquaintance. In the course of the first week she only hinted to Mr. Montague that 'some people thought his system of education rather odd; that she should be obliged to him if he would, some time or other, when he had nothing else to do, just sit down and make her understand his notions, that she might have something to say to her acquaintance, as she always wished to have when she heard any friend attacked, or any friend's opinions.'

Mr. Montague declining to sit down and make this lady understand a system of education only to give her something to say, and showing unaccountable indifference about the attacks with which he was threatened, Mrs. Tattle next addressed herself to Mrs. Montague, prophesying, in a most serious whisper, 'that the charming Miss Marianne would shortly and inevitably grow quite crooked, if she were not immediately provided with a back-board, a French dancing-master, and a pair of stocks.'

This alarming whisper could not, however, have a permanent effect upon Mrs. Montague's understanding, because three days afterwards Mrs. Theresa, upon the most anxious inspection, entirely mistook the just and natural proportions of the hip and shoulder.

This danger vanishing, Mrs. Tattle presently, with a rueful length of face, and formal preface, 'hesitated to assure Mrs. Montague that she was greatly distressed about her daughter Sophy; that she was convinced her lungs were affected; and that she certainly ought to drink the waters morning and evening; and, above all things, must keep one of the patirosa lozenges constantly in her mouth, and directly consult Dr. Cardamum, the best physician in the world, and the person she would send for herself upon her death-bed; because, to her certain knowledge, he had recovered a young lady, a relation of her own, after she had lost one whole *globe*14 of her lungs.'

The medical opinion of a lady of so much anatomical precision could not have much weight. Neither was this universal adviser more successful in an attempt to introduce a tutor to Frederick, who, she apprehended, must want some one to perfect him in the Latin and Greek, and dead languages, of which, she observed, it would be impertinent for a woman to talk; only she might venture to repeat what she had heard said by good authority, that a competency of the dead tongues could be had nowhere but at a public school, or else from a private tutor who had been abroad (after the advantage of a classical education, finished in one of the universities) with a good family; without which introduction it was idle to think of reaping solid advantages from any continental tour; all which requisites, from personal knowledge, she could aver to be concentrated in the gentleman she had the honour to recommend, as having been tutor to a young nobleman, who had no further occasion for him, having, unfortunately for himself and his family, been killed in an untimely duel.

All Mrs. Theresa Tattle's suggestions being lost upon these stoical parents, her powers were next tried upon the children, and her success soon became apparent. On Sophy, indeed, she could not make any impression, though she had expended on her some of her finest strokes of flattery. Sophy, though very desirous of the approbation of her friends, was not very desirous of winning the favour of strangers. She was about thirteen—that dangerous age at which ill-educated girls, in their anxiety to display their accomplishments, are apt to become dependent for applause upon the praise of every idle visitor; when the habits not being formed, and the attention being suddenly turned to dress and manners, girls are apt to affect and imitate, indiscriminately, everything that they conceive to be agreeable.

Sophy, whose taste had been cultivated at the same time with her powers of reasoning, was not liable to fall into these errors. She found that she could please those whom she wished to please, without affecting to be anything but what she really was; and her friends listened to what she said, though she never repeated the sentiments, or adopted the phrases, which she might easily have copied from the conversation of those who were older or more fashionable than herself.

This word *fashionable*, Mrs. Theresa Tattle knew, had usually a great effect, even at thirteen; but she had not observed that it had much power upon Sophy; nor were her remarks concerning grace and manners much attended to. Her mother had taught Sophy that it was best to let herself alone, and not to distort either her person or her mind in acquiring grimace, which nothing but the fashion of the moment can support, and which is always detected and despised by people of real good sense and politeness.

'Bless me!' said Mrs. Tattle, to herself, 'if I had such a tall daughter, and so unformed, before my eyes from morning to night, it would certainly break my poor heart. Thank heaven, I am not a mother! if I were, Miss Marianne for me!'

Miss Marianne had heard so often from Mrs. Tattle that she was very charming, that she could not help believing it; and from being a very pleasing, unaffected little girl, she in a short time grew so conceited, that she could neither speak, look, move, nor be silent, without imagining that everybody was, or ought to be, looking at her; and when Mrs. Theresa saw that Mrs. Montague looked very grave upon these occasions, she, to repair the ill she had done, would say, after praising Marianne's hair or her eyes, 'Oh, but little ladies should never think about their beauty, you know. Nobody loves anybody for being handsome, but for being good.' People must think children are very silly, or else they can never have reflected upon the nature of belief in their own minds, if they imagine that children will believe the words that are said to them, by way of moral, when the countenance, manner, and every concomitant circumstance tell them a different tale. Children are excellent physiognomists—they quickly learn the universal language of looks; and what is said *of* them always makes a greater impression than what is said *to* them, a truth of which those prudent people surely cannot be aware who comfort themselves, and apologise to parents, by saying, 'Oh, but I would not say so and so to the child.'

Mrs. Theresa had seldom said to Frederick Montague 'that he had a vast deal of drollery, and was a most incomparable mimic'; but she had said so of him in whispers, which magnified the sound to his imagination, if not to his ear. He was a boy of much vivacity, and had considerable abilities; but his appetite for vulgar praise had not yet been surfeited. Even Mrs. Theresa Tattle's flattery pleased him, and he exerted himself for her entertainment so much that he became quite a buffoon. Instead of observing characters and manners, that he might judge of them, and form his own, he now watched every person he saw, that he might detect some foible, or catch some singularity in their gesture or pronunciation, which he might successfully mimic.

Alarmed by the rapid progress of these evils, Mr. and Mrs. Montague, who, from the first day that they had been honoured with Mrs. Tattle's visit, had begun to look out for new lodgings, were now extremely impatient to decamp. They were not people who, from the weak fear of offending a silly acquaintance, would hazard the happiness of their family. They had heard of a house in the country which was likely to suit them, and they determined to go directly to look at it. As they were to be absent all day, they foresaw that their officious neighbour would probably interfere with their children. They did not choose to exact any promise from them which they might be tempted to break, and therefore they only said at parting, 'If Mrs. Theresa Tattle should ask you to come to her, do as you think proper.'

Scarcely had Mrs. Montague's carriage got out of hearing when a note was brought, directed to 'Frederick Montague, Junior, Esq.,' which he immediately opened, and read as follows:—

'Mrs. Theresa Tattle presents her very best compliments to the entertaining Mr. Frederick Montague; she hopes he will have the charity to drink tea with her this evening, and bring his charming sister, Miss Marianne, with him, as Mrs. Theresa will be quite alone with a shocking headache, and is sensible her nerves are affected; and Dr. Cardamum says that (especially in Mrs. T. T.'s case) it is downright death to nervous patients to be alone an instant. She therefore trusts Mr. Frederick will not refuse to come and make her laugh. Mrs. Theresa has taken care to provide a few macaroons for her little favourite, who said she was particularly fond of them the other day. Mrs. Theresa hopes they will all come at six, or before, not forgetting Miss Sophy, if she will condescend to be of the party.'

At the first reading of this note, 'the entertaining' Mr. Frederick and the 'charming' Miss Marianne laughed heartily, and looked at Sophy, as if they were afraid that she should think it possible they could like such gross flattery; but upon a second perusal, Marianne observed that it certainly was very good-natured of Mrs. Theresa to remember the macaroons; and Frederick allowed that it was wrong to laugh at the poor woman because she had the headache. Then twisting the note in his fingers, he appealed to Sophy:—

'Well, Sophy, leave off drawing for an instant,' said Frederick, 'and tell us what answer can we send?'

'Can!—we can send what answer we please.'

'Yes, I know that,' said Frederick; 'I would refuse if I could; but we ought not to do anything rude, should we? So I think we might as well go, because we could not refuse, if we would, I say.'

'You have made such confusion,' replied Sophy, 'between "couldn't" and "wouldn't" and "shouldn't," that I can't understand you: surely they are all different things.'

'Different! no,' cried Frederick—'*could, would, should, might*, and *ought* are all the same thing in the Latin grammar; all of 'em signs of the potential mood, you know.'

Sophy, whose powers of reasoning were not to be confounded, even by quotations from the Latin grammar, looked up soberly from her drawing, and answered 'that very likely those words might be signs of the same thing in the Latin grammar, but she believed that they meant perfectly different things in real life.'

'That's just as people please,' said her sophistical brother. 'You know words mean nothing in themselves. If I choose to call my hat my cadwallader, you would understand me just as well, after I had once explained it to you, that by cadwallader I meant this black thing that I put upon my head; cadwallader and hat would then be just the same thing to you.'

'Then why have two words for the same thing?' said Sophy; 'and what has this to do with *could* and *should*? You wanted to prove——'

'I wanted to prove,' interrupted Frederick, 'that it's not worth while to dispute for two hours about two words. Do keep to the point, Sophy, and don't dispute with me.'

'I was not disputing, I was reasoning.'

'Well, reasoning or disputing. Women have no business to do either; for, how should they know how to chop logic like men?'

At this contemptuous sarcasm upon her sex, Sophy's colour rose.

'There!' cried Frederick, exulting, 'now we shall see a philosopheress in a passion; I'd give sixpence, half-price, for a harlequin entertainment, to see Sophy in a passion. Now, Marianne, look at her brush dabbing so fast in the water!'

Sophy, who could not easily bear to be laughed at, with some little indignation, said, 'Brother, I wish——'

'There! there!' cried Frederick, pointing to the colour which rose in her cheeks almost to her temples—'rising! rising! rising! look at the thermometer! blood heat! blood! fever heat! boiling water heat! Marianne.'

'Then,' said Sophy, smiling, 'you should stand a little farther off, both of you. Leave the thermometer to itself a little while. Give it time to cool. It will come down to "temperate" by the time you look again.'

'Oh, brother!' cried Marianne, 'she's so good-humoured, don't tease her any more, and don't draw heads upon her paper, and don't stretch her india-rubber, and don't let us dirty any more of her brushes. See! the sides of her tumbler are all manner of colours.'

'Oh, I only mixed red, blue, green, and yellow to show you, Marianne, that all colours mixed together make white. But she is temperate now, and I won't plague her; she shall chop logic, if she likes it, though she is a woman.'

'But that's not fair, brother,' said Marianne, 'to say "woman" in that way. I'm sure Sophy found out how to tie that difficult knot, which papa showed us yesterday, long before you did, though you are a man.' 'Not long,' said Frederick. 'Besides, that was only a conjuring trick.'

'It was very ingenious, though,' said Marianne; 'and papa said so. Besides, she understood the "Rule of Three," which was no conjuring trick, better than you did, though she is a woman; and she can reason, too, mamma says.'

'Very well, let her reason away,' said the provoking wit. 'All I have to say is, that she'll never be able to make a pudding.'

'Why not, pray, brother?' inquired Sophy, looking up again, very gravely.

'Why, you know papa himself, the other day at dinner, said that that woman who talks Greek and Latin as well as I do, is a fool after all; and that she had better have learned something useful; and Mrs. Tattle said, she'd answer for it she did not know how to make a pudding.'

'Well! but I am not talking Greek and Latin, am I?'

'No, but you are drawing, and that's the same thing.'

'The same thing! Oh, Frederick!' said little Marianne, laughing.

'You may laugh; but I say it is the same sort of thing. Women who are always drawing and reasoning never know how to make puddings. Mrs. Theresa Tattle said so, when I showed her Sophy's beautiful drawing yesterday.'

'Mrs. Theresa Tattle might say so,' replied Sophy, calmly; 'but I do not perceive the reason, brother, why drawing should prevent me from learning how to make a pudding.'

'Well, I say you'll never learn how to make a good pudding.'

'I have learned,' continued Sophy, who was mixing her colours, 'to mix such and such colours together to make the colour that I want; and why should I not be able to learn to mix flour and butter, and sugar and egg, together, to produce the taste that I want?'

'Oh, but mixing will never do, unless you know the quantities, like a cook; and you would never learn the right quantities.'

'How did the cook learn them? Cannot I learn them as she did?'

'Yes, but you'd never do it exactly, and mind the spoonfuls right, by the recipe, like a cook.'

'Indeed! indeed! but she would,' cried Marianne, eagerly; 'and a great deal more exactly, for mamma has taught her to weigh and measure things very carefully; and when I was ill she always weighed the bark in nicely, and dropped my drops so carefully: better than the cook. When mamma took me down to see the cook make a cake once, I saw her spoonfuls, and her ounces, and her handfuls: she dashed and splashed without minding exactness, or the recipe, or anything. I'm sure Sophy would make a much better pudding, if exactness only were wanting.'

'She dashed and splashed without minding exactness, or the recipe, or anything.'

'She dashed and splashed without minding exactness, or the recipe, or anything.'
'Well, granting that she could make the best pudding in the whole world, what does that signify? I say she never would, so it comes to the same thing.'

'Never would! how can you tell that, brother?'

'Why, now look at her, with her books, and her drawings, and all this apparatus. Do you think she would ever jump up, with all her nicety, too, and put by all these things, to go down into the greasy kitchen, and plump up to the elbows in suet, like a cook, for a plum-pudding?'

'I need not plump up to the elbows, brother,' said Sophy, smiling, 'nor is it necessary that I should be a cook; but, if it were necessary, I hope I should be able to make a pudding.'

'Yes, yes,' cried Marianne, warmly; 'and she would jump up, and put by all her things in a minute if it were necessary, and run downstairs and up again like lightning, or do anything that was ever so disagreeable to her, even about the suet, with all her nicety, brother, I assure you, as she used to do anything, everything for me, when I was ill last winter. Oh, brother, she can do anything; and she could make the best plum-pudding in the whole world, I'm sure, in a minute, if it were necessary.'

CHAPTER II

A knock at the door, from Mrs. Theresa Tattle's servant, recalled Marianne to the business of the day.

'There,' said Frederick, 'we have sent no answer all this time. It's necessary to think of that in a minute.'

The servant came with his mistress's compliments, to let the young ladies and Mr. Frederick know that she was waiting tea for them.

'Waiting! then we must go,' said Frederick.

The servant opened the door wider, to let him pass, and Marianne thought she must follow her brother; so they went downstairs together, while Sophy gave her own message to the servant, and quietly stayed at her usual occupations.

Mrs. Tattle was seated at her tea-table, with a large plate of macaroons beside her, when Frederick and Marianne entered. She was 'delighted' they were come, and 'grieved' not to see Miss Sophy along with them. Marianne coloured a little; for though she had precipitately followed her brother, and though he had quieted her conscience for a moment by saying, 'You know, papa and mamma told us to do what we thought best,' yet she did not feel quite pleased with herself; and it was not till after Mrs. Theresa had exhausted all her compliments and half her macaroons, that she could restore her spirits to their usual height.

'Come, Mr. Frederick,' said she after tea, 'you promised to make me laugh; and nobody can make me laugh so well as yourself.'

'Oh, brother,' said Marianne, 'show Mrs. Theresa Dr. Carbuncle eating his dinner; and I'll be Mrs. Carbuncle.'

Marianne. Now, my dear, what shall I help you to?

Frederick. 'My dear!' she never calls him my dear, you know, but always Doctor.

Mar. Well then, doctor, what will you eat to-day?

Fred. Eat, madam! eat! nothing! nothing! I don't see anything here I can eat, ma'am.

Mar. Here's eels, sir; let me help you to some eel—stewed eel;—you used to be fond of stewed eel.

Fred. Used, ma'am, used! But I'm sick of stewed eels. You would tire one of anything. Am I to see nothing but eels? And what's this at the bottom?

Mar. Mutton, doctor, roast mutton; if you'll be so good as to cut it.

Fred. Cut it, ma'am! I can't cut it, I say; it's as hard as a deal board. You might as well tell me to cut the table, ma'am. Mutton, indeed! not a bit of fat. Roast mutton, indeed! not a drop of gravy. Mutton, truly! quite a cinder. I'll have none of it. Here, take it away; take it downstairs to the cook. It's a very hard case, Mrs. Carbuncle, that I can never have a bit of anything that I can eat at my own table, Mrs. Carbuncle, since I was married, ma'am, I that am the easiest man in the whole world to please about my dinner. It's really very extraordinary, Mrs. Carbuncle! What have you at that corner there, under the cover?

Mar. Patties, sir; oyster patties.

Fred. Patties, ma'am! kickshaws! I hate kickshaws. Not worth putting under a cover, ma'am. And why not have glass covers, that one may see one's dinner before one, before it grows cold with asking questions, Mrs. Carbuncle, and lifting up covers? But nobody has any sense; and I see no water plates anywhere, lately.

Mar. Do, pray, doctor, let me help you to a bit of chicken before it gets cold, my dear.

Fred. (*aside*). 'My dear,' again, Marianne!

Mar. Yes, brother, because she is frightened, you know, and Mrs. Carbuncle always says 'my dear' to him when she's frightened, and looks so pale from side to side; and sometimes she cries before dinner's done, and then all the company are quite silent, and don't know what to do.

'Oh, such a little creature; to have so much sense, too!' exclaimed Mrs. Theresa, with rapture. 'Mr. Frederick, you'll make me die with laughing! Pray go on, Dr. Carbuncle.'

Fred. Well, ma'am, then if I must eat something, send me a bit of fowl; a leg and wing, the liver wing, and a bit of the breast, oyster sauce, and a slice of that ham, if you please, ma'am.

(*Dr. Carbuncle eats voraciously, with his head down to his plate, and, dropping the sauce, he buttons up his coat tight across the breast.*)

Fred. Here; a plate, knife and fork, bit o' bread, a glass of Dorchester ale!

'Oh, admirable!' exclaimed Mrs. Tattle, clapping her hands.

'Now, brother, suppose that it is after dinner,' said Marianne; 'and show us how the doctor goes to sleep.'

Frederick threw himself back in an arm-chair, leaning his head back, with his mouth open, snoring; nodded from time to time, crossed and uncrossed his legs, tried to awake himself by twitching his wig, settling his collar, blowing his nose, and rapping on the lid of his snuff-box.

All which infinitely diverted Mrs. Tattle, who, when she could stop herself from laughing, declared 'it made her sigh, too, to think of the life poor Mrs. Carbuncle led with that man, and all for nothing, too; for her jointure was nothing, next to nothing, though a great thing, to be sure, her friends thought, for her, when she was only Sally Ridgeway before she was married. Such a wife as she makes,' continued Mrs. Theresa, lifting up her hands and eyes to heaven, 'and so much as she has gone through, the brute ought to be ashamed of himself if he does not leave her something extraordinary in his will; for turn it which way she will, she can never keep a carriage, or live like anybody else, on her jointure, after all, she tells me, poor soul! A sad prospect, after her husband's death, to look forward to, instead of being comfortable, as her friends expected; and she, poor young thing! knowing no better when they married her! People should look into these things beforehand, or never marry at all, I say, Miss Marianne.'

Miss Marianne, who did not clearly comprehend this affair of the jointure, or the reason why Mrs. Carbuncle would be so unhappy after her husband's death, turned to Frederick, who was at that instant studying Mrs. Theresa as a future character to mimic. 'Brother,' said

Marianne, 'now sing an Italian song for us like Miss Croker. Pray, Miss Croker, favour us with a song. Mrs. Theresa Tattle has never had the pleasure of hearing you sing; she's quite impatient to hear you sing.'

'Yes, indeed, I am,' said Mrs. Theresa.

Frederick put his hands before him affectedly. 'Oh, indeed, ma'am! indeed, ladies! I really am so hoarse, it distresses me so to be pressed to sing; besides, upon my word, I have quite left off singing. I've never sung once, except for very particular people, this winter.'

Mar. But Mrs. Theresa Tattle is a very particular person. I'm sure you'll sing for her.

Fred. Certainly, ma'am, I allow that you use a powerful argument; but I assure you now, I would do my best to oblige you, but I absolutely have forgotten all my English songs. Nobody hears anything but Italian now, and I have been so giddy as to leave my Italian music behind me. Besides, I make it a rule never to hazard myself without an accompaniment.

Mar. Oh, try, Miss Croker, for once.

(*Frederick sings, after much preluding.*)

Violante in the pantry,
Gnawing of a mutton-bone;
   How she gnawed it,
   How she claw'd it,
When she found herself alone!

'Charming!' exclaimed Mrs. Tattle; 'so like Miss Croker, I'm sure I shall think of you, Mr. Frederick, when I hear her asked to sing again. Her voice, however, introduces her to very pleasant parties, and she's a girl that's very much taken notice of, and I don't doubt will go off vastly well. She's a particular favourite of mine, you must know; and I mean to do her a piece of service the first opportunity, by saying something or other, that shall go round to her relations in Northumberland, and make them do something for her; as well they may, for they are all rolling in gold, and won't give her a penny.

Mar. Now, brother, read the newspaper like Counsellor Puff.

'Oh, pray do, Mr. Frederick, for I declare I admire you of all things! You are quite yourself to-night. Here's a newspaper, sir, pray let us have Counsellor Puff. It's not late.'

(*Frederick reads in a pompous voice.*)

'As a delicate white hand has ever been deemed a distinguishing ornament in either sex, Messrs. Valiant and Wise conceive it to be their duty to take the earliest opportunity to advertise the nobility and gentry of Great Britain in general, and their friends in particular, that they have now ready for sale, as usual, at the Hippocrates' Head, a fresh assortment of new-invented, much-admired primrose soap. To prevent impositions and counterfeits, the public are requested to take notice, that the only genuine primrose soap is stamped on the outside, "Valiant and Wise."'

'Oh, you most incomparable mimic! 'tis absolutely the counsellor himself. I absolutely must show you, some day, to my friend Lady Battersby; you'd absolutely make her die with laughing; and she'd quite adore you,' said Mrs. Theresa, who was well aware that every pause must be filled with flattery. 'Pray go on, pray go on. I shall never be tired, if I sit looking at you these hundred years.'

Stimulated by these plaudits, Frederick proceeded to show how Colonel Epaulette blew his nose, flourished his cambric handkerchief, bowed to Lady Diana Periwinkle, and admired her work, saying, 'Done by no hands, as you may guess, but those of Fairly Fair.' Whilst Lady Diana, he observed, simpered so prettily, and took herself so quietly for Fairly Fair, not perceiving that the colonel was admiring his own nails all the while.

Next to Colonel Epaulette, Frederick, at Marianne's particular desire, came into the room like Sir Charles Slang.

'Very well, brother,' cried she, 'your hand down to the very bottom of your pocket, and your other shoulder up to your ear; but you are not quite wooden enough, and you should walk as if your hip were out of joint. There now, Mrs. Tattle, are not those good eyes? They stare so like his, without seeming to see anything all the while.'

'Excellent! admirable! Mr. Frederick. I must say that you are the best mimic of your age I ever saw, and I'm sure Lady Battersby will think so too. That is Sir Charles to the very life. But with all that, you must know he's a mighty pleasant, fashionable young man when you come to know him, and has a great deal of sense under all that, and is of a very good family—the Slangs, you know. Sir Charles will come into a fine fortune himself next year, if he can keep clear of gambling, which I hear is his foible, poor young man! Pray go on. I interrupt you, Mr. Frederick.'

'Now, brother,' said Marianne.

'No, Marianne, I can do no more. I'm quite tired, and I will do no more,' said Frederick, stretching himself at full length upon a sofa.

Even in the midst of laughter, and whilst the voice of flattery yet sounded in his ear, Frederick felt sad, displeased with himself, and disgusted with Mrs. Theresa.

'What a deep sigh was there!' said Mrs. Theresa; 'what can make you sigh so bitterly? You, who make everybody else laugh. Oh, such another sigh again!'

'Marianne,' cried Frederick, 'do you remember the man in the mask?'

'What man in the mask, brother?'

'The man—the actor—the buffoon, that my father told us of, who used to cry behind the mask that made everybody else laugh.'

'Cry! bless me,' said Mrs. Theresa, 'mighty odd! very extraordinary! but one can't be surprised at meeting with extraordinary characters amongst that race of people, actors by profession, you know; for they are brought up from the egg to make their fortune, or at least their

113

bread, by their oddities. But, my dear Mr. Frederick, you are quite pale, quite exhausted; no wonder—what will you have? a glass of cowslip-wine?'

'Oh no, thank you, ma'am,' said Frederick.

'Oh yes; indeed you must not leave me without taking something; and Miss Marianne must have another macaroon. I insist upon it,' said Mrs. Theresa, ringing the bell. 'It is not late, and my man Christopher will bring up the cowslip-wine in a minute.'

'But, Sophy! and papa and mamma, you know, will come home presently,' said Marianne.

'Oh! Miss Sophy has her books and drawings. You know she's never afraid of being alone. Besides, to-night it was her own choice. And as to your papa and mamma, they won't be home to-night, I'm pretty sure; for a gentleman, who had it from their own authority, told me where they were going, which is further off than they think; but they did not consult me; and I fancy they'll be obliged to sleep out; so you need not be in a hurry about them. We'll have candles.'

The door opened just as Mrs. Tattle was going to ring the bell again for candles and the cowslip-wine. 'Christopher! Christopher!' said Mrs. Theresa, who was standing at the fire, with her back to the door, when it opened, 'Christopher! pray bring——Do you hear?' but no Christopher answered; and, upon turning round, Mrs. Tattle, instead of Christopher, beheld two little black figures, which stood perfectly still and silent. It was so dark, that their forms could scarcely be discerned.

'In the name of heaven, who and what may you be? Speak, I conjure you! what are ye?'

'The chimney-sweepers, ma'am, an' please your ladyship.'

'Chimney-sweepers!' repeated Frederick and Marianne, bursting out a-laughing.

'Chimney-sweepers!' repeated Mrs. Theresa, provoked at the recollection of her late solemn address to them. 'Chimney-sweepers! and could not you say so a little sooner? Pray, what brings you here, gentlemen, at this time of night?'

'The bell rang, ma'am,' answered a squeaking voice.

'The bell rang! yes, for Christopher. The boy's mad, or drunk.'

'Ma'am,' said the taller of the chimney-sweepers, who had not yet spoken, and who now began in a very blunt manner; 'ma'am, your brother desired us to come up when the bell rang; so we did.'

'My brother? I have no brother, dunce,' said Mrs. Theresa.

'Mr. Eden, madam.'

'Ho, ho!' said Mrs. Tattle, in a more complacent tone, 'the boy takes me for Miss Bertha Eden, I perceive'; and, flattered to be taken in the dark by a chimney-sweeper for a young and handsome lady, Mrs. Theresa laughed, and informed him 'that they had mistaken the room; and they must go up another pair of stairs, and turn to the left.'

The chimney-sweeper with the squeaking voice bowed, thanked her ladyship for this information, said, 'Good-night to ye, quality'; and they both moved towards the door.

'Stay,' said Mrs. Tattle, whose curiosity was excited; 'what can the Edens want with chimney-sweepers at this time o' night, I wonder? Christopher, did you hear anything about it?' said the lady to her footman, who was now lighting the candles.

'Upon my word, ma'am,' said the servant, 'I can't say; but I'll step down below and inquire. I heard them talking about it in the kitchen; but I only got a word here and there, for I was hunting for the snuff-dish, as I knew it must be for candles when I heard the bell ring, ma'am; so I thought to find the snuff-dish before I answered the bell, for I knew it must be for candles you rang. But, if you please, I'll step down now, ma'am, and see about the chimney-sweepers.'

'Yes, step down, do; and, Christopher, bring up the cowslip-wine, and some more macaroons for my little Marianne.'

Marianne withdrew rather coldly from a kiss which Mrs. Tattle was going to give her; for she was somewhat surprised at the familiarity with which this lady talked to her footman. She had not been accustomed to these familiarities in her father and mother, and she did not like them.

'Well,' said Mrs. Tattle to Christopher, who was now returned, 'what is the news?'

'Ma'am, the little fellow with the squeaking voice has been telling me the whole story. The other morning, ma'am, early, he and the other were down the hill sweeping in Paradise Row. Those chimneys, they say, are difficult; and the square fellow, ma'am, the biggest of the two boys, got wedged in the chimney. The other little fellow was up at the top at the time, and he heard the cry; but in his fright, and all, he did not know what to do, ma'am; for he looked about from the top of the chimney, and not a soul could he see stirring, but a few that he could not make attend to his screech; the boy within almost stifling too. So he screeched, and screeched, all he could; and by the greatest chance in life, ma'am, old Mr. Eden was just going down the hill to fetch his morning walk.'

'Ay,' interrupted Mrs. Theresa, 'friend Ephraim is one of your early risers.'

'Well?' said Marianne, impatiently.

'So, ma'am, hearing the screech, he turns and sees the sweep; and at once he understands the matter——'

'I'm sure he must have taken some time to understand it,' interposed Mrs. Tattle, 'for he's the slowest creature breathing, and the deafest in company. Go on, Christopher. So the sweep did make him hear.'

'So he says, ma'am; and so the old gentleman went in and pulled the boy out of the chimney, with much ado, ma'am.'

'Bless me!' exclaimed Mrs. Theresa; 'but did old Eden go up the chimney himself after the boy, wig and all?'

'Why, ma'am,' said Christopher, with a look of great delight, 'that was all as one, as the very 'dentical words I put to the boy myself, when he told me his story. But, ma'am, that was what I couldn't get out of him, neither, rightly, for he is a churl—the big boy that was stuck in the chimney, I mean; for when I put the question to him about the wig, laughing like, he wouldn't take it laughing like at all; but would only make answer to us like a bear, 'He saved my life, that's all I know'; and this over again, ma'am, to all the kitchen round, that cross-

114

questioned him. But I finds him stupid and ill-mannered like, for I offered him a shilling, ma'am, myself, to tell about the wig; but he put it back in a way that did not become such as he, to no lady's butler, ma'am; whereupon I turns to the slim fellow (and he's smarterer, and more mannerly, ma'am, with a tongue in his head for his betters), but he could not resolve me my question either; for he was up at the top of the chimney the best part o' the time; and when he came down Mr. Eden had his wig on, but had his arm all bare and bloody, ma'am.'

'Poor Mr. Eden!' exclaimed Marianne.

'Oh, miss,' continued the servant, 'and the chimney-sweep himself was so bruised, and must have been killed.'

'Well, well! but he's alive now; go on with your story, Christopher,' said Mrs. T. 'Chimney-sweepers get wedged in chimneys every day; it's part of their trade, and it's a happy thing when they come off with a few bruises.15 To be sure,' added she, observing that both Frederick and Marianne looked displeased at this speech, 'to be sure, if one may believe this story, there was some real danger.'

'Real danger! yes, indeed,' said Marianne; 'and I'm sure I think Mr. Eden was very good.'

'Certainly it was a most commendable action, and quite providential. So I shall take an opportunity of saying, when I tell the story in all companies; and the boy may thank his kind stars, I'm sure, to the end of his days, for such an escape——But pray, Christopher,' said she, persisting in her conversation with Christopher, who was now laying the cloth for supper, 'pray, which house was it in Paradise Row? where the Eagles or the Miss Ropers lodge? or which?'

'It was at my Lady Battersby's, ma'am.'

'Ha! ha!' cried Mrs. Theresa, 'I thought we should get to the bottom of the affair at last. This is excellent! This will make an admirable story for my Lady Battersby the next time I see her. These Quakers are so sly! Old Eden, I know, has long wanted to obtain an introduction into that house; and a charming charitable expedient hit upon! My Lady Battersby will enjoy this, of all things.'

CHAPTER III

'Now,' continued Mrs. Theresa, turning to Frederick, as soon as the servant had left the room, 'now, Mr. Frederick Montague, I have a favour—such a favour—to ask of you; it's a favour which only you can grant; you have such talents, and would do the thing so admirably; and my Lady Battersby would quite adore you for it. She will do me the honour to be here to spend an evening to-morrow. I'm convinced Mr. and Mrs. Montague will find themselves obliged to stay out another day, and I so long to show you off to her ladyship; and your Doctor Carbuncle, and your Counsellor Puff, and your Miss Croker, and all your charming characters. You must let me introduce you to her ladyship to-morrow evening. Promise me.'

'Oh, ma'am,' said Frederick, 'I cannot promise you any such thing, indeed. I am much obliged to you; but indeed I cannot come.'

'Why not, my dear sir? why not? You don't think I mean you should promise, if you are certain your papa and mamma will be home.'

'If they do come home, I will ask them about it,' said Frederick, hesitating; for though he by no means wished to accept the invitation, he had not yet acquired the necessary power of decidedly saying No.

'Ask them!' repeated Mrs. Theresa. 'My dear sir, at your age, must you ask your papa and mamma about such things?'

'Must! no, ma'am,' said Frederick; 'but I said I would. I know I need not, because my father and mother always let me judge for myself almost about everything.'

'And about this, I am sure,' cried Marianne. 'Papa and mamma, you know, just as they were going away, said, "If Mrs. Theresa asks you to come, do as you think best."'

'Well, then,' said Mrs. Theresa, 'you know it rests with yourselves, if you may do as you please.'

'To be sure I may, madam,' said Frederick, colouring from that species of emotion which is justly called false shame, and which often conquers real shame; 'to be sure, ma'am, I may do as I please.'

'Then I may make sure of you,' said Mrs. Theresa; 'for now it would be downright rudeness to tell a lady you won't do as she pleases. Mr. Frederick Montague, I'm sure, is too well-bred a young gentleman to do so unpolite, so ungallant a thing!'

The jargon of politeness and gallantry is frequently brought by the silly acquaintance of young people to confuse their simple morality and clear good sense. A new and unintelligible system is presented to them in a language foreign to their understanding, and contradictory to their feelings. They hesitate between new motives and old principles. From the fear of being thought ignorant, they become affected; and from the dread of being thought to be children act like fools. But all this they feel only when they are in the company of such people as Mrs. Theresa Tattle.

'Ma'am,' Frederick began, 'I don't mean to be rude; but I hope you'll excuse me from coming to drink tea with you to-morrow, because my father and mother are not acquainted with Lady Battersby, and maybe they might not like——'

'Take care, take care,' said Mrs. Theresa, laughing at his perplexity; 'you want to get off from obliging me, and you don't know how. You had very nearly made a most shocking blunder in putting it all upon poor Lady Battersby. Now you know it's impossible that Mr. and Mrs. Montague could have in nature the slightest objection to introducing you to my Lady Battersby at my own house; for, don't you know, that, besides her ladyship's many unquestionable qualities, which one need not talk of, she is cousin, but once removed, to the Trotters of Lancashire—your mother's great favourites? And there is not a person at the Wells, I'll venture to say, could be of more advantage to your sister Sophy, in the way of partners, when she comes to go to balls, which it's to be supposed she will, some time or other; and as you are so good a brother, that's a thing to be looked to, you know. Besides, as to yourself, there's nothing her ladyship delights in so much as in a good mimic; and she'll quite adore you!'

'But I don't want her to adore me, ma'am,' said Frederick, bluntly; then, correcting himself, added, 'I mean for being a mimic.'

'Why not, my love? Between friends, can there be any harm in showing one's talents? You that have such talents to show. She'll keep your secret, I'll answer for her; and,' added she, 'you needn't be afraid of her criticism; for, between you and me, she's no great critic: so you'll come. Well, thank you, that's settled. How you have made me beg and pray! but you know your own value, I see; as you entertaining people always do. One must ask a wit, like a fine singer, so often. Well, but now for the favour I was going to ask you.'

Frederick looked surprised; for he thought that the favour of his company was what she meant; but she explained herself farther.

'As to the old Quaker who lodges above, old Ephraim Eden—my Lady Battersby and I have so much diversion about him. He is the best character, the oddest creature! If you were but to see him come into the rooms with those stiff skirts, or walking with his eternal sister Bertha, and his everlasting broad-brimmed hat! One knows him a mile off! But then his voice and way, and altogether, if one could get them to the life, they'd be better than anything on the stage; better even than anything I've seen to-night; and I think you'd make a capital Quaker for my Lady Battersby; but then the thing is, one can never get to hear the old quiz talk. Now you, who have so much invention and cleverness—I have no invention myself—but could you not hit upon some way of seeing him, so that you might get him by heart? I'm sure you, who are so quick, would only want to see him, and hear him, for half a minute, to be able to take him off, so as to kill one with laughing. But I have no invention.'

'Oh, as to the invention,' said Frederick, 'I know an admirable way of doing the thing, if that is all; but then remember, I don't say I will do the thing, for I will not. But I know a way of getting up into his room, and seeing him, without his knowing me to be there.'

'Oh, tell it me, you charming, clever creature!'

'But, remember, I do not say I will do it.'

'Well, well, let us hear it; and you shall do as you please afterwards. Merciful goodness!' exclaimed Mrs. Tattle, 'do my ears deceive me? I declare I looked round, and thought I heard the squeaking chimney-sweeper was in the room!'

'So did I, Frederick, I declare,' cried Marianne, laughing, 'I never heard anything so like his voice in my life.'

Frederick imitated the squeaking voice of this chimney-sweeper to great perfection.

'Now,' continued he, 'this fellow is just my height. The old Quaker, if my face were blackened, and if I were to change clothes with the chimney-sweeper, I'll answer for it, would never know me.'

'Oh, it's an admirable invention! I give you infinite credit for it!' exclaimed Mrs. Theresa. 'It shall, it must be done. I'll ring, and have the fellow up this minute.'

'Oh, no; do not ring,' said Frederick, stopping her hand, 'I don't mean to do it. You know you promised that I should do as I pleased. I only told you my invention.'

'Well, well; but only let me ring, and ask whether the chimney-sweepers are below. You shall do as you please afterwards.'

'Christopher, shut the door. Christopher,' said she to the servant who came up when she rang, 'pray are the sweeps gone yet?' 'No, ma'am.' 'But have they been up to old Eden yet?' 'Oh no, ma'am; nor be not to go till the bell rings; for Miss Bertha, ma'am, was asleep a-lying down, and her brother wouldn't have her wakened on no account whatsomever. He came down hisself to the kitchen to the sweeps, though; but wouldn't have, as I heard him say, his sister waked for no account. But Miss Bertha's bell will ring when she wakens for the sweeps, ma'am. 'Twas she wanted to see the boy as her brother saved, and I suppose sent for 'em to give him something charitable, ma'am.' 'Well, never mind your suppositions,' said Mrs. Theresa; 'run down this very minute to the little squeaking chimney-sweep, and send him up to me. Quick, but don't let the other bear come up with him.'

Christopher, who had curiosity as well as his mistress, when he returned with the chimney-sweeper, prolonged his own stay in the room by sweeping the hearth, throwing down the tongs and shovel, and picking them up again.

'That will do, Christopher! Christopher, that will do, I say,' Mrs. Theresa repeated in vain. She was obliged to say, 'Christopher, you may go,' before he would depart.

'Now,' said she to Frederick, 'step in here to the next room with this candle, and you'll be equipped in an instant. Only just change clothes with the boy; only just let me see what a charming chimney-sweeper you'd make. You shall do as you please afterwards.' 'Well, I'll only change clothes with him, just to show you for one minute.'

'But,' said Marianne to Mrs. Theresa whilst Frederick was changing his clothes, 'I think Frederick is right about——' 'About what, love?' 'I think he is in the right not to go up, though he can do it so easily, to see that gentleman; I mean on purpose to mimic and laugh at him afterwards. I don't think that would be quite right.' 'Why, pray, Miss Marianne?' 'Why, because he is so good-natured to his sister. He would not let her be wakened.' 'Dear, it's easy to be good in such little things; and he won't have long to be good to her neither; for I don't think she will trouble him long in this world, anyhow.' 'What do you mean?' said Marianne. 'That she'll die, child.' 'Die! die with that beautiful colour in her cheeks! How sorry her poor, poor brother will be! But she will not die, I'm sure, for she walks about, and runs upstairs so lightly! Oh, you must be quite mistaken, I hope.' 'If I'm mistaken, Dr. Panado Cardamum's mistaken too, then, that's my comfort. He says, unless the waters work a miracle, she stands a bad chance; and she won't follow my advice, and consult the doctor for her health.' 'He would frighten her to death, perhaps,' said Marianne. 'I hope Frederick won't go up to disturb her.' 'Lud, child, you are turned simpleton all of a sudden; how can your brother disturb her more than the real chimney-sweeper?' 'But I don't think it's right,' persisted Marianne, 'and I shall tell him so.' 'Nay, Miss Marianne, I don't commend you now. Young ladies should not be so forward to give opinions and advice to their elder brothers unasked; and I presume that Mr. Frederick and I must know what's right as well as Miss Marianne. Hush! here he is. Oh, the capital figure!' cried Mrs. Theresa. 'Bravo, bravo!' cried she, as Frederick entered in the chimney-sweeper's dress; and as he spoke, saying, 'I'm afraid, please your ladyship, to dirt your ladyship's carpet,' she broke out into immoderate raptures, calling him 'her charming chimney-sweeper!' and repeating that she knew beforehand the character would do for him.

Mrs. Theresa instantly rang the bell, in spite of all expostulation—ordered Christopher to send up the other chimney-sweeper—triumphed in observing that Christopher did not know Frederick when he came into the room; and offered to lay any wager that the other chimney-sweeper would mistake him for his companion. And so he did; and when Frederick spoke, the voice was so very like, that it was scarcely possible that he should have perceived the difference.

Marianne was diverted by this scene; but she started when, in the midst of it, they heard a bell ring. 'That's the lady's bell, and we must go,' said the blunt chimney-sweeper. 'Go, then, about your business,' said Mrs. Theresa, 'and here's a shilling for you, to drink, my honest fellow. I did not know you were so much bruised when I first saw you. I won't detain you. Go,' said she, pushing Frederick towards the door. Marianne sprang forward to speak to him; but Mrs. Theresa kept her off; and, though Frederick resisted, the lady shut the door upon him by superior force, and, having locked it, there was no retreat. Mrs. Tattle and Marianne waited impatiently for Frederick's return. 'I hear them,' cried Marianne, 'I hear them coming downstairs.' They listened again, and all was silent. At length they suddenly heard a great noise of many steps in the hall. 'Merciful!' exclaimed Mrs. Theresa, 'it must be your father and mother come back.' Marianne ran to unlock the room door, and Mrs. Theresa followed her into the hall. The hall was rather dark, but under the lamp a crowd of people; all the servants in the house having gathered together.

As Mrs. Theresa approached, the crowd opened in silence, and in the midst she beheld Frederick, with blood streaming from his face. His head was held by Christopher; and the chimney-sweeper was holding a basin for him. 'Merciful! what will become of me?' exclaimed Mrs. Theresa. 'Bleeding! he'll bleed to death! Can nobody think of anything that will stop blood in a minute? A key, a large key down his back— a key—has nobody a key? Mr. and Mrs. Montague will be here before he has done bleeding. A key! cobwebs! a puff ball! for mercy's sake! Can nobody think of anything that will stop blood in a minute? Gracious me! he'll bleed to death, I believe.'

'He'll bleed to death! Oh, my brother!' cried Marianne, catching hold of the words; and terrified, she ran upstairs, crying, 'Sophy, oh, Sophy! come down this minute, or he'll be dead! My brother's bleeding to death! Sophy! Sophy! come down, or he'll be dead!'

'Let go the basin, you,' said Christopher, pulling the basin out of the chimney-sweeper's hand, who had all this time stood in silence; 'you are not fit to hold the basin for a gentleman.' 'Let him hold it,' said Frederick; 'he did not mean to hurt me.' 'That's more than he deserves. I'm certain sure he might have known well enough it was Mr. Frederick all the time, and he'd no business to go to fight—such a one as he—with a gentleman.' 'I did not know he was a gentleman,' said the chimney-sweeper! 'how could I?' 'How could he, indeed?' said Frederick; 'he shall hold the basin.'

'Gracious me! I'm glad to hear him speak like himself again, at any rate,' cried Mrs. Theresa. 'And here comes Miss Sophy, too.' 'Sophy!' cried Frederick. 'Oh, Sophy, don't you come—don't look at me; you'll despise me.' 'My brother!—where? where?' said Sophy, looking, as she thought, at the two chimney-sweepers.

'It's Frederick,' said Marianne; 'that's my brother.'

'Miss Sophy, don't be alarmed,' Mrs. Theresa began; 'but gracious goodness! I wish Miss Bertha——'

At this instant a female figure in white appeared upon the stairs; she passed swiftly on, whilst every one gave way before her. 'Oh, Miss Bertha!' cried Mrs. Theresa, catching hold of her gown to stop her, as she came near Frederick. 'Oh, Miss Eden, your beautiful India muslin! take care of the chimney-sweeper, for heaven's sake.' But she pressed forward.

'It's my brother, will he die?' cried Marianne, throwing her arms round her, and looking up as if to a being of a superior order. 'Will he bleed to death?' 'No, my love!' answered a sweet voice; 'do not frighten thyself.'

'I've done bleeding,' said Frederick. 'Dear me, Miss Marianne, if you would not make such a rout,' cried Mrs. Tattle. 'Miss Bertha, it's nothing but a frolic. You see Mr. Frederick Montague only in a masquerade dress. Nothing in the world but a frolic, ma'am. You see he's stopped bleeding. I was frightened out of my wits at first. I thought it was his eye, but I see it's only his nose. All's well that ends well. Mr. Frederick, we'll keep your counsel. Pray, ma'am, let us ask no questions; it's only a boyish frolic. Come, Mr. Frederick, this way, into my room, and I'll give you a towel and some clean water, and you can get rid of this masquerade dress. Make haste, for fear your father and mother should drop in upon us.'

'Do not be afraid of thy father and mother. They are surely thy best friends,' said a voice. It was the voice of an elderly gentleman, who now stood behind Frederick. 'Oh, sir, oh, Mr. Eden,' said Frederick, turning to him. 'Don't betray me! for goodness' sake!' whispered Mrs. Tattle, 'say nothing about me.' 'I'm not thinking about you. Let me speak,' cried he, pushing away her hand, which stopped his mouth. 'I shall say nothing about you, I promise you,' said Frederick, with a look of contempt. 'No, but for your own sake, my dear sir, your papa and mamma. Bless me! is not that Mrs. Montague's carriage?'

'My brother, ma'am,' said Sophy, 'is not afraid of my father and mother's coming back. Let him speak; he was going to speak the truth.'

'To be sure, Miss Sophia, I wouldn't hinder him from speaking the truth; but it's not proper, I presume, ma'am, to speak truth at all times, and in all places, and before everybody, servants and all. I only wanted, ma'am, to hinder your brother from exposing himself. A hall, I apprehend, is not a proper place for explanation.'

'Here,' said Mr. Eden, opening the door of his room, which was on the opposite side of the hall to Mrs. Tattle's. 'Here is a place,' said he to Frederick, 'where thou mayst speak the truth at all times, and before everybody.' 'Nay, my room's at Mr. Frederick Montague's service, and my door's open too. This way, pray,' said she, pulling his arm. But Frederick broke from her, and followed Mr. Eden. 'Oh, sir, will you forgive me?' cried he. 'Forgive thee!—and what have I to forgive?' 'Forgive, brother, without asking what,' said Bertha, smiling.

'He shall know all!' cried Frederick; 'all that concerns myself, I mean. Sir, I disguised myself in this dress; I came up to your room to-night on purpose to see you, without your knowing it, that I might mimic you. The chimney-sweeper, where is he?' said Frederick, looking round; and he ran into the hall to seek for him. 'May he come in? he may—he is a brave, an honest, good, grateful boy. He never guessed who I was. After we left you we went down to the kitchen together, and there, fool as I was, for the pleasure of making Mr. Christopher and the servants laugh, began to mimic you. This boy said he would not stand by and hear you laughed at; that you had saved his life; that I ought to be ashamed of myself; that you had just given me half a crown; and so you had; but I went on, and told him I'd knock him down if he said another word. He did; I gave the first blow; we fought; I came to the ground; the servants pulled me up again. They found out, I don't know how, that I was not a chimney-sweeper. The rest you saw. And now can you forgive me, sir?' said Frederick to Mr. Eden, seizing hold of his hand.

'The other hand, friend,' said the Quaker, gently withdrawing his right hand, which everybody now observed was much swelled, and putting it into his bosom again. 'This, and welcome,' offering his other hand to Frederick, and shaking his with a smile. 'Oh, that other

117

hand!' said Frederick, 'that was hurt, I remember. How ill I have behaved—extremely ill! But this is a lesson that I shall never forget as long as I live. I hope for the future I shall behave like a gentleman.' 'And like a man—and like a good man, I am sure thou wilt,' said the good Quaker, shaking Frederick's hand affectionately; 'or I am much mistaken, friend, in that black countenance.'

'You are not mistaken,' cried Marianne. 'Frederick will never be persuaded again by anybody to do what he does not think right; and now, brother you may wash your black countenance.'

Just when Frederick had got rid of half his black countenance, a double knock was heard at the door. It was Mr. and Mrs. Montague. 'What will you do now?' whispered Mrs. Theresa to Frederick, as his father and mother came into the room. 'A chimney-sweeper covered with blood!' exclaimed Mr. and Mrs. Montague. 'Father, I am Frederick,' said he, stepping forward towards them, as they stood in astonishment. 'Frederick! my son!' 'Yes, mother, I'm not hurt half so much as I deserve; I'll tell you——' 'Nay,' interrupted Bertha, 'let my brother tell the story this time. Thou hast told it once, and told it well; no one but my brother could tell it better.'

'A story never tells so well the second time, to be sure,' said Mrs. Theresa; 'but Mr. Eden will certainly make the best of it.'

Without taking any notice of Mrs. Tattle, or her apprehensive looks, Mr. Eden explained all he knew of the affair in a few words. 'Your son,' concluded he, 'will quickly put off his dirty dress. The dress hath not stained the mind; that is fair and honourable. When he found himself in the wrong, he said so; nor was he in haste to conceal his adventure from his father; this made me think well of both father and son. I speak plainly, friend, for that is best. But what is become of the other chimney-sweeper? He will want to go home,' said Mr. Eden, turning to Mrs. Theresa. Without making any reply, she hurried out of the room as fast as possible, and returned in a few moments, with a look of extreme consternation.

'And like a man—and like a good man, I am sure thou wilt,' said the good Quaker shaking Frederick's hand affectionately

'And like a man—and like a good man, I am sure thou wilt,' said the good Quaker shaking Frederick's hand affectionately

'Here is a catastrophe indeed! Now, indeed, Mr. Frederick, your papa and mamma have reason to be angry. A new suit of clothes!—the barefaced villain! gone! no sign of them in my closet, or anywhere. The door was locked; he must have gone up the chimney, out upon the leads, and so escaped; but Christopher is after him. I protest, Mrs. Montague, you take it too quietly. The wretch!—a new suit of clothes, blue coat and buff waistcoat. I never heard of such a thing! I declare, Mr. Montague, you are vastly good, not to be in a passion,' added Mrs. Theresa.

'Madam,' replied Mr. Montague, with a look of much civil contempt, 'I think the loss of a suit of clothes, and even the disgrace that my son has been brought to this evening, fortunate circumstances in his education. He will, I am persuaded, judge and act for himself more wisely in future. Not will he be tempted to offend against humanity, for the sake of being called "The best mimic in the world."'

THE BARRING OUT
OR,
PARTY SPIRIT

'The mother of mischief,' says an old proverb, 'is no bigger than a midge's wing.'

At Doctor Middleton's school there was a great tall dunce of the name of Fisher, who never could be taught how to look out a word in the dictionary. He used to torment everybody with—'Do pray help me! I can't make out this one word.' The person who usually helped him in his distress was a very clever, good-natured boy, of the name of De Grey, who had been many years under Dr. Middleton's care, and who, by his abilities and good conduct, did him great credit. The doctor certainly was both proud and fond of him; but he was so well beloved, or so much esteemed, by his companions, that nobody had ever called him by the odious name of favourite, until the arrival of a new scholar of the name of Archer.

Till Archer came, the ideas of *favourites* and *parties* were almost unknown at Dr. Middleton's; but he brought all these ideas fresh from a great public school, at which he had been educated—at which he had acquired a sufficient quantity of Greek and Latin, and a superabundant quantity of party spirit. His aim, the moment he came to a new school, was to get to the head of it, or at least to form the strongest party. His influence, for he was a boy of considerable abilities, was quickly felt, though he had a powerful rival, as he thought proper to call him, in De Grey; and, with *him*, a rival was always an enemy. De Grey, so far from giving him any cause of hatred, treated him with a degree of cordiality which would probably have had an effect upon Archer's mind, if it had not been for the artifices of Fisher.

It may seem surprising that a *great dunce* should be able to work upon a boy like Archer, who was called a great genius; but when genius is joined to a violent temper, instead of being united to good sense, it is at the mercy even of dunces.

Fisher was mortally offended one morning by De Grey's refusing to translate his whole lesson for him. He went over to Archer, who, considering him as a partisan deserting from the enemy, received him with open arms, and translated his whole lesson, without expressing *much* contempt for his stupidity. From this moment Fisher forgot all De Grey's former kindness, and considered only how he could in his turn mortify the person whom he felt to be so much his superior.

De Grey and Archer were now reading for a premium, which was to be given in their class. Fisher betted on Archer's head, who had not sense enough to despise the bet of a blockhead. On the contrary, he suffered him to excite the spirit of rivalship in its utmost fury by collecting the bets of all the school. So that this premium now became a matter of the greatest consequence, and Archer, instead of taking the means to secure a judgment in his favour, was listening to the opinions of all his companions. It was a prize which was to be won by his own exertions; but he suffered himself to consider it as an affair of chance. The consequence was, that he trusted to chance—his partisans lost their wagers, and he the premium—and his temper.

'Mr. Archer,' said Dr. Middleton, after the grand affair was decided, 'you have done all that genius alone could do; but you, De Grey, have done all that genius and industry united could do.'

'Well!' cried Archer, with affected gaiety, as soon as the doctor had left the room—'well, I'm content with *my* sentence. Genius alone for me—industry for those who *want* it,' added he, with a significant look at De Grey.

Fisher applauded this as a very spirited speech; and, by insinuations that Dr. Middleton 'always gave the premium to De Grey,' and 'that those who had lost their bets might thank themselves for it, for being such simpletons as to bet against the favourite,' he raised a murmur highly flattering to Archer amongst some of the most credulous boys; whilst others loudly proclaimed their belief in Dr. Middleton's impartiality. These warmly congratulated De Grey. At this Archer grew more and more angry, and when Fisher was proceeding to speak nonsense *for* him, pushed forward into the circle to De Grey, crying, 'I wish, Mr. Fisher, you would let me fight my own battles!'

'And *I* wish,' said young Townsend, who was fonder of diversions than of premiums, or battles, or of anything else—'*I* wish that we were not to have any battles; after having worked like horses, don't set about to fight like dogs. Come,' said he, tapping De Grey's shoulder, 'let us see your new playhouse, do—it's a holiday, and let us make the most of it. Let us have the "School for Scandal," do; and I'll play Charles for you, and you, De Grey, shall be *my little Premium*. Come, do open this new playhouse of yours to-night.'

'Come then!' said De Grey, and he ran across the playground to a waste building at the farthest end of it, in which, at the earnest request of the whole community, and with the permission of Dr. Middleton, he had with much pain and ingenuity erected a theatre.

'The new theatre is going to be opened! Follow the manager! Follow the manager!' echoed a multitude of voices.

119

'*Follow the manager!*' echoed very disagreeably in Archer's ear; but as he could not be *left alone*, he was also obliged to follow the manager. The moment that the door was unlocked, the crowd rushed in; the delight and wonder expressed at the sight were great, and the applause and thanks which were bestowed upon the manager were long and loud.

Archer at least thought them long, for he was impatient till his voice could be heard. When at length the acclamations had spent themselves, he walked across the stage with a knowing air, and looking round contemptuously—

'And is *this* your famous playhouse?' cried he. 'I wish you had, any of you, seen the playhouse *I* have been used to?'

These words made a great and visible change in the feelings and opinions of the public. 'Who would be a servant of the public? or who would toil for popular applause?' A few words spoken in a decisive tone by a new voice operated as a charm, and the playhouse was in an instant metamorphosed in the eyes of the spectators. All gratitude for the past was forgotten, and the expectation of something better justified to the capricious multitude their disdain of what they had so lately pronounced to be excellent.

Every one now began to criticise. One observed 'that the green curtain was full of holes, and would not draw up.' Another attacked the scenes. 'Scenes! they were not like real scenes—Archer must know best, because he was used to these things.' So everybody crowded to hear something of the *other* playhouse. They gathered round Archer to hear the description of his playhouse, and at every sentence insulting comparisons were made. When he had done, his auditors looked round, sighed, and wished that Archer had been their manager. They turned from De Grey as from a person who had done them an injury. Some of his friends—for he had friends who were not swayed by the popular opinion—felt indignation at this ingratitude, and were going to express their feelings; but De Grey stopped them, and begged that he might speak for himself.

'Gentlemen,' said he, coming forward, as soon as he felt that he had sufficient command of himself. 'My friends, I see you are discontented with me and my playhouse. I have done my best to please you; but if anybody else can please you better, I shall be glad of it. I did not work so hard for the glory of being your manager. You have my free leave to tear down——' Here his voice faltered, but he hurried on—'You have my free leave to tear down all my work as fast as you please. Archer, shake hands first, however, to show that there's no malice in the case.'

Archer, who was touched by what his rival said, and stopping the hand of his new partisan, Fisher, cried, 'No, Fisher! no!—no pulling down. We can alter it. There is a great deal of ingenuity in it, considering.'

In vain Archer would now have recalled the public to reason,—the time for reason was past: enthusiasm had taken hold of their minds. 'Down with it! Down with it! Archer for ever!' cried Fisher, and tore down the curtain. The riot once begun, nothing could stop the little mob, till the whole theatre was demolished. The love of power prevailed in the mind of Archer; he was secretly flattered by the zeal of his *party*, and he mistook their love of mischief for attachment to himself. De Grey looked on superior. 'I said I could bear to see all this, and I can,' said he; 'now it is all over.' And now it was all over, there was silence. The rioters stood still to take breath, and to look at what they had done. There was a blank space before them.

In this moment of silence there was heard something like a female voice. 'Hush! What strange voice is that?' said Archer. Fisher caught fast hold of his arm. Everybody looked round to see where the voice came from. It was dusk. Two window-shutters at the farthest end of the building were seen to move slowly inwards. De Grey, and in the same instant Archer, went forward; and, as the shutters opened, there appeared through the hole the dark face and shrivelled hands of a very old gipsy. She did not speak; but she looked first at one and then at another. At length she fixed her eyes on De Grey. 'Well, my good woman,' said he, 'what do you want with me?' 'Want!—nothing—with *you*,' said the old woman; 'do you want nothing with *me*?' 'Nothing,' said De Grey. Her eye immediately turned upon Archer,—'*You* want something with me,' said she, with emphasis. 'I—what do I want?' replied Archer. 'No,' said she, changing her tone, 'you want nothing—nothing will you ever want, or I am much mistaken in that *face*.'

In that *watch-chain*, she should have said, for her quick eye had espied Archer's watch-chain. He was the only person in the company who had a watch, and she therefore judged him to be the richest.

'Had you ever your fortune told, sir, in your life?' 'Not I,' said he, looking at De Grey, as if he was afraid of his ridicule, if he listened to the gipsy. 'Not you! No! for you will make your own fortune, and the fortune of all that belong to you!'

'There's good news for my friends,' cried Archer. 'And I'm one of them, remember that,' cried Fisher. 'And I,' 'And I,' joined a number of voices. 'Good luck to them!' cried the gipsy, 'good luck to them all!'

Then, as soon as they had acquired sufficient confidence in her good will, they pressed up to the window. 'There,' cried Townsend, as he chanced to stumble over the carpenter's mitre box, which stood in the way, 'there's a good omen for me. I've stumbled on the mitre box; I shall certainly be a bishop.'

Happy he who had sixpence, for he bid fair to be a judge upon the bench. And happier he who had a shilling, for he was in the high road to be one day upon the woolsack, Lord High Chancellor of England. No one had half-a-crown, or no one would surely have kept it in his pocket upon such an occasion, for he might have been an archbishop, a king, or what he pleased.

Fisher, who like all weak people was extremely credulous, had kept his post immovable in the front row all the time, his mouth open, and his stupid eyes fixed upon the gipsy, in whom he felt implicit faith.

Those who have least confidence in their own powers, and who have least expectation from the success of their own exertions, are always most disposed to trust in fortune-tellers and fortune. They hope to *win*, when they cannot *earn*; and as they can never be convinced by those who speak sense, it is no wonder they are always persuaded by those who talk nonsense.

'I have a question to put,' said Fisher, in a solemn tone. 'Put it, then,' said Archer, 'what hinders you?' 'But they will hear me,' said he, looking suspiciously at De Grey. '*I* shall not hear you,' said De Grey, 'I am going.' Everybody else drew back, and left him to whisper his question in the gipsy's ear. 'What is become of my Livy?' 'Your *sister* Livy, do you mean?' said the gipsy. 'No, my *Latin* Livy.'

The gipsy paused for information. 'It had a leaf torn out in the beginning, and *I hate Dr. Middleton*——' 'Written in it,' interrupted the gipsy. 'Right—the very book!' cried Fisher with joy. 'But how *could* you know it was Dr. Middleton's name? I thought I had scratched it, so that nobody could make it out.' 'Nobody *could* make it out but *me*,' replied the gipsy. 'But never think to deceive me,' said she, shaking her head at him in a manner that made him tremble. 'I don't deceive you indeed, I tell you the whole truth. I lost it a week ago.' 'True.' 'And when shall I find it?' 'Meet me here at this hour to-morrow evening, and I will answer you. No more! I must be gone. Not a word more to-night.'

'What is become of my Livy?' 'Your sister Livy, do you mean?'

'What is become of my Livy?' 'Your sister Livy, do you mean?'

She pulled the shutters towards her, and left the youth in darkness. All his companions were gone. He had been so deeply engaged in this conference, that he had not perceived their departure. He found all the world at supper, but no entreaties could prevail upon him to disclose his secret. Townsend rallied in vain. As for Archer, he was not disposed to destroy by ridicule the effect which he saw that the old woman's predictions in his favour had had upon the imagination of many of his little partisans. He had privately slipped two good shillings into the gipsy's hand to secure her; for he was willing to pay any price for *any* means of acquiring power.

The watch-chain had not deceived the gipsy, for Archer was the richest person in the community. His friends had imprudently supplied him with more money than is usually trusted to boys of his age. Dr. Middleton had refused to give him a larger monthly allowance than the rest of his companions; but he brought to school with him secretly the sum of five guineas. This appeared to his friends and to himself an inexhaustible treasure.

Riches and talents would, he flattered himself, secure to him that ascendency of which he was so ambitious. 'Am I your manager or not?' was now his question. 'I scorn to take advantage of a hasty moment; but since last night you have had time to consider. If you desire me to be your manager, you shall see what a theatre I will make for you. In this purse,' said he, showing through the network a glimpse of the shining treasure—'in this purse is Aladdin's wonderful lamp. Am I your manager? Put it to the vote.'

It was put to the vote. About ten of the most reasonable of the assembly declared their gratitude and high approbation of their old friend, De Grey; but the numbers were in favour of the new friend. And as no metaphysical distinctions relative to the idea of a majority had ever

121

entered their thoughts, the most numerous party considered themselves as now beyond dispute in the right. They drew off on one side in triumph, and their leader, who knew the consequence of a name in party matters, immediately distinguished his partisans by the gallant name of *Archers*, stigmatising the friends of De Grey by the odious epithet of Greybeards.

Amongst the Archers was a class not very remarkable for their mental qualifications; but who, by their bodily activity, and by the peculiar advantages annexed to their way of life, rendered themselves of the highest consequence, especially to the rich and enterprising.

The judicious reader will apprehend that I allude to the persons called day scholars. Amongst these, Fisher was distinguished by his knowledge of all the streets and shops in the adjacent town; and, though a dull scholar, he had such reputation as a man of business that whoever had commissions to execute at the confectioner's was sure to apply to him. Some of the youngest of his employers had, it is true, at times complained that he made mistakes of halfpence and pence in their accounts; but as these affairs could never be brought to a public trial, Fisher's character and consequence were undiminished, till the fatal day when his Aunt Barbara forbade his visits to the confectioner's; or rather, till she requested the confectioner, who had his private reasons for obeying her, not *to receive* her nephew's visits, as he had made himself sick at his house, and Mrs. Barbara's fears for his health were incessant.

Though his visits to the confectioner's were thus at an end, there were many other shops open to him; and with officious zeal he offered his services to the new manager, to purchase whatever might be wanting for the theatre.

Since his father's death Fisher had become a boarder at Dr. Middleton's, but his frequent visits to his Aunt Barbara afforded him opportunities of going into the town. The carpenter, De Grey's friend, was discarded by Archer, for having said '*lack-a-daisy!*' when he saw that the old theatre was pulled down. A new carpenter and paper-hanger, recommended by Fisher, were appointed to attend, with their tools, for orders, at two o'clock. Archer, impatient to show his ingenuity and his generosity, gave his plan and his orders in a few minutes, in a most decided manner. 'These things,' he observed, 'should be done with some spirit.'

To which the carpenter readily assented, and added that 'gentlemen of spirit never looked to the *expense*, but always to the *effect*.' Upon this principle Mr. Chip set to work with all possible alacrity. In a few hours' time he promised to produce a grand effect. High expectations were formed. Nothing was talked of but the new playhouse; and so intent upon it was every head, that no lessons could be got. Archer was obliged, in the midst of his various occupations, to perform the part of grammar and dictionary for twenty different people.

'O ye Athenians!' he exclaimed, 'how hard do I work to obtain your praise!'

Impatient to return to the theatre, the moment the hours destined for instruction, or, as they are termed by schoolboys, school-hours, were over each prisoner started up with a shout of joy.

'Stop one moment, gentlemen, if you please,' said Dr. Middleton, in an awful voice. 'Mr. Archer, return to your place. Are you all here?' The names of all the boys were called over, and when each had answered to his name, Dr. Middleton said—

'Gentlemen, I am sorry to interrupt your amusements; but, till you have contrary orders from me, no one, on pain of my serious displeasure, must go into *that* building' (pointing to the place where the theatre was erecting). 'Mr. Archer, your carpenter is at the door. You will be so good as to dismiss him. I do not think proper to give my reasons for these orders; but you who *know* me,' said the doctor, and his eye turned towards De Grey, 'will not suspect me of caprice. I depend, gentlemen, upon your obedience.'

To the dead silence with which these orders were received, succeeded in a few minutes a universal groan. 'So!' said Townsend, 'all our diversion is over.' 'So,' whispered Fisher in the manager's ear, 'this is some trick of the Greybeards'. Did you not observe how he looked at De Grey?'

Fired by this thought, which had never entered his mind before, Archer started from his reverie, and striking his hand upon the table, swore that he 'would not be outwitted by any Greybeard in Europe—no, nor by all of them put together. The Archers were surely a match for them. He would stand by them, if they would stand by him,' he declared, with a loud voice, 'against the whole world, and Dr. Middleton himself, with "*Little Premium*" at his right hand.'

Everybody admired Archer's spirit, but was a little appalled at the sound of standing against Dr. Middleton.

'Why not?' resumed the indignant manager. 'Neither Dr. Middleton nor any doctor upon earth shall treat me with injustice. This, you see, is a stroke at me and my party, and I won't bear it.'

'Oh, you are mistaken!' said De Grey, who was the only one who dared to oppose reason to the angry orator. 'It cannot be a stroke aimed at "you and your party," for he does not know that you *have* a party.'

'I'll make him know it, and I'll make *you* know it, too,' said Archer. 'Before I came here you reigned alone; now your reign is over, Mr. De Grey. Remember my majority this morning, and your theatre last night.'

'He has remembered it,' said Fisher. 'You see, the moment he was not to be our manager, we were to have no theatre, no playhouse, no plays. We must all sit down with our hands before us—all for "*good reasons*" of Dr. Middleton's, which he does not vouchsafe to tell us.'

'I won't be governed by any man's reasons that he won't tell me,' cried Archer. 'He cannot have good reasons, or why not tell them?' 'Nonsense!' said De Grey. '*We shall not suspect him of caprice!*' 'Why not?' 'Because we who know him have never known him capricious.' 'Perhaps not. *I* know nothing about him,' said Archer. 'No,' said De Grey; 'for that very reason *I* speak who do know him. Don't be in a passion, Archer.' 'I will be in a passion. I won't submit to tyranny. I won't be made a fool of by a few soft words. You don't know me, De Grey. I'll go through with what I've begun. I am manager, and I will be manager; and you shall see my theatre finished in spite of you, and *my* party triumphant.'

'Party,' repeated De Grey. 'I cannot imagine what is in the word "party" that seems to drive you mad. We never heard of parties till you came amongst us.'

'No; before I came, I say, nobody dared oppose you; but *I* dare; and I tell you to your face, take care of me—a warm friend and a bitter enemy is my motto.' 'I am not your enemy! I believe you are out of your senses, Archer!' said he, laughing. 'Out of my senses! No; you are my enemy! Are you not my rival? Did you not win the premium? Did not you want to be manager? Answer me, are not you, in one word, a Greybeard?' 'You called me a Greybeard, but my name is De Grey,' said he, still laughing. 'Laugh on!' cried the other, furiously. 'Come,

Archers, follow me. *We* shall laugh by-and-by, I promise you.' At the door Archer was stopped by Mr. Chip. 'Oh, Mr. Chip, I am ordered to discharge you.' 'Yes, sir; and here's a little bill——' 'Bill, Mr. Chip! why, you have not been at work for two hours!' 'Not much over, sir; but if you'll please to look into it, you'll see 'tis for a few things you ordered. The stuff is all laid out and delivered. The paper and the festoon-bordering for the drawing-room scene is cut out, and left y*a*nder within.' 'Y*a*nder within! I wish you had not been in such a confounded hurry—six-and-twenty shillings!' cried he; 'but I can't stay to talk about it now. I'll tell you, Mr. Chip,' said Archer, lowering his voice, 'what you must do for me, my good fellow.'

Then, drawing Mr. Chip aside, he begged him to pull down some of the woodwork which had been put up, and to cut it into a certain number of wooden bars, of which he gave him the dimensions, with orders to place them all, when ready, under a haystack, which he pointed out.

Mr. Chip scrupled and hesitated, and began to talk of '*the doctor*.' Archer immediately began to talk of the bill, and throwing down a guinea and a half, the conscientious carpenter pocketed the money directly, and made his bow.

'Well, Master Archer,' said he, 'there's no refusing you nothing. You have such a way of talking one out of it. You manage me just like a child.'

'Ay, ay!' said Archer, knowing that he had been cheated, and yet proud of managing a carpenter, 'ay, ay! I know the way to manage everybody. Let the things be ready in an hour's time; and hark'e! leave your tools by mistake behind you, and a thousand of twenty-penny nails. Ask no questions, and keep your own counsel like a wise man. Off with you, and take care of "*the doctor*."'

'Archers, Archers, to the Archers' tree! Follow your leader,' cried he, sounding his well-known whistle as a signal. His followers gathered round him, and he, raising himself upon the mount at the foot of the tree, counted his numbers, and then, in a voice lower than usual, addressed them thus:— 'My friends, is there a Greybeard amongst us? If there is, let him walk off at once, he has my free leave.' No one stirred. 'Then we are all Archers, and we will stand by one another. Join hands, my friends.' They all joined hands. 'Promise me not to betray me, and I will go on. I ask no security but your honour.' They all gave their honour to be secret and *faithful*, as he called it, and he went on. 'Did you ever hear of such a thing as a "*Barring Out*," my friends?' They had heard of such a thing, but they had only heard of it.

Archer gave the history of a 'Barring Out' in which he had been concerned at his school, in which the boys stood out against the master, and gained their point at last, which was a week's more holidays at Easter.16 'But if *we* should not succeed,' said they, 'Dr. Middleton is so steady; he never goes back from what he has said.' 'Did you ever try to push him back? Let us be steady and he'll tremble. Tyrants always tremble when——' 'Oh,' interrupted a number of voices, 'but he is not a tyrant—is he?' 'All schoolmasters are tyrants—are not they?' replied Archer; 'and is not he a schoolmaster?' To this logic there was no answer; but, still reluctant, they asked, 'What they should *get* by a Barring Out?' 'Get!—everything!—what we want!—which is everything to lads of spirit—victory and liberty! Bar him out till he repeals his tyrannical law; till he lets us into our own theatre again, or till he tells us his "*good reasons*" against it.' 'But perhaps he has reasons for not telling us.' 'Impossible!' cried Archer; 'that's the way we are always to be governed by a man in a wig, who says he has good reasons, and can't tell them. Are you fools? Go! go back to De Grey! I see you are all Greybeards. Go! Who goes first?' Nobody would go *first*. 'I will have nothing to do with ye, if ye are resolved to be slaves!' 'We won't be slaves!' they all exclaimed at once. 'Then,' said Archer, 'stand out in the right and be free.'

'*The right*.' It would have taken up too much time to examine what 'the right' was. Archer was always sure that '*the right*' was what his party chose to do; that is, what he chose to do himself; and such is the influence of numbers upon each other, in conquering the feelings of shame and in confusing the powers of reasoning, that in a few minutes 'the right' was forgotten, and each said to himself, 'To be sure, Archer is a very clever boy, and he can't be mistaken'; or, 'To be sure, Townsend thinks so, and he would not do anything to get us into a scrape'; or, 'To be sure, everybody will agree to this but myself, and I can't stand out alone, to be pointed at as a Greybeard and a slave. Everybody thinks it is right, and everybody can't be wrong.'

By some of these arguments, which passed rapidly through the mind without his being conscious of them, each boy decided, and deceived himself—what none would have done alone, none scrupled to do as a party. It was determined, then, that there should be a Barring Out. The arrangement of the affair was left to their new manager, to whom they all pledged implicit obedience. Obedience, it seems, is necessary, even from rebels to their ringleaders; not reasonable, but implicit obedience.

Scarcely had the assembly adjourned to the Ball-alley, when Fisher, with an important length of face, came up to the manager, and desired to speak one word to him. 'My advice to you, Archer, is, to do nothing in this till we have consulted *you know who*, about whether it's right or wrong.' '"*You know who*"! Whom do you mean? Make haste, and don't make so many faces, for I'm in a hurry. Who is "*You know who*"?' 'The old woman,' said Fisher, gravely; 'the gipsy.' 'You may consult the old woman,' said Archer, bursting out a-laughing, 'about what's right and wrong, if you please, but no old woman shall decide for me.' 'No; but you don't *take* me,' said Fisher; 'you don't *take* me. By right and wrong, I mean lucky and unlucky.' 'Whatever *I* do will be lucky,' replied Archer. 'My gipsy told you that already.' 'I know, I know,' said Fisher, 'and what she said about your friends being lucky—that went a great way with many,' added he, with a sagacious nod of his head, 'I can tell you *that*—more than you think. Do you know,' said he, laying hold of Archer's button, 'I'm in the secret? There are nine of us have crooked our little fingers upon it, not to stir a step till we get her advice; and she has appointed me to meet her about particular business of my own at eight. So I'm to consult her and to bring her answer.'

Archer knew too well how to govern fools to attempt to reason with them; and, instead of laughing any longer at Fisher's ridiculous superstition, he was determined to take advantage of it. He affected to be persuaded of the wisdom of the measure; looked at his watch; urged him to be exact to a moment; conjured him to remember exactly the words of the oracle; and, above all things, to demand the lucky hour and minute when the Barring Out should begin. With these instructions Archer put his watch into the solemn dupe's hand, and left him to count the seconds till the moment of his appointment, whilst he ran off himself to prepare the oracle.

At a little gate which looked into a lane, through which he guessed that the gipsy must pass, he stationed himself, saw her, gave her half-a-crown and her instructions, made his escape, and got back unsuspected to Fisher, whom he found in the attitude in which he had left him, watching the motion of the minute hand.

123

Proud of his secret commission, Fisher slouched his hat, he knew not why, over his face, and proceeded towards the appointed spot. To keep, as he had been charged by Archer, within the letter of the law, he stood *behind* the forbidden building, and waited some minutes.

Through a gap in the hedge the old woman at length made her appearance, muffled up, and looking cautiously about her. 'There's nobody near us!' said Fisher, and he began to be a little afraid. 'What answer,' said he, recollecting himself, 'about my Livy?' 'Lost! lost! lost!' said the gipsy, lifting up her hands; 'never, never, never to be found! But no matter for that now: that is not your errand to-night; no tricks with me; speak to me of what is next your heart.'

Fisher, astonished, put his hand upon his heart, told her all that she knew before, and received the answers that Archer had dictated: 'That the Archers should be lucky as long as they stuck to their manager and to one another; that the Barring Out should end in woe, if not begun precisely as the clock should strike nine on Wednesday night; but if begun in that *lucky* moment, and all obedient to their *lucky* leader, all should end well.'

A thought, a provident thought, now struck Fisher; for even he had some foresight where his favourite passion was concerned. 'Pray, in our Barring Out shall we be starved?' 'No,' said the gipsy, 'not if you trust to me for food, and if you give me money enough. Silver won't do for so many; gold is what must cross my hand.' 'I have no gold,' said Fisher, 'and I don't know what you mean by "so many." I'm only talking of number one, you know. I must take care of that first.'

So, as Fisher thought it was possible that Archer, clever as he was, might be disappointed in his supplies, he determined to take secret measures for himself. His Aunt Barbara's interdiction had shut him out of the confectioner's shop; but he flattered himself that he could outwit his aunt; he therefore begged the gipsy to procure him twelve buns by Thursday morning, and bring them secretly to one of the windows of the schoolroom.

As Fisher did not produce any money when he made this proposal, it was at first absolutely rejected; but a bribe at length conquered his difficulties: and the bribe which Fisher found himself obliged to give—for he had no pocket money left of his own, he being as much *restricted* in that article as Archer was *indulged*—the bribe that he found himself obliged to give to quiet the gipsy was half-a-crown, which Archer had entrusted to him to buy candles for the theatre. 'Oh,' thought he to himself, 'Archer's so careless about money, he will never think of asking me for the half-crown again; and now he'll want no candles for the *theatre*; or, at any rate, it will be some time first; and maybe Aunt Barbara may be got to give me that much at Christmas; then, if the worst comes to the worst, one can pay Archer. My mouth waters for the buns, and have 'em I must now.'

So, for the hope of twelve buns, he sacrificed the money which had been entrusted to him. Thus the meanest motives, in mean minds, often prompt to the commission of those great faults to which one should think nothing but some violent passion could have tempted.

The ambassador having thus, in his opinion, concluded his own and the public business, returned well satisfied with the result, after receiving the gipsy's reiterated promise to tap *three times* at the window on Thursday morning.

The day appointed for the Barring Out at length arrived; and Archer, assembling the confederates, informed them that all was prepared for carrying their design into execution; that he now depended for success upon their punctuality and courage. He had, within the last two hours, got all their bars ready to fasten the doors and window shutters of the schoolroom; he had, with the assistance of two of the day scholars who were of the party, sent into the town for provisions, at his own expense, which would make a handsome supper for that night; he had also negotiated with some cousins of his, who lived in the town, for a constant supply in future. 'Bless me,' exclaimed Archer, suddenly stopping in this narration of his services, 'there's one thing, after all, I've forgot, we shall be undone without it. Fisher, pray did you ever buy the candles for the playhouse?' 'No, to be sure,' replied Fisher, extremely frightened; 'you know you don't want candles for the playhouse now.' 'Not for the playhouse, but for the Barring Out. We shall be in the dark, man. You must run this minute, run.' 'For candles?' said Fisher, confused; 'how many?—what sort?' 'Stupidity!' exclaimed Archer, 'you are a pretty fellow at a dead lift! Lend me a pencil and a bit of paper, do; I'll write down what I want myself! Well, what are you fumbling for?' 'For money!' said Fisher, colouring. 'Money, man! Didn't I give you half-a-crown the other day?' 'Yes,' replied Fisher, stammering; 'but I wasn't sure that that might be enough.' 'Enough! yes, to be sure it will. I don't know what you are *at*.' 'Nothing, nothing,' said Fisher; 'here, write upon this, then,' said Fisher, putting a piece of paper into Archer's hand, upon which Archer wrote his orders. 'Away, away!' cried he.

Away went Fisher. He returned; but not until a considerable time afterwards. They were at supper when he returned. 'Fisher always comes in at supper-time,' observed one of the Greybeards, carelessly. 'Well, and would you have him come in *after* supper-time?' said Townsend, who always supplied his party with ready *wit*. 'I've got the candles,' whispered Fisher as he passed by Archer to his place. 'And the tinder-box?' said Archer. 'Yes; I got back from my Aunt Barbara under pretence that I must study for repetition day an hour later to-night. So I got leave. Was not that clever?'

A dunce always thinks it clever to cheat even by *sober lies*. How Mr. Fisher procured the candles and the tinder-box without money and without credit we shall discover further on.

Archer and his associates had agreed to stay the last in the schoolroom; and as soon as the Greybeards were gone out to bed, he, as the signal, was to shut and lock one door, Townsend the other. A third conspirator was to strike a light, in case they should not be able to secure a candle. A fourth was to take charge of the candle as soon as lighted; and all the rest were to run to their bars, which were secreted in a room; then to fix them to the common fastening bars of the window, in the manner in which they had been previously instructed by the manager. Thus each had his part assigned, and each was warned that the success of the whole depended upon their order and punctuality.

Order and punctuality, it appears, are necessary even in a Barring Out; and even rebellion must have its laws.

The long-expected moment at length arrived. De Grey and his friends, unconscious of what was going forward, walked out of the schoolroom as usual at bedtime. The clock began to strike nine. There was one Greybeard left in the room, who was packing up some of his books, which had been left about by accident. It is impossible to describe the impatience with which he was watched, especially by Fisher and the nine who depended upon the gipsy oracle.

When he had got all his books together under his arm, he let one of them fall; and whilst he stooped to pick it up, Archer gave the signal. The doors were shut, locked, and double-locked in an instant. A light was struck and each ran to his post. The bars were all in the same moment put up to the windows, and Archer, when he had tried them all, and seen that they were secure, gave a loud 'Huzza!'—in which he was joined by all the party most manfully—by all but the poor Greybeard, who, the picture of astonishment, stood stock still in the midst of them with his books under his arm; at which spectacle Townsend, who enjoyed the *frolic* of the fray more than anything else, burst into an immoderate fit of laughter. 'So, my little Greybeard,' said he, holding a candle full in his eyes, 'what think you of all this?—How came you amongst the wicked ones?' 'I don't know, indeed,' said the little boy, very gravely; 'you shut me up amongst you. Won't you let me out?' 'Let you out! No, no, my little Greybeard,' said Archer, catching hold of him and dragging him to the window bars. 'Look ye here—touch these—put your hand to them—pull, push, kick—put a little spirit into it, man—kick like an Archer, if you can; away with ye. It's a pity that the king of the Greybeards is not here to admire me. I should like to show him our fortifications. But come, my merry men all, now to the feast. Out with the table into the middle of the room. Good cheer, my jolly Archers! I'm your manager!'

Townsend, delighted with the bustle, rubbed his hands and capered about the room, whilst the preparations for the feast were hurried forward. 'Four candles!—Four candles on the table. Let's have things in style when we are about it, Mr. Manager,' cried Townsend. 'Places!—Places! There's nothing like a fair scramble, my boys. Let every one take care of himself. Hallo, Greybeard! I've knocked Greybeard down here in the scuffle. Get up again, my lad, and see a little life.'

'No, no,' cried Fisher, 'he shan't *sup* with us.' 'No, no,' cried the manager, 'he shan't *live* with us; a Greybeard is not fit company for Archers.' 'No, no,' cried Townsend, 'evil communication corrupts good manners.'

So with one unanimous hiss they hunted the poor little gentle boy into a corner; and having pent him up with benches, Fisher opened his books for him, which he thought the greatest mortification, and set up a candle beside him. 'There, now he looks like a Greybeard as he is!' cried they. 'Tell me what's the Latin for cold roast beef?' said Fisher, exultingly, and they returned to their feast.

Long and loud they revelled. They had a few bottles of cider. 'Give me the corkscrew, the cider shan't be kept till it's sour,' cried Townsend, in answer to the manager, who, when he beheld the provisions vanishing with surprising rapidity, began to fear for the morrow. 'Hang to-morrow!' cried Townsend, 'let Greybeards think of to-morrow; Mr. Manager, here's your good health.'

The Archers all stood up as their cups were filled, to drink the health of their chief with a universal cheer. But at the moment that the cups were at their lips, and as Archer bowed to thank the company, a sudden shower from above astonished the whole assembly. They looked up, and beheld the rose of a watering-engine, whose long neck appeared through a trap-door in the ceiling. 'Your good health, Mr. Manager!' said a voice, which was known to be the gardener's; and in the midst of their surprise and dismay the candles were suddenly extinguished; the trap-door shut down; and they were left in utter darkness.

'The *Devil*!' said Archer. 'Don't swear, Mr. Manager,' said the same voice from the ceiling, 'I hear every word you say.' 'Mercy upon us!' exclaimed Fisher. 'The clock,' added he, whispering, 'must have been wrong, for it had not done striking when we began. Only, you remember, Archer, it had just done before you had done locking your door.' 'Hold your tongue, blockhead!' said Archer. 'Well, boys! were ye never in the dark before? You are not afraid of a shower of rain, I hope. Is anybody drowned?' 'No,' said they, with a faint laugh, 'but what shall we do here in the dark all night long, and all day to-morrow? We can't unbar the shutters.' 'It's a wonder *nobody* ever thought of the trap-door!' said Townsend.

The trap-door had indeed escaped the manager's observation. As the house was new to him, and the ceiling being newly whitewashed, the opening was scarcely perceptible. Vexed to be out-generalled, and still more vexed to have it remarked, Archer poured forth a volley of incoherent exclamations and reproaches against those who were thus so soon discouraged by a trifle; and groping for the tinder-box, he asked if anything could be easier than to strike a light again.17 The light appeared. But at the moment that it made the tinder-box visible, another shower from above, aimed, and aimed exactly, at the tinder-box, drenched it with water, and rendered it totally unfit for further service. Archer in a fury dashed it to the ground. And now for the first time he felt what it was to be the unsuccessful head of a party. He heard in his turn the murmurs of a discontented, changeable populace; and recollecting all his bars and bolts, and ingenious contrivances, he was more provoked at their blaming him for this one only oversight than he was grieved at the disaster itself.

'Oh, my hair is all wet!' cried one, dolefully. 'Wring it then,' said Archer. 'My hand's cut with your broken glass,' cried another. 'Glass!' cried a third; 'mercy! is there broken glass? and it's all about, I suppose, amongst the supper; and I had but one bit of bread all the time.' 'Bread!' cried Archer; 'eat if you want it. Here's a piece here, and no glass near it.' 'It's all wet, and I don't like dry bread by itself; that's no feast.'

'Heigh-day! What, nothing but moaning and grumbling! If these are the joys of *a Barring Out*,' cried Townsend, 'I'd rather be snug in my bed. I expected that we should have sat up till twelve o'clock, talking, and laughing, and singing.' 'So you may still; what hinders you?' said Archer. 'Sing, and we'll join you, and I should be glad those fellows overhead heard us singing. Begin, Townsend—

Come, now, all ye social Powers,
Spread your influence o'er us—

Or else—

Rule, Britannia! Britannia rules the waves!
Britons never will be slaves.'

Nothing can be more melancholy than forced merriment. In vain they roared in chorus. In vain they tried to appear gay. It would not do. The voices died away, and dropped off one by one. They had each provided himself with a greatcoat to sleep upon; but now, in the dark, there was a peevish scrambling contest for the coats, and half the company, in very bad humour, stretched themselves upon the benches for the night.

There is great pleasure in bearing anything that has the appearance of hardship, as long as there is any glory to be acquired by it; but when people feel themselves foiled, there is no further pleasure in endurance; and if, in their misfortune, there is any mixture of the ridiculous, the motives for heroism are immediately destroyed. Dr. Middleton had probably considered this in the choice he made of his first attack.

Archer, who had spent the night as a man who had the cares of government upon his shoulders, rose early in the morning, whilst everybody else was fast asleep. In the night he had resolved the affair of the trap-door, and a new danger had alarmed him. It was possible that the enemy might descend upon them through the trap-door. The room had been built high to admit a free circulation of air. It was twenty feet, so that it was in vain to think of reaching to the trap-door.

As soon as the daylight appeared, Archer rose softly, that he might *reconnoitre*, and devise some method of guarding against this new danger. Luckily there were round holes in the top of the window-shutters, which admitted sufficient light for him to work by. The remains of the soaked feast, wet candles, and broken glass spread over the table in the middle of the room, looked rather dismal this morning.

'A pretty set of fellows I have to manage!' said Archer, contemplating the group of sleepers before him. 'It is well they have somebody to think for them. Now if I wanted—which, thank goodness, I don't—but if I did want to call a cabinet council to my assistance, whom could I pitch upon?—not this stupid snorer, who is dreaming of gipsies, if he is dreaming of anything,' continued Archer, as he looked into Fisher's open mouth. 'This next chap is quick enough; but, then, he is so fond of having everything his own way. And this curl-pated monkey, who is grinning in his sleep, is all tongue and no brains. Here are brains, though nobody would think it, in this lump,' said he, looking at a fat, rolled up, heavy-breathing sleeper; 'but what signify brains to such a lazy dog? I might kick him for my football this half-hour before I should get him awake. This lank-jawed harlequin beside him is a handy fellow, to be sure; but then, if he has hands, he has no head—and he'd be afraid of his own shadow too, by this light, he is such a coward! And Townsend, why he has puns in plenty; but, when there's any work to be done, he's the worst fellow to be near one in the world—he can do nothing but laugh at his own puns. This poor little fellow that we hunted into the corner has more sense than all of them put together; but then he is a Greybeard.'

Thus speculated the chief of a party upon his sleeping friends. And how did it happen that he should be so ambitious to please and govern this set, when for each individual of which it was composed he felt such supreme contempt? He had formed them into a *party*, had given them a name, and he was at their head. If these be not good reasons, none better can be assigned for Archer's conduct.

'I wish ye could all sleep on,' said he; 'but I must waken ye, though you will be only in my way. The sound of my hammering must waken them; so I may as well do the thing handsomely, and flatter some of them by pretending to ask their advice.'

Accordingly, he pulled two or three to waken them. 'Come, Townsend, waken, my boy! Here's some diversion for you—up! up!'

'Diversion!' cried Townsend; 'I'm your man! I'm up—*up to anything.*'

So, under the name of *diversion*, Archer set Townsend to work at four o'clock in the morning. They had nails, a few tools, and several spars, still left from the wreck of the playhouse. These, by Archer's directions, they sharpened at one end, and nailed them to the ends of several forms.

All hands were now called to clear away the supper things, and to erect these forms perpendicularly under the trap-door; and with the assistance of a few braces, a *chevaux-de-frise* was formed, upon which nobody could venture to descend. At the farthest end of the room they likewise formed a penthouse of the tables, under which they proposed to breakfast, secure from the pelting storm, if it should again assail them through the trap-door. They crowded under the penthouse as soon as it was ready, and their admiration of its ingenuity paid the workmen for the job.

'Lord! I shall like to see the gardener's phiz through the trap-door, when he beholds the spikes under him!' cried Townsend. 'Now for breakfast!' 'Ay, now for breakfast,' said Archer, looking at his watch; 'past eight o'clock, and my town boys not come! I don't understand this!'

Archer had expected a constant supply of provisions from two boys who lived in the town, who were cousins of his, and who had promised to come every day, and put food in at a certain hole in the wall, in which a ventilator usually turned. This ventilator Archer had taken down, and had contrived it so that it could be easily removed and replaced at pleasure; but, upon examination, it was now perceived that the hole had been newly stopped up by an iron back, which it was impossible to penetrate or remove.

'It never came into my head that anybody would ever have thought of the ventilator but myself!' exclaimed Archer, in great perplexity. He listened and waited for his cousins; but no cousins came, and at a late hour the company were obliged to breakfast upon the scattered fragments of the last night's feast. That feast had been spread with such imprudent profusion, that little now remained to satisfy the hungry guests.

Archer, who well knew the effect which the apprehension of a scarcity would have upon his associates, did everything that could be done by a bold countenance and reiterated assertions to persuade them that his cousins would certainly come at last, and that the supplies were only delayed. The delay, however, was alarming.

Fisher alone heard the manager's calculations and saw the public fears unmoved. Secretly rejoicing in his own wisdom, he walked from window to window, slily listening for the gipsy's signal. 'There it is!' cried he, with more joy sparkling in his eyes than had ever enlightened them before. 'Come this way, Archer; but don't tell anybody. Hark! do ye hear those three taps at the window? This is the old woman with twelve buns for me. I'll give you one whole one for yourself, if you will unbar the window for me.'

'Unbar the window!' interrupted Archer; 'no, that I won't, for you or the gipsy either; but I have heard enough to get your buns without that. But stay; there is something of more consequence than your twelve buns. I must think for ye all, I see, regularly.'

So he summoned a council, and proposed that every one should subscribe, and trust the subscription to the gipsy, to purchase a fresh supply of provisions. Archer laid down a guinea of his own money for his subscription; at which sight all the company clapped their hands, and his popularity rose to a high pitch with their renewed hopes of plenty. Now, having made a list of their wants, they folded the money in the paper, put it into a bag, which Archer tied to a long string, and, having broken the pane of glass behind the round hole in the window-shutter, he let down the bag to the gipsy. She promised to be punctual, and having filled the bag with Fishers twelve buns, they were drawn up in triumph, and everybody anticipated the pleasure with which they should see the same bag drawn up at dinner-time. The buns were a little squeezed in being drawn through the hole in the window-shutter, but Archer immediately sawed out a piece of the shutter, and broke the corresponding panes in each of the other windows, to prevent suspicion, and to make it appear that they had all been broken to admit air.

What a pity that so much ingenuity should have been employed to no purpose!

It may have surprised the intelligent reader that the gipsy was so punctual to her promise to Fisher, but we must recollect that her apparent integrity was only cunning; she was punctual that she might be employed again, that she might be entrusted with the contribution which, she foresaw, must be raised amongst the famishing garrison. No sooner had she received the money than her end was gained.

Dinner-time came; it struck three, four, five, six. They listened with hungry ears, but no signal was heard. The morning had been very long, and Archer had in vain tried to dissuade them from devouring the remainder of the provisions before they were sure of a fresh supply. And now those who had been the most confident were the most impatient of their disappointment.

Archer, in the division of the food, had attempted, by the most scrupulous exactness, to content the public, and he was both astonished and provoked to perceive that his impartiality was impeached. So differently do people judge in different situations! He was the first person to accuse his master of injustice, and the least capable of bearing such an imputation upon himself from others. He now experienced some of the joys of power, and the delight of managing unreasonable numbers.

'Have not I done everything I could to please you? Have not I spent my money to buy you food? Have not I divided the last morsel with you? I have not tasted one mouthful to-day! Did not I set to work for you at sunrise? Did not I lie awake all night for you? Have not I had all the labour and all the anxiety? Look round and see *my* contrivances, *my* work, *my* generosity! And, after all, you think me a tyrant, because I want you to have common sense. Is not this bun which I hold in my hand my own? Did not I earn it by my own ingenuity from that selfish dunce (pointing to Fisher), who could never have gotten one of his twelve buns, if I had not shown him how? Eleven of them he has eaten since morning for his own share, without offering any one a morsel; but I scorn to eat even what is justly my own, when I see so many hungry creatures longing for it. I was not going to touch this last morsel myself. I only begged you to keep it till supper-time, when perhaps you'll want it more, and Townsend, who can't bear the slightest thing that crosses his own whims, and who thinks there's nothing in this world to be minded but his own diversion, calls me a *tyrant*. You all of you promised to obey me. The first thing I ask you to do for your own good, and when, if you had common sense, you must know I can want nothing but your good, you rebel against me. Traitors! fools! ungrateful fools!'

Archer walked up and down, unable to command his emotion, whilst, for the moment, the discontented multitude was silenced.

'Here,' said he, striking his hand upon the little boy's shoulder, 'here's the only one amongst you who has not uttered one word of reproach or complaint, and he has had but one bit of bread—a bit that I gave him myself this day. Here!' said he, snatching the bun, which nobody had dared to touch, 'take it—it's mine—I give it to you, though you are a Greybeard; you deserve it. Eat it, and be an Archer. You shall be my captain; will you?' said he, lifting him up in his arm above the rest.

'I like you now,' said the little boy, courageously; 'but I love De Grey better; he has always been my friend, and he advised me never to call myself any of those names, Archer or Greybeard; so I won't. Though I am shut in here, I have nothing to do with it. I love Dr. Middleton; he was never unjust to *me*, and I daresay that he has very good reasons, as De Grey said, for forbidding us to go into that house. Besides, it's his own.'

Instead of admiring the good sense and steadiness of this little lad, Archer suffered Townsend to snatch the untasted bun out of his hands. He flung it at a hole in the window, but it fell back. The Archers scrambled for it, and Fisher ate it.

Archer saw this, and was sensible that he had not done handsomely in suffering it. A few moments ago he had admired his own generosity, and though he had felt the injustice of others, he had not accused himself of any. He turned away from the little boy, and sitting down at one end of the table, hid his face in his hands. He continued immovable in this posture for some time.

'Lord!' said Townsend; 'it was an excellent joke!' 'Pooh!' said Fisher; 'what a fool, to think so much about a bun!' 'Never mind, Mr. Archer, if you are thinking about me,' said the little boy, trying gently to pull his hands from his face.

Archer stooped down and lifted him up upon the table, at which sight the partisans set up a general hiss. 'He has forsaken us! He deserts his party! He wants to be a Greybeard! After he has got us all into this scrape, he will leave us!'

'I am not going to leave you,' cried Archer. 'No one shall ever accuse me of deserting my party. I'll stick by the Archers, right or wrong, I tell you, to the last moment. But this little fellow—take it as you please, mutiny if you will, and throw me out of the window. Call me traitor! coward! Greybeard!—this little fellow is worth you all put together, and I'll stand by him against any one who dares to lay a finger upon him; and the next morsel of food that I see shall be his. Touch him who dares!'

The commanding air with which Archer spoke and looked, and the belief that the little boy deserved his protection, silenced the crowd. But the storm was only hushed.

No sound of merriment was now to be heard—no battledore and shuttlecock—no ball, no marbles. Some sat in a corner, whispering their wishes that Archer would unbar the doors and give up. Others, stretching their arms, and gaping as they sauntered up and down the room, wished for air, or food, or water. Fisher and his nine, who had such firm dependence upon the gipsy, now gave themselves up to utter despair. It was eight o'clock, growing darker and darker every minute, and no candles, no light, could they have. The prospect of another long dark night made them still more discontented.

Townsend, at the head of the yawners, and Fisher, at the head of the hungry malcontents, gathered round Archer and the few yet unconquered spirits, demanding 'How long he meant to keep them in this dark dungeon? and whether he expected that they should starve themselves for his sake?'

The idea of *giving up* was more intolerable to Archer than all the rest. He saw that the majority, his own convincing argument, was against him. He was therefore obliged to condescend to the arts of persuasion. He flattered some with hopes of food from the town boys. Some he reminded of their promises; others he praised for former prowess; and others he shamed by the repetition of their high vaunts in the beginning of the business.

It was at length resolved that at all events they *would hold out*. With this determination they stretched themselves again to sleep, for the second night, in weak and weary obstinacy.

Archer slept longer and more soundly than usual the next morning, and when he awoke, he found his hands tied behind him! Three or four boys had just got hold of his feet, which they pressed down, whilst the trembling hands of Fisher were fastening the cord round them.

With all the force which rage could inspire, Archer struggled and roared to '*his Archers*!'—his friends, his party—for help against the traitors. But all kept aloof. Townsend, in particular, stood laughing and looking on. 'I beg your pardon, Archer, but really you look so droll. All alive and kicking! Don't be angry. I'm so weak, I cannot help laughing to-day.'

The packthread cracked. 'His hands are free! He's loose!' cried the least of the boys, and ran away, whilst Archer leaped up, and seizing hold of Fisher with a powerful grasp, sternly demanded 'What he meant by this?'

'Ask my party,' said Fisher, terrified; 'they set me on; ask my party.'

'Your party!' cried Archer, with a look of ineffable contempt; 'you reptile!—*your* party? Can such a thing as *you* have a party?'

'To be sure!' said Fisher, settling his collar, which Archer in his surprise had let go; 'to be sure! Why not? Any man who chooses it may have a party as well as yourself, I suppose. I have nine Fishermen.'

At these words, spoken with much sullen importance, Archer, in spite of his vexation, could not help laughing. 'Fishermen!' cried he, '*Fishermen!*' 'And why not Fishermen as well as Archers?' cried they. 'One party is just as good as another; it is only a question which can get the upper hand; and we had your hands tied just now.'

'That's right, Townsend,' said Archer, 'laugh on, my boy! Friend or foe, it's all the same to you. I know how to value your friendship now. You are a mighty good fellow when the sun shines; but let a storm come, and how you slink away!'

Archer leaped up, and seizing hold of Fisher with a powerful grasp, sternly demanded ' What he meant by this ?'

Archer leaped-up, and seizing hold of Fisher with a powerful grasp, sternly demanded 'What he meant by this?'

At this instant, Archer felt the difference between *a good companion* and a good friend, a difference which some people do not discover till late in life.

'Have I no friend?—no real friend amongst you all? And could ye stand by and see my hands tied behind me like a thief's? What signifies such a party—all mute?'

'We want something to eat,' answered the Fishermen. 'What signifies *such* a party, indeed? and *such* a manager, who can do nothing for one?'

'And have *I* done nothing?'

'Don't let's hear any more prosing,' said Fisher; 'we are too many for you. I've advised my party, if they've a mind not to be starved, to give you up for the ringleader, as you were; and Dr. Middleton will not let us all off, I daresay.' So, depending upon the sullen silence of the assembly, he again approached Archer with a cord. A cry of 'No, no, no! Don't tie him,' was feebly raised.

Archer stood still, but the moment Fisher touched him, he knocked him down to the ground, and turning to the rest, with eyes sparkling with indignation, 'Archers!' cried he. A voice at this instant was heard at the door. It was De Grey's voice. 'I have got a large basket of provisions for your breakfast.' A general shout of joy was sent forth by the voracious public. 'Breakfast! Provisions! A large basket! De Grey for ever! Huzza!'

De Grey promised, upon his honour, that if he would unbar the door nobody should come in with him, and no advantage should be taken of them. This promise was enough even for Archer. 'I will let him in,' said he, 'myself; for I'm sure he'll never break his word.' He pulled away the bar; the door opened; and having bargained for the liberty of Melsom, the little boy who had been shut in by mistake, De Grey entered with his basket of provisions, when he locked and barred the door instantly.

Joy and gratitude sparkled in every face when he unpacked his basket and spread the table with a plentiful breakfast. A hundred questions were asked him at once. 'Eat first,' said he, 'and we will talk afterwards.' This business was quickly despatched by those who had not tasted food for a long while. Their curiosity increased as their hunger diminished. 'Who sent us breakfast? Does Dr. Middleton know?' were questions reiterated from every mouth.

'He does know,' answered De Grey; 'and the first thing I have to tell you is, that I am your fellow-prisoner. I am to stay here till you give up. This was the only condition on which Dr. Middleton would allow me to bring you food, and he will allow no more.'

Every one looked at the empty basket. But Archer, in whom half-vanquished party spirit revived with the strength he had got from his breakfast, broke into exclamations in praise of De Grey's magnanimity, as he now imagined that De Grey had become one of themselves.

'And you will join us, will you? That's a noble fellow!' 'No,' answered De Grey, calmly; 'but I hope to persuade, or rather to convince you, that you ought to join me.' 'You would have found it no hard task to have persuaded or convinced us, whichever you pleased,' said Townsend, 'if you had appealed to Archers fasting; but Archers feasting are quite other animals. Even Cæsar himself, after breakfast, is quite another thing!' added he, pointing to Archer. 'You may speak for yourself, Mr. Townsend,' replied the insulted hero, 'but not for me, or for Archers in general, if you please. We unbarred the door upon the faith of De Grey's promise—*that* was not giving up. And it would have been just as difficult, I promise you, to persuade or convince me either that I should give up against my honour before breakfast as after.'

This spirited speech was applauded by many, who had now forgotten the feelings of famine. Not so Fisher, whose memory was upon this occasion very distinct.

'What nonsense,' and the orator paused for a synonymous expression, but none was at hand. 'What nonsense and—nonsense is here! Why, don't you remember that dinner-time, and supper-time, and breakfast-time will come again? So what signifies mouthing about persuading and convincing? We will not go through again what we did yesterday! Honour me no honour. I don't understand it. I'd rather be flogged at once, as I have been many's the good time for a less thing. I say, we'd better all be flogged at once, which must be the end of it sooner or later, than wait here to be without dinner, breakfast, and supper, all only because Mr. Archer won't give up because of his honour and nonsense!'

Many prudent faces amongst the Fishermen seemed to deliberate at the close of this oration, in which the arguments were brought so 'home to each man's business and bosom.'

'But,' said De Grey, 'when we yield, I hope it will not be merely to get our dinner, gentlemen. When we yield, Archer——' 'Don't address yourself to me,' interrupted Archer, struggling with his pride; 'you have no further occasion to try to win me. I have no power, no party, you see! And now I find that I have no friends, I don't care what becomes of myself. I suppose I'm to be given up as a ringleader. Here's this Fisher, and a party of his Fishermen, were going to tie me hand and foot, if I had not knocked him down, just as you came to the door, De Grey; and now perhaps you will join Fisher's party against me.'

De Grey was going to assure him that he had no intention of joining any party, when a sudden change appeared on Archer's countenance. 'Silence!' cried Archer, in an imperious tone, and there was silence. Some one was heard to whistle the beginning of a tune, that was perfectly new to everybody present except to Archer, who immediately whistled the conclusion. 'There!' cried he, looking at De Grey with triumph; 'that's a method of holding secret correspondence, whilst a prisoner, which I learned from "Richard Cœur de Lion." I know how to make use of everything. Hallo! friend! are you there at last?' cried he, going to the ventilator. 'Yes, but we are barred out here.' 'Round to the window then, and fill our bag. We'll let it down, my lad, in a trice; bar me out who can!'

Archer let down the bag with all the expedition of joy, and it was filled with all the expedition of fear. 'Pull away! make haste, for Heaven's sake!' said the voice from without; 'the gardener will come from dinner, else, and we shall be caught. He mounted guard all yesterday at the ventilator; and though I watched and watched till it was darker than pitch, I could not get near you. I don't know what has taken him out of the way now. Make haste, pull away!' The heavy bag was soon pulled up. 'Have you any more?' said Archer. 'Yes, plenty. Let down quick! I've got the tailor's bag full, which is three times as large as yours, and I've changed clothes with the tailor's boy; so nobody took notice of me as I came down the street.'

129

'There's my own cousin!' exclaimed Archer, 'there's a noble fellow! there's my own cousin, I acknowledge. Fill the bag, then.' Several times the bag descended and ascended; and at every unlading of the crane, fresh acclamations were heard. 'I have no more!' at length the boy with the tailor's bag cried. 'Off with you, then; we've enough, and thank you.'

A delightful review was now made of their treasure. Busy hands arranged and sorted the heterogeneous mass. Archer, in the height of his glory, looked on, the acknowledged master of the whole. Townsend, who, in his prosperity as in adversity, saw and enjoyed the comic foibles of his friends, pushed De Grey, who was looking on with a more good-natured and more thoughtful air. 'Friend,' said he, 'you look like a great philosopher, and Archer a great hero.' 'And you, Townsend,' said Archer, 'may look like a wit, if you will; but you will never be a hero.' 'No, no,' replied Townsend; 'wits were never heroes, because they are wits. You are out of your wits, and therefore may set up for a hero.' 'Laugh, and welcome. I'm not a tyrant. I don't want to restrain anybody's wit; but I cannot say I admire puns.' 'Nor I, either,' said the time-serving Fisher, sidling up to the manager, and picking the ice off a piece of plum-cake, 'nor I either; I hate puns. I can never understand Townsend's *puns*. Besides, anybody can make puns; and one doesn't want wit, either, at all times; for instance, when one is going to settle about dinner, or business of consequence. Bless us all, Archer!' continued he, with sudden familiarity, '*what a sight of good things are here*! I'm sure we are much obliged to you and your cousin. I never thought he'd have come. Why, now we can hold out as long as you please. Let us see,' said he, dividing the provisions upon the table; 'we can hold out to-day, and all to-morrow, and part of next day, maybe. Why, now we may defy the doctor and the Greybeards. The doctor will surely give up to us; for, you see, he knows nothing of all this, and he'll think we are starving all this while; and he'd be afraid, you see, to let us starve quite, in reality, for three whole days, because of what would be said in the town. My Aunt Barbara, for one, would be *at him* long before that time was out; and besides, you know, in that case, he'd be hanged for murder, which is quite another thing, in law, from a *Barring Out*, you know.'

Archer had not given to this harangue all the attention which it deserved, for his eye was fixed upon De Grey. 'What is De Grey thinking of?' he asked, impatiently. 'I am thinking,' said De Grey, 'that Dr. Middleton must believe that I have betrayed his confidence in me. The gardener was ordered away from his watch-post for one half-hour when I was admitted. This half-hour the gardener has made nearly an hour. I never would have come near you if I had foreseen all this. Dr. Middleton trusted me, and now he will repent of his confidence in me.' 'De Grey!' cried Archer, with energy, 'he shall not repent of his confidence in you—nor shall you repent of coming amongst us. You shall find that we have some honour as well as yourself, and I will take care of your honour as if it were my *own*!' 'Hey-day!' interrupted Townsend; 'are heroes allowed to change sides, pray? And does the chief of the Archers stand talking sentiment to the chief of the Greybeards? In the middle of his own party too!' 'Party!' repeated Archer, disdainfully; 'I have done with parties! I see what parties are made of! I have felt the want of a friend, and I am determined to make one if I can.' 'That you may do,' said De Grey, stretching out his hand.

'Unbar the doors! unbar the windows!' exclaimed Archer. 'Away with all these things! I give up for De Grey's sake. He shall not lose his credit on my account.' 'No,' said De Grey, 'you shall not give up for my sake.' 'Well, then, I'll give up to do what is *honourable*,' said Archer. 'Why not to do what is *reasonable*?' said De Grey. '*Reasonable!* Oh, the first thing that a man of spirit should think of is, what is *honourable*.' 'But how will he find out *what is* honourable, unless he can reason?' replied De Grey. 'Oh,' said Archer, 'his own feelings always tell him what is honourable.' 'Have not *your feelings*,' asked De Grey, 'changed within these few hours?' 'Yes, with circumstances,' replied Archer; 'but, right or wrong, as long as I think it honourable to do so and so, I'm satisfied.' 'But you cannot think anything honourable, or the contrary,' observed De Grey, 'without reasoning; and as to what you call feeling, it's only a quick sort of reasoning.' 'The quicker the better,' said Archer. 'Perhaps not,' said De Grey. 'We are apt to reason best when we are not in quite so great a hurry.' 'But,' said Archer, 'we have not always time enough to reason *at first*.' 'You must, however, acknowledge,' replied De Grey, smiling, 'that no man but a fool thinks it honourable to be in the wrong *at last*. Is it not, therefore, best to begin by reasoning to find out the right *at first*?' 'To be sure,' said Archer. 'And did you reason with yourself at first? And did you find out that it was right to bar Dr. Middleton out of his own schoolroom, because he desired you not to go into one of his own houses?' 'No,' replied Archer; 'but I should never have thought of heading a Barring Out, if he had not shown partiality; and if you had flown into a passion with me openly at once for pulling down your scenery, which would have been quite natural, and not have gone slily and forbid us the house out of revenge, there would have been none of this work.' 'Why,' said De Grey, 'should you suspect me of such a mean action, when you have never seen or known me do anything mean, and when in this instance you have no proofs?' 'Will you give me your word and honour now, De Grey, before everybody here, that you did not do what I suspected?' 'I do assure you, upon my honour, I never, indirectly, spoke to Dr. Middleton about the playhouse.' 'Then,' said Archer, 'I'm as glad as if I had found a thousand pounds! Now you are my friend indeed.' 'And Dr. Middleton—why should you suspect him without reason any more than me?' 'As to that,' said Archer, 'he is your friend, and you are right to defend him; and I won't say another word against him. Will that satisfy you?' 'Not quite.' 'Not quite! Then, indeed, you are unreasonable!' 'No,' replied De Grey; 'for I don't wish you to yield out of friendship to me, any more than to honour. If you yield to reason, you will be governed by reason another time.' 'Well, but then don't triumph over me, because you have the best side of the argument.' 'Not I! How can I?' said De Grey; 'for now you are on *the best side* as well as myself, are not you? So we may triumph together.'

'You are a good friend!' said Archer; and with great eagerness he pulled down the fortifications, whilst every hand assisted. The room was restored to order in a few minutes—the shutters were thrown open, the cheerful light let in. The windows were thrown up, and the first feeling of the fresh air was delightful. The green playground opened before them, and the hopes of exercise and liberty brightened the countenances of these voluntary prisoners.

But, alas! they were not yet at liberty. The idea of Dr. Middleton, and the dread of his vengeance, smote their hearts. When the rebels had sent an ambassador with their surrender, they stood in pale and silent suspense, waiting for their doom.

'Ah!' said Fisher, looking up at the broken panes in the windows, 'the doctor will think the most of *that*—he'll never forgive us for that.'

'Hush! here he comes!' His steady step was heard approaching nearer and nearer. Archer threw open the door, and Dr. Middleton entered. Fisher instantly fell on his knees. 'It is no delight to me to see people on their knees. Stand up, Mr. Fisher. I hope you are all conscious that you have done wrong?' 'Sir,' said Archer, 'they are conscious that they have done wrong, and so am I. I am the ringleader. Punish me as you think proper. I submit. Your punishments—your vengeance ought to fall on me alone!'

'Sir,' said Dr. Middleton, calmly, 'I perceive that whatever else you may have learned in the course of your education, you have not been taught the meaning of the word punishment. Punishment and vengeance do not with us mean the same thing. *Punishment* is pain given, with the reasonable hope of preventing those on whom it is inflicted from doing, *in future*, what will hurt themselves or others. *Vengeance* never looks to the *future*, but is the expression of anger for an injury that is past. I feel no anger; you have done me no injury.'

Here many of the little boys looked timidly up to the windows. 'Yes, I see that you have broken my windows; that is a small evil.' 'Oh, sir! How good! How merciful!' exclaimed those who had been most panic-struck. 'He forgives us!'

'Stay,' resumed Dr. Middleton; 'I cannot forgive you. I shall never revenge, but it is my duty to punish. You have rebelled against the just authority which is necessary to conduct and govern you whilst you have not sufficient reason to govern and conduct yourselves. Without obedience to the laws,' added he, turning to Archer, 'as men, you cannot be suffered in society. You, sir, think yourself a man, I observe; and you think it the part of a man not to submit to the will of another. I have no pleasure in making others, whether men or children, submit to my *will*; but my reason and experience are superior to yours. Your parents at least think so, or they would not have entrusted me with the care of your education. As long as they do entrust you to my care, and as long as I have any hopes of making you wiser and better by punishment, I shall steadily inflict it, whenever I judge it to be necessary, and I judge it to be necessary *now*. This is a long sermon, Mr. Archer, not preached to show my own eloquence, but to convince your understanding. Now, as to your punishment!'

'Name it, sir,' said Archer; 'whatever it is, I will cheerfully submit to it.' 'Name it yourself,' said Dr. Middleton, 'and show me that you now understand the nature of punishment.'

Archer, proud to be treated like a reasonable creature, and sorry that he had behaved like a foolish schoolboy, was silent for some time, but at length replied, 'That he would rather not name his own punishment.' He repeated, however, that he trusted he should bear it well, whatever it might be.

'I shall then,' said Dr. Middleton, 'deprive you, for two months, of pocket-money, as you have had too much, and have made a bad use of it.'

'Sir,' said Archer, 'I brought five guineas with me to school. This guinea is all that I have left.'

Dr. Middleton received the guinea which Archer offered him with a look of approbation, and told him that it should be applied to the repairs of the schoolroom. The rest of the boys waited in silence for the doctor's sentence against them, but not with those looks of abject fear with which boys usually expect the sentence of a schoolmaster.

'You shall return from the playground, all of you,' said Dr. Middleton, 'one quarter of an hour sooner, for two months to come, than the rest of your companions. A bell shall ring at the appointed time. I give you an opportunity of recovering my confidence by your punctuality.'

'Oh, sir! we will come the instant, the very instant the bell rings; you shall have confidence in us,' cried they, eagerly.

'I deserve your confidence, I hope,' said Dr. Middleton; 'for it is my first wish to make you all happy. You do not know the pain that it has cost me to deprive you of food for so many hours.'

Here the boys, with one accord, ran to the place where they had deposited their last supplies. Archer delivered them up to the doctor, proud to show that they were not reduced to obedience merely by necessity.

'The reason,' resumed Dr. Middleton, having now returned to the usual benignity of his manner—'the reason why I desired that none of you should go to that building,' pointing out of the window, 'was this:—I had been informed that a gang of gipsies had slept there the night before I spoke to you, one of whom was dangerously ill of a putrid fever. I did not choose to mention my reason to you or your friends. I have had the place cleaned, and you may return to it when you please. The gipsies were yesterday removed from the town.'

'De Grey, you were in the right,' whispered Archer, 'and it was I that was *unjust*.'

'The old woman,' continued the doctor, 'whom you employed to buy food has escaped the fever, but she has not escaped a gaol, whither she was sent yesterday, for having defrauded you of your money.

'Mr. Fisher,' said Dr. Middleton, 'as to you, I shall not punish you: I have no hope of making you either wiser or better. Do you know this paper?'—the paper appeared to be a bill for candles and a tinder-box. 'I desired him to buy those things, sir,' said Archer, colouring. 'And did you desire him not to pay for them?' 'No,' said Archer, 'he had half-a-crown on purpose to pay for them.' 'I know he had, but he chose to apply it to his private use, and gave it to the gipsy to buy twelve buns for his own eating. To obtain credit for the tinder-box and candles, he made use of *this* name,' said he, turning to the other side of the bill, and pointing to De Grey's name, which was written at the end of a copy of one of De Grey's exercises.

He sneaked out, whimpering in a doleful voice.

He sneaked out, whimpering in a doleful voice.

'I assure you, sir——' cried Archer. 'You need not assure me, sir,' said Dr. Middleton; 'I cannot suspect a boy of your temper of having any part in so base an action. When the people in the shop refused to let Mr. Fisher have the things without paying for them, he made use of De Grey's name, who was known there. Suspecting some mischief, however, from the purchase of the tinder-box, the shopkeeper informed me of the circumstance. Nothing in this whole business gave me half so much pain as I felt, for a moment, when I suspected that De Grey was concerned in it.' A loud cry, in which Archer's voice was heard most distinctly, declared De Grey's innocence. Dr. Middleton looked round at their eager, honest faces with benevolent approbation. 'Archer,' said he, taking him by the hand, 'I am heartily glad to see that you have got the better of your party spirit. I wish you may keep such a friend as you have now beside you; one such friend is worth two such parties. As for you, Mr. Fisher, depart; you must never return hither again.' In vain he solicited Archer and De Grey to intercede for him. Everybody turned away with contempt; and he sneaked out, whimpering in a doleful voice, 'What shall I say to my Aunt Barbara?'

THE BRACELETS

In a beautiful and retired part of England lived Mrs. Villars, a lady whose accurate understanding, benevolent heart, and steady temper peculiarly fitted her for the most difficult, as well as most important, of all occupations—the education of youth. This task she had undertaken; and twenty young persons were put under her care, with the perfect confidence of their parents. No young people could be happier; they were good and gay, emulous, but not envious of each other; for Mrs. Villars was impartially just; her praise they felt to be the reward of merit, and her blame they knew to be the necessary consequence of ill-conduct. To the one, therefore, they patiently submitted, and in the other consciously rejoiced. They rose with fresh cheerfulness in the morning, eager to pursue their various occupations. They returned in the evening with renewed ardour to their amusements, and retired to rest satisfied with themselves and pleased with each other.

Nothing so much contributed to preserve a spirit of emulation in this little society as a small honorary distinction, given annually, as a prize of successful application. The prize this year was peculiarly dear to each individual, as it was the picture of a friend whom they dearly loved. It was the picture of Mrs. Villars in a small bracelet. It wanted neither gold, pearls, nor precious stones to give it value.

The two foremost candidates for this prize were Cecilia and Leonora. Cecilia was the most intimate friend of Leonora; but Leonora was only the favourite companion of Cecilia.

Cecilia was of an active, ambitious, enterprising disposition, more eager in the pursuit than happy in the enjoyment of her wishes. Leonora was of a contented, unaspiring, temperate character; not easily roused to action, but indefatigable when once excited. Leonora was proud; Cecilia was vain. Her vanity made her more dependent upon the approbation of others, and therefore more anxious to please, than Leonora; but that very vanity made her, at the same time, more apt to offend. In short, Leonora was the most anxious to avoid what was wrong; Cecilia the most ambitious to do what was right. Few of her companions loved, but many were led by, Cecilia, for she was often successful. Many loved Leonora, but none were ever governed by her, for she was too indolent to govern.

On the first day of May, about six o'clock in the evening, a great bell rang, to summon this little society into a hall, where the prize was to be decided. A number of small tables were placed in a circle in the middle of the hall. Seats for the young competitors were raised one above another, in a semicircle, some yards distant from the table, and the judges' chairs, under canopies of lilacs and laburnums, forming another semicircle, closed the amphitheatre.

Every one put their writings, their drawings, their works of various kinds, upon the tables appropriated for each. How unsteady were the last steps to these tables! How each little hand trembled as it laid down its claims! Till this moment every one thought herself secure of success; and the heart which exulted with hope now palpitated with fear.

The works were examined, the preference adjudged, and the prize was declared to be the happy Cecilia's. Mrs. Villars came forward, smiling, with the bracelet in her hand. Cecilia was behind her companions, on the highest row. All the others gave way, and she was on the floor in an instant. Mrs. Villars clasped the bracelet on her arm; the clasp was heard through the whole hall, and a universal smile of congratulation followed. Mrs. Villars kissed Cecilia's little hand. 'And now,' said she, 'go and rejoice with your companions; the remainder of the day is yours.'

Oh! you whose hearts are elated with success, whose bosoms beat high with joy in the moment of triumph, command yourselves. Let that triumph be moderate, that it may be lasting. Consider, that though you are good, you may be better; and, though wise, you may be weak.

As soon as Mrs. Villars had given her the bracelet, all Cecilia's little companions crowded round her, and they all left the hall in an instant. She was full of spirits and vanity. She ran on. Running down the flight of steps which led to the garden, in her violent haste Cecilia threw down the little Louisa, who had a china mandarin in her hand, which her mother had sent her that very morning, and which was all broken to pieces by her fall.

'Oh, my mandarin!' cried Louisa, bursting into tears. The crowd behind Cecilia suddenly stopped. Louisa sat on the lowest step, fixing her eyes upon the broken pieces. Then, turning round, she hid her face in her hands upon the step above her. In turning, Louisa threw down the remains of the mandarin. The head, which she placed in the socket, fell from the shoulders, and rolled, bounding along the gravel walk. Cecilia pointed to the head and to the socket, and burst into laughter. The crowd behind laughed too.

At any other time they would have been more inclined to cry with Louisa; but Cecilia had just been successful, and sympathy with the victorious often makes us forget justice.

Leonora, however, preserved her usual consistency. 'Poor Louisa!' said she, looking first at her, and then reproachfully at Cecilia. Cecilia turned sharply round, colouring, half with shame and half with vexation. 'I could not help it, Leonora,' said she. 'But you could have helped laughing, Cecilia.' 'I didn't laugh at Louisa; and I surely may laugh, for it does nobody any harm.' 'I am sure, however,' replied Leonora, 'I should not have laughed if I had——' 'No, to be sure, you wouldn't, because Louisa is your favourite. I can buy her another mandarin when the old peddler comes to the door, if that's all. I *can* do no more, *can* I?' said she, again turning round to her companions. 'No, to be sure,' said they; 'that's all fair.'

Cecilia looked triumphantly at Leonora. Leonora let go her hand; she ran on, and the crowd followed. When she got to the end of the garden, she turned round to see if Leonora had followed her too; but was vexed to see her still sitting on the steps with Louisa. 'I'm sure I can do no more than buy her another, *can* I?' said she, again appealing to her companions. 'No, to be sure,' said they, eager to begin their play.

How many games did these juvenile playmates begin and leave off, before Cecilia could be satisfied with any! Her thoughts were discomposed, and her mind was running upon something else. No wonder, then, that she did not play with her usual address. She grew still more impatient. She threw down the ninepins. 'Come, let us play at something else—at threading the needle,' said she, holding out her hand. They all yielded to the hand which wore the bracelet. But Cecilia, dissatisfied with herself, was discontented with everybody else. Her tone grew more and more peremptory. One was too rude, another too stiff; one too slow, another too quick; in short, everything went wrong, and everybody was tired of her humours.

The triumph of *success* is absolute, but short. Cecilia's companions at length recollected that, though she had embroidered a tulip and painted a peach better than they, yet that they could play as well, and keep their tempers better; for she was discomposed.

Walking towards the house in a peevish mood, Cecilia met Leonora, but passed on. 'Cecilia!' cried Leonora. 'Well, what do you want with me?' 'Are we friends?' 'You know best,' said Cecilia. 'We are, if you will let me tell Louisa that you are sorry——' Cecilia, interrupting her, 'Oh, pray let me hear no more about Louisa!' 'What! not confess that you were in the wrong? O Cecilia! I had a better opinion of you.' 'Your opinion is of no consequence to me now, for you don't love me.' 'No; not when you are unjust, Cecilia.' 'Unjust! I am not unjust; and

133

if I were, you are not my governess.' 'No, but am not I your friend?' 'I don't desire to have such a friend, who would quarrel with me for happening to throw down little Louisa. How could I tell that she had a mandarin in her hand? and when it was broken, could I do more than promise her another; was that unjust?' 'But you know, Cecilia——' 'I *know*,' ironically. 'I know, Leonora, that you love Louisa better than you love me; that's the injustice!' 'If I did,' replied Leonora, gravely, 'it would be no injustice, if she deserved it better.' 'How can you compare Louisa to me!' exclaimed Cecilia, indignantly.

Leonora made no answer; for she was really hurt at her friend's conduct. She walked on to join the rest of her companions. They were dancing in a round upon the grass. Leonora declined dancing; but they prevailed upon her to sing for them. Her voice was not so sprightly, but it was sweeter than usual. Who sang so sweetly as Leonora? or who danced so nimbly as Louisa? Away she was flying, all spirits and gaiety, when Leonora's eyes, full of tears, caught hers. Louisa silently let go her companion's hand, and quitting the dance, ran up to Leonora to inquire what was the matter with her. 'Nothing,' replied she, 'that need interrupt you. Go, my dear; go and dance again.'

Louisa immediately ran away to her garden, and pulling off her little straw hat, she lined it with the freshest strawberry-leaves, and was upon her knees before the strawberry-bed when Cecilia came by. Cecilia was not disposed to be pleased with Louisa at that instant, for two reasons; because she was jealous of her, and because she had injured her. The injury, however, Louisa had already forgotten. Perhaps, to tell things just as they were, she was not quite so much inclined to kiss Cecilia as she would have been before the fall of her mandarin; but this was the utmost extent of her malice, if it can be called malice.

'What are you doing there, little one?' said Cecilia, in a sharp tone. 'Are you eating your early strawberries here all alone?' 'No,' said Louisa, mysteriously, 'I am not eating them.' 'What are you doing with them? can't you answer, then? I'm not playing with you, child!' 'Oh, as to that, Cecilia, you know I need not answer you unless I choose it; not but what I would if you would only ask me civilly, and if you would not call me *child*.' 'Why should not I call you child?' 'Because—because—I don't know; but I wish you would stand out of my light, Cecilia, for you are trampling upon all my strawberries.' 'I have not touched one, you covetous little creature!' 'Indeed—indeed, Cecilia, I am not covetous. I have not eaten one of them; they are all for your friend Leonora. See how unjust you are!'

'Unjust! that's a cant word which you learnt of my friend Leonora, as you call her; but she is not my friend now.' 'Not your friend now!' exclaimed Louisa; 'then I am sure you must have done something *very* naughty.' 'How?' cried Cecilia, catching hold of her. 'Let me go, let me go!' cried Louisa, struggling. 'I won't give you one of my strawberries, for I don't like you at all!' 'You don't, don't you?' cried Cecilia, provoked, and, catching the hat from Louisa, she flung the strawberries over the hedge.

'Will nobody help me?' exclaimed Louisa, snatching her hat again, and running away with all her force.

'How?' cried Cecilia, catching hold of her.

'How?' cried Cecilia, catching hold of her.

'What have I done?' said Cecilia, recollecting herself; 'Louisa! Louisa!' she called very loud, but Louisa would not turn back: she was running to her companions, who were still dancing, hand in hand, upon the grass, whilst Leonora, sitting in the middle, was singing to them.

'Stop! stop! and hear me!' cried Louisa, breaking through them; and, rushing up to Leonora, she threw her hat at her feet, and panting for breath—'It was full—almost full of my own strawberries,' said she, 'the first I ever got out of my own garden. They should all have been for you, Leonora; but now I have not one left. They are all gone!' said she; and she hid her face in Leonora's lap.

'Gone! gone where?' said every one, at once running up to her. 'Cecilia! Cecilia!' said she, sobbing. 'Cecilia,' repeated Leonora, 'what of Cecilia?' 'Yes, it was—it was.' 'Come along with me,' said Leonora, unwilling to have her friend exposed. 'Come, and I will get you some more strawberries.' 'Oh, I don't mind the strawberries, indeed; but I wanted to have had the pleasure of giving them to you.'

Leonora took her up in her arms to carry her away, but it was too late.

'What, Cecilia! Cecilia, who won the prize! It could not surely be Cecilia,' whispered every busy tongue.

At this instant the bell summoned them in. 'There she is! There she is!' cried they, pointing to an arbour, where Cecilia was standing ashamed and alone; and, as they passed her, some lifted up their hands and eyes with astonishment, others whispered and huddled mysteriously together, as if to avoid her. Leonora walked on, her head a little higher than usual. 'Leonora!' said Cecilia, timorously, as she passed. 'Oh, Cecilia! who would have thought that you had a bad heart?' Cecilia turned her head aside and burst into tears.

'Oh no, indeed, she has not a bad heart!' cried Louisa, running up to her and throwing her arms around her neck. 'She's very sorry; are not you, Cecilia? But don't cry any more, for I forgive you, with all my heart—and I love you now, though I said I did not when I was in a passion.'

135

'Oh, you sweet-tempered girl! how I love you!' said Cecilia, kissing her. 'Well, then, if you do, come along with me, and dry your eyes, for they are so red!' 'Go, my dear, and I'll come presently.' 'Then I will keep a place for you, next to me; but you must make haste, or you will have to come in when we have all sat down to supper, and then you will be so stared at! So don't stay now.'

Cecilia followed Louisa with her eyes till she was out of sight. 'And is Louisa,' said she to herself, 'the only one who would stop to pity me? Mrs. Villars told me that this day should be mine. She little thought how it would end!'

Saying these words, Cecilia threw herself down upon the ground; her arm leaned upon a heap of turf which she had raised in the morning, and which, in the pride and gaiety of her heart, she had called her throne.

At this instant, Mrs. Villars came out to enjoy the serenity of the evening, and, passing by the arbour where Cecilia lay, she started. Cecilia rose hastily.

'Who is there?' said Mrs. Villars. 'It is I, madam.' 'And who is *I*?' 'Cecilia.' 'Why, what keeps you here, my dear? Where are your companions? This is, perhaps, one of the happiest days of your life.' 'Oh no, madam,' said Cecilia, hardly able to repress her tears. 'Why, my dear, what is the matter?' Cecilia hesitated.

'Speak, my dear. You know that when I ask you to tell me anything as your friend, I never punish you as your governess; therefore you need not be afraid to tell me what is the matter.' 'No, madam, I am not afraid, but ashamed. You asked me why I was not with my companions. Why, madam, because they have all left me, and——' 'And what, my dear?' 'And I see that they all dislike me; and yet I don't know why they should, for I take as much pains to please as any of them. All my masters seem satisfied with me; and you yourself, madam, were pleased this very morning to give me this bracelet; and I am sure you would not have given it to any one who did not deserve it.'

'Certainly not,' said Mrs. Villars. 'You well deserve it for your application—for your successful application. The prize was for the most assiduous, not for the most amiable.'

'Then, if it had been for the most amiable, it would not have been for me?'

Mrs. Villars, smiling—'Why, what do you think yourself, Cecilia? You are better able to judge than I am. I can determine whether or no you apply to what I give you to learn; whether you attend to what I desire you to do, and avoid what I desire you not to do. I know that I like you as a pupil, but I cannot know that I should like you as a companion, unless I were your companion. Therefore I must judge of what I should do, by seeing what others do in the same circumstances.'

'Oh, pray don't, madam! for then you would not love me either. And yet I think you would love me; for I hope that I am as ready to oblige, and as good-natured as——'

'Yes, Cecilia, I don't doubt but that you would be very good-natured to me; but I'm afraid that I should not like you unless you were good-tempered too.' 'But, madam, by good-natured I mean good-tempered—it's all the same thing.' 'No, indeed, I understand by them two very different things. You are good-natured, Cecilia; for you are desirous to oblige and serve your companions—to gain them praise, and save them from blame—to give them pleasure, and relieve them from pain; but Leonora is good-tempered, for she can bear with their foibles, and acknowledge her own. Without disputing about the right, she sometimes yields to those who are in the wrong. In short, her temper is perfectly good; for it can bear and forbear.' 'I wish that mine could!' said Cecilia, sighing. 'It may,' replied Mrs. Villars; 'but it is not wishes alone which can improve us in anything. Turn the same exertion and perseverance which have won you the prize to-day to this object, and you will meet with the same success; perhaps not on the first, the second, or the third attempt; but depend upon it that you will at last. Every new effort will weaken your bad habits and strengthen your good ones. But you must not expect to succeed all at once. I repeat it to you, for habit must be counteracted by habit. It would be as extravagant in us to expect that all our faults could be destroyed by one punishment, were it ever so severe, as it was in the Roman emperor we were reading of a few days ago to wish that all the heads of his enemies were upon one neck, that he might cut them off at one blow.'

Here Mrs. Villars took Cecilia by the hand, and they began to walk home. Such was the nature of Cecilia's mind, that when any object was forcibly impressed on her imagination, it caused a temporary suspension of her reasoning faculties. Hope was too strong a stimulus for her spirits; and when fear did take possession of her mind, it was attended with total debility. Her vanity was now as much mortified as in the morning it had been elated. She walked on with Mrs. Villars in silence, until they came under the shade of the elm-tree walk, and there, fixing her eyes upon Mrs. Villars, she stopped short.

'Do you think, madam,' said she, with hesitation—'do you think, madam, that I have a bad heart?' 'A bad heart, my dear! why, what put that into your head?' 'Leonora said that I had, madam, and I felt ashamed when she said so.' 'But, my dear, how can Leonora tell whether your heart be good or bad? However, in the first place, tell me what you mean by a bad heart.' 'Indeed, I do not know what is meant by it, madam; but it is something which everybody hates.' 'And why do they hate it?' 'Because they think that it will hurt them, ma'am, I believe; and that those who have bad hearts take delight in doing mischief; and that they never do anybody any good but for their own ends.'

'Then the best definition,' said Mrs. Villars, 'which you can give me of a bad heart is, that it is some constant propensity to hurt others, and to do wrong for the sake of doing wrong.' 'Yes, madam; but that is not all either. There is still something else meant; something which I cannot express—which, indeed, I never distinctly understood; but of which, therefore, I was the more afraid.'

'Well, then, to begin with what you do understand, tell me, Cecilia, do you really think it possible to be wicked merely for the love of wickedness? No human being becomes wicked all at once. A man begins by doing wrong because it is, or because he thinks it, for his interest. If he continue to do so, he must conquer his sense of shame and lose his love of virtue. But how can you, Cecilia, who feel such a strong sense of shame, and such an eager desire to improve, imagine that you have a bad heart?'

'Indeed, madam, I never did, until everybody told me so, and then I began to be frightened about it. This very evening, madam, when I was in a passion, I threw little Louisa's strawberries away, which, I am sure, I was very sorry for afterwards; and Leonora and everybody cried out that I had a bad heart—but I am sure I was only in a passion.'

'Very likely. And when you are in a passion, as you call it, Cecilia, you see that you are tempted to do harm to others. If they do not feel angry themselves, they do not sympathise with you. They do not perceive the motive which actuates you; and then they say that you have a bad heart. I daresay, however, when your passion is over, and when you recollect yourself, you are very sorry for what you have done and said; are not you?' 'Yes, indeed, madam—very sorry.' 'Then make that sorry of use to you, Cecilia, and fix it steadily in your thoughts, as you hope to be good and happy, that if you suffer yourself to yield to your passion upon every trifling occasion, anger and its consequences will become familiar to your mind; and, in the same proportion, your sense of shame will be weakened, till what you began with doing from sudden impulse you will end with doing from habit and choice; and then you would, indeed, according to our definition, have a bad heart.' 'Oh, madam! I hope—I am sure I never shall.' 'No, indeed, Cecilia; I do, indeed, believe that you never will; on the contrary, I think that you have a very good disposition, and what is of infinitely more consequence to you, an active desire of improvement. Show me that you have as much perseverance as you have candour, and I shall not despair of your becoming everything that I could wish.'

Here Cecilia's countenance brightened, and she ran up the steps in almost as high spirits as she ran down them in the morning.

'Good-night to you, Cecilia,' said Mrs. Villars, as she was crossing the hall. 'Good-night to you, madam,' said Cecilia; and she ran upstairs to bed. She could not go to sleep; but she lay awake, reflecting upon the events of the preceding day, and forming resolutions for the future, at the same time considering that she had resolved, and resolved without effect, she wished to give her mind some more powerful motive. Ambition she knew to be its most powerful incentive. 'Have I not,' said she to herself, 'already won the prize of application, and cannot the same application procure me a much higher prize? Mrs. Villars said that if the prize had been promised to the most amiable, it would not have been given to me. Perhaps it would not yesterday, perhaps it might not to-morrow; but that is no reason that I should despair of ever deserving it.'

In consequence of this reasoning, Cecilia formed a design of proposing to her companions that they should give a prize, the first of the ensuing month (the 1st of June), to the most amiable. Mrs. Villars applauded the scheme, and her companions adopted it with the greatest alacrity.

'Let the prize,' said they, 'be a bracelet of our own hair'; and instantly their shining scissors were produced, and each contributed a lock of her hair. They formed the most beautiful gradation of colours, from the palest auburn to the brightest black. Who was to have the honour of plaiting them? was now the question. Caroline begged that she might, as she could plait very neatly, she said. Cecilia, however, was equally sure that she could do it much better; and a dispute would have inevitably ensued, if Cecilia, recollecting herself just as her colour rose to scarlet, had not yielded—yielded, with no very good grace indeed, but as well as could be expected for the first time. For it is habit which confers ease; and without ease, even in moral actions, there can be no grace.

The bracelet was plaited in the neatest manner by Caroline, finished round the edge with silver twist, and on it was worked, in the smallest silver letters, this motto, 'To the Most Amiable.' The moment it was completed, everybody begged to try it on. It fastened with little silver clasps, and as it was made large enough for the eldest girls, it was too large for the youngest. Of this they bitterly complained, and unanimously entreated that it might be cut to fit them.

'How foolish!' exclaimed Cecilia; 'don't you perceive that if any of you win it, you have nothing to do but to put the clasps a little further from the edge, but, if we get it, we can't make it larger?' 'Very true,' said they; 'but you need not to have called us foolish, Cecilia.'

It was by such hasty and unguarded expressions as these that Cecilia offended. A slight difference in the manner makes a very material one in the effect. Cecilia lost more love by general petulance than she could gain by the greatest particular exertions.

How far she succeeded in curing herself of this defect—how far she became deserving of the bracelet, and to whom the bracelet was given—shall be told in the History of the First of June.

The First of June was now arrived, and all the young competitors were in a state of the most anxious suspense. Leonora and Cecilia continued to be the foremost candidates. Their quarrel had never been finally adjusted, and their different pretensions now retarded all thoughts of a reconciliation. Cecilia, though she was capable of acknowledging any of her faults in public before all her companions, could not humble herself in private to Leonora. Leonora was her equal; they were her inferiors, and submission is much easier to a vain mind, where it appears to be voluntary, than when it is the necessary tribute to justice or candour. So strongly did Cecilia feel this truth, that she even delayed making any apology, or coming to any explanation with Leonora, until success should once more give her the palm.

'If I win the bracelet to-day,' said she to herself, 'I will solicit the return of Leonora's friendship; it will be more valuable to me than even the bracelet, and at such a time, and asked in such a manner, she surely cannot refuse it to me.' Animated with this hope of a double triumph, Cecilia canvassed with the most zealous activity. By constant attention and exertion she had considerably abated the violence of her temper, and changed the course of her habits. Her powers of pleasing were now excited, instead of her abilities to excel; and, if her talents appeared less brilliant, her character was acknowledged to be more amiable. So great an influence upon our manners and conduct have the objects of our ambition.

Cecilia was now, if possible, more than ever desirous of doing what was right, but she had not yet acquired sufficient fear of doing wrong. This was the fundamental error of her mind; it arose in a great measure from her early education. Her mother died when she was very young; and though her father had supplied her place in the best and kindest manner, he had insensibly infused into his daughter's mind a portion of that enterprising, independent spirit which he justly deemed essential to the character of her brother. This brother was some years older than Cecilia, but he had always been the favourite companion of her youth. What her father's precepts inculcated, his example enforced; and even Cecilia's virtues consequently became such as were more estimable in a man than desirable in a female. All small objects and small errors she had been taught to disregard as trifles; and her impatient disposition was perpetually leading her into more material faults; yet her candour in confessing these, she had been suffered to believe, was sufficient reparation and atonement.

Leonora, on the contrary, who had been educated by her mother in a manner more suited to her sex, had a character and virtues more peculiar to a female. Her judgment had been early cultivated, and her good sense employed in the regulation of her conduct. She had been habituated to that restraint which, as a woman, she was to expect in life, and early accustomed to yield. Compliance in her seemed natural and graceful; yet, notwithstanding the gentleness of her temper, she was in reality more independent than Cecilia. She had more reliance upon her own judgment, and more satisfaction in her own approbation. The uniform kindness of her manner, the consistency and equality of her character, had fixed the esteem and passive love of her companions.

By passive love we mean that species of affection which makes us unwilling to offend rather than anxious to oblige, which is more a habit than an emotion of the mind. For Cecilia her companions felt active love, for she was active in showing her love to them.

Active love arises spontaneously in the mind, after feeling particular instances of kindness, without reflection on the past conduct or general character. It exceeds the merits of its object, and is connected with a feeling of generosity, rather than with a sense of justice.

Without determining which species of love is the most flattering to others, we can easily decide which is the most agreeable feeling to our minds. We give our hearts more credit for being generous than for being just; and we feel more self-complacency when we give our love voluntarily, than when we yield it as a tribute which we cannot withhold. Though Cecilia's companions might not know all this in theory, they proved it in practice; for they loved her in a much higher proportion to her merits than they loved Leonora.

Each of the young judges was to signify her choice by putting a red or a white shell into a vase prepared for the purpose. Cecilia's colour was red, Leonora's white.

In the morning nothing was to be seen but these shells; nothing talked of but the long-expected event of the evening. Cecilia, following Leonora's example, had made it a point of honour not to inquire of any individual her vote, previously to their final determination.

They were both sitting together in Louisa's room. Louisa was recovering from the measles. Every one during her illness had been desirous of attending her; but Leonora and Cecilia were the only two that were permitted to see her, as they alone had had the distemper. They were both assiduous in their care of Louisa, but Leonora's want of exertion to overcome any disagreeable feelings of sensibility often deprived her of presence of mind, and prevented her from being so constantly useful as Cecilia. Cecilia, on the contrary, often made too much noise and bustle with her officious assistance, and was too anxious to invent amusements and procure comforts for Louisa, without perceiving that illness takes away the power of enjoying them.

As she was sitting at the window in the morning, exerting herself to entertain Louisa, she heard the voice of an old peddler who often used to come to the house. Downstairs, they ran immediately, to ask Mrs. Villars's permission to bring him into the hall. Mrs. Villars consented, and away Cecilia ran to proclaim the news to her companions. Then, first returning into the hall, she found the peddler just unbuckling his box, and taking it off his shoulders.

'What would you be pleased to want, miss?' said the peddler; 'I've all kinds of tweezer-cases, rings, and lockets of all sorts,' continued he, opening all the glittering drawers successively.

'Oh!' said Cecilia, shutting the drawer of lockets which tempted her most, 'these are not the things which I want. Have you any china figures? any mandarins?'

'Alack-a-day, miss, I had a great stock of that same chinaware; but now I'm quite out of them kind of things; but I believe,' said he, rummaging one of the deepest drawers, 'I believe I have one left, and here it is.' 'Oh, that is the very thing! what's its price?' 'Only three shillings, ma'am.' Cecilia paid the money, and was just going to carry off the mandarin, when the peddler took out of his greatcoat pocket a neat mahogany case. It was about a foot long, and fastened at each end by two little clasps. It had, besides, a small lock in the middle.

'What is that?' said Cecilia, eagerly. 'It's only a china figure, miss, which I am going to carry to an elderly lady, who lives nigh hand, and who is mighty fond of such things.' 'Could you let me look at it?' 'And welcome, miss,' said he, and opened the case. 'Oh, goodness! how beautiful!' exclaimed Cecilia.

It was a figure of Flora, crowned with roses, and carrying a basket of flowers in her hand. Cecilia contemplated it with delight. 'How I should like to give this to Louisa!' said she to herself; and, at last, breaking silence, 'Did you promise it to the old lady?' 'Oh no, miss, I didn't promise it—she never saw it; and if so be that you'd like to take it, I'd make no more words about it.' 'And how much does it cost?' 'Why, miss, as to that, I'll let you have it for half-a-guinea.'

Cecilia immediately produced the box in which she kept her treasure, and, emptying it upon the table, she began to count the shillings. Alas! there were but six shillings. 'How provoking!' said she; 'then I can't have it. Where's the mandarin? Oh, I have it,' said she, taking it up, and looking at it with the utmost disgust. 'Is this the same that I had before?' 'Yes, miss, the very same,' replied the peddler, who, during this time, had been examining the little box out of which Cecilia had taken her money—it was of silver. 'Why, ma'am,' said he, 'since you've taken such a fancy to the piece, if you've a mind to make up the remainder of the money, I will take this here little box, if you care to part with it.'

Now this box was a keepsake from Leonora to Cecilia. 'No,' said Cecilia hastily, blushing a little, and stretching out her hand to receive it.

'Oh, miss!' said he, returning it carelessly, 'I hope there's no offence. I meant but to serve you, that's all. Such a rare piece of china-work has no cause to go a-begging,' added he. Then, putting the Flora deliberately into the case, and turning the key with a jerk, he let it drop into his pocket; when, lifting up his box by the leather straps, he was preparing to depart.

'Oh, stay one minute!' said Cecilia.

'Oh, stay one minute!' said Cecilia, in whose mind there had passed a very warm conflict during the peddler's harangue. 'Louisa would so like this Flora,' said she, arguing with herself. 'Besides, it would be so generous in me to give it to her instead of that ugly mandarin; that would be doing only common justice, for I promised it to her, and she expects it. Though, when I come to look at this mandarin, it is not even so good as hers was. The gilding is all rubbed off, so that I absolutely must buy this for her. Oh yes! I will, and she will be so delighted! and then everybody will say it is the prettiest thing they ever saw, and the broken mandarin will be forgotten for ever.'

Here Cecilia's hand moved, and she was just going to decide: 'Oh, but stop,' said she to herself, 'consider—Leonora gave me this box, and it is a keepsake. However, we have now quarrelled, and I daresay that she would not mind my parting with it. I'm sure that I should not care if she was to give away my keepsake, the smelling-bottle, or the ring which I gave her. Then what does it signify? Besides, is it not my own? and have I not a right to do what I please with it?'

At this moment, so critical for Cecilia, a party of her companions opened the door. She knew that they came as purchasers, and she dreaded her Flora's becoming the prize of some higher bidder. 'Here,' said she, hastily putting the box into the peddler's hand, without looking at it, 'take it, and give me the Flora.' Her hand trembled, though she snatched it impatiently. She ran by, without seeming to mind any of her companions.

Let those who are tempted to do wrong by the hopes of future gratification, or the prospect of certain concealment and impunity, remember that, unless they are totally depraved, they bear in their own hearts a monitor, who will prevent their enjoying what they ill obtained.

In vain Cecilia ran to the rest of her companions, to display her present, in hopes that the applause of others would restore her own self-complacency; in vain she saw the Flora pass in due pomp from hand to hand, each vying with the other in extolling the beauty of the gift

139

and the generosity of the giver. Cecilia was still displeased with herself, with them, and even with their praise. From Louisa's gratitude, however, she yet expected much pleasure, and immediately she ran upstairs to her room.

In the meantime, Leonora had gone into the hall to buy a bodkin; she had just broken hers. In giving her change, the peddler took out of his pocket, with some halfpence, the very box which Cecilia had sold to him. Leonora did not in the least suspect the truth, for her mind was above suspicion; and besides, she had the utmost confidence in Cecilia.

'I should like to have that box,' said she, 'for it is like one of which I was very fond.'

The peddler named the price, and Leonora took the box. She intended to give it to little Louisa. On going to her room she found her asleep, and she sat softly down by her bedside. Louisa opened her eyes.

'I hope I didn't disturb you,' said Leonora. 'Oh no; I didn't hear you come in; but what have you got there?' 'It is only a little box; would you like to have it? I bought it on purpose for you, as I thought perhaps it would please you, because it's like that which I gave Cecilia.' 'Oh yes! that out of which she used to give me Barbary drops. I am very much obliged to you; I always thought *that* exceedingly pretty, and this, indeed, is as like it as possible. I can't unscrew it; will you try?'

Leonora unscrewed it. 'Goodness!' exclaimed Louisa, 'this must be Cecilia's box. Look, don't you see a great L at the bottom of it?'

Leonora's colour changed. 'Yes,' she replied calmly, 'I see that; but it is no proof that it is Cecilia's. You know that I bought this box just now of the peddler.' 'That may be,' said Louisa; 'but I remember scratching that L with my own needle, and Cecilia scolded me for it, too. Do go and ask her if she has lost her box—do,' repeated Louisa, pulling her by the ruffle, as she did not seem to listen.

Leonora, indeed, did not hear, for she was lost in thought. She was comparing circumstances which had before escaped her attention. She recollected that Cecilia had passed her as she came into the hall, without seeming to see her, but had blushed as she passed. She remembered that the peddler appeared unwilling to part with the box, and was going to put it again in his pocket with the halfpence. 'And why should he keep it in his pocket, and not show it with his other things?' Combining all these circumstances, Leonora had no longer any doubt of the truth, for though she had an honourable confidence in her friends, she had too much penetration to be implicitly credulous.

'Louisa,' she began, but at this instant she heard a step, which, by its quickness, she knew to be Cecilia's, coming along the passage.

'If you love me, Louisa,' said Leonora, 'say nothing about the box.' 'Nay, but why not? I daresay she had lost it.' 'No, my dear, I'm afraid she has not.' Louisa looked surprised. 'But I have reasons for desiring you not to say anything about it.' 'Well, then, I won't, indeed.'

Cecilia opened the door, came forward smiling, as if secure of a good reception, and taking the Flora out of the case, she placed it on the mantelpiece, opposite to Louisa's bed.

'Dear, how beautiful!' cried Louisa, starting up. 'Yes,' said Cecilia, 'and guess who it's for.' 'For me, perhaps!' said the ingenuous Louisa. 'Yes, take it, and keep it for my sake. You know that I broke your mandarin.' 'Oh, but this is a great deal prettier and larger than that.' 'Yes, I know it is; and I meant that it should be so. I should only have done what I was bound to do if I had only given you a mandarin.'

'Well,' replied Louisa, 'and that would have been enough, surely; but what a beautiful crown of roses! and then that basket of flowers! they almost look as if I could smell them. Dear Cecilia, I'm very much obliged to you; but I won't take it by way of payment for the mandarin you broke; for I'm sure you could not help that, and, besides, I should have broken it myself by this time. You shall give it to me entirely; and, as your keepsake, I'll keep it as long as I live.'

Louisa stopped short and coloured; the word keepsake recalled the box to her mind, and all the train of ideas which the Flora had banished. 'But,' said she, looking up wistfully in Cecilia's face, and holding the Flora doubtfully, 'did you——'

Leonora, who was just quitting the room, turned her head back, and gave Louisa a look, which silenced her.

Cecilia was so infatuated with her vanity, that she neither perceived Leonora's sign nor Louisa's confusion, but continued showing off her present, by placing it in various situations, till at length she put it into the case, and laying it down with an affected carelessness upon the bed, 'I must go now, Louisa. Good-bye,' said she, running up and kissing her; 'but I'll come again presently'; then, clapping the door after her, she went. But as soon as the fermentation of her spirits subsided, the sense of shame, which had been scarcely felt when mixed with so many other sensations, rose uppermost in her mind. 'What!' said she to herself, 'is it possible that I have sold what I promised to keep for ever? and what Leonora gave me? and I have concealed it too, and have been making a parade of my generosity. Oh! what would Leonora, what would Louisa—what would everybody think of me if the truth were known?'

Humiliated and grieved by these reflections, Cecilia began to search in her own mind for some consoling idea. She began to compare her conduct with that of others of her own age; and at length, fixing her comparison upon her brother George, as the companion of whom, from her infancy, she had been habitually the most emulous, she recollected that an almost similar circumstance had once happened to him, and that he had not only escaped disgrace, but had acquired glory, by an intrepid confession of his fault. Her father's word to her brother, on the occasion, she also perfectly recollected.

'Come to me, George,' he said, holding out his hand, 'you are a generous, brave boy: they who dare to confess their faults will make great and good men.'

These were his words; but Cecilia, in repeating them to herself, forgot to lay that emphasis on the word *men* which would have placed it in contradistinction to the word women. She willingly believed that the observation extended equally to both sexes, and flattered herself that she should exceed her brother in merit if she owned a fault which she thought that it would be so much more difficult to confess. 'Yes, but,' said she, stopping herself, 'how can I confess it? This very evening, in a few hours, the prize will be decided. Leonora or I shall win it. I have now as good a chance as Leonora, perhaps a better; and must I give up all my hopes—all that I have been labouring for this month past? Oh, I never can! If it were but to-morrow, or yesterday, or any day but this, I would not hesitate; but now I am almost certain of the prize, and if I win it—well, why then I will—I think I will tell all—yes I will; I am determined,' said Cecilia.

Here a bell summoned them to dinner. Leonora sat opposite to her, and she was not a little surprised to see Cecilia look so gay and unconstrained. 'Surely,' said she to herself, 'if Cecilia had done that which I suspect, she would not, she could not, look as she does.' But

Leonora little knew the cause of her gaiety. Cecilia was never in higher spirits, or better pleased with herself, than when she had resolved upon a sacrifice or a confession.

'Must not this evening be given to the most amiable? Whose, then, will it be?' All eyes glanced first at Cecilia, and then at Leonora. Cecilia smiled; Leonora blushed. 'I see that it is not yet decided,' said Mrs. Villars; and immediately they ran upstairs, amidst confused whisperings.

Cecilia's voice could be distinguished far above the rest. 'How can she be so happy!' said Leonora to herself. 'O Cecilia, there was a time when you could not have neglected me so! when we were always together the best of friends and companions; our wishes, tastes, and pleasures the same! Surely she did once love me,' said Leonora; 'but now she is quite changed. She has even sold my keepsake; and she would rather win a bracelet of hair from girls whom she did not always think so much superior to Leonora than have my esteem, my confidence, and my friendship for her whole life—yes, for her whole life, for I am sure she will be an amiable woman. Oh that this bracelet had never been thought of, or that I were certain of her winning it; for I am sure that I do not wish to win it from her. I would rather—a thousand times rather—that we were as we used to be than have all the glory in the world. And how pleasing Cecilia can be when she wishes to please!—how candid she is!—how much she can improve herself! Let me be just, though she has offended me; she is wonderfully improved within this last month. For one fault, and *that* against myself, shall I forget all her merits?'

As Leonora said these last words, she could but just hear the voices of her companions. They had left her alone in the gallery. She knocked softly at Louisa's door. 'Come in,' said Louisa; 'I'm not asleep. Oh,' said she, starting up with the Flora in her hand, the instant that the door was opened, 'I'm so glad you are come, Leonora, for I did so long to hear what you all were making such a noise about. Have you forgot that the bracelet——' 'Oh yes! is this the evening?' inquired Leonora. 'Well, here's my white shell for you,' said Louisa. 'I've kept it in my pocket this fortnight; and though Cecilia did give me this Flora, I still love you a great deal better.' 'I thank you, Louisa,' said Leonora, gratefully. 'I will take your shell, and I shall value it as long as I live; but here is a red one, and if you wish to show me that you love me, you will give this to Cecilia. I know that she is particularly anxious for your preference, and I am sure that she deserves it.' 'Yes, if I could I would choose both of you,' said Louisa, 'but you know I can only choose which I like the best.' 'If you mean, my dear Louisa,' said Leonora, 'that you like me the best, I am very much obliged to you, for, indeed, I wish you to love me; but it is enough for me to know it in private. I should not feel the least more pleasure at hearing it in public, or in having it made known to all my companions, especially at a time when it would give poor Cecilia a great deal of pain.' 'But why should it give her pain?' asked Louisa; 'I don't like her for being jealous of you.' 'Nay, Louisa, surely you don't think Cecilia jealous? She only tries to excel, and to please; she is more anxious to succeed than I am, it is true, because she has a great deal more activity, and perhaps more ambition. And it would really mortify her to lose this prize— you know that she proposed it herself. It has been her object for this month past, and I am sure she has taken great pains to obtain it.' 'But, dear Leonora, why should you lose it?' 'Indeed, my dear, it would be no loss to me; and, if it were, I would willingly suffer it for Cecilia; for, though we seem not to be such good friends as we used to be, I love her very much, and she will love me again—I'm sure she will; when she no longer fears me as a rival, she will again love me as a friend.'

Here Leonora heard a number of her companions running along the gallery. They all knocked hastily at the door, calling 'Leonora! Leonora! will you never come? Cecilia has been with us this half-hour.' Leonora smiled. 'Well, Louisa,' said she, smiling, 'will you promise me?' 'Oh, I am sure, by the way they speak to you, that they won't give you the prize!' said the little Louisa, and the tears started into her eyes. 'They love me, though, for all that,' said Leonora; 'and as for the prize, you know whom I wish to have it.'

'Leonora! Leonora!' called her impatient companions; 'don't you hear us? What are you about?' 'Oh, she never will take any trouble about anything,' said one of the party; 'let's go away.' 'Oh, go, go! make haste!' cried Louisa; 'don't stay; they are so angry.' 'Remember, then, that you have promised me,' said Leonora, and she left the room.

During all this time, Cecilia had been in the garden with her companions. The ambition which she had felt to win the first prize—the prize of superior talents and superior application—was not to be compared to the absolute anxiety which she now expressed to win this simple testimony of the love and approbation of her equals and rivals.

To employ her exuberant activity, Cecilia had been dragging branches of lilacs and laburnums, roses and sweet brier, to ornament the bower in which her fate was to be decided. It was excessively hot, but her mind was engaged, and she was indefatigable. She stood still at last to admire her works. Her companions all joined in loud applause. They were not a little prejudiced in her favour by the great eagerness which she expressed to win their prize, and by the great importance which she seemed to affix to the preference of each individual. At last, 'Where is Leonora?' cried one of them; and immediately, as we have seen, they ran to call her.

Cecilia was left alone. Overcome with heat and too violent exertion, she had hardly strength to support herself; each moment appeared to her intolerably long. She was in a state of the utmost suspense, and all her courage failed her. Even hope forsook her; and hope is a cordial which leaves the mind depressed and enfeebled.

'The time is now come,' said Cecilia; 'in a few moments all will be decided. In a few moments—goodness! How much do I hazard? If I should not win the prize, how shall I confess what I have done? How shall I beg Leonora to forgive me? I, who hoped to restore my friendship to her as an honour! They are gone to seek for her. The moment she appears I shall be forgotten. What—what shall I do?' said Cecilia, covering her face with her hands.

Such was Cecilia's situation when Leonora, accompanied by her companions, opened the hall door. They most of them ran forwards to Cecilia. As Leonora came into the bower, she held out her hand to Cecilia. 'We are not rivals, but friends, I hope,' said she. Cecilia clasped her hand; but she was in too great agitation to speak.

The table was now set in the arbour—the vase was now placed in the middle. 'Well,' said Cecilia, eagerly, 'who begins?' Caroline, one of her friends, came forward first, and then all the others successively. Cecilia's emotion was hardly conceivable. 'Now they are all in! Count them, Caroline!'

'One, two, three, four; the numbers are both equal.' There was a dead silence. 'No, they are not,' exclaimed Cecilia, pressing forward, and putting a shell into a vase. 'I have not given mine, and I give it to Leonora.' Then, snatching the bracelet, 'It is yours, Leonora,' said she; 'take it, and give me back your friendship.' The whole assembly gave one universal clap and a general shout of applause.

'I cannot be surprised at this from you, Cecilia,' said Leonora; 'and do you then still love me as you used to do?'

'O Leonora, stop! don't praise me; I don't deserve this,' said she, turning to her loudly-applauding companions. 'You will soon despise me. O Leonora, you will never forgive me! I have deceived you; I have sold——'

At this instant Mrs. Villars appeared. The crowd divided. She had heard all that passed, from her window. 'I applaud your generosity, Cecilia,' said she, 'but I am to tell you that in this instance it is unsuccessful. You have it not in your power to give the prize to Leonora. It is yours. I have another vote to give to you. You have forgotten Louisa.'

'Louisa!' exclaimed Cecilia; 'but surely, ma'am, Louisa loves Leonora better than she does me.' 'She commissioned me, however,' said Mrs. Villars, 'to give you a red shell; and you will find it in this box.'

Cecilia started, and turned as pale as death; it was the fatal box!

Mrs. Villars produced another box. She opened it; it contained the Flora. 'And Louisa also desired me,' said she, 'to return you this Flora.' She put it into Cecilia's hand. Cecilia trembled so that she could not hold it. Leonora caught it.

'Oh, madam! Oh, Leonora!' exclaimed Cecilia; 'now I have no hope left. I intended—I was just going to tell——' 'Dear Cecilia,' said Leonora, 'you need not tell it me; I know it already; and I forgive you with all my heart.'

'Yes, I can prove to you,' said Mrs. Villars, 'that Leonora has forgiven you. It is she who has given you the prize; it was she who persuaded Louisa to give you her vote. I went to see her a little while ago; and perceiving, by her countenance, that something was the matter, I pressed her to tell me what it was.

'"Why, madam," said she, "Leonora has made me promise to give my shell to Cecilia. Now I don't love Cecilia half so well as I do Leonora. Besides, I would not have Cecilia think I vote for her because she gave me a Flora." Whilst Louisa was speaking,' continued Mrs. Villars, 'I saw this silver box lying on the bed. I took it up, and asked if it was not yours, and how she came by it. "Indeed, madam," said Louisa, "I could have been almost certain that it was Cecilia's; but Leonora gave it me, and she said that she bought it of the peddler this morning. If anybody else had told me so, I could not have believed them, because I remember the box so well; but I can't help believing Leonora." "But did not you ask Cecilia about it?" said I. "No, madam," replied Louisa; "for Leonora forbade me." I guessed her reason. "Well," said I, "give me the box, and I will carry your shell in it to Cecilia." "Then, madam," said she, "if I must give it her, pray do take the Flora, and return it to her first, that she may not think it is for that I do it."'

'Oh, generous Leonora!' exclaimed Cecilia; 'but, indeed, Louisa, I cannot take your shell.'

'Then, dear Cecilia, accept of mine instead of it! you cannot refuse it; I only follow your example. As for the bracelet,' added Leonora, taking Cecilia's hand, 'I assure you I don't wish for it, and you do, and you deserve it.' 'No,' said Cecilia, 'indeed I do not deserve it. Next to you, surely Louisa deserves it best.'

'Louisa! oh yes, Louisa,' exclaimed everybody with one voice.

'Yes,' said Mrs. Villars, 'and let Cecilia carry the bracelet to her; she deserves that reward. For one fault I cannot forget all your merits, Cecilia, nor, I am sure, will your companions.' 'Then, surely, not your best friend,' said Leonora, kissing her.

Everybody present was moved. They looked up to Leonora with respectful and affectionate admiration.

'Oh, Leonora, how I love you! and how I wish to be like you!' exclaimed Cecilia—'to be as good, as generous!'

'Rather wish, Cecilia,' interrupted Mrs. Villars, 'to be as just; to be as strictly honourable, and as invariably consistent. Remember, that many of our sex are capable of great efforts—of making what they call great sacrifices to virtue or to friendship; but few treat their friends with habitual gentleness, or uniformly conduct themselves with prudence and good sense.'

THE LITTLE MERCHANTS

CHAPTER I

Chi di gallina nasce, convien che rozole.
As the old cock crows, so crows the young.

Those who have visited Italy give us an agreeable picture of the cheerful industry of the children of all ages in the celebrated city of Naples. Their manner of living and their numerous employments are exactly described in the following 'Extract from a Traveller's Journal.'[18]

'The children are busied in various ways. A great number of them bring fish for sale to town from Santa Lucia; others are very often seen about the arsenals, or wherever carpenters are at work, employed in gathering up the chips and pieces of wood; or by the seaside, picking up sticks, and whatever else has drifted ashore, which, when their basket is full, they carry away.

'Children of two or three years old, who can scarcely crawl along upon the ground, in company with boys of five or six, are employed in this petty trade. Hence they proceed with their baskets into the heart of the city, where in several places they form a sort of little market, sitting round with their stock of wood before them. Labourers, and the lower order of citizens, buy it of them to burn in the tripods for warming themselves, or to use in their scanty kitchens.

'Other children carry about for sale the water of the sulphurous wells, which, particularly in the spring season, is drunk in great abundance. Others again endeavour to turn a few pence by buying a small matter of fruit, of pressed honey, cakes, and comfits, and then, like little peddlers, offer and sell them to other children, always for no more profit than that they may have their share of them free of expense.

'It is really curious to see how an urchin, whose whole stock and property consist in a board and a knife, will carry about a water-melon, or a half-roasted gourd, collect a troup of children round him, set down his board, and proceed to divide the fruit into small pieces among them.

'The buyers keep a sharp look-out to see that they have enough for their little piece of copper; and the Lilliputian tradesmen act with no less caution as the exigencies of the case may require, to prevent his being cheated out of a morsel.'

The advantages of truth and honesty, and the value of a character for integrity, are very early felt amongst these little merchants in their daily intercourse with each other. The fair dealer is always sooner or later seen to prosper. The most cunning cheat is at last detected and disgraced.

Numerous instances of the truth of this common observation were remarked by many Neapolitan children, especially by those who were acquainted with the characters and history of Piedro and Francisco, two boys originally equal in birth, fortune, and capacity, but different in their education, and consequently in their habits and conduct. Francisco was the son of an honest gardener, who, from the time he could speak, taught him to love to speak the truth, showed him that liars are never believed—that cheats and thieves cannot be trusted, and that the shortest way to obtain a good character is to deserve it.

Youth and white paper, as the proverb says, take all impressions. The boy profited much by his father's precepts, and more by his example; he always heard his father speak the truth, and saw that he dealt fairly with everybody. In all his childish traffic, Francisco, imitating his parents, was scrupulously honest, and therefore all his companions trusted him—'As honest as Francisco,' became a sort of proverb amongst them.

'As honest as Francisco,' repeated Piedro's father, when he one day heard this saying. 'Let them say so; I say, "As sharp as Piedro"; and let us see which will go through the world best.' With the idea of making his son *sharp* he made him cunning. He taught him, that to make a *good bargain* was to deceive as to the value and price of whatever he wanted to dispose of; to get as much money as possible from customers by taking advantage of their ignorance or of their confidence. He often repeated his favourite proverb—'The buyer has need of a hundred eyes; the seller has need but of one.'[19] And he took frequent opportunities of explaining the meaning of this maxim to his son. He was a fisherman; and as his gains depended more upon fortune than upon prudence, he trusted habitually to his good luck. After being idle for a whole day, he would cast his line or his nets, and if he was lucky enough to catch a fine fish, he would go and show it in triumph to his neighbour the gardener.

'You are obliged to work all day long for your daily bread,' he would say. 'Look here; I work but five minutes, and I have not only daily bread, but daily fish.'

Upon these occasions, our fisherman always forgot, or neglected to count, the hours and days which were wasted in waiting for a fair wind to put to sea, or angling in vain on the shore.

Little Piedro, who used to bask in the sun upon the sea-shore beside his father, and to lounge or sleep away his time in a fishing-boat, acquired habits of idleness, which seemed to his father of little consequence whilst he was *but a child*.

'What will you do with Piedro as he grows up, neighbour?' said the gardener. 'He is smart and quick enough, but he is always in mischief. Scarcely a day has passed for this fortnight but I have caught him amongst my grapes. I track his footsteps all over my vineyard.' '*He is but a child* yet, and knows no better,' replied the fisherman. 'But if you don't teach him better now he is a child, how will he know when he is a man?' said the gardener. 'A mighty noise about a bunch of grapes, truly!' cried the fisherman; 'a few grapes more or less in your vineyard, what does it signify?' 'I speak for your son's sake, and not for the sake of my grapes,' said the gardener; 'and I tell you again, the boy will not do well in the world, neighbour, if you don't look after him in time.' 'He'll do well enough in the world, you will find,' answered the fisherman, carelessly. 'Whenever he casts my nets, they never come up empty. "It is better to be lucky than wise."'[20]

This was a proverb which Piedro had frequently heard from his father, and to which he most willingly trusted, because it gave him less trouble to fancy himself fortunate than to make himself wise.

'Come here, child,' said his father to him, when he returned home after the preceding conversation with the gardener; 'how old are you, my boy?—twelve years old, is not it?' 'As old as Francisco, and older by six months,' said Piedro. 'And smarter and more knowing by six years,' said his father. 'Here, take these fish to Naples, and let us see how you'll sell them for me. Venture a small fish, as the proverb says, to catch a great one.[21] I was too late with them at the market yesterday, but nobody will know but what they are just fresh out of the water, unless you go and tell them.'

'Not I; trust me for that; I'm not such a fool,' replied Piedro, laughing; 'I leave that to Francisco. Do you know, I saw him the other day miss selling a melon for his father by turning the bruised side to the customer, who was just laying down the money for it, and who was a raw servant-boy, moreover—one who would never have guessed there were two sides to a melon, if he had not, as you say, father, been told of it?'

'Off with you to market. You are a droll chap,' said his father, 'and will sell my fish cleverly, I'll be bound. As to the rest, let every man take care of his own grapes. You understand me, Piedro?'

'Perfectly,' said the boy, who perceived that his father was indifferent as to his honesty, provided he sold fish at the highest price possible. He proceeded to the market, and he offered his fish with assiduity to every person whom he thought likely to buy it, especially to those upon whom he thought he could impose. He positively asserted to all who looked at his fish that they were just fresh out of the water. Good judges of men and fish knew that he said what was false, and passed him by with neglect; but it was at last what he called *good luck* to meet with the very same young raw servant-boy who would have bought the bruised melon from Francisco. He made up to him directly, crying, 'Fish! Fine fresh fish! fresh fish!'

'Was it caught to-day?' said the boy.

I saw him the other day miss selling a melon for his father by turning the bruised side to the customer.'

'I saw him the other day miss selling a melon for his father by turning the bruised side to the customer.'

'Yes, this morning; not an hour ago,' said Piedro, with the greatest effrontery.

The servant-boy was imposed upon; and being a foreigner, speaking the Italian language but imperfectly, and not being expert at reckoning the Italian money, he was no match for the cunning Piedro, who cheated him not only as to the freshness but as to the price of the commodity. Piedro received nearly half as much again for his fish as he ought to have done.

On his road homewards from Naples to the little village of Resina, where his father lived, he overtook Francisco, who was leading his father's ass. The ass was laden with large panniers, which were filled with the stalks and leaves of cauliflowers, cabbages, broccoli, lettuces, etc.—all the refuse of the Neapolitan kitchens, which are usually collected by the gardeners' boys, and carried to the gardens round Naples, to be mixed with other manure.

'Well-filled panniers, truly,' said Piedro, as he overtook Francisco and the ass. The panniers were indeed not only filled to the top, but piled up with much skill and care, so that the load met over the animal's back.

'It is not a very heavy load for the ass, though it looks so large,' said Francisco. 'The poor fellow, however, shall have a little of this water,' added he, leading the ass to a pool by the roadside.

'I was not thinking of the ass, boy; I was not thinking of any ass, but of you, when I said, "Well-filled panniers, truly!" This is your morning's work, I presume, and you'll make another journey to Naples to-day, on the same errand, I warrant, before your father thinks you have done enough?'

'Not before *my father* thinks I have done enough, but before I think so myself,' replied Francisco.

'I do enough to satisfy myself and my father too,' said Piedro, 'without slaving myself after your fashion. Look here,' producing the money he had received for the fish; 'all this was had for asking. It is no bad thing, you'll allow, to know how to ask for money properly.'

'I should be ashamed to beg, or borrow either,' said Francisco.

'Neither did I get what you see by begging, or borrowing either,' said Piedro, 'but by using my wits; not as you did yesterday, when, like a novice, you showed the bruised side of your melon, and so spoiled your market by your wisdom.'

'Wisdom I think it still,' said Francisco.

'And your father?' asked Piedro.

'And my father,' said Francisco.

'Mine is of a different way of thinking,' said Piedro. 'He always tells me that the buyer has need of a hundred eyes, and if one can blind the whole hundred, so much the better. You must know, I got off the fish to-day that my father could not sell yesterday in the market—got it off for fresh just out of the river—got twice as much as the market price for it; and from whom, think you? Why, from the very booby that would have bought the bruised melon for a sound one if you would have let him. You'll allow I'm no fool, Francisco, and that I'm in a fair way to grow rich, if I go on as I have begun.'

'Stay,' said Francisco; 'you forgot that the booby you took in to-day will not be so easily taken in to-morrow. He will buy no more fish from you, because he will be afraid of your cheating him; but he will be ready enough to buy fruit from me, because he will know I shall not cheat him—so you'll have lost a customer, and I gained one.'

'With all my heart,' said Piedro. 'One customer does not make a market; if he buys no more from me, what care I? there are people enough to buy fish in Naples.'

'And do you mean to serve them all in the same manner?' asked Francisco.

'If they will be only so good as to give me leave,' said Piedro, laughing, and repeating his father's proverb, "'Venture a small fish to catch a large one.'"22 He had learned to think that to cheat in making bargains was witty and clever.

'And you have never considered, then,' said Francisco, 'that all these people will, one after another, find you out in time?'

'Ay, in time; but it will be some time first. There are a great many of them, enough to last me all the summer, if I lose a customer a day,' said Piedro.

'And next summer,' observed Francisco, 'what will you do?'

'Next summer is not come yet; there is time enough to think what I shall do before next summer comes. Why, now, suppose the blockheads, after they had been taken in and found it out, all joined against me, and would buy none of our fish—what then? Are there no trades but that of a fisherman? In Naples, are there not a hundred ways of making money for a smart lad like me? as my father says. What do you think of turning merchant, and selling sugar-plums and cakes to the children in their market? Would they be hard to deal with, think you?'

'I think not,' said Francisco; 'but I think the children would find out in time if they were cheated, and would like it as little as the men.'

'I don't doubt them. Then *in time* I could, you know, change my trade—sell chips and sticks in the wood-market—hand about the lemonade to the fine folks, or twenty other things. There are trades enough, boy.'

'Yes, for the honest dealer,' said Francisco, 'but for no other; for in all of them you'll find, as *my* father says, that a good character is the best fortune to set up with. Change your trade ever so often, you'll be found out for what you are at last.'

'And what am I, pray?' said Piedro, angrily. 'The whole truth of the matter is, Francisco, that you envy my good luck, and can't bear to hear this money jingle in my hand. Ay, stroke the long ears of your ass, and look as wise as you please. It's better to be lucky than wise, as *my* father says. Good morning to you. When I am found out for what I am, or when the worst comes to the worst, I can drive a stupid ass, with his panniers filled with rubbish, as well as you do now, *honest Francisco*?'

'Not quite so well. Unless you were *honest Francisco*, you would not fill his panniers quite so readily.'

This was certain, that Francisco was so well known for his honesty amongst all the people at Naples with whom his father was acquainted, that every one was glad to deal with him; and as he never wronged any one, all were willing to serve him—at least, as much as they could without loss to themselves; so that after the market was over, his panniers were regularly filled by the gardeners and others with whatever he wanted. His industry was constant, his gains small but certain, and he every day had more and more reason to trust to his father's maxim—That honesty is the best policy.

The foreign servant lad, to whom Francisco had so honestly, or, as Piedro said, so sillily, shown the bruised side of the melon, was an Englishman. He left his native country, of which he was extremely fond, to attend upon his master, to whom he was still more attached. His master was in a declining state of health, and this young lad waited on him a little more to his mind than his other servants. We must, in consideration of his zeal, fidelity, and inexperience, pardon him for not being a good judge of fish. Though he had simplicity enough to be easily cheated once, he had too much sense to be twice made a dupe. The next time he met Piedro in the market, he happened to be in company with several English gentlemen's servants, and he pointed Piedro out to them all as an arrant knave. They heard his cry of 'Fresh fish! fresh fish! fine fresh fish!' with incredulous smiles, and let him pass, but not without some expressions of contempt, though uttered in English, he tolerably well understood; for the tone of contempt is sufficiently expressive in all languages. He lost more by not selling his fish to these people than he had gained the day before by cheating the *English booby*. The market was well supplied, and he could not get rid of his cargo.

'Is not this truly provoking?' said Piedro, as he passed by Francisco, who was selling fruit for his father. 'Look, my basket is as heavy as when I left home; and look at 'em yourself, they really are fine fresh fish to-day; and yet, because that revengeful booby told how I took him in yesterday, not one of yonder crowd would buy them; and all the time they really are fresh to-day!'

'So they are,' said Francisco; 'but you said so yesterday, when they were not; and he that was duped then is not ready to believe you to-day. How does he know that you deserve it better?'

'He might have looked at the fish,' repeated Piedro; 'they are fresh to-day. I am sure he need not have been afraid.'

145

'Ay,' said Francisco; 'but as my father said to you once—the scalded dog fears cold water.'23

Here their conversation was interrupted by the same English lad, who smiled as he came up to Francisco, and taking up a fine pine-apple, he said, in a mixture of bad Italian and English—'I need not look at the other side of this; you will tell me if it is not as good as it looks. Name your price; I know you have but one, and that an honest one; and as to the rest, I am able and willing to pay for what I buy; that is to say, my master is, which comes to the same thing. I wish your fruit could make him well, and it would be worth its weight in gold—to me, at least. We must have some of your grapes for him.'

'Is he not well?' inquired Francisco. 'We must, then, pick out the best for him,' at the same time singling out a tempting bunch. 'I hope he will like these; but if you could some day come as far as Resina (it is a village but a few miles out of town, where we have our vineyard), you could there choose for yourself, and pluck them fresh from the vines for your poor master.'

'Bless you, my good boy; I should take you for an Englishman, by your way of dealing. I'll come to your village. Only write me down the name; for your Italian names slip through my head. I'll come to the vineyard if it was ten miles off; and all the time we stay in Naples (may it not be so long as I fear it will!), with my master's leave, which he never refuses me to anything that's proper, I'll deal with you for all our fruit, as sure as my name's Arthur, and with none else, with my good will. I wish all your countrymen would take after you in honesty, indeed I do,' concluded the Englishman, looking full at Piedro, who took up his unsold basket of fish, looking somewhat silly, and gloomily walked off.

Arthur, the English servant, was as good as his word. He dealt constantly with Francisco, and proved an excellent customer, buying from him during the whole season as much fruit as his master wanted. His master, who was an Englishman of distinction, was invited to take up his residence, during his stay in Italy, at the Count de F.'s villa, which was in the environs of Naples—an easy walk from Resina. Francisco had the pleasure of seeing his father's vineyard often full of generous visitors, and Arthur, who had circulated the anecdote of the bruised melon, was, he said, 'proud to think that some of this was his doing, and that an Englishman never forgot a good turn, be it from a countryman or foreigner.'

'My dear boy,' said Francisco's father to him, whilst Arthur was in the vineyard helping to tend the vines, 'I am to thank you and your honesty, it seems, for our having our hands so full of business this season. It is fair you should have a share of our profits.'

'So I have, father, enough and enough, when I see you and mother going on so well. What can I want more?'

'Oh, my brave boy, we know you are a grateful, good son; but I have been your age myself; you have companions, you have little expenses of your own. Here; this vine, this fig-tree, and a melon a week next summer shall be yours. With these make a fine figure amongst the little Neapolitan merchants; and all I wish is that you may prosper as well, and by the same honest means, in managing for yourself, as you have done managing for me.'

'Thank you, father; and if I prosper at all, it shall be by those means, and no other, or I should not be worthy to be called your son.'

Piedro the cunning did not make quite so successful a summer's work as did Francisco the honest. No extraordinary events happened, no singular instance of bad or good luck occurred; but he felt, as persons usually do, the natural consequences of his own actions. He pursued his scheme of imposing, as far as he could, upon every person he dealt with; and the consequence was, that at last nobody would deal with him.

'It is easy to outwit one person, but impossible to outwit all the world,' said a man24 who knew the world at least as well as either Piedro or his father.

Piedro's father, amongst others, had reason to complain. He saw his own customers fall off from him, and was told, whenever he went into the market, that his son was such a cheat there was no dealing with him. One day, when he was returning from the market in a very bad humour, in consequence of these reproaches, and of his not having found customers for his goods, he espied his *smart* son Piedro at a little merchant's fruit-board, devouring a fine gourd with prodigious greediness. 'Where, glutton, do you find money to pay for these dainties?' exclaimed his father, coming close up to him, with angry gestures. Piedro's mouth was much too full to make an immediate reply, nor did his father wait for any, but darting his hand into the youth's pocket, pulled forth a handful of silver.

'The money, father,' said Piedro, 'that I got for the fish yesterday, and that I meant to give you to-day, before you went out.'

'Then I'll make you remember it against another time, sirrah!' said his father. 'I'll teach you to fill your stomach with my money. Am I to lose my customers by your tricks, and then find you here eating my all? You are a rogue, and everybody has found you out to be a rogue; and the worst of rogues I find you, who scruples not to cheat his own father.'

Saying these words, with great vehemence he seized hold of Piedro, and in the very midst of the little fruit-market gave him a severe beating. This beating did the boy no good; it was vengeance not punishment. Piedro saw that his father was in a passion, and knew that he was beaten because he was found out to be a rogue, rather than for being one. He recollected perfectly that his father once said to him: 'Let every one take care of his own grapes.'

Indeed, it was scarcely reasonable to expect that a boy who had been educated to think that he might cheat every customer he could in the way of trade, should be afterwards scrupulously honest in his conduct towards the father whose proverbs encouraged his childhood in cunning.

Piedro writhed with bodily pain as he left the market after his drubbing, but his mind was not in the least amended. On the contrary, he was hardened to the sense of shame by the loss of reputation. All the little merchants were spectators of this scene, and heard his father's words: 'You *are* a rogue, and the worst of rogues, who scruples not to cheat his own father.'

These words were long remembered, and long did Piedro feel their effects. He once flattered himself that, when his trade of selling fish failed him, he could readily engage in some other; but he now found, to his mortification, that what Francisco's father said proved true: 'In all trades the best fortune to set up with is a good character.'

Not one of the little Neapolitan merchants would either enter into partnership with him, give him credit, or even trade with him for ready money.—'If you would cheat your own father, to be sure you will cheat us,' was continually said to him by these prudent little people.

Piedro was taunted and treated with contempt at home and abroad. His father, when he found that his son's *smartness* was no longer useful in making bargains, shoved him out of his way whenever he met him. All the food or clothes that he had at home seemed to be given to him grudgingly, and with such expressions as these: 'Take that; but it is too good for you. You must eat this, now, instead of gourds and figs—and be thankful you have even this.'

Piedro spent a whole winter very unhappily. He expected that all his old tricks, and especially what his father had said of him in the market-place, would be soon forgotten; but month passed after month, and still these things were fresh in the memory of all who had known them.

It is not easy to get rid of a bad character. A very great rogue25 was once heard to say, that he would, with all his heart, give ten thousand pounds for a good character, because he knew that he could make twenty thousand by it.

Something like this was the sentiment of our cunning hero when he experienced the evils of a bad reputation, and when he saw the numerous advantages which Francisco's good character procured. Such had been Piedro's wretched education, that even the hard lessons of experience could not alter its pernicious effects. He was sorry his knavery had been detected, but he still thought it clever to cheat, and was secretly persuaded that, if he had cheated successfully, he should have been happy. 'But I know I am not happy now,' said he to himself one morning, as he sat alone disconsolate by the sea-shore, dressed in tattered garments, weak and hungry, with an empty basket beside him. His fishing-rod, which he held between his knees, bent over the dry sands instead of into the water, for he was not thinking of what he was about; his arms were folded, his head hung down, and his ragged hat was slouched over his face. He was a melancholy spectacle.

Francisco, as he was coming from his father's vineyard with a large dish of purple and white grapes upon his head, and a basket of melons and figs hanging upon his arm, chanced to see Piedro seated in this melancholy posture. Touched with compassion, Francisco approached him softly; his footsteps were not heard upon the sands, and Piedro did not perceive that any one was near him till he felt something cold touch his hand; he then started, and, looking up, saw a bunch of ripe grapes, which Francisco was holding over his head.

'Eat them; you'll find them very good, I hope,' said Francisco, with a benevolent smile.

'They are excellent—most excellent, and I am much obliged to you, Francisco,' said Piedro. 'I was very hungry, and that's what I am now, without anybody's caring anything about it. I am not the favourite I was with my father, but I know it is all my own fault.'

'Well, but cheer up,' said Francisco; 'my father always says, "One who knows he has been in fault, and acknowledges it, will scarcely be in fault again." Yes, take as many figs as you will,' continued he; and held his basket closer to Piedro, who, as he saw, cast a hungry eye upon one of the ripe figs.

'But,' said Piedro, after he had taken several, 'shall not I get you into a scrape by taking so many? Won't your father be apt to miss them?'

'Do you think I would give them to you if they were not my own?' said Francisco, with a sudden glance of indignation.

'Well, don't be angry that I asked the question; it was only from fear of getting you into disgrace that I asked it.'

'It would not be easy for anybody to do that, I hope,' said Francisco, rather proudly.

'And to me less than anybody,' replied Piedro, in an insinuating tone, '*I*, that am so much obliged to you!'

'A bunch of grapes and a few figs are no mighty obligation,' said Francisco, smiling; 'I wish I could do more for you. You seem, indeed, to have been very unhappy of late. We never see you in the markets as we used to do.'

'No; ever since my father beat me, and called me rogue before all the children there, I have never been able to show my face without being gibed at by one or t'other. If you would but take me along with you amongst them, and only just *seem* my friend for a day or two, or so, it would quite set me up again; for they all like you.'

'I would rather *be* than seem your friend, if I could,' said Francisco.

'Ay, to be sure; that would be still better,' said Piedro, observing that Francisco, as he uttered his last sentence, was separating the grapes and other fruits into two equal divisions. 'To be sure I would rather you would *be* than *seem* a friend to me; but I thought that was too much to ask at first, though I have a notion, notwithstanding I have been so *unlucky* lately—I have a notion you would have no reason to repent of it. You would find me no bad hand, if you were to try, and take me into partnership.'

'Partnership!' interrupted Francisco, drawing back alarmed; 'I had no thoughts of that.'

'But won't you? can't you?' said Piedro, in a supplicating tone; '*can't* you have thoughts of it? You'd find me a very active partner.'

Francisco still drew back, and kept his eyes fixed upon the ground. He was embarrassed; for he pitied Piedro, and he scarcely knew how to point out to him that something more is necessary in a partner in trade besides activity, and that is honesty.

'Can't you?' repeated Piedro, thinking that he hesitated from merely mercenary motives. 'You shall have what share of the profits you please.'

'I was not thinking of the profits,' said Francisco; 'but without meaning to be ill-natured to you, Piedro, I must say that I cannot enter into any partnership with you at present; but I will do what, perhaps, you will like as well,' said he, taking half the fruit out of his basket; 'you are heartily welcome to this; try and sell it in the children's fruit-market.' 'I'll go on before you, and speak to those I am acquainted with, and tell them you are going to set up a new character, and that you hope to make it a good one.'

'Hey, shall I! Thank you for ever, dear Francisco,' cried Piedro, seizing his plentiful gift of fruit. 'Say what you please for me.'

'But don't make me say anything that is not true,' said Francisco, pausing.

'No, to be sure not,' said Piedro; 'I *do* mean to give no room for scandal. If I could get them to trust me as they do you, I should be happy indeed.'

147

'That is what you may do, if you please,' said Francisco. 'Adieu, I wish you well with all my heart; but I must leave you now, or I shall be too late for the market.'

CHAPTER II

Chi va piano va sano, e anché lontano.
Fair and softly goes far in a day.

Piedro had now an opportunity of establishing a good character. When he went into the market with his grapes and figs, he found that he was not shunned or taunted as usual. All seemed disposed to believe in his intended reformation, and to give him a fair trial.

These favourable dispositions towards him were the consequence of Francisco's benevolent representations. He told them that he thought Piedro had suffered enough to cure him of his tricks, and that it would be cruelty in them, because he might once have been in fault, to banish him by their reproaches from amongst them, and thus to prevent him from the means of gaining his livelihood honestly.

Piedro made a good beginning, and gave what several of the younger customers thought excellent bargains. His grapes and figs were quickly sold, and with the money that he got for them he the next day purchased from a fruit-dealer a fresh supply; and thus he went on for some time, conducting himself with scrupulous honesty, so that he acquired some credit among his companions. They no longer watched him with suspicious eyes. They trusted to his measures and weights, and they counted less carefully the change which they received from him.

The satisfaction he felt from this alteration in their manners was at first delightful, to Piedro; but in proportion to his credit, his opportunities of defrauding increased; and these became temptations which he had not the firmness to resist. His old manner of thinking recurred.

'I make but a few shillings a day, and this is but slow work,' said he to himself. 'What signifies my good character, if I make so little by it?'

Light gains, and frequent, make a heavy purse,26 was one of Francisco's proverbs. But Piedro was in too great haste to get rich to take time into his account. He set his invention to work, and he did not want for ingenuity, to devise means of cheating without running the risk of detection. He observed that the younger part of the community were extremely fond of certain coloured sugar-plums, and of burnt almonds.

With the money he had earned by two months' trading in fruit he laid in a large stock of what appeared to these little merchants a stock of almonds and sugar-plums, and he painted in capital gold coloured letters upon his board, 'Sweetest, largest, most admirable sugar-plums of all colours ever sold in Naples, to be had here; and in gratitude to his numerous customers, Piedro adds to these "Burnt almonds gratis."'

This advertisement attracted the attention of all who could read; and many who could not read heard it repeated with delight. Crowds of children surrounded Piedro's board of promise, and they all went away the first day amply satisfied. Each had a full measure of coloured sugar-plums at the usual price, and along with these a burnt almond gratis. The burnt almond had such an effect upon the public judgment, that it was universally allowed that the sugar-plums were, as the advertisement set forth, the largest, sweetest, most admirable ever sold in Naples; though all the time they were, in no respect, better than any other sugar-plums.

It was generally reported that Piedro gave full measure—fuller than any other board in the city. He measured the sugar-plums in a little cubical tin box; and this, it was affirmed, he heaped up to the top and pressed down before he poured out the contents into the open hands of his approving customers. This belief, and Piedro's popularity, continued longer even than he had expected; and, as he thought his sugar-plums had secured their reputation with the *generous public*, he gradually neglected to add burnt almonds gratis.

One day a boy of about ten years old passed carelessly by, whistling as he went along, and swinging a carpenter's rule in his hand. 'Ha! what have we here?' cried he, stopping to read what was written on Piedro's board. 'This promises rarely. Old as I am, and tall of my age, which makes the matter worse, I am still as fond of sugar-plums as my little sister, who is five years younger than I. Come, Signor, fill me quick, for I'm in haste to taste them, two measures of the sweetest, largest, most admirable sugar-plums in Naples—one measure for myself, and one for my little Rosetta.'

'You'll pay for yourself and your sister, then,' said Piedro, 'for no credit is given here.'

'No credit do I ask,' replied the lively boy; 'when I told you I loved sugar-plums, did I tell you I loved them, or even my sister, so well as to run in debt for them? Here's for myself, and here's for my sister's share,' said he, laying down his money; 'and now for the burnt almonds gratis, my good fellow.'

'They are all out; I have been out of burnt almonds this great while,' said Piedro.

'Then why are they in your advertisement here?' said Carlo.

'I have not had time to scratch them out of the board.'

'What! not when you have, by your own account, been out of them a great while? I did not know it required so much time to blot out a few words—let us try'; and as he spoke, Carlo, for that was the name of Piedro's new customer, pulled a bit of white chalk out of his pocket, and drew a broad score across the line on the board which promised burnt almonds gratis.

'You are most impatient,' said Piedro; 'I shall have a fresh stock of almonds to-morrow.' 'Why must the board tell a lie to-day?' 'It would ruin me to alter it,' said Piedro. 'A lie may ruin you, but I could scarcely think the truth could.' 'You have no right to meddle with me or my board,' said Piedro, put off his guard, and out of his usual soft voice of civility, by this last observation. 'My character, and that of my board, are too firmly established now for any chance customer like you to injure.' 'I never dreamed of injuring you or any one else,' said Carlo—'I wish, moreover, you may not injure yourself. Do as you please with your board, but give me my sugar-plums, for I have some right to meddle with those, having paid for them.' 'Hold out your hand, then.' 'No, put them in here, if you please; put my sister's, at least, in here; she likes to have them in this box: I bought some for her in it yesterday, and she'll think they'll taste the better out of the same box. But how is this? your measure does not fill my box nearly; you give us very few sugar-plums for our money.' 'I give you full measure, as I give to everybody.' 'The measure should be an inch cube, I know,' said Carlo; 'that's what all the little merchants have agreed to, you

148

know.' 'True,' said Piedro, 'so it is.' 'And so it is, I must allow,' said Carlo, measuring the outside of it with the carpenter's rule which he held in his hand. 'An inch every way; and yet by my eye—and I have no bad one, being used to measuring carpenter's work for my father—by my eye, I should think this would have held more sugar-plums.' 'The eye often deceives us,' said Piedro. 'There's nothing like measuring, you find.' 'There's nothing like measuring, I find, indeed,' replied Carlo, as he looked closely at the end of his rule, which, since he spoke last, he had put into the tin cube to take its depth in the inside. 'This is not as deep by a quarter of an inch, Signor Piedro, measured within as it is measured without.'

Piedro changed colour terribly, and seizing hold of the tin box, endeavoured to wrest it from the youth who measured so accurately. Carlo held his prize fast, and lifting it above his head, he ran into the midst of the square where the little market was held, exclaiming, 'A discovery! a discovery! that concerns all who love sugar-plums. A discovery! a discovery! that concerns all who have ever bought the sweetest, largest, and most admirable sugar-plums ever sold in Naples.'

The crowd gathered from all parts of the square as he spoke.

'We have bought,' and 'We have bought of those sugar-plums,' cried several little voices at once, 'if you mean Piedro's.'

'The same,' continued Carlo—'he who, out of gratitude to his numerous customers, gives, or promises to give, burnt almonds gratis.'

'Excellent they were!' cried several voices. 'We all know Piedro well; but what's your discovery?'

'My discovery is,' said Carlo, 'that you, none of you, know Piedro. Look you here; look at this box—this is his measure; it has a false bottom—it holds only three-quarters as much as it ought to do; and his numerous customers have all been cheated of one-quarter of every measure of the admirable sugar-plums they have bought from him. "Think twice of a good bargain," says the proverb.'

'So we have been finely duped, indeed,' cried some of the bystanders, looking at one another with a mortified air. Full of courtesy, full of craft!27 'So this is the meaning of his burnt almonds gratis,' cried others; all joined in an uproar of indignation, except one, who, as he stood behind the rest, expressed in his countenance silent surprise and sorrow.

'Is this Piedro a relation of yours?' said Carlo, going up to this silent person. 'I am sorry, if he be, that I have published his disgrace, for I would not hurt *you*. You don't sell sugar-plums as he does, I'm sure; for my little sister Rosetta has often bought from you. Can this Piedro be a friend of yours?'

'I wished to have been his friend, but I see I can't,' said Francisco. 'He is a neighbour of ours, and I pitied him; but since he is at his old tricks again, there's an end of the matter. I have reason to be obliged to you, for I was nearly taken in. He has behaved so well for some time past, that I intended this very evening to have gone to him, and to have told him that I was willing to do for him what he has long begged of me to do—to enter into partnership with him.'

'Francisco! Francisco! your measure, lend us your measure!' exclaimed a number of little merchants crowding round him. 'You have a measure for sugar-plums; and we have all agreed to refer to that, and to see how much we have been cheated before we go to break Piedro's bench and declare him bankrupt,28—the punishment for all knaves.'

They pressed on to Francisco's board, obtained his measure, found that it held something more than a quarter above the quantity that could be contained in Piedro's. The cries of the enraged populace were now most clamorous. They hung the just and the unjust measures upon high poles; and, forming themselves into a formidable phalanx, they proceeded towards Piedro's well-known yellow-lettered beard, exclaiming, as they went along, 'Common cause! common cause! The little Neapolitan merchants will have no knaves amongst them! Break his bench! break his bench! He is a bankrupt in honesty.'

Piedro saw the mob, heard the indignant clamour, and terrified at the approach of numbers, he fled with the utmost precipitation, having scarcely time to pack up half his sugar-plums. There was a prodigious number, more than would have filled many honest measures, scattered upon the ground and trampled under foot by the crowd. Piedro's bench was broken, and the public vengeance wreaked itself also upon his treacherous painted board. It was, after being much disfigured by various inscriptions expressive of the universal contempt for Piedro, hung up in a conspicuous part of the market-place; and the false measure was fastened like a cap upon one of its corners. Piedro could never more show his face in this market, and all hopes of friendship—all hopes of partnership with Francisco—were for ever at an end.

If rogues would calculate, they would cease to be rogues; for they would certainly discover that it is most for their interest to be honest—setting aside the pleasure of being esteemed and beloved, of having a safe conscience, with perfect freedom from all the various embarrassments and terror to which knaves are subject. Is it not clear that our crafty hero would have gained rather more by a partnership with Francisco, and by a fair character, than he could possibly obtain by fraudulent dealing in comfits?

When the mob had dispersed, after satisfying themselves with executing summary justice upon Piedro's bench and board, Francisco found a carpenter's rule lying upon the ground near Piedro's broken bench, which he recollected to have seen in the hands of Carlo. He examined it carefully, and he found Carlo's name written upon it, and the name of the street where he lived; and though it was considerably out of his way, he set out immediately to restore the rule, which was a very handsome one, to its rightful owner. After a hot walk through several streets, he overtook Carlo, who had just reached the door of his own house. Carlo was particularly obliged to him, he said, for restoring this rule to him, as it was a present from the master of a vessel, who employed his father to do carpenter's work for him. 'One should not praise one's self, they say,' continued Carlo; 'but I long so much to gain your good opinion, that I must tell you the whole history of the rule you have restored. It was given to me for having measured the work and made up the bill of a whole pleasure-boat myself. You may guess I should have been sorry enough to have lost it. Thank you for its being once more in my careless hands, and tell me, I beg, whenever I can do you any service. By-the-bye, I can make up for you a fruit stall. I'll do it to-morrow, and it shall be the admiration of the market. Is there anything else you could think of for me?'

'Why, yes,' said Francisco; 'since you are so good-natured, perhaps you'd be kind enough to tell me the meaning of some of those lines and figures that I see upon your rule. I have a great curiosity to know their use.'

'That I'll explain to you with pleasure, as far as I know them myself; but when I'm at fault, my father, who is cleverer than I am, and understands trigonometry, can help us out.'

'Trigonometry!' repeated Francisco, not a little alarmed at the high-sounding word; 'that's what I certainly shall never understand.'

'Oh, never fear,' replied Carlo, laughing. 'I looked just as you do now—I felt just as you do now—all in a fright and a puzzle, when I first heard of angles and sines, and co-sines, and arcs and centres, and complements and tangents.'

'Oh, mercy! mercy!' interrupted Francisco, whilst Carlo laughed, with a benevolent sense of superiority.

'Why,' said Carlo, 'you'll find all these things are nothing when you are used to them. But I cannot explain my rule to you here broiling in the sun. Besides, it will not be the work of a day, I promise you; but come and see us at your leisure hours, and we'll study it together. I have a great notion we shall become friends; and, to begin, step in with me now,' said Carlo, 'and eat a little macaroni with us. I know it is ready by this time. Besides, you'll see my father, and he'll show you plenty of rules and compasses, as you like such things; and then I'll go home with you in the cool of the evening, and you shall show me your melons and vines, and teach me, in time, something of gardening. Oh, I see we must be good friends, just made for each other; so come in—no ceremony.'

Carlo was not mistaken in his predictions; he and Francisco became very good friends, spent all their leisure hours together, either in Carlo's workshop or in Francisco's vineyard, and they mutually improved each other. Francisco, before he saw his friend's rule, knew but just enough of arithmetic to calculate in his head the price of the fruit which he sold in the market; but with Carlo's assistance, and the ambition to understand the tables and figures upon the wonderful rule, he set to work in earnest, and in due time satisfied both himself and his master.

'Who knows but these things that I am learning now may be of some use to me before I die?' said Francisco, as he was sitting one morning with his tutor, the carpenter.

'To be sure it will,' said the carpenter, putting down his compasses, with which he was drawing a circle. 'Arithmetic is a most useful, and I was going to say necessary thing to be known by men in all stations; and a little trigonometry does no harm. In short, my maxim is, that no knowledge comes amiss; for a man's head is of as much use to him as his hands; and even more so.

'A word to the wise will always suffice.

'Besides, to say nothing of making a fortune, is not there a great pleasure in being something of a scholar, and being able to pass one's time with one's book, and one's compasses and pencil? Safe companions these for young and old. No one gets into mischief that has pleasant things to think of and to do when alone; and I know, for my part, that trigonometry is——'

Here the carpenter, just as he was going to pronounce a fresh panegyric upon his favourite trigonometry, was interrupted by the sudden entrance of his little daughter Rosetta, all in tears: a very unusual spectacle, for, taking the year round, she shed fewer tears than any child of her age in Naples.

'Why, my dear good-humoured little Rosetta, what has happened? Why these large tears?' said her brother Carlo, and he went up to her, and wiped them from her cheeks. 'And these that are going over the bridge of the nose so fast? I must stop these tears too,' said Carlo.

Rosetta, at this speech, burst out laughing, and said that she did not know till then that she had any bridge on her nose.

'And were these shells the cause of the tears?' said her brother, looking at a heap of shells which she held before her in her frock.

'Yes, partly,' said Rosetta. 'It was partly my own fault, but not all. You know I went out to the carpenters' yard, near the arsenal, where all the children are picking up chips and sticks so busily; and I was as busy as any of them, because I wanted to fill my basket soon; and then I thought I should sell my basketful directly in the little wood-market. As soon as I had filled my basket, and made up my faggot (which was not done, brother, till I was almost baked by the sun, for I was forced to wait by the carpenters for the bits of wood to make up my faggot)—I say, when it was all ready, and my basket full, I left it all together in the yard.' 'That was not wise to leave it,' said Carlo. 'But I only left it for a few minutes, brother, and I could not think anybody would be so dishonest as to take it whilst I was away. I only just ran to tell a boy, who had picked up all these beautiful shells upon the sea-shore, and who wanted to sell them, that I should be glad to buy them from him, if he would only be so good as to keep them for me, for an hour or so, till I had carried my wood to market, and till I had sold it, and so had money to pay him for the shells.'

'Your heart was set mightily on these shells, Rosetta.'

'Yes; for I thought you and Francisco, brother, would like to have them for your nice grotto that you are making at Resina. That was the reason I was in such a hurry to get them. The boy who had them to sell was very good-natured; he poured them into my lap, and said I had such an honest face he would trust me, and that as he was in a great hurry, he could not wait an hour whilst I sold my wood; but that he was sure I would pay him in the evening, and he told me that he would call here this evening for the money. But now what shall I do, Carlo? I shall have no money to give him: I must give him back his shells, and that's a great pity.'

'But how happened it that you did not sell your wood?'

'Oh, I forgot; did not I tell you that? When I went back for my basket, do you know it was empty, quite empty, not a chip left? Some dishonest person had carried it all off. Had not I reason to cry now, Carlo?'

'I'll go this minute into the wood-market, and see if I can find your faggot. Won't that be better than crying?' said her brother. 'Should you know any one of your pieces of wood again if you were to see them?'

'Yes, one of them, I am sure, I should know again,' said Rosetta. 'It had a notch at one end of it, where one of the carpenters cut it off from another piece of wood for me.'

'And is this piece of wood from which the carpenter cut it still to be seen?' said Francisco. 'Yes, it is in the yard; but I cannot bring it to you, for it is very heavy.'

'We can go to it,' said Francisco, 'and I hope we shall recover your basketful.'

Carlo and his friend went with Rosetta immediately to the yard, near the arsenal, saw the notched piece of wood, and then proceeded to the little wood-market, and searched every heap that lay before the little factors; but no notched bit was to be found, and Rosetta declared that she did not see one stick that looked at all like any of hers.

On their part, her companions eagerly untied their faggots to show them to her, and exclaimed, 'that they were incapable of taking what did not belong to them; that of all persons they should never have thought of taking anything from the good-natured little Rosetta, who was always ready to give to others, and to help them in making up their loads.'

Despairing of discovering the thief, Francisco and Carlo left the market. As they were returning home, they were met by the English servant Arthur, who asked Francisco where he had been, and where he was going.

As soon as he heard of Rosetta's lost faggot, and of the bit of wood, notched at one end, of which Rosetta drew the shape with a piece of chalk which her brother had lent her, Arthur exclaimed, 'I have seen such a bit of wood as this within this quarter of an hour; but I cannot recollect where. Stay! this was at the baker's, I think, where I went for some rolls for my master. It was lying beside his oven.'

To the baker's they all went as fast as possible, and they got there but just in time. The baker had in his hand the bit of wood with which he was that instant going to feed his oven.

'Stop, good Mr. Baker!' cried Rosetta, who ran into the baker's shop first; and as he heard 'Stop! stop!' re-echoed by many voices, the baker stopped; and turning to Francisco, Carlo, and Arthur, begged, with a countenance of some surprise, to know why they had desired him to stop.

The case was easily explained, and the baker told them that he did not buy any wood in the little market that morning; that this faggot he had purchased between the hours of twelve and one from a lad about Francisco's height, whom he met near the yard of the arsenal.

'This is my bit of wood, I am sure; I know it by this notch,' said Rosetta.

'Well,' said the baker, 'if you will stay here a few minutes, you will probably see the lad who sold it to me. He desired to be paid in bread, and my bread was not quite baked when he was here. I bid him call again in an hour, and I fancy he will be pretty punctual, for he looked desperately hungry.'

The baker had scarcely finished speaking when Francisco, who was standing watching at the door, exclaimed, 'Here comes Piedro! I hope he is not the boy who sold you the wood, Mr. Baker?' 'He is the boy, though,' replied the baker, and Piedro, who now entered the shop, started at the sight of Carlo and Francisco, whom he had never seen since the day of disgrace in the fruit-market.

'Your servant, Signor Piedro,' said Carlo; 'I have the honour to tell you that this piece of wood, and all that you took out of the basket, which you found in the yard of the arsenal, belongs to my sister.' 'Yes, indeed,' cried Rosetta.

Piedro being very certain that nobody saw him when he emptied Rosetta's basket, and imagining that he was suspected only upon the bare assertion of a child like Rosetta, who might be baffled and frightened out of her story, boldly denied the charge, and defied any one to prove him guilty.

'He has a right to be heard in his own defence,' said Arthur, with the cool justice of an Englishman; and he stopped the angry Carlo's arm, who was going up to the culprit with all the Italian vehemence of oratory and gesture. Arthur went on to say something in bad Italian about the excellence of an English trial by jury, which Carlo was too much enraged to hear, but to which Francisco paid attention, and turning to Piedro, he asked him if he was willing to be judged by twelve of his equals. 'With all my heart,' said Piedro, still maintaining an unmoved countenance, and they returned immediately to the little wood-market. On their way, they had passed through the fruit-market, and crowds of those who were well acquainted with Piedro's former transactions followed, to hear the event of the present trial.

Arthur could not, especially as he spoke wretched Italian, make the eager little merchants understand the nature and advantages of an English trial by jury. They preferred their own summary mode of proceeding. Francisco, in whose integrity all had perfect confidence, was chosen with unanimous shouts for the judge; but he declined the office, and another was appointed. He was raised upon a bench, and the guilty but insolent-looking Piedro, and the ingenuous, modest Rosetta stood before him. She made her complaint in a very artless manner; and Piedro, with ingenuity, which in a better cause would have deserved admiration, spoke volubly and craftily in his own defence. But all that he could say could not alter facts. The judge compared the notched bit of wood found at the baker's with a piece from which it was cut, which he went to see in the yard of the arsenal. It was found to fit exactly. The judge then found it impossible to restrain the loud indignation of all the spectators. The prisoner was sentenced never more to sell wood in the market; and the moment sentence was pronounced, Piedro was hissed and hooted out of the market-place. Thus a third time he deprived himself of the means of earning his bread.

We shall not dwell upon all his petty methods of cheating in the trades he next attempted. He handed lemonade about in a part of Naples where he was not known, but he lost his customers by putting too much water and too little lemon into this beverage. He then took to the waters from the sulphurous springs, and served them about to foreigners; but one day, as he was trying to jostle a competitor from the coach door, he slipped his foot and broke his glasses. They had been borrowed from an old woman who hired out glasses to the boys who sold lemonade. Piedro knew that it was the custom to pay, of course, for all that was broken; but this he was not inclined to do. He had a few shillings in his pocket, and thought that it would be very clever to defraud this poor woman of her right, and to spend his shillings upon what he valued much more than he did his good name—macaroni. The shillings were soon gone.

We shall now for the present leave Piedro to his follies and his fate; or, to speak more properly, to his follies and their inevitable consequences.

Piedro was hissed and hooted out of the market-place.

Piedro was hissed and hooted out of the market-place.

Francisco was all this time acquiring knowledge from his new friends, without neglecting his own or his father's business. He contrived, during the course of autumn and winter, to make himself a tolerable arithmetician. Carlo's father could draw plans in architecture neatly; and, pleased with the eagerness Francisco showed to receive instruction, he willingly put a pencil and compasses into his hand, and taught him all he knew himself. Francisco had great perseverance, and, by repeated trials, he at length succeeded in copying exactly all the plans which his master lent him. His copies, in time, surpassed the originals, and Carlo exclaimed, with astonishment: 'Why, Francisco, what an astonishing *genius* you have for drawing!—Absolutely you draw plans better than my father!'

'As to genius,' said Francisco, honestly, 'I have none. All that I have done has been done by hard labour. I don't know how other people do things; but I am sure that I never have been able to get anything done well but by patience. Don't you remember, Carlo, how you and even Rosetta laughed at me the first time your father put a pencil into my awkward, clumsy hands?'

'Because,' said Carlo, laughing again at the recollection, 'you held your pencil so drolly; and when you were to cut it, you cut it just as if you were using a pruning-knife to your vines; but now it is your turn to laugh, for you surpass us all. And the times are changed since I set about to explain this rule of mine to you.'

'Ay, that rule,' said Francisco—'how much I owe to it! Some great people, when they lose any of their fine things, cause the crier to promise a reward of so much money to anyone who shall find and restore their trinket. How richly have you and your father rewarded me for returning this rule!'

Francisco's modesty and gratitude, as they were perfectly sincere, attached his friends to him most powerfully; but there was one person who regretted our hero's frequent absences from his vineyard at Resina. Not Francisco's father, for he was well satisfied his son never neglected his business; and as to the hours spent in Naples, he had so much confidence in Francisco, that he felt no apprehensions of his

152

getting into bad company. When his son had once said to him, 'I spend my time at such a place, and in such and such a manner,' he was as well convinced of its being so as if he had watched and seen him every moment of the day. But it was Arthur who complained of Francisco's absence.

'I see, because I am an Englishman,' said he, 'you don't value my friendship, and yet that is the very reason you ought to value it; no friends so good as the English, be it spoken without offence to your Italian friend, for whom you now continually leave me to dodge up and down here in Resina, without a soul that I like to speak to, for you are the only Italian I ever liked.'

'You *shall* like another, I promise you,' said Francisco. 'You must come with me to Carlo's, and see how I spend my evenings; then complain of me, if you can.'

It was the utmost stretch of Arthur's complaisance to pay this visit; but, in spite of his national prejudices and habitual reserve of temper, he was pleased with the reception he met with from the generous Carlo and the playful Rosetta. They showed him Francisco's drawings with enthusiastic eagerness; and Arthur, though no great judge of drawing, was in astonishment, and frequently repeated, 'I know a gentleman who visits my master who would like these things. I wish I might have them to show him.'

'Take them, then,' said Carlo; 'I wish all Naples could see them, provided they might be liked half as well as I like them.'

Arthur carried off the drawings, and one day, when his master was better than usual, and when he was at leisure, eating a dessert of Francisco's grapes, he entered respectfully, with his little portfolio under his arm, and begged permission to show his master a few drawings done by the gardener's son, whose grapes he was eating.

Though not quite so partial a judge as the enthusiastic Carlo, this gentleman was both pleased and surprised at the sight of these drawings, considering how short a time Francisco had applied himself to this art, and what slight instructions he had received. Arthur was desired to summon the young artist. Francisco's honest, open manner, joined to the proofs he had given of his abilities, and the character Arthur gave him for strict honesty, and constant kindness to his parents, interested Mr. Lee, the name of this English gentleman, much in his favour. Mr. Lee was at this time in treaty with an Italian painter, whom he wished to engage to copy for him exactly some of the cornices, mouldings, tablets, and antique ornaments which are to be seen amongst the ruins of the ancient city of Herculaneum.29

29 We must give those of our young English readers who may not be acquainted with the ancient city of Herculaneum some idea of it. None can be ignorant that near Naples is the celebrated volcanic mountain of Vesuvius;—that, from time to time, there happen violent eruptions from this mountain; that is to say, flames and immense clouds of smoke issue from different openings, mouths, or *craters*, as they are called, but more especially from the summit of the mountain, which is distinguished by the name of *the* crater. A rumbling, and afterwards a roaring noise is heard within, and prodigious quantities of stones and minerals burnt into masses (scoriæ) are thrown out of the crater, sometimes to a great distance. The hot ashes from Mount Vesuvius have often been seen upon the roofs of the houses of Naples, from which it is six miles distant. Streams of lava run down the sides of the mountain during the time of an eruption, destroying everything in their way, and overwhelm the houses and vineyards which are in the neighbourhood.

About 1700 years ago, during the reign of the Roman Emperor Titus, there happened a terrible eruption of Mount Vesuvius; and a large city called Herculaneum, which was situated at about four miles' distance from the volcano, was overwhelmed by the streams of lava which poured into it, filled up the streets, and quickly covered over the tops of the houses, so that the whole was no more visible. It remained for many years buried. The lava which covered it became in time fit for vegetation, plants grew there, a new soil was formed, and a new town called Portici was built over the place where Herculaneum formerly stood. The little village of Resina is also situated near the spot. About fifty years ago, in a poor man's garden at Resina, a hole in a well about thirty feet below the surface of the earth was observed. Some persons had the curiosity to enter into this hole, and, after creeping underground for some time, they came to the foundations of houses. The peasants, inhabitants of the village, who had probably never heard of Herculaneum, were somewhat surprised at their discovery.30 About the same time, in a pit in the town of Portici, a similar passage under ground was discovered, and, by orders of the King of Naples, workmen were employed to dig away the earth, and clear the passages. They found, at length, the entrance into the town, which, during the reign of Titus, was buried under lava. It was about eighty-eight Neapolitan palms (a palm contains near nine inches) below the top of the pit. The workmen, as they cleared the passages, marked their way with chalk when they came to any turning, lest they should lose themselves. The streets branched out in many directions, and, lying across them, the workmen often found large pieces of timber, beams, and rafters; some broken in the fall, others entire. These beams and rafters are burned quite black, and look like charcoal, except those that were found in moist places, which have more the colour of rotten wood, and which are like a soft paste, into which you might run your hand. The walls of the houses slant, some one way, some another, and some are upright. Several magnificent buildings of brick, faced with marble of different colours, are partly seen, where the workmen have cleared away the earth and lava with which they were encrusted. Columns of red and white marble, and flights of marble steps, are seen in different places; and out of the ruins of the palaces some very fine statues and pictures have been dug. Foreigners who visit Naples are very curious to see this subterraneous city, and are desirous to carry with them into their own country some proofs of their having examined this wonderful place.

CHAPTER III

Tutte le gran faciende si fanno di foca cosa.
What great events from trivial causes spring.

Signor Camillo, the artist employed by Mr. Lee to copy some of the antique ornaments in Herculaneum, was a liberal-minded man, perfectly free from that mean jealousy which would repress the efforts of rising genius.

'Here is a lad scarcely fifteen, a poor gardener's son, who, with merely the instructions he could obtain from a common carpenter, has learned to draw these plans and elevations, which you see are tolerably neat. What an advantage your instruction would be to him,' said Mr. Lee, as he introduced Francisco to Signor Camillo. 'I am interested in this lad from what I have learned of his good conduct. I hear he is strictly honest, and one of the best of sons. Let us do something for him. If you will give him some knowledge of your art, I will, as far as money can recompense you for your loss of time, pay whatever you may think reasonable for his instruction.'

Signor Camillo made no difficulties; he was pleased with his pupil's appearance, and every day he liked him better and better. In the room where they worked together there were some large books of drawings and plates, which Francisco saw now and then opened by his master, and which he had a great desire to look over; but when he was left in the room by himself he never touched them, because he had not permission. Signor Camillo, the first day he came into his room with his pupil, said to him, 'Here are many valuable books and drawings, young man. I trust, from the character I have heard of you, that they will be perfectly safe here.'

Some weeks after Francisco had been with the painter, they had occasion to look for the front of a temple in one of these large books. 'What! don't you know in which book to look for it, Francisco?' cried his master, with some impatience. 'Is it possible that you have been here so long with these books, and that you cannot find the print I mean? Had you half the taste I gave you credit for, you would have singled it out from all the rest, and have it fixed in your memory.'

'But, signor, I never saw it,' said Francisco, respectfully, 'or perhaps I should have preferred it.'

'That you never saw it, young man, is the very thing of which I complain. Is a taste for the arts to be learned, think you, by looking at the cover of a book like this? Is it possible that you never thought of opening it?'

'Often and often,' cried Francisco, 'have I longed to open it; but I thought it was forbidden me, and however great my curiosity in your absence, I have never touched them. I hoped, indeed, that the time would come when you would have the goodness to show them to me.'

'And so the time is come, excellent young man,' cried Camillo; 'much as I love taste, I love integrity more. I am now sure of your having the one, and let me see whether you have, as I believe you have, the other. Sit you down here beside me; and we will look over these books together.'

The attention with which his young pupil examined everything, and the pleasure he unaffectedly expressed in seeing these excellent prints, sufficiently convinced his judicious master that it was not from the want of curiosity or taste that he had never opened these tempting volumes. His confidence in Francisco was much increased by this circumstance, slight as it may appear.

One day Signor Camillo came behind Francisco, as he was drawing with much intentness, and tapping him upon the shoulder, he said to him: 'Put up your pencils and follow me. I can depend upon your integrity; I have pledged myself for it. Bring your note-book with you, and follow me; I will this day show you something that will entertain you at least as much as my large book of prints. Follow me.'

Francisco followed, till they came to the pit near the entrance of Herculaneum. 'I have obtained leave for you to accompany me,' said his master, 'and you know, I suppose, that this is not a permission granted to every one?' Paintings of great value, besides ornaments of gold and silver, antique bracelets, rings, etc., are from time to time found amongst these ruins, and therefore it is necessary that no person should be admitted whose honesty cannot be depended upon. Thus, even Francisco's talents could not have advanced him in the world, unless they had been united to integrity. He was much delighted and astonished by the new scene that was now opened to his view; and as, day after day, he accompanied his master to this subterraneous city, he had leisure for observation. He was employed, as soon as he had gratified his curiosity, in drawing. There are niches in the walls in several places, from which pictures have been dug, and these niches are often adorned with elegant masks, figures and animals, which have been left by the ignorant or careless workmen, and which are going fast to destruction. Signor Camillo, who was copying these for his English employer, had a mind to try his pupil's skill, and, pointing to a niche bordered with grotesque figures, he desired him to try if he could make any hand of it. Francisco made several trials, and at last finished such an excellent copy, that his enthusiastic and generous master, with warm encomiums, carried it immediately to his patron, and he had the pleasure to receive from Mr. Lee a purse containing five guineas, as a reward and encouragement for his pupil.

Francisco had no sooner received this money than he hurried home to his father and mother's cottage. His mother, some months before this time, had taken a small dairy farm; and her son had once heard her express a wish that she was but rich enough to purchase a remarkably fine brindled cow, which belonged to a farmer in the neighbourhood.

'Here, my dear mother,' cried Francisco, pouring the guineas into her lap; 'and here,' continued he, emptying a bag, which contained about as much more, in small Italian coins, the profits of trade-money he had fairly earned during the two years he sold fruit amongst the little Neapolitan merchants; 'this is all yours, dearest mother, and I hope it will be enough to pay for the brindled cow. Nay, you must not refuse me—I have set my heart upon the cow being milked by you this very evening; and I'll produce my best bunches of grapes, and my father, perhaps, will give us a melon, for I've had no time for melons this season; and I'll step to Naples and invite—may I, mother?—my good friends, dear Carlo and your favourite little Rosetta, and my old drawing master, and my friend Arthur, and we'll sup with you at your dairy.'

The happy mother thanked her son, and the father assured him that neither melon nor pine-apple should be spared, to make a supper worthy of his friends.

The brindled cow was bought, and Arthur and Carlo and Rosetta most joyfully accepted the invitation.

The carpenter had unluckily appointed to settle a long account that day with one of his employers, and he could not accompany his children. It was a delicious evening; they left Naples just as the sea-breeze, after the heats of the day, was most refreshingly felt. The walk to Resina, the vineyard, the dairy, and most of all, the brindled cow, were praised by Carlo and Rosetta with all the Italian superlatives which signify, 'Most beautiful! most delightful! most charming!' Whilst the English Arthur, with as warm a heart, was more temperate in his praise, declaring that this was 'the most like an English summer's evening of any he had ever felt since he came to Italy; and that, moreover, the cream was almost as good as what he had been used to drink in Cheshire.' The company, who were all pleased with each other, and with the gardener's good fruit, which he produced in great abundance, did not think of separating till late.

It was a bright moonlight night, and Carlo asked his friend if he would walk with them part of the way to Naples. 'Yes, all the way most willingly,' cried Francisco, 'that I may have the pleasure of giving to your father, with my own hands, this fine bunch of grapes, that I have reserved for him out of my own share.' 'Add this fine pine-apple for my share, then,' said his father, 'and a pleasant walk to you, my young friends.'

They proceeded gaily along, and when they reached Naples, as they passed through the square where the little merchants held their market, Francisco pointed to the spot where he found Carlo's rule. He never missed an opportunity of showing his friends that he did not forget their former kindness to him. 'That rule,' said he, 'has been the cause of all my present happiness, and I thank you for——'

'Oh, never mind thanking him now,' interrupted Rosetta, 'but look yonder, and tell me what all those people are about.' She pointed to a group of men, women, and children, who were assembled under a piazza, listening in various attitudes of attention to a man, who was standing upon a flight of steps, speaking in a loud voice, and with much action, to the people who surrounded him. Francisco, Carlo, and Rosetta joined his audience. The moon shone full upon his countenance, which was very expressive, and which varied frequently according to the characters of the persons whose history he was telling, and according to all the changes of their fortune. This man was one of those who are called Improvisatori—persons who, in Italian towns, go about reciting verses or telling stories, which they are supposed to invent as they go on speaking. Some of these people speak with great fluency, and collect crowds round them in the public streets. When an Improvisatore sees the attention of his audience fixed, and when he comes to some very interesting part of his narrative, he dexterously drops his hat upon the ground, and pauses till his auditors have paid tribute to his eloquence. When he thinks the hat sufficiently full, he takes it up again, and proceeds with his story. The hat was dropped just as Francisco and his two friends came under the piazza. The orator had finished one story, and was going to commence another. He fixed his eyes upon Francisco, then glanced at Carlo and Rosetta, and after a moment's consideration he began a story which bore some resemblance to one that our young English readers may, perhaps, know by the name of 'Cornaro, or the Grateful Turk.'

Francisco was deeply interested in this narrative, and when the hat was dropped, he eagerly threw in his contribution. At the end of the story, when the speaker's voice stopped, there was a momentary silence, which was broken by the orator himself, who exclaimed, as he took up the hat which lay at his feet, 'My friends, here is some mistake! this is not my hat; it has been changed whilst I was taken up with my story. Pray, gentlemen, find my hat amongst you; it was a remarkably good one, a present from a nobleman for an epigram I made. I would not lose my hat for twice its value. It has my name written withinside of it, Dominicho, Improvisatore. Pray, gentlemen, examine your hats.'

Everybody present examined their hats, and showed them to Dominicho, but his was not amongst them. No one had left the company; the piazza was cleared, and searched in vain. 'The hat has vanished by magic.' said Dominicho. 'Yes, and by the same magic a statue moves,' cried Carlo, pointing to a figure standing in a niche, which had hitherto escaped observation. The face was so much in the shade, that Carlo did not at first perceive that the statue was Piedro. Piedro, when he saw himself discovered, burst into a loud laugh, and throwing down Dominicho's hat, which he held in his hand behind him, cried, 'A pretty set of novices! Most excellent players at hide-and-seek you would make.'

Whether Piedro really meant to have carried off the poor man's hat, or whether he was, as he said, merely in jest, we leave it to those who know his general character to decide.

Carlo shook his head. 'Still at your old tricks, Piedro,' said he. 'Remember the old proverb: No fox so cunning but he comes to the furrier's at last.'[31]

'I defy the furrier and you too,' replied Piedro, taking up his own ragged hat. 'I have no need to steal hats; I can afford to buy better than you'll have upon your head. Francisco, a word with you, if you have done crying at the pitiful story you have been listening to so attentively.'

'And what would you say to me?' said Francisco, following him a few steps. 'Do not detain me long, because my friends will wait for me.'

'If they are friends, they can wait,' said Piedro. 'You need not be ashamed of being seen in my company now, I can tell you; for I am, as I always told you I should be, the richest man of the two.'

'Rich! you rich?' cried Francisco. 'Well, then, it was impossible you could mean to trick that poor man out of his good hat.'

'Impossible!' said Piedro. Francisco did not consider that those who have habits of pilfering continue to practise them often, when the poverty which first tempted them to dishonesty ceases. 'Impossible! You stare when I tell you I am rich; but the thing is so. Moreover, I am well with my father at home. I have friends in Naples, and I call myself Piedro the Lucky. Look you here,' said he, producing an old gold coin. 'This does not smell of fish, does it? My father is no longer a fisherman, nor I either. Neither do I sell sugar-plums to children; nor do I slave myself in a vineyard, like some folks; but fortune, when I least expected it, has stood my friend. I have many pieces of gold like this. Digging in my father's garden, it was my luck to come to an old Roman vessel full of gold. I have this day agreed for a house in Naples for my father. We shall live, whilst we can afford it, like great folks, you will see; and I shall enjoy the envy that will be felt by some of my old friends, the little Neapolitan merchants, who will change their note when they see my change of fortune. What say you to all this, Francisco the Honest?'

'That I wish you joy of your prosperity, and hope you may enjoy it long and well.'

'Well, no doubt of that. Every one who has it enjoys it *well*. He always dances well to whom fortune pipes.'[32]

'Yes, no longer pipe, no longer dance,' replied Francisco; and here they parted; for Piedro walked away abruptly, much mortified to perceive that his prosperity did not excite much envy, or command any additional respect from Francisco.

'I would rather,' said Francisco, when he returned to Carlo and Rosetta, who waited for him under the portico, when he left them—'I would rather have such good friends as you, Carlo and Arthur, and some more I could name, and, besides that, have a clear conscience, and work honestly for my bread, than be as lucky as Piedro. Do you know he has found a treasure, he says, in his father's garden—a vase full of gold? He showed me one of the gold pieces.'

'Much good may they do him. I hope he came honestly by them,' said Carlo; 'but ever since the affair of the double measure, I suspect double-dealing always from him. It is not our affair, however. Let him make himself happy his way, and we ours.

'He that would live in peace and rest,
Must hear, and see, and say the best.'[33]

All Piedro's neighbours did not follow this peaceable maxim; for when he and his father began to circulate the story of the treasure found in the garden, the village of Resina did not give them implicit faith. People nodded and whispered, and shrugged their shoulders; then crossed themselves and declared that they would not, for all the riches of Naples, change places with either Piedro or his father. Regardless, or pretending to be regardless, of these suspicions, Piedro and his father persisted in their assertions. The fishing-nets were sold, and everything in their cottage was disposed of; they left Resina, went to live at Naples, and, after a few weeks, the matter began to be almost forgotten in the village.

The old gardener, Francisco's father, was one of those who endeavoured to *think the best*; and all that he said upon the subject was, that he would not exchange Francisco the Honest for Piedro the Lucky; that one can't judge of the day till one sees the evening as well as the morning.34

Not to leave our readers longer in suspense, we must inform them that the peasants of Resina were right in their suspicions. Piedro had never found any treasure in his father's garden, but he came by his gold in the following manner:—

After he was banished from the little wood-market for stealing Rosetta's basketful of wood, after he had cheated the poor woman, who let glasses out to hire, out of the value of the glasses which he broke, and, in short, after he had entirely lost his credit with all who knew him, he roamed about the streets of Naples, reckless of what became of him.

He found the truth of the proverb, 'that credit lost is like a Venice glass broken—it can't be mended again.' The few shillings which he had in his pocket supplied him with food for a few days. At last he was glad to be employed by one of the peasants who came to Naples to load their asses with manure out of the streets. They often follow very early in the morning, or during the night-time, the trace of carriages that are gone, or that are returning from the opera; and Piedro was one night at this work, when the horses of a nobleman's carriage took fright at the sudden blaze of some fireworks. The carriage was overturned near him; a lady was taken out of it, and was hurried by her attendants into a shop, where she stayed till her carriage was set to rights. She was too much alarmed for the first ten minutes after her accident to think of anything; but after some time, she perceived that she had lost a valuable diamond cross, which she had worn that night at the opera. She was uncertain where she had dropped it; the shop, the carriage, the street were searched for it in vain.

Piedro saw it fall as the lady was lifted out of the carriage, seized upon it, and carried it off. Ignorant as he was of the full value of what he had stolen, he knew not how to satisfy himself as to this point, without trusting some one with the secret.

After some hesitation, he determined to apply to a Jew, who, as it was whispered, was ready to buy everything that was offered to him for sale, without making any *troublesome* inquiries. It was late; he waited till the streets were cleared, and then knocked softly at the back door of the Jew's house. The person who opened the door for Piedro was his own father. Piedro started back; but his father had fast hold of him.

'What brings you here?' said the father, in a low voice, a voice which expressed fear and rage mixed.

'Only to ask my way—my shortest way,' stammered Piedro.

'No equivocations! Tell me what brings you here at this time of the night? I *will* know.'

Piedro, who felt himself in his father's grasp, and who knew that his father would certainly search him, to find out what he had brought to sell, thought it most prudent to produce the diamond cross. His father could but just see its lustre by the light of a dim lamp which hung over their heads in the gloomy passage in which they stood.

'You would have been duped, if you had gone to sell this to the Jew. It is well it has fallen into my hands. How came you by it?' Piedro answered that he had found it in the street. 'Go your ways home, then,' said the father; 'it is safe with me. Concern yourself no more about it.'

Piedro was not inclined thus to relinquish his booty, and he now thought proper to vary in his account of the manner in which he found the cross. He now confessed that it had dropped from the dress of a lady, whose carriage was overturned as she was coming home from the opera, and he concluded by saying that, if his father took his prize from him without giving him his share of the profits, he would go directly to the shop where the lady stopped whilst her servants were raising the carriage, and that he would give notice of his having found the cross.

Piedro's father saw that his *smart* son, though scarcely sixteen years of age, was a match for him in villainy. He promised him that he should have half of whatever the Jew would give for the diamonds, and Piedro insisted upon being present at the transaction.

The Jew, who was a man old in all the arts of villainy, contrived to cheat both his associates.

The Jew, who was a man old in all the arts of villainy, contrived to cheat both his associates.

We do not wish to lay open to our young readers scenes of iniquity. It is sufficient to say that the Jew, who was a man old in all the arts of villainy, contrived to cheat both his associates, and obtained the diamond cross for less than half its value. The matter was managed so that the transaction remained undiscovered. The lady who lost the cross, after making fruitless inquiries, gave up the search, and Piedro and his father rejoiced in the success of their manœuvres.

It is said that 'Ill-gotten wealth is quickly spent';<u>35</u> and so it proved in this instance. Both father and son lived a riotous life as long as their money lasted, and it did not last many months. What his bad education began, bad company finished, and Piedro's mind was completely ruined by the associates with whom he became connected during what he called his *prosperity*. When his money was at an end, these unprincipled friends began to look cold upon him, and at last plainly told him—'If you mean to *live with us*, you must *live as we do*.' They lived by robbery.

Piedro, though familiarised to the idea of fraud, was shocked at the thought of becoming a robber by profession. How difficult it is to stop in the career of vice! Whether Piedro had power to stop, or whether he was hurried on by his associates, we shall, for the present, leave in doubt.

CHAPTER IV

We turn with pleasure from Piedro the Cunning to Francisco the Honest. Francisco continued the happy and useful course of his life. By his unremitting perseverance he improved himself rapidly under the instructions of his master and friend, Signor Camillo; his friend, we say, for the fair and open character of Francisco won, or rather earned, the friendship of this benevolent artist. The English gentleman seemed to take a pride in our hero's success and good conduct. He was not one of those patrons who think that they have done enough

157

when they have given five guineas. His servant Arthur always considered every generous action of his master's as his own, and was particularly pleased whenever this generosity was directed towards Francisco.

As for Carlo and the little Rosetta, they were the companions of all the pleasant walks which Francisco used to take in the cool of the evening, after he had been shut up all day at his work. And the old carpenter, delighted with the gratitude of his pupil, frequently repeated—'That he was proud to have given the first instructions to such a *genius*; and that he had always prophesied Francisco would be a *great* man.' 'And a good man, papa,' said Rosetta; 'for though he has grown so great, and though he goes into palaces now, to say nothing of that place underground, where he has leave to go, yet, notwithstanding all this, he never forgets my brother Carlo and you.'

'That's the way to have good friends,' said the carpenter. 'And I like his way; he does more than he says. Facts are masculine, and words are feminine.'36

These good friends seemed to make Francisco happier than Piedro could be made by his stolen diamonds.

One morning, Francisco was sent to finish a sketch of the front of an ancient temple, amongst the ruins of Herculaneum. He had just reached the pit, and the men were about to let him down with cords, in the usual manner, when his attention was caught by the shrill sound of a scolding woman's voice. He looked, and saw at some paces distant this female fury, who stood guarding the windlass of a well, to which, with threatening gestures and most voluble menaces, she forbade all access. The peasants—men, women, and children, who had come with their pitchers to draw water at this well—were held at bay by the enraged female. Not one dared to be the first to advance; whilst she grasped with one hand the handle of the windlass, and, with the other tanned muscular arm extended, governed the populace, bidding them remember that she was padrona, or mistress of the well. They retired, in hopes of finding a more gentle padrona at some other well in the neighbourhood; and the fury, when they were out of sight, divided the long black hair which hung over her face, and, turning to one of the spectators, appealed to them in a sober voice, and asked if she was not right in what she had done. 'I, that am padrona of the well,' said she, addressing herself to Francisco, who, with great attention, was contemplating her with the eye of a painter—'I, that am padrona of the well, must in times of scarcity do strict justice, and preserve for ourselves alone the water of our well. There is scarcely enough even for ourselves. I have been obliged to make my husband lengthen the ropes every day for this week past. If things go on at this rate, there will soon be not one drop of water left in my well.'

'Nor in any of the wells of the neighbourhood,' added one of the workmen, who was standing by; and he mentioned several in which the water had lately suddenly decreased; and a miller affirmed that his mill had stopped for want of water.

Francisco was struck by these remarks. They brought to his recollection similar facts, which he had often heard his father mention in his childhood, as having been observed previous to the last eruption of Mount Vesuvius.37 He had also heard from his father, in his childhood, that it is better to trust to prudence than to fortune; and therefore, though the peasants and workmen, to whom he mentioned his fears, laughed, and said, 'That as the burning mountain had been favourable to them for so many years, they would trust to it and St. Januarius one day longer,' yet Francisco immediately gave up all thoughts of spending this day amidst the ruins of Herculaneum. After having inquired sufficiently, after having seen several wells, in which the water had evidently decreased, and after having seen the mill-wheels that were standing still for want of their usual supply, he hastened home to his father and mother, reported what he had heard and seen, and begged of them to remove, and to take what things of value they could to some distance from the dangerous spot where they now resided.

Some of the inhabitants of Resina, whom he questioned, declared that they had heard strange rumbling noises underground; and a peasant and his son, who had been at work the preceding day in a vineyard, a little above the village, related that they had seen a sudden puff of smoke come out of the earth, close to them; and that they had, at the same time, heard a noise like the going off of a pistol.38

The villagers listened with large eyes and open ears to these relations; yet such was their habitual attachment to the spot they lived upon, or such the security in their own good fortune, that few of them would believe that there could be any necessity for removing. 'We'll see what will happen to-morrow; we shall be safe here one day longer,' said they.

Francisco's father and mother, more prudent than the generality of their neighbours, went to the house of a relation, at some miles' distance from Vesuvius, and carried with them all their effects.

In the meantime, Francisco went to the villa where his English friends resided. The villa was in a most dangerous situation, near Torre del Greco—a town that stands at the foot of Mount Vesuvius. He related all the facts that he had heard to Arthur, who, not having been, like the inhabitants of Resina, familiarised to the idea of living in the vicinity of a burning mountain and habituated to trust in St. Januarius, was sufficiently alarmed by Francisco's representations. He ran to his master's apartment, and communicated all that he had just heard. The Count de Flora and his lady, who were at this time in the house, ridiculed the fears of Arthur, and could not be prevailed upon to remove even as far as Naples. The lady was intent upon preparations for her birthday, which was to be celebrated in a few days with great magnificence at their villa; and she observed that it would be a pity to return to town before that day, and they had everything arranged for the festival. The prudent Englishman had not the gallantry to appear to be convinced by these arguments, and he left the place of danger. He left it not too soon, for the next morning exhibited a scene—a scene which we shall not attempt to describe.

We refer our young readers to the account of this dreadful eruption of Mount Vesuvius, published by Sir W. Hamilton in the *Philosophical Transactions*. It is sufficient here to say that, in the space of about five hours, the wretched inhabitants of Torre del Greco saw their town utterly destroyed by the streams of burning lava which poured from the mountain. The villa of Count de Flora, with some others, which were at a little distance from the town, escaped; but they were absolutely surrounded by the lava. The count and countess were obliged to fly from their house with the utmost precipitation in the night-time; and they had not time to remove any of their furniture, their plate, clothes, or jewels.

A few days after the eruption, the surface of the lava became so cool that people could walk upon it, though several feet beneath the surface it was still exceedingly hot. Numbers of those who had been forced from their houses now returned to the ruins to try to save whatever they could. But these unfortunate persons frequently found their houses had been pillaged by robbers, who, in these moments of general confusion, enrich themselves with the spoils of their fellow-creatures.

'Has the count abandoned his villa? and is there no one to take care of his plate and furniture? The house will certainly be ransacked before morning,' said the old carpenter to Francisco, who was at his house giving him an account of their flight. Francisco immediately went to the count's house in Naples, to warn him of his danger. The first person he saw was Arthur, who, with a face of terror, said to him, 'Do you know what has happened? It is all over with Resina!' 'All over with Resina! What, has there been a fresh eruption? Has the lava reached Resina?' 'No; but it will inevitably be blown up. There,' said Arthur, pointing to a thin figure of an Italian, who stood pale and trembling, and looking up to heaven as he crossed himself repeatedly—'There,' said Arthur, 'is a man who has left a parcel of his cursed rockets and fireworks, with I don't know how much gunpowder, in the count's house, from which we have just fled. The wind blows that way. One spark of fire, and the whole is blown up.'

Francisco waited not to hear more; but instantly, without explaining his intentions to any one, set out for the count's villa, and, with a bucket of water in his hand, crossed the beds of lava with which the house was encompassed; when, reaching the hall where the rockets and gunpowder were left, he plunged them into the water, and returned with them in safety over the lava, yet warm under his feet.

What was the surprise and joy of the poor firework-maker when he saw Francisco return from this dangerous expedition! He could scarcely believe his eyes, when he saw the rockets and the gunpowder all safe.

Returned in safety over the lava, yet warm under his feet.

The count, who had given up the hopes of saving his palace, was in admiration when he heard of this instance of intrepidity, which probably saved not only his villa, but the whole village of Resina, from destruction. These fireworks had been prepared for the celebration of the countess's birthday, and were forgotten in the hurry of the night on which the inhabitants fled from Torre del Greco.

'Brave young man!' said the count to Francisco, 'I thank you, and shall not limit my gratitude to thanks. You tell me that there is danger of my villa being pillaged by robbers. It is from this moment your interest as well as mine to prevent their depredations; for (trust to my liberality) a portion of all that is saved of mine shall be yours.'

'Bravo! bravissimo!' exclaimed one who started from a recessed window in the hall where all this passed. 'Bravo! bravissimo!' Francisco thought he knew the voice and the countenance of this man, who exclaimed with so much enthusiasm. He remembered to have seen him before, but when, or where, he could not recollect. As soon as the count left the hall, the stranger came up to Francisco. 'Is it possible,' said he, 'that you don't know me? It is scarcely a twelvemonth since I drew tears from your eyes.' 'Tears from my eyes?' repeated Francisco, smiling; 'I have shed but few tears. I have had but few misfortunes in my life.' The stranger answered him by two extempore Italian lines, which conveyed nearly the same idea that has been so well expressed by an English poet:—

To each their sufferings—all are men
Condemn'd alike to groan;
The feeling for another's woes,
Th' unfeeling for his own.

'I know you now perfectly well,' cried Francisco; 'you are the Improvisatore who, one fine moonlight night last summer, told us the story of Cornaro the Turk.'

'The same,' said the Improvisatore; 'the same, though in a better dress, which I should not have thought would have made so much difference in your eyes, though it makes all the difference between man and man in the eyes of the stupid vulgar. My genius has broken through the clouds of misfortune of late. A few happy impromptu verses I made on the Count de Flora's fall from his horse attracted attention. The count patronises me. I am here now to learn the fate of an ode I have just composed for his lady's birthday. My ode was to have been set to music, and to have been performed at his villa near Torre del Greco, if these troubles had not intervened. Now that the mountain is quiet again, people will return to their senses. I expect to be munificently rewarded. But perhaps I detain you. Go; I shall not forget to celebrate the heroic action you have performed this day. I still amuse myself amongst the populace in my tattered garb late in the evenings, and I shall sound your praises through Naples in a poem I mean to recite on the late eruption of Mount Vesuvius. Adieu.'

The Improvisatore was as good as his word. That evening, with more than his usual enthusiasm, he recited his verses to a great crowd of people in one of the public squares. Amongst the crowd were several to whom the name of Francisco was well known, and by whom he was well beloved. These were his young companions, who remembered him as a fruit-seller amongst the little merchants. They rejoiced to hear his praises, and repeated the lines with shouts of applause.

'Let us pass. What is all this disturbance in the streets?' said a man, pushing his way through the crowd. A lad who held by his arm stopped suddenly on hearing the name of Francisco, which the people were repeating with so much enthusiasm.

'Ha! I have found at last a story that interests you more than that of Cornaro the Turk,' cried the Improvisatore, looking in the face of the youth who had stopped so suddenly. 'You are the young man who, last summer, had liked to have tricked me out of my new hat. Promise me you won't touch it now,' said he, throwing down the hat at his feet, 'or you hear not one word I have to say. Not one word of the heroic action performed at the villa of the Count de Flora, near Torre del Greco, this morning, by Signor Francisco.'

'*Signor* Francisco!' repeated the lad with disdain. 'Well, let us hear what you have to tell of him,' added he. 'Your hat is very safe, I promise you; I shall not touch it. What of *Signor* Francisco?'

'*Signor* Francisco I may, without impropriety, call him,' said the Improvisatore, 'for he is likely to become rich enough to command the title from those who might not otherwise respect his merit.'

'Likely to become rich! how?' said the lad, whom our readers have probably before this time discovered to be Piedro. 'How, pray, is he likely to become rich enough to be a signor?'

'The Count de Flora has promised him a liberal portion of all the fine furniture, plate, and jewels that can be saved from his villa at Torre del Greco. Francisco is gone down hither now with some of the count's domestics to protect the valuable goods against those villainous plunderers, who robbed their fellow-creatures of what even the flames of Vesuvius would spare.'

'Come, we have had enough of this stuff,' cried the man whose arm Piedro held. 'Come away,' and he hurried forwards.

This man was one of the villains against whom the honest orator expressed such indignation. He was one of those with whom Piedro got acquainted during the time that he was living extravagantly upon the money he gained by the sale of the stolen diamond cross. That robbery was not discovered; and his *success*, as he called it, hardened him in guilt. He was both unwilling and unable to withdraw himself from the bad company with whom his ill-gotten wealth connected him. He did not consider that bad company leads to the gallows.39

The universal confusion which followed the eruption of Mount Vesuvius was to these villains a time of rejoicing. No sooner did Piedro's companion hear of the rich furniture, plate, etc., which the imprudent orator had described as belonging to the Count de Flora's villa, than he longed to make himself master of the whole.

'It is a pity,' said Piedro, 'that the count has sent Francisco with his servants down to guard it.' 'And who is this Francisco of whom you seem to stand in so much awe?' 'A boy, a young lad only, of about my own age; but I know him to be sturdily honest. The servants we might corrupt; but even the old proverb of "Angle with a silver hook,"40 won't hold good with him.'

'And if he cannot be won by fair means, he must be conquered by foul,' said the desperate villain; 'but if we offer him rather more than the count has already promised for his share of the booty, of course he will consult at once his safety and his interest.'

'No,' said Piedro; 'that is not his nature. I know him from a child, and we'd better think of some other house for to-night's business.'

'None other; none but this,' cried his companion, with an oath. 'My mind is determined upon this, and you must obey your leader: recollect the fate of him who failed me yesterday.'

The person to whom he alluded was one of the gang of robbers who had been assassinated by his companions for hesitating to commit some crime suggested by their leader. No tyranny is so dreadful as that which is exercised by villains over their young accomplices, who become their slaves. Piedro, who was of a cowardly nature, trembled at the threatening countenance of his captain, and promised submission.

In the course of the morning, inquiries were made secretly amongst the count's servants; and the two men who were engaged to sit up at the villa that night along with Francisco were bribed to second the views of this gang of thieves. It was agreed that about midnight the robbers should be let into the house; that Francisco should be tied hand and foot, whilst they carried off their booty. 'He is a stubborn chap, though so young, I understand,' said the captain of the robbers to his men; 'but we carry poniards, and know how to use them. Piedro, you look pale. You don't require to be reminded of what I said to you when we were alone just now?'

Piedro's voice failed, and some of his comrades observed that he was young and new to the business. The captain, who, from being his pretended friend during his wealthy days, had of late become his tyrant, cast a stern look at Piedro, and bid him be sure to be at the old Jew's, which was the place of meeting, in the dusk of the evening. After saying this he departed.

Piedro, when he was alone, tried to collect his thoughts—all his thoughts were full of horror. 'Where am I?' said he to himself; 'what am I about? Did I understand rightly what he said about poniards? Francisco; oh, Francisco! Excellent, kind, generous Francisco! Yes, I recollect your look when you held the bunch of grapes to my lips, as I sat by the sea-shore deserted by all the world; and now, what friends have I? Robbers and——' The word *murderers* he could not utter. He again recollected what had been said about poniards, and the longer his mind fixed upon the words, and the look that accompanied them, the more he was shocked. He could not doubt that it was the serious intention of his accomplices to murder Francisco, if he should make any resistance.

Piedro had at this moment no friend in the world to whom he could apply for advice or assistance. His wretched father died some weeks before this time, in a fit of intoxication. Piedro walked up and down the street, scarcely capable of thinking, much less of coming to any rational resolution.

The hours passed away, the shadows of the houses lengthened under his footsteps, the evening came on, and when it grew dusk, after hesitating in great agony of mind for some time, his fear of the robbers' vengeance prevailed over every other feeling, and he went at the appointed hour to the place of meeting.

The place of meeting was at the house of that Jew to whom he, several months before, sold the diamond cross. That cross which he thought himself so lucky to have stolen, and to have disposed of undetected, was, in fact, the cause of his being in his present dreadful situation. It was at the Jew's that he connected himself with this gang of robbers, to whom he was now become an absolute slave.

'Oh that I dared to disobey!' said he to himself, with a deep sigh, as he knocked softly at the back door of the Jew's house. The back door opened into a narrow, unfrequented street, and some small rooms at this side of the house were set apart for the reception of guests who desired to have their business kept secret. These rooms were separated by a dark passage from the rest of the house, and numbers of people came to the shop in the front of the house, which looked into a creditable street, without knowing anything more, from the ostensible appearance of the shop, than that it was a kind of pawnbroker's, where old clothes, old iron, and all sorts of refuse goods might be disposed of conveniently.

At the moment Piedro knocked at the back door, the front shop was full of customers; and the Jew's boy, whose office it was to attend to these signals, let Piedro in, told him that none of his comrades were yet come, and left him in a room by himself.

He was pale and trembling, and felt a cold dew spread over him. He had a leaden image of Saint Januarius tied round his neck, which, in the midst of his wickedness, he superstitiously preserved as a sort of charm, and on this he kept his eyes stupidly fixed, as he sat alone in this gloomy place.

He listened from time to time, but he heard no noise at the side of the house where he was. His accomplices did not arrive, and, in a sort of impatient terror, the attendant upon an evil conscience, he flung open the door of his cell, and groped his way through the passage which he knew led to the public shop. He longed to hear some noise, and to mix with the living. The Jew, when Piedro entered the shop, was bargaining with a poor, thin-looking man about some gunpowder.

'I don't deny that it has been wet,' said the man, 'but since it was in the bucket of water, it has been carefully dried. I tell you the simple truth, that so soon after the grand eruption of Mount Vesuvius, the people of Naples will not relish fireworks. My poor little rockets, and even my Catherine-wheels, will have no effect. I am glad to part with all I have in this line of business. A few days ago I had fine things in readiness for the Countess de Flora's birthday, which was to have been celebrated at the count's villa.'

'Why do you fix your eyes on me, friend? What is your discourse to me?' said Piedro, who imagined that the man fixed his eyes upon him as he mentioned the name of the count's villa.

'I did not know that I fixed my eyes upon you; I was thinking of my fireworks,' said the poor man, simply. 'But now that I do look at you and hear your voice, I recollect having had the pleasure of seeing you before.'

'When? where?' said Piedro.

'A great while ago; no wonder you have forgotten me,' said the man; 'but I can recall the night to your recollection. You were in the street with me the night I let off that unlucky rocket which frightened the horses, and was the cause of overturning a lady's coach. Don't you remember the circumstance?'

'I have a confused recollection of some such thing,' said Piedro, in great embarrassment; and he looked suspiciously at this man, in doubt whether he was cunning, and wanted to sound him, or whether he was so simple as he appeared.

'You did not, perhaps, hear, then,' continued the man 'that there was a great search made, after the overturn, for a fine diamond cross belonging to the lady in the carriage? That lady, though I did not know it till lately, was the Countess de Flora.'

'I know nothing of the matter,' interrupted Piedro, in great agitation. His confusion was so marked that the firework-maker could not avoid taking notice of it; and a silence of some moments ensued. The Jew, more practised in dissimulation than Piedro, endeavoured to turn the man's attention back to his rockets and his gunpowder—agreed to take the gunpowder—paid for it in haste, and was, though apparently unconcerned, eager to get rid of him. But this was not so easily done. The man's curiosity was excited, and his suspicions of Piedro were increased every moment by all the dark changes of his countenance. Piedro, overpowered with the sense of guilt, surprised at the unexpected mention of the diamond cross, and of the Count de Flora's villa, stood like one convicted, and seemed fixed to the spot, without power of motion.

'I want to look at the old cambric that you said you had—that would do for making—that you could let me have cheap for artificial flowers,' said the firework-maker to the Jew; and as he spoke, his eye from time to time looked towards Piedro.

Piedro felt for the leaden image of the saint, which he wore round his neck. The string which held it cracked, and broke with the pull he gave it. This slight circumstance affected his terrified and superstitious mind more than all the rest. He imagined that at this moment his fate was decided; that Saint Januarius deserted him, and that he was undone. He precipitately followed the firework-man the instant he left the shop, and seizing hold of his arm, whispered, 'I must speak to you.' 'Speak, then,' said the man, astonished. 'Not here; this way,' said he, drawing him towards the dark passage; 'what I have to say must not be overheard. You are going to the Count de Flora's, are not you?' 'I am,' said the man. He was going there to speak to the countess about some artificial flowers; but Piedro thought he was going to speak to her about the diamond cross. 'You are going to give information against me? Nay, hear me, I confess that I purloined that diamond cross; but I can do the count a great service, upon condition that he pardons me. His villa is to be attacked this night by four well-armed men. They will set out five hours hence. I am compelled, under the threat of assassination, to accompany them; but I shall do no more. I throw myself upon the count's mercy. Hasten to him—we have no time to lose.'

The poor man, who heard this confession, escaped from Piedro the moment he loosed his arm. With all possible expedition he ran to the count's palace in Naples, and related to him all that had been said by Piedro. Some of the count's servants, on whom he could most depend, were at a distant part of the city attending their mistress, but the English gentleman offered the services of his man Arthur. Arthur no sooner heard the business, and understood that Francisco was in danger, than he armed himself without saying one word, saddled his English horse, and was ready to depart before any one else had finished his exclamations and conjectures.

'But we are not to set out yet,' said the servant; 'it is but four miles to Torre del Greco; the sbirri (officers of justice) are summoned—they are to go with us—we must wait for them.'

They waited, much against Arthur's inclination, a considerable time for these sbirri. At length they set out, and just as they reached the villa, the flash of a pistol was seen from one of the apartments in the house. The robbers were there. This pistol was snapped by their captain at poor Francisco, who had bravely asserted that he would, as long as he had life, defend the property committed to his care. The pistol missed fire, for it was charged with some of the damaged powder which the Jew had bought that evening from the firework-maker, and which he had sold as excellent immediately afterwards to his favourite customers—the robbers who met at his house.

Arthur, as soon as he perceived the flash of the piece, pressed forward through all the apartments, followed by the count's servants and the officers of justice. At the sudden appearance of so many armed men, the robbers stood dismayed. Arthur eagerly shook Francisco's hand, congratulating him upon his safety, and did not perceive, till he had given him several rough friendly shakes, that his arm was wounded, and that he was pale with the loss of blood.

'It is not much—only a slight wound,' said Francisco; 'one that I should have escaped if I had been upon my guard; but the sight of a face that I little expected to see in such company took from me all presence of mind; and one of the ruffians stabbed me here in the arm, whilst I stood in stupid astonishment.'

'Oh! take me to prison! take me to prison—I am weary of life—I am a wretch not fit to live!' cried Piedro, holding his hands to be tied by the sbirri.

The next morning Piedro was conveyed to prison; and as he passed through the streets of Naples he was met by several of those who had known him when he was a child. 'Ay,' said they, as he went by, 'his father encouraged him in cheating when he was *but a child*; and see what he is come to, now he is a man!' He was ordered to remain twelve months in solitary confinement. His captain and his accomplices were sent to the galleys, and the Jew was banished from Naples.

And now, having got these villains out of the way, let us return to honest Francisco. His wound was soon healed. Arthur was no bad surgeon, for he let his patient get well as fast as he pleased; and Carlo and Rosetta nursed him with so much kindness, that he was almost sorry to find himself perfectly recovered.

'Now that you are able to go out,' said Francisco's father to him, 'you must come and look at my new house, my dear son.' 'Your new house, father?' 'Yes, son, and a charming one it is, and a handsome piece of land near it—all at a safe distance, too, from Mount Vesuvius; and can you guess how I came by it?—it was given to me for having a good son.'

'Yes,' cried Carlo; 'the inhabitants of Resina, and several who had property near Torre del Greco, and whose houses and lives were saved by your intrepidity in carrying the materials for the fireworks and the gunpowder out of this dangerous place, went in a body to the duke, and requested that he would mention your name and these facts to the king, who, amongst the grants he has made to the sufferers by the late eruption of Mount Vesuvius, has been pleased to say that he gives this house and garden to your father, because you have saved the property and lives of many of his subjects.'

The value of a handsome portion of furniture, plate, etc., in the Count de Flora's villa, was, according to the count's promise, given to him; and this money he divided between his own family and that of the good carpenter who first put a pencil into his hands. Arthur would not accept of any present from him. To Mr. Lee, the English gentleman, he offered one of his own drawings—a fruit-piece. 'I like this very well,' said Arthur, as he examined the drawing, 'but I should like this melon better if it was a little bruised. It is now three years ago since I was going to buy that bruised melon from you; you showed me your honest nature then, though you were but a boy; and I have found you the same ever since. A good beginning makes a good ending—an honest boy will make an honest man; and honesty is the best policy, as you have proved to all who wanted the proof, I hope.'

'Yes,' added Francisco's father, 'I think it is pretty plain that Piedro the Cunning has not managed quite so well as Francisco the Honest.'

TARLTON

Delightful task! to rear the tender thought,—
To teach the young idea how to shoot,—
To pour the fresh instruction o'er the mind,—
To breathe th' enlivening spirit,—and to fix
The generous purpose in the glowing breast.

Thomson.

Young Hardy was educated by Mr. Trueman, a very excellent master, at one of our rural Sunday schools. He was honest, obedient, active, and good-natured, hence he was esteemed by his master; and being beloved by all his companions who were good, he did not desire to be loved by the bad; nor was he at all vexed or ashamed when idle, mischievous, or dishonest boys attempted to plague or ridicule him. His friend Loveit, on the contrary, wished to be universally liked, and his highest ambition was to be thought the best-natured boy in the school—and so he was. He usually went by the name of *Poor Loveit*, and everybody pitied him when he got into disgrace, which he frequently did, for, though he had a good disposition, he was often led to do things which he knew to be wrong merely because he could never have the courage to say '*No*,' because he was afraid to offend the ill-natured, and could not bear to be laughed at by fools.

One fine autumn evening, all the boys were permitted to go out to play in a pleasant green meadow near the school. Loveit and another boy, called Tarlton, began to play a game at battledore and shuttlecock, and a large party stood by to look on, for they were the best players at battledore and shuttlecock in the school, and this was a trial of skill between them. When they had got it up to three hundred and twenty, the game became very interesting. The arms of the combatants grew so tired that they could scarcely wield the battledores. The shuttlecock began to waver in the air; now it almost touched the ground, and now, to the astonishment of the spectators, mounted again high over their heads; yet the strokes became feebler and feebler; and 'Now, Loveit!' 'Now, Tarlton!' resounded on all sides. For another minute the victory was doubtful; but at length the setting sun, shining full in Loveit's face, so dazzled his eyes that he could no longer see the shuttlecock, and it fell at his feet.

After the first shout for Tarlton's triumph was over, everybody exclaimed, 'Poor Loveit! he's the best-natured fellow in the world! What a pity that he did not stand with his back to the sun!'

'Now, I dare you all to play another game with me,' cried Tarlton, vauntingly; and as he spoke, he tossed the shuttlecock up with all his force—with so much force that it went over the hedge and dropped into a lane which went close beside the field. 'Heyday!' said Tarlton, 'what shall we do now?'

The boys were strictly forbidden to go into the lane; and it was upon their promise not to break this command, that they were allowed to play in the adjoining field.

No other shuttlecock was to be had, and their play was stopped. They stood on the top of the bank, peeping over the hedge. 'I see it yonder,' said Tarlton; 'I wish somebody would get it. One could get over the gate at the bottom of the field, and be back again in half a minute,' added he, looking at Loveit. 'But you know we must not go into the lane,' said Loveit, hesitatingly. 'Pugh!' said Tarlton, 'why, now, what harm could it do?' 'I don't know,' said Loveit, drumming upon his battledore; 'but——' 'You don't know, man! why, then, what are you afraid of, I ask you?' Loveit coloured, went on drumming, and again, in a lower voice, said '*he didn't know*.' But upon Tarlton's repeating, in a more insolent tone, 'I ask you, man, what you're afraid of?' he suddenly left off drumming, and looking round, said, 'he was not afraid of anything that he knew of.' 'Yes, but you are,' said Hardy, coming forward. 'Am I?' said Loveit; 'of what, pray, am I afraid?' 'Of doing wrong!' '*Afraid of doing wrong*!' repeated Tarlton, mimicking him, so that he made everybody laugh. 'Now, hadn't you better say afraid of being flogged?' 'No,' said Hardy, coolly, after the laugh had somewhat subsided, 'I am as little afraid of being flogged as you are, Tarlton; but I meant——' 'No matter what you meant; why should you interfere with your wisdom and your meanings; nobody thought of asking *you* to stir a step for us; but we asked Loveit, because he's the best fellow in the world.' 'And for that very reason you should not ask him, because you know he can't refuse you anything.' 'Indeed, though,' cried Loveit, piqued, '*there* you're mistaken, for I could refuse if I chose it.'

Hardy smiled; and Loveit, half afraid of his contempt, and half afraid of Tarlton's ridicule, stood doubtful, and again had recourse to his battledore, which he balanced most curiously upon his forefinger. 'Look at him!—now do look at him!' cried Tarlton; 'did you ever in your life see anybody look so silly!—Hardy has him quite under his thumb; he's so mortally afraid of Parson Prig, that he dare not, for the soul of him, turn either of his eyes from the tip of his nose; look how he squints!' 'I don't squint,' said Loveit, looking up, 'and nobody has me under his thumb! and what Hardy said was only for fear I should get in disgrace; he's the best friend I have.'

Loveit spoke this with more than usual spirit, for both his heart and his pride were touched. 'Come along, then,' said Hardy, taking him by the arm in an affectionate manner; and he was just going, when Tarlton called after him, 'Ay, go along with its best friend, and take care it does not get into a scrape;—good-bye, Little Panado!' 'Whom do they call Little Panado?' said Loveit, turning his head hastily back. 'Never mind,' said Hardy, 'what does it signify?' 'No,' said Loveit, 'to be sure it does not signify; but one does not like to be called Little Panado; besides,' added he, after going a few steps farther, 'they'll all think it so ill-natured. I had better go back, and just tell them that I'm very sorry I can't get their shuttlecock;—do come back with me.' 'No,' said Hardy, 'I can't go back; and you'd better not.' 'But, I assure you, I won't stay a minute; wait for me,' added Loveit; and he slunk back again to prove that he was not Little Panado.

Once returned, the rest followed, of course; for to support his character of good nature he was obliged to yield to the entreaties of his companions, and, to show his spirit, leapt over the gate, amidst the acclamations of the little mob:—he was quickly out of sight.

'Here,' cried he, returning in about five minutes, quite out of breath, 'I've got the shuttlecock; and I'll tell you what I've seen,' cried he, panting for breath. 'What?' cried everybody, eagerly. 'Why, just at the turn of the corner, at the end of the lane'—panting. 'Well,' said Tarlton, impatiently, 'do go on.' 'Let me just take breath first.' 'Pugh—never mind your breath.' 'Well, then, just at the turn of the corner, at

163

the end of the lane, as I was looking about for the shuttlecock, I heard a great rustling somewhere near me, and so I looked where it could come from; and I saw, in a nice little garden, on the opposite side of the way, a boy, about as big as Tarlton, sitting in a great tree, shaking the branches; so I called to the boy, to beg one; but he said he could not give me one, for that they were his grandfather's; and just at that minute, from behind a gooseberry bush, up popped the uncle; the grandfather poked his head out of the window; so I ran off as fast as my legs would carry me, though I heard him bawling after me all the way.'

'And let him bawl,' cried Tarlton; 'he shan't bawl for nothing; I'm determined we'll have some of his fine large rosy apples before I sleep to-night.'

At this speech a general silence ensued; everybody kept his eyes fixed upon Tarlton, except Loveit, who looked down, apprehensive that he should be drawn on much farther than he intended. 'Oh, indeed!' said he to himself, 'as Hardy told me, I had better not have come back!'

Regardless of this confusion, Tarlton continued, 'But before I say any more, I hope we have no spies amongst us. If there is any one of you afraid to be flogged, let him march off this instant!'

Loveit coloured, bit his lips, wished to go, but had not the courage to move first. He waited to see what everybody else would do: nobody stirred; so Loveit stood still.

'Well, then,' cried Tarlton, giving his hand to the boy next him, then to the next, 'your word and honour that you won't betray me; but stand by me, and I'll stand by you.' Each boy gave his hand and his promise, repeating, 'Stand by me, and I'll stand by you.'

Loveit hung back till the last; and had almost twisted off the button of the boy's coat who screened him, when Tarlton came up, holding out his hand, 'Come, Loveit, lad, you're in for it: stand by me, and I'll stand by you.' 'Indeed, Tarlton,' expostulated he, without looking him in the face, 'I do wish you'd give up this scheme; I daresay all the apples are gone by this time; I wish you would. Do, pray, give up this scheme.' 'What scheme, man? you haven't heard it yet; you may as well know your text before you begin preaching.'

The corners of Loveit's mouth could not refuse to smile, though in his heart he felt not the slightest inclination to laugh.

'Why, I don't know you, I declare I don't know you to-day,' said Tarlton; 'you used to be the best-natured, most agreeable lad in the world, and would do anything one asked you; but you're quite altered of late, as we were saying just now, when you skulked away with Hardy; come,—do, man, pluck up a little spirit, and be one of us, or you'll make us all *hate you*.' '*Hate* me!' repeated Loveit, with terror; 'no, surely, you won't all *hate* me!' and he mechanically stretched out his hand, which Tarlton shook violently, saying, '*Ay, now, that's right.*' '*Ay, now, that's wrong!*' whispered Loveit's conscience; but his conscience was of no use to him, for it was always overpowered by the voice of numbers; and though he had the wish, he never had the power, to do right. 'Poor Loveit! I knew he would not refuse us,' cried his companions; and even Tarlton, the moment he shook hands with him, despised him. It is certain that weakness of mind is despised both by the good and the bad.

The league being thus formed, Tarlton assumed all the airs of commander, explained his schemes, and laid the plan of attack upon the poor old man's apple-tree. It was the only one he had in the world. We shall not dwell upon their consultation; for the amusement of contriving such expeditions is often the chief thing which induces idle boys to engage in them.

There was a small window at the end of the back staircase, through which, between nine and ten o'clock at night, Tarlton, accompanied by Loveit and another boy, crept out. It was a moonlight night, and after crossing the field, and climbing the gate, directed by Loveit, who now resolved to go through the affair with spirit, they proceeded down the lane with rash yet fearful steps.

At a distance Loveit saw the whitewashed cottage, and the apple-tree beside it. They quickened their pace, and with some difficulty scrambled through the hedge which fenced the garden, though not without being scratched and torn by the briers. Everything was silent. Yet now and then, at every rustling of the leaves, they started, and their hearts beat violently. Once, as Loveit was climbing the apple-tree, he thought he heard a door in the cottage open, and earnestly begged his companions to desist and return home. This, however, he could by no means persuade them to do, until they had filled their pockets with apples; then, to his great joy, they returned, crept in at the staircase window, and each retired, as softly as possible, to his own apartment.

Loveit slept in the room with Hardy, whom he had left fast asleep, and whom he now was extremely afraid of awakening. All the apples were emptied out of Loveit's pockets, and lodged with Tarlton till the morning, for fear the smell should betray the secret to Hardy. The room door was apt to creak, but it was opened with such precaution that no noise could be heard, and Loveit found his friend as fast asleep as when he left him.

'Ah,' said he to himself, 'how quietly he sleeps! I wish I had been sleeping too.' The reproaches of Loveit's conscience, however, served no other purpose but to torment him; he had not sufficient strength of mind to be good. The very next night, in spite of all his fears, and all his penitence, and all his resolutions, by a little fresh ridicule and persuasion he was induced to accompany the same party on a similar expedition. We must observe that the necessity for continuing their depredations became stronger the third day; for, though at first only a small party had been in the secret, by degrees it was divulged to the whole school; and it was necessary to secure secrecy by sharing the booty.

Every one was astonished that Hardy, with all his quickness and penetration, had not yet discovered their proceedings; but Loveit could not help suspecting that he was not quite so ignorant as he appeared to be. Loveit had strictly kept his promise of secrecy; but he was by no means an artful boy; and in talking to his friend, conscious that he had something to conceal, he was perpetually on the point of betraying himself; then, recollecting his engagement, he blushed, stammered, bungled; and upon Hardy's asking what he meant, would answer with a silly, guilty countenance that he did not know; or abruptly break off, saying, 'Oh, nothing! nothing at all!'

It was in vain that he urged Tarlton to permit him to consult his friend. A gloom overspread Tarlton's brow when he began to speak on the subject, and he always returned a peremptory refusal, accompanied with some such taunting expression as this—'I wish we had nothing to do with such a sneaking fellow; he'll betray us all, I see, before we have done with him.' 'Well,' said Loveit to himself, 'so I am abused after all, and called a sneaking fellow for my pains; that's rather hard, to be sure, when I've got so little by the job.'

In truth he had not got much; for in the division of the booty only one apple, and half of another which was only half ripe, happened to fall to his share; though, to be sure, when they had all eaten their apples, he had the satisfaction to hear everybody declare they were very sorry they had forgotten to offer some of theirs to '*poor Loveit.*'

In the meantime, the visits to the apple-tree had been now too frequently repeated to remain concealed from the old man who lived in the cottage. He used to examine his only tree very frequently, and missing numbers of rosy apples, which he had watched ripening, he, though not prone to suspicion, began to think that there was something going wrong; especially as a gap was made in his hedge, and there were several small footsteps in his flower-beds.

The good old man was not at all inclined to give pain to any living creature, much less to children, of whom he was particularly fond. Nor was he in the least avaricious, for though he was not rich, he had enough to live upon, because he had been very industrious in his youth; and he was always very ready to part with the little he had. Nor was he a cross old man. If anything would have made him angry, it would have been the seeing his favourite tree robbed, as he had promised himself the pleasure of giving his red apples to his grandchildren on his birthday. However, he looked up at the tree in sorrow rather than in anger, and leaning upon his staff, he began to consider what he had best do.

'If I complain to their master,' said he to himself, 'they will certainly be flogged, and that I should be sorry for; yet they must not be let to go on stealing; that would be worse still, for it would surely bring them to the gallows in the end. Let me see—oh, ay, that will do; I will borrow farmer Kent's dog Barker, he'll keep them off, I'll answer for it.'

Farmer Kent lent his dog Barker, cautioning his neighbour, at the same time, to be sure to chain him well, for he was the fiercest mastiff in England. The old man, with farmer Kent's assistance, chained him fast to the trunk of the apple-tree.

Night came; and Tarlton, Loveit, and his companions returned at the usual hour. Grown bolder now by frequent success, they came on talking and laughing. But the moment they had set their foot in the garden, the dog started up; and, shaking his chain as he sprang forward, barked with unremitting fury. They stood still as if fixed to the spot. There was just moonlight enough to see the dog. 'Let us try the other side of the tree,' said Tarlton. But to whichever side they turned, the dog flew round in an instant, barking with increased fury.

'He'll break his chain and tear us to pieces,' cried Tarlton; and, struck with terror, he immediately threw down the basket he had brought with him, and betook himself to flight, with the greatest precipitation. 'Help me! oh, pray, help me! I can't get through the hedge,' cried Loveit, in a lamentable tone, whilst the dog growled hideously, and sprang forward to the extremity of his chain. 'I can't get out! Oh, for God's sake, stay for me one minute, dear Tarlton!' He called in vain; he was left to struggle through his difficulties by himself; and of all his dear friends not one turned back to help him. At last, torn and terrified, he got through the hedge and ran home, despising his companions for their selfishness. Nor could he help observing that Tarlton, with all his vaunted prowess, was the first to run away from the appearance of danger.

The next morning Loveit could not help reproaching the party with their conduct. 'Why could not you, any of you, stay one minute to help me?' said he. 'We did not hear you call,' answered one. 'I was so frightened,' said another, 'I would not have turned back for the whole world.' 'And you, Tarlton?' 'I,' said Tarlton; 'had not I enough to do to take care of myself, you blockhead? Every one for himself in this world!' 'So I see,' said Loveit, gravely. 'Well, man! is there anything strange in that?' 'Strange! why, yes; I thought you all loved me!' 'Lord love you, lad! so we do; but we love ourselves better.' 'Hardy would not have served me so, however,' said Loveit, turning away in disgust. Tarlton was alarmed. 'Pugh!' said he; 'what nonsense have you taken into your brain? Think no more about it. We are all very sorry, and beg your pardon; come, shake hands,—forgive and forget.'

Loveit gave his hand, but gave it rather coldly. 'I forgive it with all my heart,' said he; 'but I cannot forget it so soon!' 'Why, then, you are not such a good-humoured fellow as we thought you were. Surely you cannot bear malice, Loveit.' Loveit smiled, and allowed that he certainly could not bear malice. 'Well, then, come; you know at the bottom we all love you, and would do anything in the world for you.' Poor Loveit, flattered in his foible, began to believe that they did love him at the bottom, as they said, and even with his eyes open consented again to be duped.

'How strange it is,' thought he, 'that I should set such value upon the love of those I despise! When I'm once out of this scrape, I'll have no more to do with them, I'm determined.'

Compared with his friend Hardy, his new associates did indeed appear contemptible; for all this time Hardy had treated him with uniform kindness, avoided to pry into his secrets, yet seemed ready to receive his confidence, if it had been offered.

After school in the evening, as he was standing silently beside Hardy, who was ruling a sheet of paper for him, Tarlton, in his brutal manner, came up, and seizing him by the arm, cried, 'Come along with me, Loveit, I've something to say to you.' 'I can't come now,' said Loveit, drawing away his arm. 'Ah, do come now,' said Tarlton, in a voice of persuasion. 'Well, I'll come presently.' 'Nay, but do, pray; there's a good fellow, come now, because I've something to say to you.' 'What is it you've got to say to me? I wish you'd let me alone,' said Loveit; yet at the same time he suffered himself to be led away.

Tarlton took particular pains to humour him and bring him into temper again; and even, though he was not very apt to part with his playthings, went so far as to say, 'Loveit, the other day you wanted a top; I'll give you mine if you desire it.' Loveit thanked him, and was overjoyed at the thoughts of possessing this top. 'But what did you want to say to me just now?' 'Ay, we'll talk of that presently; not yet—when we get out of hearing.' 'Nobody is near us,' said Loveit. 'Come a little farther, however,' said Tarlton, looking round suspiciously. 'Well now, well?' 'You know the dog that frightened us so last night?' 'Yes.' 'It will never frighten us again.' 'Won't it? how so?' 'Look here,' said Tarlton, drawing something from his pocket wrapped in a blue handkerchief. 'What's that?' Tarlton opened it. 'Raw meat!' exclaimed Loveit. 'How came you by it?' 'Tom, the servant boy, Tom got it for me, and I'm to give him sixpence.' 'And is it for the dog?' 'Yes, I vowed I'd be revenged on him, and after this he'll never bark again.' 'Never bark again! What do you mean? Is it poison?' exclaimed Loveit, starting back with horror. 'Only poison for *a dog*;' said Tarlton, confused; 'you could not look more shocked if it was poison for a Christian.'

Loveit stood for nearly a minute in profound silence. 'Tarlton,' said he at last, in a changed tone and altered manner, 'I did not know you; I will have no more to do with you.' 'Nay, but stay,' said Tarlton, catching hold of his arm, 'stay; I was only joking.' 'Let go my arm—you were in earnest.' 'But then that was before I knew there was any harm. If you think there's any harm?' '*If*,' said Loveit. 'Why, you know, I might not know; for Tom told me it's a thing that's often done. Ask Tom.' 'I'll ask nobody! Surely we know better what's right and wrong than Tom does.' 'But only just ask him, to hear what he'll say.' 'I don't want to hear what he'll say,' cried Loveit, vehemently; 'the dog will die in agonies—in agonies! There was a dog poisoned at my father's—I saw him in the yard. Poor creature! He lay and howled and writhed himself!' 'Poor creature! Well, there's no harm done now,' cried Tarlton, in a hypocritical tone. But though he thought fit to dissemble with Loveit, he was thoroughly determined in his purpose.

Poor Loveit, in haste to get away, returned to his friend Hardy; but his mind was in such agitation, that he neither talked nor moved like himself; and two or three times his heart was so full that he was ready to burst into tears.

'Is it poison?' exclaimed Loveit, starting back with horror.

'Is it poison?' exclaimed Loveit, starting back with horror.

'How good-natured you are to me,' said he to Hardy, as he was trying vainly to entertain him; 'but if you knew——' Here he stopped short, for the bell for evening prayer rang, and they all took their places and knelt down. After prayers, as they were going to bed, Loveit stopped Tarlton,—'*Well?*' asked he, in an inquiring manner, fixing his eyes upon him. '*Well?*' replied Tarlton, in an audacious tone, as if he meant to set his inquiring eye at defiance. 'What do you mean to do to-night?' 'To go to sleep, as you do, I suppose,' replied Tarlton, turning away abruptly, and whistling as he walked off.

'Oh, he has certainly changed his mind!' said Loveit to himself, 'else he could not whistle.'

About ten minutes after this, as he and Hardy were undressing, Hardy suddenly recollected that he had left his new kite out upon the grass. 'Oh,' said he, 'it will be quite spoiled before morning!' 'Call Tom,' said Loveit, 'and bid him bring it in for you in a minute.' They both went to the top of the stairs to call Tom; no one answered. They called again louder, 'Is Tom below?' 'I'm here,' answered he at last, coming out of Tarlton's room with a look of mixed embarrassment and effrontery. And as he was receiving Hardy's commission, Loveit saw the corner of the blue handkerchief hanging out of his pocket. This excited fresh suspicions in Loveit's mind; but, without saying one word, he immediately stationed himself at the window in his room, which looked out towards the lane; and, as the moon was risen, he could see if any one passed that way. 'What are you doing there?' said Hardy, after he had been watching some time; 'why don't you come to bed?' Loveit returned no answer, but continued standing at the window. Nor did he watch long in vain. Presently he saw Tom gliding slowly along a bypath, and get over the gate into the lane.

'He's gone to do it!' exclaimed Loveit aloud, with an emotion which he could not command. 'Who's gone? to do what?' cried Hardy, starting up. 'How cruel! how wicked!' continued Loveit. 'What's cruel—what's wicked? speak out at once!' returned Hardy, in that commanding tone which, in moments of danger, strong minds feel themselves entitled to assume towards weak ones. Loveit instantly, though in an incoherent manner, explained the affair to him. Scarcely had the words passed his lips, when Hardy sprang up and began dressing himself without saying one syllable. 'For God's sake, what are you going to do?' said Loveit in great anxiety. 'They'll never forgive me! don't betray me! they'll never forgive! pray, speak to me! only say you won't betray us.' 'I will not betray you, trust to me,' said Hardy; and he left the room, and Loveit stood in amazement; whilst, in the meantime, Hardy, in hopes of overtaking Tom before the fate of the poor dog was decided, ran with all possible speed across the meadow, and then down the lane. He came up with Tom just as he was climbing the bank into the old man's garden. Hardy, too much out of breath to speak, seized hold of him, dragged him down, detaining him with a firm grasp, whilst he panted for utterance. 'What, Master Hardy, is it you? what's the matter? what do you want?' 'I want the poisoned meat that you have in your pocket.' 'Who told you that I had any such thing?' said Tom, clapping his hand upon his guilty pocket. 'Give it me quietly, and I'll let you off.' 'Sir, upon my word, I haven't! I didn't! I don't know what you mean,' said Tom, trembling, though he was by far the stronger of the two. 'Indeed, I don't know what you mean.' 'You do,' said Hardy, with great indignation, and a violent struggle immediately commenced.

The dog, now alarmed by the voices, began to bark outrageously. Tom was terrified lest the old man should come out to see what was the matter; his strength forsook him, and flinging the handkerchief and meat over the hedge, he ran away with all his speed. The handkerchief fell within reach of the dog, who instantly snapped at it; luckily it did not come untied. Hardy saw a pitchfork on a dunghill close beside him, and, seizing upon it, stuck it into the handkerchief. The dog pulled, tore, growled, grappled, yelled; it was impossible to get the handkerchief from between his teeth; but the knot was loosed, the meat, unperceived by the dog, dropped out, and while he dragged off the handkerchief in triumph, Hardy, with inexpressible joy, plunged the pitchfork into the poisoned meat and bore it away.

Never did hero retire with more satisfaction from a field of battle. Full of the pleasure of successful benevolence, Hardy tripped joyfully home, and vaulted over the window-sill, when the first object he beheld was Mr. Power, the usher, standing at the head of the stairs, with his candle in his hand.

'Come up, whoever you are,' said Mr. William Power, in a stern voice; 'I thought I should find you out at last. Come up, whoever you are!' Hardy obeyed without reply.—'Hardy!' exclaimed Mr. Power, starting back with astonishment; 'is it you, Mr. Hardy?' repeated he, holding the light to his face. 'Why, sir,' said he, in a sneering tone, 'I'm sure if Mr. Trueman was here he wouldn't believe his own eyes; but for my part I saw through you long since; I never liked saints, for my share. Will you please do me the favour, sir, if it is not too much trouble, to empty your pockets?' Hardy obeyed in silence. 'Heyday! meat! raw meat! what next?' 'That's all,' said Hardy, emptying his pockets inside out. 'This is *all*,' said Mr. Power, taking up the meat. 'Pray, sir,' said Hardy, eagerly, 'let that meat be burned; it is poisoned.' 'Poisoned!' cried Mr. William Power, letting it drop out of his fingers; 'you wretch!' looking at him with a menacing air, 'what is all this? Speak.' Hardy was silent. 'Why don't you speak?' cried he, shaking him by the shoulder impatiently. Still Hardy was silent. 'Down upon your knees this minute and confess all; tell me where you've been, what you've been doing, and who are your accomplices, for I know there is a gang of you; so,' added he, pressing heavily upon Hardy's shoulder, 'down upon your knees this minute, and confess the whole, that's your only way now to get off yourself. If you hope for *my* pardon, I can tell you it's not to be had without asking for.'

'Sir,' said Hardy, in a firm but respectful voice, 'I have no pardon to ask, I have nothing to confess; I am innocent; but if I were not, I would never try to get off myself by betraying my companions.' 'Very well, sir! very well! very fine! stick to it, stick to it, I advise you, and we shall see. And how will you look to-morrow, Mr. Innocent, when my uncle, the doctor, comes home?' 'As I do now, sir,' said Hardy, unmoved.

His composure threw Mr. Power into a rage too great for utterance. 'Sir,' continued Hardy, 'ever since I have been at school, I never told a lie, and therefore, sir, I hope you will believe me now. Upon my word and honour, sir, I have done nothing wrong.' 'Nothing wrong? Better and better! what, when I caught you going out at night?' '*That*, to be sure, was wrong,' said Hardy, recollecting himself; 'but except that——' 'Except that, sir! I will except nothing. Come along with me, young gentleman, your time for pardon is past.'

Saying these words, he pulled Hardy along a narrow passage to a small closet, set apart for desperate offenders, and usually known by the name of the *Black Hole*. 'There, sir, take up your lodging there for to-night,' said he, pushing him in; 'to-morrow I'll know more, or I'll know why,' added he, double-locking the door, with a tremendous noise, upon his prisoner, and locking also the door at the end of the passage, so that no one could have access to him. 'So now I think I have you safe!' said Mr. William Power to himself, stalking off with steps which made the whole gallery resound, and which made many a guilty heart tremble.

The conversation which had passed between Hardy and Mr. Power at the head of the stairs had been anxiously listened to; but only a word or two here and there had been distinctly overheard.

The locking of the Black Hole door was a terrible sound—some knew not what it portended, and others knew *too well*. All assembled in the morning with faces of anxiety. Tarlton's and Loveit's were the most agitated: Tarlton for himself, Loveit for his friend, for himself, for everybody. Every one of the party, and Tarlton at their head, surrounded him with reproaches; and considered him as the author of the evils which hung over them. 'How could you do so? and why did you say anything to Hardy about it? when you had promised, too! Oh! what shall we all do? what a scrape you have brought us into! Loveit, it's all your fault!' '*All my fault!*' repeated poor Loveit, with a sigh; 'well, that is hard.'

'Goodness! there's the bell,' exclaimed a number of voices at once. 'Now for it!' They all stood in a half-circle for morning prayers. They listened—'Here he is coming! No—Yes—Here he is!' And Mr. William Power, with a gloomy brow, appeared and walked up to his place at the head of the room. They knelt down to prayers, and the moment they rose, Mr. William Power, laying his hand upon the table, cried, 'Stand still, gentlemen, if you please.' Everybody stood stock still; he walked out of the circle; they guessed that he was gone for Hardy, and the whole room was in commotion. Each with eagerness asked each what none could answer, '*Has he told?*' '*What* has he told?' 'Who has he told of?' 'I hope he has not told of me,' cried they. 'I'll answer for it he has told of all of us,' said Tarlton. 'And I'll answer for it he has told of none of us,' answered Loveit, with a sigh. 'You don't think he's such a fool, when he can get himself off,' said Tarlton.

At this instant the prisoner was led in, and as he passed through the circle, every eye was fixed upon him. His eye fell upon no one, not even upon Loveit, who pulled him by the coat as he passed—every one felt almost afraid to breathe. 'Well, sir,' said Mr. Power, sitting down in Mr. Trueman's elbow-chair, and placing the prisoner opposite to him; 'well, sir, what have you to say to me this morning?' 'Nothing, sir,' answered Hardy, in a decided, yet modest manner; 'nothing but what I said last night.' 'Nothing more?' 'Nothing more, sir.' 'But I have something more to say to you, sir, then; and a great deal more, I promise you, before I have done with you;' and then, seizing him in a fury, he was just going to give him a severe flogging, when the schoolroom door opened, and Mr. Trueman appeared, followed by an old man whom Loveit immediately knew. He leaned upon his stick as he walked, and in his other hand carried a basket of apples. When they came within the circle, Mr. Trueman stopped short 'Hardy!' exclaimed he, with a voice of unfeigned surprise, whilst Mr. William Power stood with his hand suspended. 'Ay, Hardy, sir,' repeated he. 'I told him you'd not believe your own eyes.'

Mr. Trueman advanced with a slow step. 'Now, sir, give me leave,' said the usher, eagerly drawing him aside and whispering.

'So, sir,' said Mr. T. when the whisper was done, addressing himself to Hardy, with a voice and manner which, had he been guilty, must have pierced him to the heart, 'I find I have been deceived in you; it is but three hours ago that I told your uncle I never had a boy in my school in whom I placed so much confidence; but, after all this show of honour and integrity, the moment my back is turned, you are the first to set an example of disobedience of my orders. Why do I talk of disobeying my commands,—you are a thief!' 'I, sir?' exclaimed Hardy, no longer able to repress his feelings. 'You, sir,—you and some others,' said Mr. Trueman, looking round the room with a penetrating glance—'you and some others,' 'Ay, sir,' interrupted Mr. William Power, 'get that out of him if you can—ask him.' 'I will ask him nothing; I shall neither put his truth nor his honour to the trial; truth and honour are not to be expected amongst thieves.' 'I am not a thief! I have never had anything to do with thieves,' cried Hardy, indignantly. 'Have you not robbed this old man? Don't you know the taste of these apples?' said Mr. Trueman, taking one out of the basket. 'No, sir; I do not. I never touched one of that old man's apples.' 'Never touched one of them! I suppose this is some vile equivocation; you have done worse, you have had the barbarity, the baseness, to attempt to poison his dog; the poisoned meat was found in your pocket last night.' 'The poisoned meat was found in my pocket, sir; but I never intended to poison the dog—I saved his life.' 'Lord bless him!' said the old man. 'Nonsense—cunning!' said Mr. Power. 'I hope you won't let him impose upon you, sir.' 'No, he cannot impose upon me; I have a proof he is little prepared for,' said Mr. Trueman, producing the blue handkerchief in which the meat had been wrapped.

Tarlton turned pale; Hardy's countenance never changed. 'Don't you know this handkerchief, sir?' 'I do, sir.' 'Is it not yours?' 'No, sir.' 'Don't you know whose it is?' cried Mr. Power. Hardy was silent.

'Now, gentlemen,' said Mr. Trueman, 'I am not fond of punishing you; but when I do it, you know, it is always in earnest. I will begin with the eldest of you; I will begin with Hardy, and flog you with my own hands till this handkerchief is owned.' 'I'm sure it's not mine,' and 'I'm sure it's none of mine,' burst from every mouth, whilst they looked at each other in dismay; for none but Hardy, Loveit, and Tarlton knew the secret. 'My cane,' said Mr. Trueman, and Mr. Power handed him the cane. Loveit groaned from the bottom of his heart. Tarlton leaned back against the wall with a black countenance. Hardy looked with a steady eye at the cane.

'But first,' said Mr. Trueman, laying down the cane, 'let us see. Perhaps we may find out the owner of this handkerchief another way,' examining the corners. It was torn almost to pieces; but luckily the corner that was marked remained.

'May God bless you!'

'May God bless you!'

'J. T.!' cried Mr. Trueman. Every eye turned upon the guilty Tarlton, who, now as pale as ashes and trembling in every limb, sank down upon his knees, and in a whining voice begged for mercy. 'Upon my word and honour, sir, I'll tell you all; I should never have thought of stealing the apples if Loveit had not first told me of them; and it was Tom who first put the poisoning the dog into my head. It was he that carried the meat; *wasn't it?*' said he, appealing to Hardy, whose word he knew must be believed. 'Oh, dear sir!' continued he as Mr. Trueman began to move towards him, 'do let me off; do pray let me off this time! I'm not the only one, indeed, sir! I hope you won't make me an example for the rest. It's very hard I'm to be flogged more than they!' 'I'm not going to flog you.' 'Thank you, sir,' said Tarlton, getting up and wiping his eyes. 'You need not thank me,' said Mr. Trueman. 'Take your handkerchief—go out of this room—out of this house; let me never see you more.'

'If I had any hopes of him,' said Mr. Trueman, as he shut the door after him—'if I had any hopes of him, I would have punished him; but I have none. Punishment is meant only to make people better; and those who have any hopes of themselves will know how to submit to it.'

At these words Loveit first, and immediately all the rest of the guilty party, stepped out of the ranks, confessed their fault and declared themselves ready to bear any punishment their master thought proper.

'Oh, they have been punished enough,' said the old man; 'forgive them, sir.'

Hardy looked as if he wished to speak. 'Not because you ask it,' said Mr. Trueman to the guilty penitents, 'though I should be glad to oblige you—it wouldn't be just; but there,' pointing to Hardy, 'there is one who has merited a reward; the highest I can give him is that of pardoning his companions.'

Hardy bowed and his face glowed with pleasure, whilst everybody present sympathised in his feelings.

'I am sure,' thought Loveit, 'this is a lesson I shall never forget.'

'Gentlemen,' said the old man, with a faltering voice, 'it wasn't for the sake of my apples that I spoke; and you, sir,' said he to Hardy, 'I thank you for saving my dog. If you please, I'll plant on that mount, opposite the window, a young apple-tree, from my old one. I will water it, and take care of it with my own hands for your sake, as long as I am able. And may God bless you!' laying his trembling hand on Hardy's head; 'may God bless you—I'm sure God *will* bless all such boys as you are.'

THE BASKET-WOMAN.

Toute leur étude était de se complaire et de s'entr'aider. <u>41</u>

Paul et Virginie.

At the foot of a steep, slippery, white hill, near Dunstable, in Bedfordshire, called Chalk Hill, there is a hut, or rather a hovel, which travellers could scarcely suppose could be inhabited, if they did not see the smoke rising from its peaked roof. An old woman lives in this hovel,<u>42</u> and with her a little boy and girl, the children of a beggar who died and left these orphans perishing with hunger. They thought themselves very happy when the good old woman first took them into her hut and bid them warm themselves at her small fire, and gave them a crust of mouldy bread to eat. She had not much to give, but what she had she gave with good-will. She was very kind to these poor children, and worked hard at her spinning-wheel and at her knitting, to support herself and them. She earned money also in another way. She used to follow all the carriages as they went up Chalk Hill, and when the horses stopped to take breath or to rest themselves, she put stones behind the carriage wheels to prevent them from rolling backwards down the steep, slippery hill.

The little boy and girl loved to stand beside the good-natured old woman's spinning-wheel when she was spinning, and to talk to her. At these times she taught them something which, she said, she hoped they would remember all their lives. She explained to them what is meant by telling the truth, and what it is to be honest. She taught them to dislike idleness, and to wish that they could be useful.

One evening, as they were standing beside her, the little boy said to her, 'Grandmother,' for that was the name by which she liked that these children should call her—'grandmother, how often you are forced to get up from your spinning-wheel, and to follow the chaises and coaches up that steep hill, to put stones underneath the wheels, to hinder them from rolling back! The people who are in the carriages give you a halfpenny or a penny for doing this, don't they?' 'Yes, child.' 'But it is very hard work for you to go up and down that hill. You often say that you are tired, and then you know that you cannot spin all that time. Now if we might go up the hill, and put the stones behind the wheels, you could sit still at your work, and would not the people give us the halfpence? and could not we bring them all to you? Do, pray, dear grandmother, try us for one day—to-morrow, will you?'

'Yes,' said the old woman; 'I will try what you can do; but I must go up the hill along with you for the first two or three times, for fear you should get yourselves hurt.'

So, the next day, the little boy and girl went with their grandmother, as they used to call her, up the steep hill; and she showed the boy how to prevent the wheels from rolling back, by putting stones behind them; and she said, 'This is called scotching the wheels'; and she took off the boy's hat and gave it to the little girl, to hold up to the carriage-windows, ready for the halfpence.

When she thought that the children knew how to manage by themselves, she left them, and returned to her spinning-wheel. A great many carriages happened to go by this day, and the little girl received a great many halfpence. She carried them all in her brother's hat to her grandmother in the evening; and the old woman smiled, and thanked the children. She said that they had been useful to her, and that her spinning had gone on finely, because she had been able to sit still at her wheel all day. 'But, Paul, my boy,' said she, 'what is the matter with your hand?'

'Only a pinch—only one pinch that I got, as I was putting a stone behind a wheel of a chaise. It does not hurt me much, grandmother; and I've thought of a good thing for to-morrow. I shall never be hurt again, if you will only be so good as to give me the old handle of the broken crutch, grandmother, and the block of wood that lies in the chimney-corner, and that is of no use. I'll make it of some use, if I may have it.'

'Take it then, dear,' said the old woman; 'and you'll find the handle of the broken crutch under my bed.'

Paul went to work immediately, and fastened one end of the pole into the block of wood, so as to make something like a dry-rubbing brush. 'Look, grandmamma, look at my *scotcher*. I call this thing my *scotcher*,' said Paul, 'because I shall always scotch the wheels with it. I shall never pinch my fingers again; my hands, you see, will be safe at the end of this long stick; and, sister Anne, you need not be at the trouble of carrying any more stones after me up the hill; we shall never want stones any more. My scotcher will do without anything else, I hope. I wish it was morning, and that a carriage would come, that I might run up the hill and try my scotcher.'

'And I wish that as many chaises may go by to-morrow as there did to-day, and that we may bring you as many halfpence, too, grandmother,' said the little girl.

'So do I, my dear Anne,' said the old woman; 'for I mean that you and your brother shall have all the money that you get to-morrow. You may buy some gingerbread for yourselves, or some of those ripe plums that you saw at the fruit-stall, the other day, which is just going into Dunstable. I told you then that I could not afford to buy such things for you; but now that you can earn halfpence for yourselves, children, it is fair you should taste a ripe plum and bit of gingerbread for once and a way in your lives.'

'We'll bring some of the gingerbread home to her, shan't we, brother?' whispered little Anne. The morning came; but no carriages were heard, though Paul and his sister had risen at five o'clock, that they might be sure to be ready for early travellers. Paul kept his scotcher poised upon his shoulder, and watched eagerly at his station at the bottom of the hill. He did not wait long before a carriage came. He followed it up the hill; and the instant the postillion called to him, and bid him stop the wheels, he put his scotcher behind them, and found that it answered the purpose perfectly well.

Many carriages went by this day, and Paul and Anne received a great many halfpence from the travellers.

When it grew dusk in the evening, Anne said to her brother—'I don't think any more carriages will come by to-day. Let us count the halfpence, and carry them home now to grandmother.'

'No, not yet,' answered Paul, 'let them alone—let them lie still in the hole where I have put them. I daresay more carriages will come by before it is quite dark, and then we shall have more halfpence.'

Paul had taken the halfpence out of his hat, and he had put them into a hole in the high bank by the roadside; and Anne said she would not meddle with them, and that she would wait till her brother liked to count them; and Paul said—'If you will stay and watch here, I will go and gather some blackberries for you in the hedge in yonder field. Stand you hereabouts, half-way up the hill, and the moment you see any carriage coming along the road, run as fast as you can and call me.'

Anne waited a long time, or what she thought a long time; and she saw no carriage, and she trailed her brother's scotcher up and down till she was tired. Then she stood still, and looked again, and she saw no carriage; so she went sorrowfully into the field, and to the hedge where her brother was gathering blackberries, and she said, 'Paul, I'm sadly tired, *sadly tired*!' said she, 'and my eyes are quite strained with looking for chaises; no more chaises will come to-night; and your scotcher is lying there, of no use, upon the ground. Have not I waited long enough for to-day, Paul?' 'Oh no,' said Paul; 'here are some blackberries for you; you had better wait a little bit longer. Perhaps a carriage might go by whilst you are standing here talking to me.'

Anne, who was of a very obliging temper, and who liked to do what she was asked to do, went back to the place where the scotcher lay; and scarcely had she reached the spot, when she heard the noise of a carriage. She ran to call her brother, and, to their great joy, they now saw four chaises coming towards them. Paul, as soon as they went up the hill, followed with his scotcher; first he scotched the wheels of one carriage, then of another; and Anne was so much delighted with observing how well the scotcher stopped the wheels, and how much better it was than stones, that she forgot to go and hold her brother's hat to the travellers for halfpence, till she was roused by the voice of a little rosy girl, who was looking out of the window of one of the chaises. 'Come close to the chaise-door,' said the little girl; 'here are some halfpence for you.'

Anne held the hat; and she afterwards went on to the other carriages. Money was thrown to her from each of them; and when they had all gotten safely to the top of the hill, she and her brother sat down upon a large stone by the roadside, to count their treasure. First they began by counting what was in the hat—'One, two, three, four halfpence.'

'But, oh, brother, look at this!' exclaimed Anne; 'this is not the same as the other halfpence.'

'No, indeed, it is not,' cried Paul, 'it is no halfpenny; it is a guinea, a bright golden guinea!' 'Is it?' said Anne, who had never seen a guinea in her life before, and who did not know its value; 'and will it do as well as a halfpenny to buy gingerbread? I'll run to the fruit-stall and ask the woman; shall I?'

'No, no,' said Paul, 'you need not ask any woman, or anybody but me; I can tell you all about it, as well as anybody in the whole world.'

'The whole world! Oh, Paul, you forgot. Not so well as my grandmother.'

'Why, not so well as my grandmother, perhaps; but, Anne, I can tell you that you must not talk yourself, Anne, but you must listen to me quietly, or else you won't understand what I am going to tell you, for I can assure you that I don't think I quite understood it myself, Anne, the first time my grandmother told it to me, though I stood stock still listening my best.'

Prepared by this speech to hear something very difficult to be understood, Anne looked very grave, and her brother explained to her that, with a guinea, she might buy two hundred and fifty-two times as many plums as she could get for a penny.

'Why, Paul, you know the fruit-woman said she would give us a dozen plums for a penny. Now, for this little guinea, would she give us two hundred and fifty-two dozen?'

'If she has so many, and if we like to have so many, to be sure she will,' said Paul, 'but I think we should not like to have two hundred and fifty-two dozen of plums; we could not eat such a number.'

'But, oh, brother, look at this! this is not the same as the other halfpence.'

'But, oh, brother, look at this! this is not the same as the other halfpence.'

'But we could give some of them to my grandmother,' said Anne. 'But still there would be too many for her, and for us too,' said Paul, 'and when we had eaten the plums, there would be an end to all the pleasure. But now I'll tell you what I am thinking of, Anne, that we might buy something for my grandmother that would be very useful to her indeed, with the guinea—something that would last a great while.'

'What, brother? What sort of thing?' 'Something that she said she wanted very much last winter, when she was so ill with the rheumatism—something that she said yesterday, when you were making her bed, she wished she might be able to buy before next winter.'

'I know, I know what you mean!' said Anne—'a blanket. Oh, yes, Paul, that will be much better than plums; do let us buy a blanket for her; how glad she will be to see it! I will make her bed with the new blanket, and then bring her to look at it. But, Paul, how shall we buy a blanket? Where are blankets to be got?'

'Leave that to me, I'll manage that. I know where blankets can be got; I saw one hanging out of a shop the day I went last to Dunstable.'

'You have seen a great many things at Dunstable, brother.'

'Yes, a great many; but I never saw anything there or anywhere else that I wished for half so much as I did for the blanket for my grandmother. Do you remember how she used to shiver with the cold last winter? I'll buy the blanket to-morrow. I'm going to Dunstable with her spinning.'

'And you'll bring the blanket to me, and I shall make the bed very neatly, that will be all right—all happy!' said Anne, clapping her hands.

'But stay! Hush! don't clap your hands so, Anne; it will not be all happy, I'm afraid,' said Paul, and his countenance changed, and he looked very grave. 'It will not be all right, I'm afraid, for there is one thing we have neither of us thought of, but that we ought to think about. We cannot buy the blanket, I'm afraid.' 'Why, Paul, why?' 'Because I don't think this guinea is honestly ours.'

'Nay, brother, but I'm sure it is honestly ours. It was given to us, and grandmother said all that was given to us to-day was to be our own.' 'But who gave it to you, Anne?' 'Some of the people in those chaises, Paul. I don't know which of them, but I daresay it was the little rosy girl.'

'No,' said Paul, 'for when she called you to the chaise door, she said, "Here's some halfpence for you." Now, if she gave you the guinea, she must have given it to you by mistake.'

'Well, but perhaps some of the people in the other chaises gave it to me, and did not give it to me by mistake, Paul. There was a gentleman reading in one of the chaises and a lady, who looked very good-naturedly at me, and then the gentleman put down his book and put his head out of the window, and looked at your scotcher, brother, and he asked me if that was your own making; and when I said yes, and that I was your sister, he smiled at me, and put his hand into his waistcoat pocket, and threw a handful of halfpence into the hat, and I daresay he gave us the guinea along with them because he liked your scotcher so much.' 'Why,' said Paul, 'that might be, to be sure, but I wish I was quite certain of it.' 'Then, as we are not quite certain, had not we best go and ask my grandmother what she thinks about it?'

Paul thought this was excellent advice; and he was not a silly boy, who did not like to follow good advice. He went with his sister directly to his grandmother, showed her the guinea, and told her how they came by it.

'My dear, honest children,' said she, 'I am very glad you told me all this. I am very glad that you did not buy either the plums or the blanket with this guinea. I'm sure it is not honestly ours. Those who threw it you gave it you by mistake, I warrant; and what I would have you do is, to go to Dunstable, and try if you can at either of the inns find out the person who gave it to you. It is now so late in the evening that perhaps the travellers will sleep at Dunstable, instead of going on the next stage; and it is likely that whosoever gave you a guinea instead of a halfpenny has found out their mistake by this time. All you can do is to go and inquire for the gentleman who was reading in the chaise.'

'Oh!' interrupted Paul, 'I know a good way of finding him out. I remember it was a dark green chaise with red wheels: and I remember I read the innkeeper's name upon the chaise, "*John Nelson*." (I am much obliged to you for teaching me to read, grandmother.) You told me yesterday, grandmother, that the names written upon chaises are the innkeepers to whom they belong. I read the name of the innkeeper upon that chaise. It was John Nelson. So Anne and I will go to both the inns in Dunstable, and try to find out this chaise—John Nelson's. Come, Anne, let us set out before it gets quite dark.'

Anne and her brother passed with great courage the tempting stall that was covered with gingerbread and ripe plums, and pursued their way steadily through the streets of Dunstable; but Paul, when he came to the shop where he had seen the blanket, stopped for a moment and said, 'It is a great pity, Anne, that the guinea is not ours. However, we are doing what is honest, and that is a comfort. Here, we must go through this gateway, into the inn-yard; we are come to the "Dun Cow."' 'Cow!' said Anne, 'I see no cow.' 'Look up, and you'll see the cow over your head,' said Paul—'the sign—the picture. Come, never mind looking at it now; I want to find out the green chaise that has John Nelson's name upon it.'

Paul pushed forward, through a crowded passage, till he got into the inn-yard. There was a great noise and bustle. The hostlers were carrying in luggage. The postillions were rubbing down the horses, or rolling the chaises into the coachhouse.

'What now? What business have you here, pray?' said a waiter, who almost ran over Paul, as he was crossing the yard in a great hurry to get some empty bottles from the bottle-rack. 'You've no business here, crowding up the yard. Walk off, young gentleman, if you please.'

'Pray give me leave, sir,' said Paul, 'to stay a few minutes, to look amongst these chaises for one dark green chaise with red wheels, that has Mr. John Nelson's name written upon it.'

'What's that he says about a dark green chaise?' said one of the postillions.

'What should such a one as he is know about chaises?' interrupted the hasty waiter, and he was going to turn Paul out of the yard; but the hostler caught hold of his arm and said, 'Maybe the child *has* some business here; let's know what he has to say for himself.'

The waiter was at this instant luckily obliged to leave them to attend the bell; and Paul told his business to the hostler, who, as soon as he saw the guinea and heard the story, shook Paul by the hand, and said, 'Stand steady, my honest lad; I'll find the chaise for you, if it is to be found here; but John Nelson's chaises almost always drive to the "Black Bull."'

After some difficulty, the green chaise, with John Nelson's name upon it, and the postillion who drove that chaise, were found; and the postillion told Paul that he was just going into the parlour to the gentleman he had driven, to be paid, and that he would carry the guinea with him.

'No,' said Paul, 'we should like to give it back ourselves.'

'Yes,' said the hostler; 'that they have a right to do.'

The postillion made no reply, but looked vexed, and went on towards the house, desiring the children would wait in the passage till his return. In the passage there was standing a decent, clean, good-natured-looking woman, with two huge straw baskets on each side of her. One of the baskets stood a little in the way of the entrance. A man who was pushing his way in, and carried in his hand a string of dead larks hung to a pole, impatient at being stopped, kicked down the straw basket, and all its contents were thrown out. Bright straw hats, and boxes, and slippers were all thrown in disorder upon the dirty ground.

'Oh, they will be trampled upon! They will be all spoiled!' exclaimed the woman to whom they belonged.

'We'll help you to pick them up, if you will let us,' cried Paul and Anne, and they immediately ran to her assistance.

When the things were all safe in the basket again, the children expressed a desire to know how such beautiful things could be made of straw; but the woman had not time to answer before the postillion came out of the parlour, and with him a gentleman's servant, who came to Paul, and clapping him upon the back, said, 'So, my little chap, I gave you a guinea for a halfpenny, I hear; and I understand you've brought it back again; that's right, give me hold of it.' 'No, brother,' said Anne, 'this is not the gentleman that was reading.' 'Pooh, child, I came in Mr. Nelson's green chaise. Here's the postillion can tell you so. I and my master came in that chaise. I and my master that was

173

reading, as you say, and it was he that threw the money out to you. He is going to bed; he is tired and can't see you himself. He desires that you'll give me the guinea.'

Paul was too honest himself to suspect that this man was telling him a falsehood; and he now readily produced his bright guinea, and delivered it into the servant's hands. 'Here's sixpence apiece for you, children,' said he, 'and goodnight to you.' He pushed them towards the door; but the basket-woman whispered to them as they went out, 'Wait in the street till I come to you.'

'Pray, Mrs. Landlady,' cried this gentleman's servant, addressing himself to the landlady, who just then came out of a room where some company were at supper—'Pray, Mrs. Landlady, please to let me have roasted larks for my supper. You are famous for larks at Dunstable; and I make it a rule to taste the best of everything wherever I go; and, waiter, let me have a bottle of claret. Do you hear?'

'Larks and claret for his supper,' said the basket-woman to herself, as she looked at him from head to foot. The postillion was still waiting, as if to speak to him; and she observed them afterwards whispering and laughing together. '*No bad hit,*' was a sentence which the servant pronounced several times.

Now it occurred to the basket-woman that this man had cheated the children out of the guinea to pay for the larks and claret; and she thought that perhaps she could discover the truth. She waited quietly in the passage.

'Waiter! Joe! Joe!' cried the landlady, 'why don't you carry in the sweetmeat-puffs and the tarts here to the company in the best parlour?'

'Coming, ma'am,' answered the waiter; and with a large dish of tarts and puffs, the waiter came from the bar; the landlady threw open the door of the best parlour, to let him in; and the basket-woman had now a full view of a large cheerful company, and amongst them several children, sitting round a supper-table.

'Ay,' whispered the landlady, as the door closed after the waiter and the tarts, 'there are customers enough, I warrant, for you in that room, if you had but the luck to be called in. Pray, what would you have the conscience, I wonder now, to charge me for these here half-dozen little mats to put under my dishes?'

'A trifle, ma'am,' said the basket-woman. She let the landlady have the mats cheap, and the landlady then declared she would step in and see if the company in the best parlour had done supper. 'When they come to their wine,' added she, 'I'll speak a good word for you, and get you called in afore the children are sent to bed.'

The landlady, after the usual speech of, '*I hope the supper and everything is to your liking, ladies and gentlemen,*' began with, 'If any of the young gentlemen or ladies would have a *cur'osity* to see any of our famous Dunstable straw-work, there's a decent body without would, I daresay, be proud to show them her pincushion-boxes, and her baskets and slippers, and her other *cur'osities.*'

The eyes of the children all turned towards their mother; their mother smiled, and immediately their father called in the basket-woman, and desired her to produce her *curiosities*. The children gathered round her large pannier as it opened, but they did not touch any of her things.

'Ah, papa!' cried a little rosy girl, 'here are a pair of straw slippers that would just fit you, I think; but would not straw shoes wear out very soon? and would not they let in the wet?'

'Yes, my dear,' said her father, 'but these slippers are meant——' 'For powdering-slippers, miss,' interrupted the basket-woman. 'To wear when people are powdering their hair,' continued the gentleman, 'that they may not spoil their other shoes.' 'And will you buy them, papa?' 'No, I cannot indulge myself,' said her father, 'in buying them now. I must make amends,' said he, laughing, 'for my carelessness; and as I threw away a guinea to-day, I must endeavour to save sixpence at least?'

'Ah, the guinea that you threw by mistake into the little girl's hat as we were coming up Chalk Hill. Mamma, I wonder that the little girl did not take notice of its being a guinea, and that she did not run after the chaise to give it back again. I should think, if she had been an honest girl, she would have returned it.'

'Miss!—ma'am!—sir!' said the basket-woman, 'if it would not be impertinent, may I speak a word? A little boy and girl have just been here inquiring for a gentleman who gave them a guinea instead of a halfpenny by mistake; and not five minutes ago I saw the boy give the guinea to a gentleman's servant, who is there without, and who said his master desired it should be returned to him.'

'There must be some mistake, or some trick in this,' said the gentleman. 'Are the children gone? I must see them—send after them.' 'I'll go for them myself,' said the good-natured basket-woman; 'I bid them wait in the street yonder, for my mind misgave me that the man who spoke so short to them was a cheat, with his larks and his claret.'

Paul and Anne were speedily summoned, and brought back by their friend the basket-woman; and Anne, the moment she saw the gentleman, knew that he was the very person who smiled upon her, who admired her brother's scotcher, and who threw a handful of halfpence into the hat; but she could not be certain, she said, that she received the guinea from him; she only thought it most likely that she did.

'But I can be certain whether the guinea you returned be mine or no,' said the gentleman. 'I marked the guinea; it was a light one; the only guinea I had, which I put into my waistcoat pocket this morning.' He rang the bell, and desired the waiter to let the gentleman who was in the room opposite to him know that he wished to see him. 'The gentleman in the white parlour, sir, do you mean?' 'I mean the master of the servant who received a guinea from this child.' 'He is a Mr. Pembroke, sir,' said the waiter.

Mr. Pembroke came; and as soon as he heard what had happened, he desired the waiter to show him to the room where his servant was at supper. The dishonest servant, who was supping upon larks and claret, knew nothing of what was going on; but his knife and fork dropped from his hand, and he overturned a bumper of claret as he started up from the table, in great surprise and terror, when his master came in with a face of indignation, and demanded '*The guinea*—the *guinea, sir*! that you got from this child; that guinea which you said I ordered you to ask for from this child.'

The servant, confounded and half-intoxicated, could only stammer out that he had more guineas than one about him, and that he really did not know which it was. He pulled his money out, and spread it upon the table with trembling hands. The marked guinea appeared. His master instantly turned him out of his service with strong expressions of contempt.

'And now, my little honest girl,' said the gentleman who had admired her brother's scotcher, turning to Anne, 'and now tell me who you are, and what you and your brother want or wish for most in the world.'

In the same moment Anne and Paul exclaimed, 'The thing we wish for the most in the world is a blanket for our grandmother.'

His master came in with a face of indignation, and demanded 'The guinea—*the* guinea, sir!'

His master came in with a face of indignation, and demanded 'The guinea—*the* guinea, sir!'

'She is not our grandmother in reality, I believe, sir,' said Paul; 'but she is just as good to us, and taught me to read, and taught Anne to knit, and taught us both that we should be honest—so she has; and I wish she had a new blanket before next winter, to keep her from the cold and the rheumatism. She had the rheumatism sadly last winter, sir; and there is a blanket in this street that would be just the thing for her.'

'She shall have it, then; and,' continued the gentleman, 'I will do something more for you. Do you like to be employed or to be idle best?'

'We like to have something to do always, if we could, sir,' said Paul; 'but we are forced to be idle sometimes, because grandmother has not always things for us to do that we *can* do well.'

'Should you like to learn how to make such baskets as these?' said the gentleman, pointing to one of the Dunstable straw-baskets. 'Oh, very much!' said Paul. 'Very much!' said Anne. 'Then I should like to teach you how to make them,' said the basket-woman; 'for I'm sure of one thing, that you'd behave honestly to me.'

The gentleman put a guinea into the good-natured basket-woman's hand, and told her that he knew she could not afford to teach them her trade for nothing. 'I shall come through Dunstable again in a few months,' added he; 'and I hope to see that you and your scholars are going on well. If I find that they are, I will do something more for you.' 'But,' said Anne, 'we must tell all this to grandmother, and ask her about it; and I'm afraid—though I'm very happy—that it is getting very late, and that we should not stay here any longer.' 'It is a fine moonlight night,' said the basket-woman; 'and is not far. I'll walk with you, and see you safe home myself.'

175

The gentleman detained them a few minutes longer, till a messenger whom he had dispatched to purchase the much-wished-for blanket returned.

'Your grandmother will sleep well upon this good blanket, I hope,' said the gentleman, as he gave it into Paul's opened arms. 'It has been obtained for her by the honesty of her adopted children.'

THE END

Made in the USA
Middletown, DE
09 July 2024

57066708R00099